## Praise for

"*The It Girls* is a glorious romp through the lives and loves of the scintillating Sutherland sisters! Karen Harper does a wonderful job of bringing Lucile and Elinor to life in this richly imagined and impeccably researched novel. Readers who enjoy historical fiction are in for a treat!"

—Hazel Gaynor, *New York Times* bestselling author of *The Girl Who Came Home*

## Praise for *The Royal Nanny*

"Veteran author Harper fills her tale with exquisite details of clothing, habits, palace intrigue, and everyday life. Fans of period dramas will enjoy the engaging plot, well-drawn characters, and vivid setting." —*Booklist*

"This is a beautifully told novel of a woman who was surrounded by all the glitz and glamour of royalty but remained unaffected . . . Readers will greatly admire the protagonist while learning about the quirks of the royal family and the events that shook the world in the early 20th century."

—Historical Novel Society

"Emotional and sweet, brimming over with details of the daily life of the household, traveling to exotic locals, city and county experiences. From palaces to nurseries, this behind-the-scenes story is a testament to Harper's skill for bringing readers straight into her novels . . . Harper at her best." —*RT Book Reviews*

"Told through the eyes of an endearing narrator, *The Royal Nanny* is a gem, revealing that those forgotten in history are often the true treasures."

—Erika Robuck, nationally bestselling author of *Hemingway's Girl*

"Fans of *Downton Abbey* will devour this vivid tale of one nanny's unwavering love and sacrifices endured for the sake of the royal children in her care. Full of emotion and heart, Lala redefines the meaning of motherhood while Harper gives us a behind-the-scenes look into the lives of the Royals."

—Renée Rosen, author of *White Collar Girl*

# *The* IT GIRLS

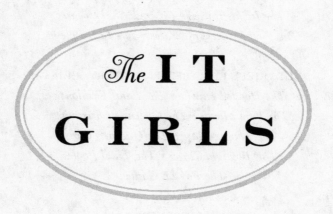

**Also by Karen Harper**

HISTORICAL NOVELS

*The Royal Nanny • The Queen's Governess*

*The Irish Princess • Mistress Shakespeare*

*The First Princess of Wales • The Last Boleyn*

THE QUEEN ELIZABETH I MYSTERY SERIES

*The Hooded Hawke • The Fatal Fashione*

*The Fyre Mirror • The Queene's Christmas*

*The Thorne Maze • The Queene's Cure*

*The Twylight Tower • The Tidal Poole*

*The Poyson Garden*

SUSPENSE

*Chasing Shadows • Drowning Tides*

*Falling Darkness • Broken Bonds*

*Shattered Secrets • Upon a Winter's Night*

*Dark Crossings • Finding Mercy*

*Return to Grace • Fall from Pride*

*Down River • Deep Down*

*The Hiding Place • Below the Surface*

*Inferno • Hurricane*

*Dark Angel • Dark Harvest*

*Dark Road Home • The Falls*

*The Stone Forest • Shaker Run*

*Down to the Bone • The Baby Farm*

*Empty Cradle • Black Orchid*

# The IT GIRLS

KAREN HARPER

WILLIAM MORROW
An Imprint of HarperCollins*Publishers*

HarperCollins
PUBLISHERS
*Since 1817*

This book is a work of fiction. References to real people, events, establishments, organizations, or locales are intended only to provide a sense of authenticity, and are used fictitiously. All other characters, and all incidents and dialogue, are drawn from the author's imagination and are not to be construed as real.



HarperCollins books may be purchased for educational, business, or sales promotional use. For information, please email the Special Markets Department at SPsales@harpercollins.com.

FIRST EDITION

*Designed by Diahann Sturge*
*Background art throughout © by MSSA/Shutterstock, Inc.*

Library of Congress Cataloging-in-Publication Data has been applied for.

ISBN 978-0-06-256777-2
ISBN 978-0-06-269844-5 (library edition)

17 18 19 20 21 LSC 10 9 8 7 6 5 4 3 2 1

# Acknowledgments

Thanks to Don for living with an Anglophile and proofreading my manuscripts. Also, I greatly appreciate my support team at HarperCollins, especially my editor, Lucia Macro, as well as my agent, Annelise Robey—both modern "It Girls."

# Prologue

*The Isle of Jersey*
*April 1875*

"If we are caught, we'll be in beastly trouble for this," Nellie said, tugging at her sister's sleeve as they opened the door to the ladies' cloakroom of Government House and darted inside.

"Not if we don't get caught. Don't be in such a fret," Lucy scolded in a whisper. "She will surely come in here before the reception, and we'll catch a glimpse of her."

"Mother will be furious, and since the lieutenant governor and Mrs. Norcott are hosts for this party, then—"

"They won't even know. Oh look! Ada was right. We can crawl under the skirt of that ruffled dressing table and cut little peekholes in it to see out."

"*Peepholes,*" Nellie corrected.

"Never you mind. I brought my best sewing scissors," Lucy declared, brandishing them like a sword.

At age ten, Nellie was hardly as bold as her sister, who was sixteen months older and the family tomboy to Nellie's wallflower. But they'd agreed it was worth a risk to catch a glimpse of Lillie Langtry, the toast of London and a native of this small island snagged between France and England. Nellie had been writing reams about Lillie in her own *Complete and True Diary of Miss Elinor Sutherland*. *Snagged,* a lovely word, she reminded herself again. Indeed, they were snagged here with a terrible stepfather who was so mean to their lovely mother. Why, it was like some fairy tale with an ogre after their father—the true prince—had died.

"All right," Nellie agreed. "I'll crawl under, though you know I abhor closed places. At least it won't be pitch-dark under there." Four years ago, the sisters and their mother had sailed from Canada, on a trip so harrowing Nellie had never gotten over it.

After all, Nellie thought, trying to buck herself up, anything to see the so-called Jersey Lily who was so beautiful that she'd been painted by artists and invited to dinners by important people in London. Simply everyone in little Jersey had crowded the streets the day Lillie wed the widower Mr. Langtry last year. The streets had been awash with flowers and crowds. But they had heard she'd wed him just to escape on his yacht. Lucy had repeated ad nauseam that she'd heard Lillie was so clever that even at London events she wore simple black gowns with no jewelry to accent her stunning face and form.

Nellie sighed and watched as Lucy cut two peepholes in the white muslin and pink glazed calico folds of the dressing table skirt. The top of the table boasted little cut-glass bottles, combs, brushes, and a silver-backed hand mirror.

"I can't wait to see what she wears," Lucy was saying. "I'll sketch every stitch of her gown."

"And I'll record everything about it, everything. I just hope Ada doesn't catch it for tipping us off when she arrives."

Ada Norcott was the daughter of the channel island's lieutenant governor, a representative of Queen Victoria, no less. Ada was often allowed to play with the Sutherland sisters. They lived in a rented, furnished house just outside the capital, St. Helier, so Ada often invited them to stay with her in town. That had been the case today, though the girls were not to attend the reception and dinner, only gaze out windows at arriving carriages, and that wasn't good enough.

"All right, get under straightaway," Lucy ordered.

"But Ada hasn't given us the high sign yet."

"Good gracious, do you want to be in a scramble when she does? This isn't a story in one of those books you bury yourself in where people escape through magic doors and such nonsense. If we are scolded for this, Mother will have the vapors, and our I-am-ill-help-me-right-now Mr. Kennedy will be meaner than ever."

Nellie gathered her skirts and crawled in the small space, followed by Lucy. They hunched together, straining to listen for Ada's telltale knock on the door that would mean Mrs. Lillie Le Breton Langtry had arrived and was coming upstairs to leave her wrap.

Not only had their idol Lillie escaped the little English Channel island of Jersey but she'd escaped a father who, despite his religious position as dean of Jersey, had a racy reputation. Gossip said that the senior clergyman of the island diocese had taken numerous paramours. Why, 'twas said poor Lillie had at first fallen for a handsome young man she did not know was her half brother, and the dean had been forced to tell her to keep her from incest. Oh my, sin and scandal here on "just" Jersey, supposedly only the haunt of rural folk, day-trippers, and cows!

Both girls jolted when Ada's triple knock resounded on the door. Lucy pulled the dressing table skirt tighter and peered out the larger slit she'd made for herself. Nellie looked out too, holding her breath in their dusty little tent.

And in swept Lillie Langtry. *Oh crumbs,* Lucy thought. Ada's mother was with her, when they'd hoped she'd come in alone. Even inside here, Lucy inhaled in a sniff of powder and perfume as she gaped at Lillie's white satin corded gown with a tight bodice and puffed bustle and the flaming scarlet flowers that perched behind each ear.

Nellie noted with a sigh Lillie's upswept, golden-brown hair so fashionably curled and fringed. She rued her own red hair, which was considered too loud and too Mediterranean, whereas Lucy's was light brown and Ada's was absolutely flaxen. And, oh, Lillie Langtry already had a glass of what looked to be champagne in her hand, but it might as well have been ambrosia of the Greek gods.

The sisters stared as Lillie put her glass on the table above their heads and proceeded to primp, though they couldn't see the top half of her now. Her petticoats pushed toward them, and they both leaned back, losing their peepholes. Then Nellie sneezed.

"Oh!" Lillie cried and stepped away from the dressing table.

"Whoever was that?" Ada's mother demanded.

Lillie lifted the muslin skirt that hid them and peered closer. "Dear me, whatever are you two doing here?"

Feeling ever so childish when she considered herself, at twelve nearly of age, nearly a young lady, Lucy crawled out and stood.

Nellie, though she admitted she was scared of horses and the dark and a few other things, followed her older sister's move.

"Why, it's the Sutherland girls!" Mrs. Norcott cried. "What pluck! Mrs. Langtry, these are friends of my daughter Ada's, but there is surely no excuse for such improper, cheeky behavior."

"Well," Lillie said in her melodious voice Lucy vowed right then to imitate forever, "their excuse is they wanted to say hello and knew they wouldn't have an opportunity later, yes?"

"Yes, that's it," Lucy declared, grateful for the assistance.

Nellie felt tongue-tied but bobbed a slight curtsy. After all, the islanders were treating this woman as if she were a princess, and such romantic stories were the solid stuff of Nellie's fanciful and far-flung imaginings.

"Indeed, I am delighted to make the acquaintance of such enterprising and bold young ladies," Lillie said, extending a gloved hand to each of them. "And I know Mrs. Norcott will be certain you do not get a telling off."

Ignoring the older woman's continued sputtering—about Ada being something called complicit—Lillie squeezed their hands and then released them. She leaned closer to lift her crystal champagne glass and raised it toward her Cupid-bow lips in a graceful motion.

"I salute the Sutherland sisters," she said, as if she were leading the grandest toast at a castle instead of old Government House in just Jersey. "Success to you both, which I have no doubt will come to you for your aplomb and determination. It is as important as a woman's wiles and smiles."

Lucy didn't know what aplomb or wiles meant, but Nellie no doubt did. Lucy broke into a smile, and Nellie blinked back tears of gratitude and adoration.

Lucy dared to put in, "Our real names are Lucile and Elinor."

"Ah, far grander. Dare I hope you two will fly away from quiet, old Jersey someday too? Here's to wonderful people and their endeavors."

She drained her drink. "I vow you are girls after my own heart—and remember to guard your hearts, Lucile and Elinor Sutherland. Ta, ta, then," she said and, with a wave and a swish of skirts, headed for the door.

Mrs. Norcott hastened to hold it open and out sailed Lillie into the hall, followed by the older woman and a brisk slam of the door.

"Oh my, what a gown and what an exit," Lucy said with a sigh.

"An exit for her, but a new beginning for me," Nellie declared. "I shall write about her and be just like her."

"Nonsense. We will be just like Lucile and Elinor Sutherland and make our own way in the world."

"Only not marry for a yacht and an escape, like she did. I intend to find romance."

"I don't give a straw for that, just that I get on famously, and not on Jersey. Onward and upward as Grandmama used to say. Now let's get going."

# PART I

# The Island

1879–1885

# CHAPTER *One*

"My dearest girls, you are fretting Mr. Kennedy too much," their mother told them, even shaking her finger at them this time over their bothering their stepfather.

She was still a lovely woman, which, Lucy thought, was probably what got them in this pickle. One must know what to spend one's face and future for, she thought, and this marriage bargain their mother had made to get them away from rural Canada and back to Europe was not worth it. She had promised their beloved father on his deathbed she would return here but at what price?

The three "Sutherland girls," as they still sometimes called themselves out of David Kennedy's earshot, were huddled in the parlor of their rented house called Richelieu. "However mild we find the climate here, your stepfather has his difficult days," Mother went on, wringing her hands.

"As do we—and you, Mother," Lucy insisted, "with all his bitterness and scolding."

"We mustn't judge someone who is ill, my dears. As the Bible says, we must look out not only for our own interests but also for the interests of others."

"He doesn't look out for yours," Lucy said, hands on her hips. At nearly age sixteen now, she had stepped forward more than once to defend her mother to the curmudgeon. "Good gracious, he runs you ragged."

"Lucy," Elinor put in, "best we leave it alone."

"A fine thing for you to say," Lucy went on with a frown at her younger sister. "You often hide out in this very room if we're not with Ada—alone with these portraits of beautiful women who just stare down from their frames and don't make a peep, when Mother's always at his beck and call."

"Lucile!" Mother said. "You dare not scold your sister for making what escape she can. You love these paintings too, or at least the gowns in them, as much as Nellie loves making up their stories. Now I must get back upstairs for he needs his hot posset. Oh, how different Jersey is from those days your father and I lived here, our—our first wonderful, romantic days together." Her eyelashes clumped with tears. "I've told you both so much about him, so please never forget him and his fine family ties as I shan't so that—"

Her voice caught on a sob. She squeezed both their shoulders and hurried from the room as the thuds of her second husband's cane sounded on the ceiling overhead.

Lucy said, "She loved Father so much she'll never love anyone else. She married *him*," she added with a slanted look at the ceiling, "to get us out of that farm in wilderness Canada, to give us a chance in England. And here we are in just Jersey after a stay in Mr. Kennedy's family's gloomy castle, which I hated, hated, hated. Especially the horrid governesses, especially that one that locked us up so she could have illicit trysts with the valet!"

"Just Jersey is far better than that. At least before we ran off the last governess here, we improved our French, *oui*? I long to see France—well, someday."

"At least we can get out of this house, right now, together," Lucy said. "Your mere mention of our Ontario days makes me feel doubly trapped here."

"We can't just leave."

"Write Mother a note that we went for a walk to see Ada or to look in shop windows in town."

"But did we?"

"Good gracious, Nellie, you adore reading fiction, so make it up! We'll walk out the causeway to old Elizabeth Castle. As grim and weathered as the old stone pile is, you've said it's so romantic with its stone towers, and it was named for 'the Virgin Queen.' I'm sure it's low tide."

"But we'll have to listen for the warning bell when to leave. I don't care if we learned how to swim years ago, you know you can get caught there when the tide rises."

"Ah, when the tide rises," Lucy said, slapping a piece of paper and pen on the table next to Nellie, then fetching the inkwell. "Sounds like the title of a book you could use when you become a famous writer someday."

"Don't tease. I shall keep my diary but find someone wonderful to wed," Nellie insisted as she bent over the paper. "And you will draw and sew pretty dresses like the ones in these Lely and Reynolds portraits, *oui*?"

"*Sacre bleu!* When the cows come home!"

"Which, of course, they do in Jersey all the time."

Lucy almost laughed at that. "The cows may come home, but I won't be here. I'm going to follow the Jersey Lily to London."

"Can you believe it? She's won the favor of the Prince of Wales. I overheard that she's his mistress—his lover. I didn't tell you anything about that, because it is just *too* risqué, but I overheard Mrs. Norcott telling mother something Lillie said to the prince in public. In public!"

"Tell me now. Tell me!" Lucy demanded, putting her elbows on the table and her face close to Nellie's.

In a quiet voice, though there was no one else to hear, blushing to the roots of her red hair, Nellie said, "He told her—as a joke, I guess—that he had spent enough on her to build a battleship."

"Oh my. I can just imagine the wardrobe he's paying for and the jewels. No more plain black gowns. But she wasn't cowed one bit by that, I'll wager. So she said?" Lucy prompted.

"She told him right back, 'And you've spent enough in me to float one!'"

Lucy gasped and clapped both hands over her mouth. She bounced back from the table, eyes wide. She was shocked at that, but also at the fact that Nellie must know what that meant. "And did she get scolded, snubbed, or shunned?"

"Our Lillie? I take it whoever overheard laughed, and it's spread like wildfire—obviously, even to Jersey! Can you believe it?" Nellie repeated.

Lucy heaved a huge sigh. "It doesn't matter a whit if I believe it. She believes in herself, and so the world's her oyster."

"I knew you would be shocked. And to think, she believed in us. There," Nellie said, signing both their names with a flourish. "I told Mother we won't be late. Since I'm named after her, I should sign as Elinor the second. One of my goals in life is to be presented at court someday. You just wait and see. I adore hearing and reading about royalty."

"And I adore getting clear of this house. Just Jersey, here we come."

* * *

They walked quickly toward the harbor through St. Helier's quaint, narrow streets and cheek-by-jowl shops with French names over their doors. Others were abroad, both the British islanders, mostly retired officers and small pensioners drawn by the low income-tax haven of the Crown dependency. But there were the descendants of the Norman-French, too, who had been here for centuries and spoke a half-French dialect none of the British bothered to learn.

The native Jerseyites made their livelihoods by cider production and selling crafts like walking sticks fashioned from tall cabbage stalks. The women knitted stockings and the famous dark blue sweaters called jerseys worn by island fishermen. Besides tending their brown Jersey cows for their rich milk, farmers enriched their small gardens with seaweed compost and, of course, cow manure. Out in the green countryside, gardens could smell to high heaven, but the patches of golden gorse had a sweet scent that sometimes drowned that out.

Potatoes were the prime crop here, especially small ones called *chats*, which the islanders boiled or fried. *Vive la pomme de terre!* sometimes seemed to be the island motto in this forty-five square miles that used to be the home for seafarers and smugglers of fancy French goods. After all, France was still but a two-hour steamer trip away.

The girls were forever trying to spot cottages with the so-called witches' seats on the chimney tops. Nellie pointed at one now, and they both nodded without having to say a word. It was an island tradition that, if a house didn't have that slab for the crones to sit on, smoke their pipes, and keep warm from the chimney draft, they would come right down and sit by the fire, and then the householder would be cursed.

Seagulls screeched overhead, and the sea this late afternoon glittered azure in the sun, then plunged to darker blue when a cloud raced overhead. Despite what they'd written about going to see Ada, they passed stolid Government House and started out on the stone walkway around the harbor. A steamer was approaching, and fishing boats and a few stray pleasure crafts nodded at anchor. Over it all loomed the huge fortress named for Queen Elizabeth, which could always be reached by boat or sometimes on foot over the causeway when the tide was out.

Nellie stretched her strides to keep up with Lucy. However petite Lucy was, she walked like the very dickens. "It's as if this pathway presents damp treasures from Poseidon's realm, like seaweed hair from mermaids and polished pebbles for their jewels on this magic road to another time."

"Mm," Lucy said. "It's the military men in their natty uniforms I like looking at."

"Just think, you're ready to come out—well, if you can say that in a forsaken place like this, however many dances and soirees the Norcotts offer at Government House in the season. If you wed a naval man, hopefully one who will someday become an admiral, he could get assigned to some wonderful place, and you could see the world."

"I'll see the world. Somehow."

"But you'd rather see Paris, right? Ah, me too. Look," Nellie said with a sweep of her hand. "It's so clear today you can even see the houses in France, only about twelve miles away and yet so far. Too bad Mother's letter to her distant relations will mean an invitation for you to visit only old England and cold Scotland."

"She wants me out of the house because I stand up to him, and he can't abide me. Nice to have mutual feelings, I warrant."

"I would miss you if you went—terribly," Nellie admitted as they climbed stone stairs to the walkway along the walls. It had the best view, but the wind tugged at their hats and hair.

"I know you long to see Paris too," Lucy said, "especially after all those wonderful tales Grandmama told of all her relations living there. Remember those barrels of goods she'd get near Christmas? You loved the books, but I loved the clothes, the latest Paris fashions in cold, rough Canada."

"And made such for your dolls. I vow, it was the only reason you liked dolls. You preferred to roughhouse with the neighboring boys."

"And Grandmama was so strict. Always proper manners, learning to sit still in silence, to be self-contained, as she called it. You could do it, but I could not."

"I just made up stories in my head," Nellie said as they walked through the entrance gate under the grim walls. "Stories about castles and princesses. I never told you, but I used to think my fate was to be that of the heroine in *The Princess and the Goblin.* I fully expected to learn later I was really a princess in disguise after all."

Lucy leaned her elbows on one of the narrow, deep windows of the fortress wall and inhaled the tangy sea breeze. "If you are the princess, then poor mother is really a queen who has married a goblin."

"And you then?"

"I don't deal in fancies or fiction. I want things real and ready. I want to look outward, not in some book."

Nellie looked hurt. They stood in silence, gazing out for a while, watching the waves bash the rocks below. At least, Lucy thought, Nellie wasn't going to stage one of her dramatic scenes or use a bunch of big words like *castigate* and *incorrigible*.

"It's true," Lucy spoke finally, putting her hand on her younger sister's shoulder, "that we're as different as night and day, looks and interests, but we will stick together, no matter what, whoever we marry or where we go or what we do. Promise? I do."

"And not ever argue again."

"Really, don't go overboard. Oh, there's the tidal warning bell, so we'd best head back already. Mother or the maid would cover for us, no doubt, but I don't want to get my feet wet on such a windy day."

"Just get your feet wet with exciting people and having things your way," Nellie dared as they set out back down the stone stairs at a good clip, amid the crowd of others hurrying back. Already the tide was licking at the causeway, and the occasional gust of October wind blew spray on them so they could taste salt when they licked their lips. No doubt Mother would know they'd been to the shore. *Oh crumbs,* Lucy thought, she couldn't think of everything.

Lost in their separate thoughts and warmed by having pledged even a ragged oath to each other, the sisters held hands and quickened their steps.

# CHAPTER *Two*

Nellie was miserable, more so than usual. Not only was Lucy off visiting Mother's relations in England, but Ada's father had been recalled to London, so she'd lost her best friend, too.

"That is, except for all of you," she whispered to the pile of books she was unpacking and shelving.

Mr. Kennedy had moved the family, such as it was, into town to a small house called Colomerberie. Most houses here had names, and Nellie was convinced she could have done a better job picking this place or its name. *Forlorn* might do. Yes, Forlorn House, even though her stepfather's books had been shipped from Scotland, and she was going to read most of them as well as keep up her visits to the town library. And the kind, elderly widower next door, who knew Mr. Kennedy, had encouraged that and told her she could borrow books from his private library too.

Hungry and feeling cramped from so much kneeling and stretching, Nellie got up and went out into the hall to ask Cook for something to eat. She was not a live-in cook but a girl who came for the afternoon with groceries and prepared tea and then dinner. Mother had a guest for once, a retired naval captain's wife, Mrs. Ruth Rancal, and Nellie could hear their voices as she passed in the hall.

"That flaming red hair of hers will be a problem when she comes out in her first season," Mrs. Rancal was saying. "It may look come-hither, but she's rather shy, isn't she?"

Nellie wilted against the wall. They were talking about her. She'd heard whispers before that what she liked to think of as her ruby red hair made her look brazen. That's what one of their banished governesses had said, the same one who had scolded that it was unladylike to devour books and read about "naked" Greek and Roman gods and goddesses.

"Her lovely green eyes may not be the usual blue and her eyebrows are quite dark, but they only accent her fine features," Mother said. At least Mother was defending her. She had her dander up.

"But overly striking in color," the woman insisted. "Quite. And draws the wrong sort of attention. But I have something that may help. I truly came to help, you see."

Nellie didn't see. Mother said, "I know the ideal of beauty is pale brown or golden hair but—"

"Indeed it is, and you and your eldest have softer coloring. But here, this is an iron comb of a particular ilk. They say, if you comb her hair with it, it will darken that bright red."

Their voices went on, Mother's on edge now. Nellie nearly staggered back into the library. She was ugly. Everyone thought she was ugly. Now she knew why, when she'd done charades or amateur theatricals with Ada, she had always been given the comic parts with padded or disguised faces, sometimes even wigs. Almost sixteen years old and ugly! Of course, Mother loved her and would never say so, but she hadn't thrown the woman out.

Nellie grabbed her cloak and bonnet off the hat tree and tore outside into the chilly fog. At least Lucy was coming home soon, but that would make things worse. Lucy would have her first social season here, even if it was in "just" Jersey. And poor, shy, lonely, ugly Nellie might as well go talk to the cows in the fields or witches on the chimney seats!

She leaned against the front door, wishing she could disappear into the fog. How hard she'd worked to fashion her hair, twisted round her head in a thick plait ending in a small Grecian knot at the nape of her neck. It was graceful, even if it was roaring red. She swirled her cape around her shoulders and popped her bonnet on, yanking its ribbons tight.

"Hello, there, Miss Sutherland!" came a jaunty call as Nigel Wicker emerged from a hired hackney and headed toward his house next door. He was the kindly, retired gentleman who talked about books with her, recommending and loaning her some. Upon occasion, they sometimes walked together to the library. But the most fascinating thing about Mr. Wicker was that he had actually held a post called Queen's Messenger for Queen Victoria. He regaled Nellie with all sorts of stories, and, after all, she too believed in the Divine Right of Kings and Queens. So romantic, the royals of the realm, even—almost—Mr. Wicker.

"How is the bright and beautiful Nellie Sutherland today?" he asked, stopping partway toward his door to doff his hat. Evidently, when he saw her storm cloud face, he went on hastily, "By the by, my nephew Charles will be visiting me on his break from Eton soon. I would hope you might have time to meet him. He is sixteen, and I want him to realize the beauties of this place," he added with a smile and a wink.

Nellie stared at first like a simpleton, then found herself nodding. "Of course, and Mother would—would love to meet him too," she managed.

Had that sounded too forward? Or too cowardly? As if she didn't trust Mr. Wicker's judgment? As if she couldn't trust this Charles from Eton if Mother didn't meet him to approve?

"Lovely," he said with a smile and another a tip of his hat. "And you are that. I warrant poor young Charles will be swept away. Ah, if I were only half a century younger!"

He smiled and plodded toward his front door. Clasping her hands between her breasts, Nellie just stared. This man was once Queen's Messenger, and it was as if he had brought her a message from lofty realms, just when she needed it the most. Perhaps not everyone—mayhap, men at least—thought she was ugly. And Mr. Wicker must know that his nephew Charles would like her appearance too, else why would he promote the young man's making her acquaintance?

Suddenly, she could have flown into the fog instead of walked. But she turned back and went into "Forlorn House" again. Maybe she'd call it "Future House" now, as things suddenly seemed so much better, especially when she saw her mother's guest leaving. Mother was not only showing her out but hurrying her from the parlor into the hallway, so perhaps she'd given the carper a telling off.

Mrs. Rancal's eyes went to Nellie's hair, so she untied her bonnet and swept it off in defiance. Nellie stood her ground and smiled, deliberately showing her teeth. She hadn't observed her bolder sister all these years for nothing.

"Oh dear, I see the fog is worse," the woman said after Nellie swept the door open for her.

"Well, one good thing about it, I'm sure you'll find," Nellie said, squinting at the woman's light brown tresses frosted with gray, "is that the fog lends some shine to those with dull hair."

Mrs. Rancal gasped. Mother's eyes widened, and she cleared her throat. Nellie thought one or the other would scold her, but Mrs. Rancal bustled off, and Nellie firmly closed the door behind her.

"I dare say you overheard her talking to me," Mother said.

"I did."

"Just when I started to stand up for your lovely hair, she switched to news of Mrs. Langtry, so did you hear that, too?"

"No. Last I knew her dalliance with the Prince of Wales was ended but what else? She's gone back to Mr. Langtry? After all, he was complicit in everything and, no doubt, profited a pretty penny from all that."

"Come into the parlor," Mother said, hustling her inside and closing the door. Though Mother almost always stood ramrod straight, she leaned back against it. "Word has just reached Jersey that Mrs. Langtry is estranged from her husband. She's in a family way without a family, and it's debatable who—well, who is the father of the child."

"Pregnant? By the prince and he won't say so?"

"Evidently not. Although some say the child is that of Prince Louis of Battenberg. And she's evidently dallied with someone named Arthur Jones, too, and she's leaving for Paris with him. She's ruined herself, and, without Prince Edward's favor, the creditors are at her door. It seems the Langtrys have declared bankruptcy."

Nellie sank onto the settee, propped her elbows on her knees, and put her chin in her hands, glaring at the floor. She had to write Lucy, though since she was in England, she might already know. Poor Lillie, her and Lucy's shining star that lit the way out of Jersey into the realms of the great and grand. And now disaster. It made red hair seem like the smallest of problems. It made the world of men and money so much more terrifying.

"My dear, you aren't ill, are you?" Mother asked and sat down beside her to put her arm around her slumped shoulders.

"Just sick of some things, that's all, but I'll be better soon. You'll see."

* * *

With a roll of her eyes and Mother and Nellie watching, Lucy bent over the dining room table, madly cutting gray satin without a pattern. She had been back in Jersey for over a year and had turned eighteen when she declared to Nellie and Mother that she was going to not only sew clothing but also design dresses for the three of them. Even though they were, she argued, on too strict a budget, and "stuck in a backwater of the realm," they could still be stylish.

"He doesn't give us an extra farthing beyond necessities for clothes," Lucy said with a narrowed glance at the ceiling of the dining room.

"Mr. Kennedy is an absolute layabout, Mother," Nellie chimed in.

"Both of you, mind your tongue," Mother chided. "He's ill, and we are to help the sick."

Lucy went on, "You could use a new church gown and neither Nellie nor I can look our best in old rags with our young set even here."

"Now, Lucy," Mother said in her gentle tone, "hardly old rags.

But, my, I admire how you can simply eye a form and figure and cut away. I will treasure that gown and such fine material."

"Good enough for here," Lucy said and stuck pins in her mouth to assemble the pieces. She had to mutter now. "But not if Nellie and I were in London or Paris, dining with"—here her pins spilled from her lips onto the fabric—"the uppers, the absolute nobs of the kingdom . . ."

"Or I with Charles and you with Cecil," Nellie put in.

Lucy straightened and sighed. "Charles and Cecil. Sounds like romantic names from one of your books, does it not, my fair ladies?"

Mother said, "You're quite taken with Cecil, I know, dear, but you've already won and refused three others since you've been back, so I'll wager this is just another passing fancy."

"Mother, I'm not juggling beaus. And Cecil isn't a fancy. He's upstanding. Charming. Dashing in his officer's navy uniform. From a good family. He adores me and I him."

Lucy knew Nellie was not as moony over her long-distant Eton beau Charles as she herself was over Cecil. She needed him. She wanted him. Of course they would be married, so there was no comparison to Lillie, who had gone so astray. Cecil was tall and handsome and well spoken. Piercing blue eyes and from a good family in Kent with a town house in London. She could live somewhere at his first posting and escape all this.

Mother, clucking like a mother hen, bustled off to play more endless backgammon with Mr. Kennedy. Time after time, Lucy had warned herself never to become involved with a man who so much as coughed, for their stepfather's asthma had turned to chronic bronchitis, even here on sunny Jersey. But the handsome, polite, and very attentive Cecil Lockley seemed hale and hearty. He was such a skilled kisser. And his caresses, careful and clever with their chaperones always about—

"You really do love Cecil, then," Nellie said, interrupting her thoughts.

"Madly. I'm over the moon. But I'm not one to be simply swept away like one of those swooning maidens in the novels you read. And you?"

"I'm being very careful and not because of the example of our poor Lillie Langtry. I want a love like Father was to Mother. They had enough romance to live on for a lifetime. Lucy, since you've been home," she blurted, "I've ever so much wanted to ask you something, and I know you'll give me an honest answer straightaway."

"No, I'm not going to elope with Cecil, though I'd like to."

"Not that," Nellie said, standing and leaning stiff-armed on the table as if to brace herself. "Do you think I'm unattractive, even ugly? I mean, with my hair and dark brows, green eyes and all, compared to—well, to you or someone like Lillie—though, I mean to say, I would never compare my appearance to hers or yours with your lighter coloring."

Lucy laid down the pieces for the bodice she was pinning together. Though she was the shorter of the two, she put a hand on the table for balance and stood on tiptoe to look Nellie straight in the eye.

"Ugly? Never! Not you. Your features are more regular than mine, though anyone could tell we are sisters. Your hair is magnificent—if a bit of a surprise at first, as if—as if someone gazed upon a special sunrise. And you know that I tell true."

"Oh, I do!" Nellie cried and nearly dove around the corner of the table to hug her.

They clung for a moment as they had not for years. Then Nellie stepped back and brushed tears from her cheeks. Lucy, surprised at the burst of emotion from her subdued sister, though she did seem to be more confident since she'd been back, just stood there.

"Well," Lucy said, clearing her throat, "that's set then, and let no one else say otherwise, or they'll have words with me. You know"—she put hands to hips and eyed the gown, all in pieces yet—"I wish to high heaven we didn't have scratchy boned neck-pieces. But that's not as bad as the strangling corsets—"

"I thought you said strangling corpses for a minute."

They both giggled. "That's what the fashions men design do to us, make of us," Lucy declared. "Our corsets force us into a swooping spine shape."

"Ha. *S* also for silly? Or better yet, *S* for your swell and smashing sewing?"

"Stunning."

"Superior! Oh, Lucile Sutherland, the things you say and do!"

"Indeed! The things you read and ought to do!"

They smiled at each other. "More to come," Lucy promised and bent back to her task.

* * *

This wasn't going well, Lucy thought, as she tugged up her long, white gloves again. *Oh crumbs*—the left one had a stain from a drop of red punch on it, but the pale green gown she'd made for herself looked fine.

In the awkward silence between her and Cecil as they sat out a waltz in one of the alcoves in the upstairs ballroom at Government House, she tried one more time to get her beloved beau on track. Why was he suddenly speechless? It was surely not that he was being posted to Gibraltar, for he was excited about that, though she considered it another exile assignment. Why not someplace exotic and romantic, somewhere in the Mediterranean? But he was to be off in a fortnight, so they had to settle their relationship and plan a future wedding now, as she'd been heavily hinting to him.

"What I meant was that I shall miss you terribly," she tried to explain again, backtracking a bit on her emotion. "My feelings for you are so strong that I wanted you to know I feel committed to future plans—especially since you're leaving, so I pledge you my trust."

He shifted on the wooden seat again. He was sitting even more bolt upright than usual. She should have tried this outside in the moonlight, but he'd seemed so avid as they had danced, and Mother had always said to strike while the iron was hot.

"Ah," he said, "it sounded for a moment as if you were pledging me your troth—you know, wedding words." He forced a stiff smile.

With a nod, she looked into his wide, blue eyes, waiting, waiting. For heaven's sake, the man was not dense. He was twenty-two and well enough educated. She had been so certain he would not only take her pledge of love to heart, but respond in kind, so they could make some serious plans. More than once over the last few months, he'd whispered that he adored her and could not live without her. So was that all a ploy to get her alone in the gardens?

"I will miss you, too, of course," he said, looking as jumpy as if his seat were suddenly hot. "And write to you."

*All those kisses and caresses,* she thought. Was she the dense one? Hadn't that all meant love? How dare he lead her on. At the least he should ask her to wait for him!

"I need some more punch," he said, "and to talk to Gareth about something. Of course, I'll fetch more for you, too, and be back in a trice."

Her handsome, nattily attired, beloved military man nearly fled in full retreat. Dashed, devastated, she blinked back tears. Did he intend to ask Gareth what to do? Gareth had liked her too. Should she try to make Cecil jealous with Gareth? He needed something to wake him up to his feelings for her. Their union made sense and would be quite proper. His family was not noble, though well respected; through her own father, though he was long gone, she could claim some well-do-do relatives. She'd been so confident that her first real love would be her eternal one, just like Mother's had been. She'd even told Nellie that Cecil would ask for her hand before he left for Gibraltar, and now this catastrophe!

# CHAPTER *Three*

Nellie adored Paris. With Mother's help, she'd been invited to visit by the kindly Mlle Duret, a dear old French lady who had enjoyed a respite in Jersey and taken pity on her. Mademoiselle spoke very little English, and Nellie had been shocked to learn that she couldn't follow rapid speech. Still, she was learning to improve her schoolgirl version of that lovely language. And though she missed Mother—Lucy had gone off in a huge snit to revisit friends in England after Cecil failed to propose—Nellie loved Paris! She didn't even mind that the old lady hardly had any young people around.

Oh, the wide boulevards, like the one she was staying on, the Boulevard Malesherbes, were so spacious compared to Jersey's narrow streets. The cafés, the handsome, well-attired people seemed so charming. The city was ablaze with lights at night. They were going this very evening to the Comédie Française to see a play with the famous British actress Sarah Bernhardt! Nellie wondered if she'd died and gone to heaven, well at least the French version of heaven.

"Nellie, *cherie,*" Mademoiselle said in French as she looked up from opening the mail her butler had brought in, "the young man Trevor who called on us yesterday has asked to accompany us to the theater tonight."

At Mademoiselle's announcement, Nellie's heartbeat dashed to a faster pace. Trevor was an acquaintance of Mr. Kennedy's relatives, so he'd come with an introductory letter, his intent being to pay his respects. And he obviously wanted to see her again. Dear Charles at Eton had never seemed so far away.

"Oh, how kind of him," Nellie said in her best French. Trevor Gingerich spoke both French and English—and usually whispered to her in her native tongue. Mlle Duret was also hard of hearing, so Trevor had murmured compliments that only *ma cher femme* could understand.

"I hope your mama would not object," her hostess went on. "My eyesight and hearing may not be as good as before, but I am as watchful as an owl, especially at night. Trevor seemed quite taken with you, yes, so I shall be watching his behavior, my dear."

*And I too,* Nellie thought with another shivery thrill. *I too.*

* * *

Still deeply bruised and grieving from her Prince Charming turning into a frog, Lucy threw herself into social events at her friends' estate at King's Walden in Hertfortshire, England. A young set swarmed about the house, so there was not a dull moment. Yet she felt dull, as if her emotions were buried. She had adored Cecil and still longed for him to realize his mistake and, filled with jealousy she might meet someone else, come to beg for her hand. So she'd put on quite a show here, forcing herself to smile, to be chatty and—well, to seem interested as well as interesting.

Indeed, she had met someone else, and he was paying her a great deal of attention, paying her court, as Nellie would put it from those medieval romance books she read.

"James, there you are," she said as James Wallace approached the garden bench where she'd been sitting and brooding. She held a parasol as the sun was warm. She realized she'd been nervously twirling it and held it still.

Yet a bachelor at age forty, James was good-looking—almost handsome—and pleasant. He seemed quite smitten with her, which should have helped her loss of Cecil. His family was Scottish and his middle name was Stuart, which she imagined would please Nellie heartily, as that was the family name of Scots and English kings. She'd only known James for the week she'd been here, but he'd told her he had met her mother when she visited relatives near here and, he'd said, had found her almost as charming as her lovely daughter.

Her interests matched his in that he loved to travel and went often abroad to France, even to Greece, Italy, and Egypt, where she longed to visit. He enjoyed other people and seemed to hold his liquor. He had a drink of his favorite whiskey in his hand right now as well as a glass of white wine he extended to her before evidently changing his mind and putting both drinks down on the bench beside her.

"Walk with me, then?" he asked, extending his hands.

She clasped his and he pulled her up, right into his arms. Her parasol tumbled and her poise did too. He had held her hands, hugged her, kissed her good night before, but this . . .

A full-fledged, commanding kiss, lips moving, his hand skimming her hip. Finally, they came up for air. Even in the warmth of the day, she felt goose bumps skim her skin.

"Lucile Sutherland, I adore you," he whispered, nearly out of breath. "I want to hold you and keep you forever. Come, walk with me down the paths out here, I dare say, walk with me forever down life's path."

She wondered when Cecil heard she was betrothed if he would come for her, write to her. Maybe he would protest her wedding someone else. Maybe . . .

Behind the yew hedge at the edge of the small maze, James was kissing her again. His hands ran riot on her back, her bum, too, crushing her to him. It was entirely exhilarating. She would not have to go back to live off Mr. Kennedy's funds. Mother and Nellie could visit her at the house James had vowed to rent in a lovely-sounding place called Cranford Park located at Hounslow, a town near London where he had influential and well-to-do friends. He had praised the gowns she wore and complimented her cleverness to design them.

"Marry me, my darling, marry me, and we'll go away to fabulous places together. The world will be ours," he vowed.

Lucy was pretty certain she said yes.

* * *

The passionate, violent drama *Theodora* stunned Nellie. Sarah Bernhardt was like no one she'd ever seen.

Sarah Bernhardt was wafer thin, a far cry from the plump actresses Nellie had seen in drawings of newspapers or gazettes. Bernhardt was wide- and almost hollow-eyed in her dramatic grief and passion.

Nellie felt she'd drunk the love potion Theodora downed in

the play. And to see a woman take the lead in romance, seducing a man she was not wed to was thrilling. Indeed, even though Trevor surreptitiously held her hand in the dark and moved his knee against her skirts and whispered compliments in her ear, it was the passion of the play that moved her.

She was nearly trembling with the impact of it all when she bid him good night at Mademoiselle's home. Had Trevor been jesting when he had suggested they "fly away" together? The compliments he whispered in her ear would have set her hostess to booting him out the door, but the old lady had missed most of it. She must not realize his polite attentions hid his ardor.

After all, Mademoiselle had accepted for both of them a visit with him to the gardens called Jardin des Plantes tomorrow. That no doubt seemed harmless enough, for Mademoiselle had whispered to her, "I hope your mother doesn't think you are too young to have seen that tragedy, but I so wanted you to experience the Comédie Française and Sarah Bernhardt, quite the rage here as well as in your country."

As for Nellie, once Trevor had bid them good night and departed, kissing their gloved hands, she could not stop talking about Bernhardt's amazing performance. Nellie recalled the news that their long-lost Lillie Langtry had become an actress, but could she emote like that?

Evidently relieved her young guest was not in raptures over Trevor, Mademoiselle declared Nellie must have caught a touch of fever and sent her to bed after she drank a tisane to calm her nerves.

But Nellie was mostly heated from the impact of the story and the vibrant emotions of the characters. Hatred and fear. Love. Yes, lust. And the power of a woman to control her own destiny, despite the strength of her husband, whatever the pain and passion!

* * *

As the three of them strolled through the gardens the next day, it seemed Mlle Duret was smitten with tropical flowers and Trevor seemed smitten by Nellie. But she could not help but stare at the caged animals she'd never seen before—so rare and unusual, at least to her, especially the so-called Bengal tiger from India with its tawny orange fur and black stripes. It prowled; it slunk and roared.

"That big, beautiful cat has your coloring exactly, *mon cherie,*" Trevor whispered in her ear, and his warm breath heated her. He squeezed her arm he held next to his ribs.

"Frightening, the power of it," Mademoiselle said in French from Trevor's other side where he escorted the elderly lady also. "It—why, thank the Lord for this cage, for that beast looks ready to strike."

"The nature of the breed, the fierce female, looking for her mate," Trevor said in French, again reserving his flirty bon mots for Nellie's ears alone. And just wait until she told Lucy about being courted—maybe seduced—in two languages!

As Mlle Duret turned away to look into the lion cage nearby, Trevor held Nellie back. "I still beg you to run away with me. To Italy, Spain, anywhere your heart desires, for I desire and adore you."

It sounded so romantic, so enticing, yet Nellie knew she had enough good sense not to promise to leave one place for another as Mother had done with Mr. Kennedy. And Trevor hadn't mentioned marriage.

"I shall consider it," she told him with a smile, "but for a rather long while."

"Ah, you strike me to the heart!" he whispered, placing his free hand on his chest and managing a look wretchedly forlorn. "Your beauty, your coloring, golden red with your raven eyebrows. You are and will always be the striking tigress of my heart and in my dreams, *ma Belle Tigresse*!"

* * *

The very afternoon Nellie returned to Jersey, Mother opened the letter from Lucy, who was still in England, even before Nellie could tell her all about seeing Sarah Bernhardt. She began to read the letter aloud, then gasped and screamed, collapsing on the divan in the parlor.

"What? Is she all right? Mother, what?" Nellie cried and sat beside her. She seized her wrist that held the letter. "Is she ill? Worse?"

"Worse," Mother croaked out and burst into tears.

Nellie seized the letter and skimmed it. Betrothed? Lucy was betrothed! But to whom? She had hoped for Cecil to get final leave before Gibraltar to follow her to England, but—who was James Stuart Wallace?

"Is it just that we don't know him?" Nellie asked. She put her hand on Mother's arm to pull it away from her face.

"I know him. Know of him too," she choked out.

"Tell me. She must have met him before. She's only been gone a little over a week."

Mother gripped her hands hard in her lap. Nellie could not recall seeing her in such panic or distress. She'd always been disciplined, a good soldier in this campaign—this battle—to leave her own family behind in Canada and care for Mr. Kennedy, whom she could never love.

"We'd best read the entire letter," Mother said, swiping at the tears on her cheeks and then producing a handkerchief she slid under her eyes. "James Wallace can be smooth, but he's a rounder, a roué with a taste for liquor, gambling, and women. He must be near forty and doesn't have a home, travels a lot, I take it."

"W-well," Nellie stammered, "she would like that. And she's much more practical than me, though she's so very opinionated."

"I heard he's a spendthrift and has debts—gambling debts, creditors."

"Surely she knows all that. Lucy's whip-smart. Someone must have told her, or we can reason with her."

Mother just stared into space, as if seeing something that wasn't there—or looking for answers. Nellie read the entire letter aloud. Lucy would design and sew her own wedding gown. They would rent a house in someplace called Cranford Park in Hounslow near London, where they could enjoy all the city had to offer. James had some lovely friends she had yet to meet . . . Please, would Nellie stand up with her? The wedding would be small and was set for 18 September this momentous year, 1884, in London . . . They hoped to travel to wonderful places, especially to the Mediterranean in the winter months . . . Mother and Nellie would always be welcome to visit and, of course, Mr. and Mrs. James Wallace would come to Jersey now and again . . . please be happy for her, since this was best . . .

"She's done this on the rebound from Cecil," Nellie muttered and started to cry too. "Our little family—the three of us—our real family—will never be the same. Oh, Mother, we've lost her!"

"Dear God in heaven, she's lost her mind."

# CHAPTER *Four*

Lucy's desire as a young bride was to look both virginal yet grand, and she felt she'd managed to pull that off with the gown she'd made for herself. The candlelight satin, pleated and draped in front and blooming in back over a bustle, was enhanced by a lace train attached to her forehead circlet of late rose blossoms. The train of the skirt pulled several feet of scallop-hemmed and embroidered skirt. The effect, she knew from staring at herself for hours in a full-length looking glass, was to make her seem to float down the aisle.

In truth, she felt she dragged. Her eyes were still rimmed with red from sobbing herself to sleep.

"Oh, Nellie, what have I done? I hardly know him." She'd admitted her worst fears to her sister last night. Nellie had sat on the bench at the foot of Lucy's bed while Lucy paced in a swirl of skirts from her night robe. "I know James drinks too much, but so do a lot of men. At least he's never sloppy or loud about it. Well, now that he's settling down at last and declared his undying love, he'll have to change some of his ways," she'd insisted, hitting a fist repeatedly into the palm of her other hand.

"I know Mr. Kennedy only got worse, but—well, at least James has money. He wants a son, and he's observed more than once that girls seem to run in our family, but he loves me anyway."

Nellie had tried to comfort her, but she'd been listening and nodding. Finally, they'd lain down on the bed in exhausted silence and held hands. In her heart, in the quiet, Lucy had vowed to forget her foolish first love and be a good wife to her husband.

"Lucile Christiana," the presiding vicar's voice intoned as James held her hand, jolting her back to the present, "do you solemnly pledge . . ."

Things seemed to be happening around her but not to her. It was like a dream, like that drama Nellie had described with Sarah Bernhardt as Theodora who had drunk a love potion and then fallen madly in love with the first man she saw. Like a tragedy, only one where everyone did not end up dead on the stage.

Strangely, when the service was over and they turned to face the small gathering of family and friends—more his than hers—as she paraded with James down the aisle with Nellie and her two other bridesmaids behind her, she had a strange idea, almost a vision, one that hardly seemed suitable on her wedding day, but that gave her hope nonetheless. She could *show* these people a parade of women wearing her designs and that she could create frocks and gowns not only for Mother, Nellie, and herself, but for others.

She'd met a lovely couple near where they were to live, really their landlords for the house, and they'd been most kind. There they were, seated in the second pew, nodding at her and James, Lord Fitzharding so short and thin and Lady Fitzharding so huge a woman—Jack Sprat and his wife, Nellie had whispered after she'd met them. Could she dare to hope someone of the peerage would wear her designs? Lady Fitzharding was smiling so broadly at her.

But, oh no, Mother was crying.

* * *

Lucy considered the wedding night more than a disappointment. If she were honest with herself, it was a disaster. She had imagined being slowly wooed and worshipped, but instead James was rushed and impatient. Perhaps she should have expected as much, given his behavior before the wedding, but even a hint of Nellie's fragile, fanciful ideas of storybook romance would have been nice. Perhaps James thought he had now moved from adoration to ownership.

Still, this was marriage. But it wasn't long after breakfast that James downed his first drink of the day, and it was not fruit juice or tea. "I thought," he said—when he'd said precious little of what he'd thought on their wedding night, except that her body looked like alabaster—"that we'd enjoy a wedding trip later and just settle into our new home this first month or so."

"You said I could decorate it fashionably, but I suppose I should wait on that."

"I have the money, now, darling, so 'fashion' away. I'm glad to see the autumn weather's holding. We'll want to take some brisk walks with the hunt dogs. But the sky's the limit when you get to London to buy curtain goods or upholstery fabric or whatever. And, remember, you can purchase a few new frocks instead of sewing your own. No need for that anymore."

"But I love sketching and sewing them, not only for me but for Mother and Nellie."

"I want to see them well dressed, too, of course. But, as pretty as your dresses and gowns are, I can't have someone of our gentrified station—perhaps with the best yet to come—laboring like a seamstress. We'll be out in the Fitzharding set now. So glad they've taken a fancy to you and your sister. Your mama tries to be agreeable, but I don't think she's weathering losing you as well as I thought she would. I'll win her over, just as I did you—you'll see," he said and poured another glass of liquor from the sideboard.

* * *

"Lucy," Nellie said, looking round the sitting room at Cranford Park two months after the wedding, "I adore your friends here, especially the kindly Fitzhardings. And what you've done with these rooms—absolutely spiffing!"

"I'm glad you enjoy them at least—as does Lady Fitzharding. James really doesn't care one way or the other, though he likes me to make him proud and he basks in any compliments I receive. But he's balked at paying some of the bills when he told me to spend away, anything I wanted."

They sat on the mauve-silk and golden-tasseled Louis XIV–style divan. Nellie knew Lucy had an upset stomach and, with the holidays coming soon, it had crimped her style. James had gone off without her today, shooting whatever birds were available now. Nellie knew she could have accompanied him to the outdoor luncheon in place of Lucy, but it was nippy out, and she'd worried that Lucy looked so shaky she might heave up her breakfast, meager as it was of tea, toast, and honey.

"This room is almost my ideal of a romantic bower—an escape to the past," Nellie said, hoping to perk Lucy up. "I adore the way you've draped the ceiling so beautifully that it seems we are in a summer tent with all these silk ribbon roses you've made. The pretty china plates and flowered rug are so sweet I can almost smell the blossoms."

"Coming from you, the queen of old-fashioned romance, a great compliment."

"Well, as James has teased me more than once, since he knows I often read about royalty, his middle name is Stuart. But I told him, one of them had his head chopped off."

"Nellie, neither of us are good at this but—" Here she popped up and made for a rose-patterned porcelain ewer she had on display at the piano she loved to play. She sat on the piano bench and propped the ewer on her lap and looked into it, as if she had something hidden there.

"Neither of us are good at what?" Nellie asked. "I've never decorated a room in my life, only arranged the few things I have, but I'd like to. I imagine I would do it up quite exotically, something inspired by the scenery from Bernhardt's *Theodora*. I've been keeping extensive journals, you know. The Fitzhardings have been so kind not only to you but to me, admiring my stories and the caricature sketches I've made of them and their friends, so—"

"I don't mean decorating," Lucy interrupted, her voice shaky. It was as if she had not been listening at all. "Dear Lord, I meant that, after but these few months married, I think I'm pregnant. Worse, I don't want to be."

She retched into the ewer and collapsed onto the piano keys with a dissonant chord.

Nellie hurried to her, put one arm around her shoulders and one hand on her forehead, while Lucy vomited into the ewer again.

"Oh. Oh dear—dearest," Nellie managed, whipping her handkerchief from her sleeve to wipe her sister's face. "I'll summon your lady's maid."

"That bell cord—there," she said, pointing. "Violets on it. Tha—that one."

*Silk violets and roses and pregnant,* Nellie thought. Poor Lucy wasn't happy, didn't want a child now, or at least James's child. And just when Mother was getting resigned to the marriage, especially since the rented house was nice and James and Lucy had been taken in by a lord and lady, and James had seemed—sometimes, that is—to have money.

Nellie pulled the correct cord twice and hurried back to sit on the piano bench with her arm around Lucy. Nellie glanced out the window through the flower-patterned curtains into the distance. James was walking back with one of the Fitzhardings' footmen, who was carrying a slew of dead birds. And James was drinking from a small metal flask.

*Oh drat!* Suddenly Mother's worries about James's drinking seemed justified. At least he was with a man, not a woman, so Nellie hoped his womanizing reputation Mother fretted over was not true. But with Lucy pregnant and disheartened, Nellie would have to keep any of the bounder's secret she learned, at least for now.

Nellie knew she was learning a good but hard lesson. Mixing matrimony and men seemed more than dangerous and dim-witted—it could be disastrous.

* * *

"Lucy insisted on a French name for the child," James groused to Nellie when he came back in from seeing his newborn daughter months later. "Es-may, spelled E-s-m-e. Never heard it before," he muttered and took a swig from a silver pocket flask, though Nellie knew by his tone and expression that it was hardly a congratulatory toast. Everyone knew James had wanted a son. "Whatever does Lucy have to do with France?" he asked and banged out of the sitting room off Lucy's bedroom where the baby had been born after nearly twenty hours of labor.

He was barely gone a moment and came back in. As much as Nellie had appreciated him letting Mother and her visit here—she now preferred to stay with the Fitzhardings nearby—he had thoroughly upset her.

Before he could say another word, she told him, "She picked a French name because we have a proud French heritage through our Canadian grandmama. We still have relatives near Paris, as you well know. And please stop shouting. You told her if it wasn't a son, she could choose the name."

"That aside, is it true what I heard yesterday?" he demanded, all too obviously switching topics as he did when bored or cornered. "About your turning down that millionaire who took a fancy to you on top of refusing the hand of the Duke of Newcastle last spring? A duke! Hell, Queen Elinor, you could have been a duchess and helped us all up the damned social ladder. Granted the duke was an old man—"

"And I've noted from observation somewhere that a marriage can be ill served by huge differences in the ages of the couple. I'm barely beyond twenty to his lofty sixty years, but on this day which should be so happy here for the birth of your child—"

"Listen, Nellie," he said, pointing a finger at her. "I know your clever comments and sketches of people amuse the Fitzhardings and their friends, but you don't amuse me. Do you intend to keep living off your poor mother—or that curmudgeon Kennedy—the Fitzhardings, or me?"

"I'll make my own way. I'd rather jump into the sea than wed someone I don't love like the duke or that wealthy acquaintance you hauled in here with his yacht. I knew someone once who married for a yacht and a grand escape, and she ended up badly."

"Say no more!" he said, holding up a hand and the flask toward her as if to ward her off. "I don't do battles with words. I prefer to love rather than fight!"

Nellie gave an inelegant snort. Oh yes, Lucy might be the one with the strongest spine in the past, but she could fend for herself now. "I realize you'd rather love—or your form of so-called love," she hissed, fighting to keep her voice down so Lucy and Mother would not hear from the other side of the door. "I've heard about your dancing and singing friends in town."

"And you've kept your mouth closed for once, I take it, since Lucy never mentioned that." He pretended to applaud her, one hand against his flask. "Look, Elinor the great," he said, lowering his voice too and stalking toward her, though she stood her ground. "All Lucile Christiana Sutherland Wallace adores is thinking up pretty things like room decorations and dresses. She wasn't even enamored of having my child, as far as I can tell."

"She will be a good mother to Esme."

"How about being the wife I need? Going shooting or watching me fish? Not spending so much money on fabric and bibelots and knickknacks," he said with such a sweeping gesture around the room that some of his liquor sloshed out to mar two silk throw pillows in a slash of darker blue.

"You courted and wooed her. You knew what she was like from the start! Maybe the world would be the better for it if the woman would choose and propose."

"That's the dumbest damn thing I've ever heard come out of your pretty mouth," he said and wiped the back of his hand across his own.

She stared hard at him. He acted as if he'd say more, do more, then he slammed out of the room again.

Though Nellie felt weak-kneed, she did not collapse, but went over to the sitting room door to the upstairs hall and firmly turned the key to lock him out.

# CHAPTER *Five*

Lucy wished she felt well enough to pace or even venture outside, whatever the weather. These four walls—everything was closing in around her here in Hounslow. Esme's birth and a fever that had lingered had sapped her strength.

Now she only had a fever to get out of this house for a spell. And without her adorable, two-month-old daughter. Yet guilt rode her hard that she had few maternal feelings for the child.

Simpson, the young nursemaid, knocked and brought cherubic Esme in as she did twice a day. Lucy took the baby, held her the way she'd seen others do. Why did it not feel instinctive and natural? Why couldn't she want to do all this?

"There, there, my sweet little doll," Lucy crooned, but she sounded silly to herself. What was wrong with her that she didn't need to coo and fuss over Esme the way even Nellie had?

It terrified her that she only loved her child in an abstract way, not with a rush of emotion. Granted, she would love to take Esme places when she was older and to teach her things.

Actually, her fiercest feeling for the child was to protect her from her own father as she grew up, not that he would hurt her as he was seldom near her. He had become a layabout when he wasn't drinking or gaming. He was also sulking because Lucy and even Nellie had criticized his long absences and his love of his brandy. This time the cad had been away in London for three days, doing who knows what and seeing—no doubt, chasing—who knows whom? Why had he swept her off her feet if he now simply wanted to sweep her under the rug? Granted, she'd been pregnant and then ill, but was her company so distasteful? She feared he would someday break the child's heart as he had broken hers.

"Let's give her the sterling silver rattle that Lady Fitzharding brought, Simpson," Lucy said and pointed at the shiny rattle.

"Oh, I think she'd hurt her gums with that, and we'd best just let her look at it—not that it's teething time yet, Mrs. Wallace," the girl said. Again, Lucy felt she didn't know what she was doing with Esme. It annoyed her that Simpson picked up the rattle and shook it as the baby gurgled and watched with her blue eyes wide.

After Simpson took Esme back to the nursery and she was alone, Lucy reached for Nellie's latest letter from Paris, where she'd gone to visit their cousins Margot and Auguste, family connections through their grandmama. Despite the fact James dared to banish Nellie from here—and then wasn't around to keep her out anyway—this letter annoyed and even angered her.

*Dearest Lucy, what lovely fun I am having! I have discovered that English women have more freedom than do French women, but I would still rather be here!*

"Indeed, what a cheery letter," Lucy said, frowning at it and speaking in a biting voice. "Why, I am having the most smashing fun here, married to James Wallace who ignores me." If Nellie thought these frequent, gushy epistles were helping, she was wrong. And it got worse.

> *You would adore the fashions here, and Margot has so kindly given me her last year's gowns by Jacques Doucet, a women's fashion designer who is simply all the rage. Lower necklines, which you would love. Lace, lace, lace, spills of lace. I have a peach gown with a tiered, full skirt all in gathers and folds, layers of lace, so wait until you see that. And I've had my hair done by Marcel Grateau, all with a hot comb and then finger waves. I'm sure you'd agree that sort of hair dressing goes so well with Doucet's fancy dresses!*
>
> *So far, we have divided our time between our relatives' town house on the Champs-Elysées and a charming family château in the country, though I far prefer Paris. Versailles was a marvel! Our cousins' family is amazingly well placed in Parisienne society, so different from dear Mlle Duret on my last visit. Auguste is the perfect gentleman to escort Margot and me about.*

Lucy couldn't help herself. She wadded up that first page and tossed it on the floor under her daybed. But, as if to punish herself, she read on.

> *What I mean about English girls having more freedom—even here—is that, since everyone knows I have no dowry—they call it a dot—the young women are willing to introduce me to the men they hope to wed or even their fiancés, because they know I will not—cannot—*

*steal their men! The young men live a fast life, but the young ladies a carefully watched one. Of course I must be on my guard against flirtations, because I don't want to lose the friendship of our cousins and the charming people in their circle, so I am keeping a diary of everything here, all my visits . . .*

"While you, dear Lucy, enjoy yourself to no end." Lucy created her own next line and tossed that page too. "And, of course," she went on imitating Nellie's voice, "all your dreams, dearest Lucy, are in ashes while your husband is off gallivanting in London."

But she did read the last paragraph just before the signature, because it mentioned their former idol Lillie Langtry:

*So did you hear that Lillie has been a huge success in her stage career in the States? They say Prince Edward urged her to try it! And maybe partly sponsored her! Lily has become an American citizen, where, I warrant, there is even more freedom for us younger women, those not wed at least, for then the man rules the roost as well we know! And that reminds me of one more thing—the French make it clear that love and romance are rarely the same thing!*

"And don't I know that," Lucy said in her own voice and heaved a huge sigh. But, she promised herself, she would still strive for romance, at least in her designs, in her heart. Though, somehow, it felt as if the grand possibilities for all that were over, and even her sister and mother could not understand the black depths of that. It made her angry at Nellie all over again.

"And I know," Lucy said aloud to her fancy, empty room, "that, for a would-be authoress, my sister, you use far too many exclamation points when you write to your sister who is distressed and depressed." She ended by muttering "ding damn!"—one of James's favorite curses—and meant the exclamation point.

The man who ruled her roost had told her to stop drawing and sewing her own fashions, Mother's dresses too, but she was going to do it anyway. It fed her soul.

She turned over the last page of Nellie's letter, grabbed the pen she had intended to use to write her back and sketched herself in an evening gown she was certain would be far better than one of this Jacques Doucet's, not with the stiffer lace but clouds and clouds of something she'd seen only once in a French fashion gazette—soft, heavenly chiffon.

Why was it she could pour out her emotions like this, but not when she saw her own daughter, her flesh and blood? This drawing was a gown of emotion, one she could imagine cutting out even now, one she would entitle *Exotic Escape*.

# PART II

# London

1886–1907

# CHAPTER *Six*

At least they had all moved to London, so Lucy hoped that would help the ennui that she had experienced at Cranford Park, however kind the Fitzhardings had been to include them in society there. She worried James wanted to be in London for ulterior motives, but the best part was that Mother and Mr. Kennedy had moved to London also.

As his health had taken yet another turn for the worse, the old man had wanted to be closer to his doctors. Actually, the sicker he got, the more Lucy and Nellie, too, felt they got on with him. Besides, he doted on Esme, giving her little trinkets she loved, more than he'd ever given a straw for her or Nellie, but then they'd hardly been toddling, babbling babies when he'd taken them on.

James was gone a great deal, often with male friends at night, but he didn't object if Lucy went to the theater with Nellie, who was living with Mother in their small house on Davies Street. Unlike Mr. Kennedy, James didn't fuss over the baby but merely patted her on her head on his way out the door. But Lucy had learned to love the company of her daughter.

But she could not even abide James's presence anymore, nor evidently could he stand hers. Today he'd been berating her for having a friend who was divorced, and she'd defied him to keep up that friendship, and they'd been arguing about that off and on. How dare he chase after other women and hold a simple friendship with her own sex against her. She almost wondered if he feared it would give her ideas—and it had.

"Ding damn, Lucy, a woman like that divorced friend is what others call 'not quite nice,' and you know it! An outcast, a social pariah!"

"I imagine she had a husband who deserted her as you have us."

"Are you daft, woman? Defiant and disobedient, I know, but quite daft? I will not have my wife designing her own clothes, let alone that of others! And I know how you think—you'd like to sew fancy dresses for your betters, and where would that put us then? Outrageous! Besides, my finances may not stretch to cover the fees you pay for materials and dry goods and decorations in this modest little house now, but I've hardly deserted you!"

"Perhaps that would not be a fate worse than death, anyway."

He raised his hand as if to slap her. They argued a great deal, but he'd never raised a hand to her. Lucy glared at him, standing her ground. She heard Nellie come partway down the stairs from seeing Esme.

"I love," James muttered for her ears alone, "the pantomime theater, but I can't even pantomime that I care for you anymore."

"Anymore? Your so-called care for me hardly lasted until Esme was born, then you were emotionally—physically and morally—out the door. Which would not be such a bad idea now," she said brazenly and reached for the brass doorknob.

He narrowed his eyes and heaved an exasperated sigh. The sharp smell of liquor on his breath nearly knocked her over. His shoulders slumped. She thought for one moment he would crush the top hat he held in his other hand. He shoved her hand away from the knob, yanked the door open, and went out into the night.

Lucy stood in the doorway, staring after him. In the twilight, some people were afoot, some in carriages or hansoms as the gas lantern lighter went by with his little ladder from post to post. She hoped those people had calm and happy lives. She heard Nellie come the rest of the way downstairs.

"I'm sorry, Lucy," she said. "Best close the door. The night air is cold."

"It feels cold in here, too, all the time, but worst when he's here," she said and closed the door and locked it. They went into the narrow parlor and sank onto the settee Lucy had brought from the other house since she well knew their funds were dwindling.

"Sometimes, Nellie," she said, her voice small, "I don't know how I got to this place—in my life, I mean. I want to do so much to create beautiful designs and bring them to life but can do so little. You wrote from Paris that the French knew the difference between love and romance. Well, I do too, and I have neither."

"He is a driven man for some reason—difficult, but he may change. Perhaps if he had a son—"

"Not from me, though I fear he's sowing wild oats with others. He's besotted not only with liquor but with those so-called pantomime girls. I overheard him tell a friend about them the other day, how sweet and pliable they are, how lovely—"

Lucy's voice broke, but she sniffed hard and went on. "I can't abide him anymore, I just can't. You are wise to turn down your admirers and callers at the door, however much it is expected of you to wed. I know you regret depending financially on Mother and Mr. Kennedy still, and I wish I had some funds to help with that. My whole life like this—Esme's too? James called me daft. I'll go mad—I think I am mad to keep sketching my designs, sewing my gowns. I need a friend who is out in society to wear one of my creations, to attract attention from others, and then—"

Nellie gasped. "You mean go into trade? But—but, even at our place in the great social wheel of things—Lucy, it just isn't done! Not without absolute ruin. I have to agree with James on that."

"I know. I know! Mother would be shocked too. The few and far between new friends I have might drop me, and see—you were shocked. Now if I were only a man . . ."

"I can't believe you said that."

"Well, if you, of all people, don't understand, I am doomed."

"Not that I don't understand your longing. I just mean I can't believe you said that, however much the bold and brave tomboy you used to be and then how you stood up to Mr. Kennedy and now to James. Honestly, Lucile Sutherland Wallace, I sometimes know what you mean. Not that I'd like to be a man, but that I'd like to be a woman and not have to act like one."

Lucy seized Nellie's hand and squeezed it. "Something good has to be coming soon," Lucy vowed. "Something beyond sweet Esme and living in London at last. Something way beyond marriage, I swear it!"

Instead of sobbing and hugging, they shook each other's hands like men.

* * *

"I might as well say it right out," Lucy told her mother and Nellie as she entered the largest upstairs bedroom of her mother's house on Davies Street.

David Kennedy had died, and they were in his bedroom where his things were being packed or stacked to be given away. Lucy had left five-year-old Esme home—if it was home anymore—with her nursemaid, Simpson. Now she wended her way into the clutter and chaos, which was nothing like the chaos in her heart. She had vowed to herself she would be strong through this and would not dissolve in tears—and not over Mr. Kennedy's demise, but over the news she was about to give.

She took a deep breath, gripped her hands together, then gritted out, "James has run off with one of his pantomime girls. He has deserted me, and our marriage is over."

Mother gasped and sank into the chair that had been Mr. Kennedy's favorite. Nellie, looking angry but not surprised, said, "A pantomime girl! A perfect match for one of his level of morality and mental acuity. Except for you, the man has terrible taste, and he leaves a terrible taste in one's mouth."

Lucy yanked her coat off and threw it amid the piles of Mr. Kennedy's earthly goods. His funeral had been last month, and now James Wallace was dead too—that is, as far as she was concerned. It meant social and financial ruin, but she was glad James was gone. Still, she grieved for Esme, however terrible a father he had been. She and Nellie had missed their own long-gone father for years.

"Dear me," Mother said, waving her hand before her face to give herself air. She looked so pale in her black mourning widow weeds, while Lucy and Nellie had only kept to black bonnets and cloaks, and that for Mother's sake. She looked as if she'd faint, so Lucy went to kneel beside her while Nellie sat on the nearby ottoman.

"I was right about him from the first," Mother said between deep breaths. "A bad apple to say the least. You, my dear, and darling Esme are what matter now." She reached out to hold Lucy's hand with her free one.

"But are you all right?" Lucy asked. "You're not going to get the vapors? I didn't, and you mustn't."

"You, faint? Hardly. And of late I've discovered I'm made of sterner stuff too—I've had to be. But this will mean disgrace for you and Esme, when she's old enough. It will hang about her like—like an albatross round her neck. It's always the woman who takes the brunt and blame of all this. Mr. Kennedy is gone, and I thought at last we would come into our own, so to speak. But unspeakable—this."

*Damn men*, Lucy thought. God forgive her for that, but "ding damn" them. Not only the cruel, departed Mr. Kennedy but cruel, departed James Stuart Wallace.

"I just want both of you to know I eventually will demand a divorce," she told them.

"But—but that would bring even more difficulties," Mother insisted, "however much you want James completely out of your life. At least you must not rush to it straightaway."

"Lucy," Nellie put in, "think of it from this angle. You'd not escape him if you ever began to sell your designs. You'd have to be known as Mrs. James Wallace. Besides, we've seen it's the men designers who have the prestige and power. And with James's name on your designs, what if the blackguard demanded a fee, so—"

"I know. I know! But somehow I am going to find a way to be just Lucile Ltd. for my designs, I swear I am. I have to try to get someone interested, to hire an extra seamstress. Even with meager finances as they are—as they will be . . ."

Tears welled up at last, blinding her. She blinked them away, but they clumped her lashes and speckled her flushed cheeks. She forced a stiff smile. "You know," she told them in a quiet voice, "Esme doesn't even ask about him—where he's gone, when he's coming back. He's been gone from her for a long time, I guess. Mother, I'm sorry. I rushed into the marriage. I see that now."

"I know you did. I know you did, my dearest."

"So," Nellie put in, "best you not rush into a scandalous divorce and ruin any chance to build a career in design for proper women."

"If things are too tight or too awful," Mother said, "you and Esme can move in here with Nellie and me. There will be so much more room now, and I've been left some money."

"If I do—and I don't want to uproot Esme now," Lucy told her, "I will help here, and when I begin to sell my designs, I—when I can get my life together again, as if it's ever really been together—except with both of you and now Esme . . . I'll—I'll be right back."

Avoiding stacks of books and piles of shoes and clothing, Lucy rushed from the room and down the hall to the water closet where she could curse and cry.

* * *

"Now, Lucy," Nellie told her sister in a sotto voce tone as they left the Lyceum theater and hailed a hansom. "I'm not sure that you should have accepted that party invitation. I know you've been on your own for over six months, but you are not divorced."

"So you've reminded me time and again. This is not the court of King Arthur or Louis of France, you know. Times are quite different now."

"Sadly, not for women in limbo. Anyway, I've missed you while I've been away visiting again, and it was kind of you to introduce me to the play's cast, but shouldn't we get home to Mother and Esme? I'm sure your nursemaid Simpson will wait up too, but—really—to an actress's house? These and other friends you've made while I've been gone and you and Esme have moved in with Mother sound so—well, Bohemian."

"They are uplifting and supportive, so please don't judge them," Lucy said. "You liked the drama, and you will like my new friends."

"Well, yes, Ellen Terry is a fine actress. But just because she and her set don't give a straw if you've been deserted and are considering a formal divorce, that makes them friendly? I mean, Lucy, really, what about that couple over there, who waved at you, the strange man with long, golden hair, obviously dyed."

"Oh, back in the line for hackneys? He's terribly clever and quite a critic of the way things are. That's Oscar Wilde and his wife."

"Wild indeed. And Ellen Terry is downright indifferent to her personal appearance and dress once she's off the stage. You admitted that, and I can see it. I thought you wanted to seek out socially fit persons to wear your designs and so promote them among their class."

"Don't lecture me, Nellie. And don't sound like a snob. If you don't want to accompany me, I will drop you at home."

"No. No, I said I'd go and you should have someone with you. I've missed you while I've been away. I'll behave, big sister."

"Perhaps all this will be fodder for your precious diary, which you claim you will turn into a novel."

Nellie kept her mouth shut after that. The book she was hoping to write, inspired by memories of the people and places she'd traveled, could probably use some eccentrics—not that everyone wasn't that to some degree. But that Oscar Wilde person, however witty, was dressed in black velvet knee breeches and had a huge sunflower in his buttonhole. And Mrs. Wilde was in a family way, yet was flaunting her bulbous belly with a tight dress when everyone from Victoria's court down was diligent to hide the shape of a baby, even if everyone knew how pregnant one was. How in the world could Lucy be associated with romantic, lovely fashions when she was friends with people who dressed like that? And Nellie had the distinct, uneasy feeling she hadn't seen anything yet.

* * *

Unfortunately, Mr. and Mrs. Oscar Wilde fit right in at the party, Nellie thought after their arrival. The actress's house was in an area called Barkston Gardens in Chelsea near the Thames. Young girls that Ellen Terry had gotten off the streets offered everyone wine and tiny shrimp sandwiches. When they—the guests, too—sat, it was on huge ottomans with no backs, forcing them to recline as if they were at a Roman party or in a harem.

For a while, Lucy played the piano. She'd always taken to that, had even entertained passengers years ago on their ship from Canada to England.

"I'm a woman with a past," Nellie overheard their hostess say more than once in a brief lull. Nellie wondered if that's why the actress and Lucy seemed to be getting on, as Lucy now draped folds of fabric over Ellen while others remarked and applauded and Lucy promised to sew her a dress.

At least one man who came in late and in a hurry knew how to dress. Oh, and he seemed to know Lucy and went right to her. He took her hands and kissed her on each cheek but then he did the same with their hostess. Nellie overheard Ellen introduce him to everyone as "Dr. Morell Mackenzie, our own famous, brilliant throat surgeon, and one knighted by the queen! Besides, he makes sure my theater throat stays healthy."

Nellie gasped. *The* not only famous but infamous Dr. Mackenzie! Surely everyone had read in the newspapers and gazettes how he had been summoned to Germany to treat the cancerous throat of Crown Prince Frederick of Prussia, who was wed to Queen Victoria's daughter. There was some sort of brouhaha between the German militant conservatives headed by someone named Otto von Bismarck, and the so-called enlightened, parliament party, which Frederick's family was caught up in. But there had been a scandal involving the English doctor.

She racked her brain for the details. Though the German doctors had declared Prince Frederick was suffering from throat cancer and should have his larynx removed—which would have meant the loss of his voice and the impossibility of him becoming German emperor—the eminent Dr. Mackenzie had examined the prince and insisted it was not cancer and could be treated, thus preserving his right to the throne. But when Frederick ascended, he only lived and ruled for a short time.

The German doctors had accused Mackenzie of ignorance, even of long-distance murder, though Frederick had lived long enough to attend Queen Victoria's Diamond Jubilee celebrating her sixty years on the throne and promoting continued German-English ties.

In answer to the German doctors' slurs against Mackenzie—and his being chastised by the Royal College of Surgeons for writing a book in defense of his actions—the once glorified doctor had lately been vilified in England. But he was obviously welcome here among these people, despite a larger scandal than Lucy's desertion by her husband.

Yet, Nellie wondered, was this famous man so familiar with Lucy only from his attending the same gatherings here at Ellen Terry's? If he'd been here before, why had Ellen Terry introduced him to everyone? He did look like a fish out of water.

*Talk about drama and theater*, Nellie thought. *This is like watching a play right here*. In the cast of characters, Morell Mackenzie was dark haired and wiry, with a purposeful, serious air about himself. He stood very straight, almost stiffly. His conservative dark suit made him stand out too. He spoke to everyone, greeting them, including, eventually her, whom Lucy had seemed to point out to him.

Nellie thought him almost dashing, but she decided he lingered with her because she was Lucy's—Lucile, he called her—sister. They chatted easily, and he kept asking her questions about Lucy, their early years and time on Jersey, though he seemed to know a great deal about them already. Indeed, doctors were used to asking a great many questions.

Finally, Nellie managed to slip in one of her own. "So where and when did you meet Lucy?"

"She brought Esme to my office when the child was about one year old and had a hacking cough the little dear could not shake.

Some soothing medicine and elixir drops solved that, and she was very grateful."

"I see." So he'd known Lucy for almost four years!

"And I see that charm and beauty and talent runs in the family. Lucile says you like to write."

"Yes, someday perhaps for publication. Fiction, hardly the subject of your medical books."

"I wrote three before this last catastrophe. Choose your subjects carefully then, I would warn, but believe in what you write and then go ahead, only be prepared for criticism and conflict."

He heaved a sigh, and his shoulders seemed to slump before he straightened them. His features crumpled for a moment, and he sighed again. She yearned to ask him how well he really knew Lucy. And, though Nellie had been back from her travels this time barely three days, why hadn't Lucy—his Lucile?—so much as mentioned him?

He took her hand and bowed over it, then worked his way back toward Lucy. Nellie watched them chat. Shift positions. Smile into each other's eyes, then look away. They talked more, earnestly this time, almost whispering. About what? The doctor moved stiffly as he bent toward Lucy, as a flash of pain crossed his face. Lucy was actually blushing, which, even with her pale skin, she almost never did.

Lucy's laugh floated to Nellie over the buzz of voices. She hardly ever laughed lately as she struggled to rear Esme, help their mother, and find someone outside the family with enough panache and power to promote her fashions, but a medical man? One who spent a great deal of time in his office or a hospital, looking down patients' throats? One who might be a lifelong bachelor and have a knighthood but one who was under public scrutiny for being untrustworthy and even dangerous?

* * *

Lucy could tell Nellie was seething as they climbed into the hansom and their driver started the horse through the dark London streets toward Mother's house. Lucy could only hope it was because she had not stayed by her sister's side every minute at the party.

"Dr. Mackenzie is charming," Nellie said. "And charmed by you."

"And I him. We've been friends for a while," she said, shrugging.

"Since Esme was one year old, I take it."

"Yes, that's right. Listen, Nellie, if you've read any slanders aimed at him, discount them. That's all spawned by German propaganda and English doctors jealous of his talents."

"And his talents include?"

Lucy turned toward her but kept her voice low so their driver would not overhear. "I don't care for the tone of your voice. I said we are friends, and we are."

"He looks at you with longing and you blush."

"Do I?"

"You care for him—deeply. Did James know?"

"Why should he? We basically live apart—he's too busy with pantomime girls to notice much of what I do." She sighed. "Look, Nellie, leave this alone. Yes, I do respect and love him in a way."

"In a way! You're having an *affaire de coeur* with him at the very least. Does Mother know? I can't believe Mother knows and didn't say a thing to me."

"Perhaps she is not a busybody and a moral critic of the highest order. Besides, she knows Morell. I've played the piano for him at the house more than once. She, too, enjoys his company."

"I know this isn't my business, but—"

"Quite correct. You are my sister, not my keeper."

"But what if James drags him into the case if you pursue a divorce? It will sully you and the doctor."

"James does not have a leg to stand on. I don't care if the man usually comes out the best in such cases. Morell Mackenzie is an upstanding, gifted, generous, decent man. Despite a childhood back injury, he's dedicated to his work and he—he's been so browbeaten lately, that he's—he's ill. It is all I can do to keep his spirits up when mine are so low, but it's helped me, helped us both."

Her voice broke. Nellie reached out and grasped her hand.

"He didn't seem ill," she told Lucy, "only tired and melancholy. What kind of ill? Not cancer like the emperor?"

Lucy shook her head and blinked back tears. "He wears a back brace, but that's not the worst of it. Heart trouble. He's very weak at times of—of physical exertion, which he ignores. Because he's in danger from enemies now, foreign and domestic, those damned Germans and even his former colleagues who were always jealous of his brilliance, he wants us not to see each other anymore, but I cannot desert him. He needs me. Can't you honor that? Can't you admit it sounds like one of your romantic novels where the two lovers cannot wed and tragedy is on the horizon? I just pray that someday such suffering of the soul will not be your fate or Esme's, either."

Nellie squeezed her hand as their hansom rattled over cobblestones through the gaslit yet so dim streets of London.

# CHAPTER *Seven*

Finally, a nibble from all this fashion fishing, but not as big a catch as Nellie had hoped for, circled back to her again. This was the fourth costume designed and sewn by Lucy that she had worn today for the huge house party given by millionaire Billy Grant at his estate in Devon. Her assignment was to make herself into a living clothes mannequin to display Lucy's designs and try to get someone well connected to agree to wear a Lucile Ltd. frock in a prominent place. The men had gone outside with their port and cigars, but the women were still mingling in here, so she'd best make her rounds again.

So many people were here this evening; some she knew, most she did not. She was becoming known as a travel writer for small London gazettes. But better yet, these last few months had been such a heady experience with men noticing her and trying to impress her that she almost could imagine herself the belle of the ball.

How thrilled she was to have come into her own, as Lucy put it, to have grown into her striking features and richly colored hair and eyes. Sometimes Nellie almost had to pinch herself to believe she was no longer a nervous wallflower, not just an extra person invited to fill out a list of preferred guests. And Lucy's designs gave her the frame for her blossoming beauty, poise, and growing self-confidence.

"Oh, there you are, my dear," the young woman who was eyeing her said. "I was admiring that gown during dinner, quite as lovely as your earlier tea gown this afternoon. I'm told your sister creates all your lovely clothes. You simply seem to float in them, and I noted quite a few of the gentlemen looking and whispering, though I realize it was not only the allure of the gown that caused that."

The young, pretty, and chatty Honorable Mrs. Arthur Brand was someone Nellie had pegged as a clotheshorse with social aspirations and a small budget. It wasn't exactly like catching a duchess, but it was a start.

"I overheard you say your sister would design specially for a client," she rushed on, sounding suddenly anxious.

"Indeed, she would be honored. She would meet you, of course, and hear your needs and wishes. As she's just establishing her designs, she would be so affordable compared to Worth and those other Paris designers everyone runs to. The fashions would be yours alone, not what others are wearing, though very much in vogue, of course. Lucile is very attuned to matching individual beauty with the perfect frame for their future fame."

"Ah, you are a poet and don't show it, but you have shown me the most marvelous possibility," Mrs. Brand said, blatantly perusing the gown again.

She laughed and tucked her arm into Nellie's as if they were now longtime companions. "Everyone thinks you are so clever with your personality sketches and gazette articles. I read one recently. I do believe your red hair and green eyes are a magnet too, for the men, at least. Oh, I wonder whatever is that much ado out on the patio," she said, turning them toward the windows. "If they're telling ribald jokes, I hope my Arthur isn't among them."

For dinner and dancing tonight, Nellie had to admit the gown Lucy had made for her was a dream in softest lilac and cream satin with tiny ribbon roses scattered over the paneled skirt and echoed in the elaborate hemline. The draped satin bustle balanced the beaded bodice. By observation and practice, Nellie had learned to flirt by peeking over the rim of her lace fan and fluttering it to accent the swell of her breasts of the décolleté gown. She had met so many new acquaintances these last two days, several of them admiring men, but it was truly the women she was trying to attract right now with Lucy's dress, and this eager woman might mean victory at last.

Nellie was careful with the fluted champagne glass so she wouldn't splash the expensive fabric. Perhaps she'd even had a few too many glasses of the bubbly liquid, but it all went down so smoothly. At the corner of the ballroom stood a champagne fountain of overflowing, stacked goblets to echo the larger water fountain on the terrace, just outside the sweep of ballroom windows where most of the men had gathered.

She also wore Mother's only pearl necklace and the second pair of elbow-length kid gloves of the four she'd brought along. Of course the men also wore gloves for dancing. Properly, no flesh ever touched, at least here in public, though, as ever, she noticed the bedrooms in the country house placed certain people in close proximity. She'd been partnered in dances by several swains—an old word from her romantic readings over the years—but none, she thought with a sigh, who would want more than a liaison with her, for everyone knew she had hardly a penny to her name.

Despite her increasing popularity, she yearned for romance, for someone to truly love and trust, but duty first—and research for the book she longed to write, one about her own travels but with a fictional heroine. This was the least she could do for Lucy, who was desperately trying to make ends meet and launch her business, however déclassé it was for married women to be in trade.

As shocked as Nellie had been four months ago over Lucy's affair with Dr. Mackenzie, she felt sympathy for her sister now. Word was the doctor was dying from shame, grief, and heart failure. Recently, after his country house had been ransacked, he had again told Lucy to stay away because he might not be safe even in London where he was living now. His looming loss was breaking Lucy's heart. Terribly romantic, but terribly terrible!

The two women moved—with other ladies—toward the sweep of windows to see what was going on outside. Shouts, cheers, maybe jeers floated to them.

"You won't believe it, Nellie," their host Billy Grant told them as he came inside and took her other arm. "Four of the men whose hearts you've conquered were speaking of you and ended up—with their too-full stomachs and port glasses—in a scuffle in the fountain, fully dressed!"

"No! You're teasing," Nellie insisted, and her stomach cartwheeled. Would this hurt or enhance her reputation?

"I'm not teasing. And I'd advise you not to go outside right now or that lovely gown might end up soaking wet if one of them insisted on embracing you."

"You see," Mrs. Brand said calmly, as if men fought and made fools of themselves over Nellie every day, "even gentlemen admire your costumes, although they are acting more like ruffians right now. But I must be certain my Arthur is standing clear. Stay there, dear, and please tell your sister I'll call upon her very soon."

The shouting and splashing sounded louder as a footman opened the door for Mrs. Brand to go out. Were other gentlemen joining in the fracas? Was she dreaming this? Elinor "Nellie" Sutherland had smitten hearts and caused this upheaval?

Wait until she told Lucy, but she wasn't sure she was going to tell Mother.

"I think they've had enough fun," Billy said as he raised and kissed her gloved hand. "Before someone drowns and all for love, best I put an end to this. Oh, Clayton, keep the object of the war company until I can return law and order, won't you?" he said and headed back toward the door.

A nice-looking, blue-eyed man a head taller than Nellie bowed slightly over their briefly linked hands. Oh yes, although she hadn't been formally introduced to him, she'd overheard him talking about his travels to several others, trips sounding extensive, expensive, and so exciting. How she yearned to travel more than she had—and write about it all too. Though he must be in his thirties, he had a head of thick, wavy silver hair. He clinked his glass to her goblet.

"Clayton Glyn at your service," he said in a pleasant voice with another charming smile. The man had perfect teeth. "*Enchante, Mademoiselle Sutherland*. I am grieved not to have made your acquaintance before now, even at another gathering, but I've been traveling in the Far East and have just returned. I've barely spent time at my estate in Essex. When I overheard who the hubbub was about outside, I came in to meet and to protect the paragon of beauty to be certain she does not become a damsel in distress."

She liked the sound of all that, the formality, the bit of perfect French, the touch of his gloved hand, and his protective nature. He'd actually used one of her favorite romantic lines from books she'd read and would, no doubt, use in hers, *At your service*. And he didn't want her to be *a damsel in distress,* as if he yearned to rescue her. His eyes seemed to drink her all in as he drained his beverage, then reached to set hers aside on a table as if she'd already agreed to dance with him in this suddenly not crowded room, while the orchestra calmly played yet another waltz.

She smiled and nodded as if all his praise was her due. Good heavens, had she gone conceited as well as tongue-tied for once?

"So I admit," Clayton Glyn went on, "I had to see the object of affection of the four men scuffling in a fountain. In my travels I have seen famous fountains such as Trevi in Rome and the Fontaines de la Concorde in Paris—and those at Versailles." Then with a wink and a tip of his head, he said, "But suddenly, that one outside has become my favorite, since it's taken all your beaus away so that I may meet you and have you to myself for a few moments. Shall we dance?"

Nellie's heart raced. A world traveler. One who probably loved Paris. Who had an estate. One who must be unattached. And she was so drawn to the slight hint of arrogance in his voice and attitude—so noble and superior, above all the fray.

For once, she was indeed speechless.

* * *

Lucy was beside herself over the rumors that Dr. Morell Mackenzie was dying. He had written her to stay away after he was certain he was being watched by German spies—or possibly, someone hired by the Royal College of Surgeons of London who felt he had betrayed their trust. But if he were truly fatally ill, she had to see him one more time.

She'd agonized over this, but then, ever since James had deserted her, she was used to agony. Not that he'd gone but that he'd left ruin in his wake. Could she risk a divorce and still have her dream of designing and selling fashions—and for fashionable women? That had obsessed her during the day and kept her awake at night.

And now she knew she must go at night. The fact Morell had once given her carte blanche to visit him at his office at any time, allowing her to immediately be taken into his waiting room ahead of patients, had spawned rumors. He was an attractive catch, so she'd been closely watched by some of his patients. But he had taken leave from practicing medicine at this difficult time. It was a great wrench for him, and she understood that, too. She had to risk all, not only to see him tonight, but also to not give up on her dream of serving others. Oh, not by healing bodies, but by healing women's hearts—possibly her own, too, with her fanciful, fabulous designs.

Previously, she and Morell had met mostly after dark. The doctor's own driver would come to call, taking her to their meeting spots. Mother was in a snit when she went out unchaperoned. But tonight, Lucy was taking Mother's lady's maid, Bradford, with her to add an aura of respectability to her visit.

A hired hackney took them to Morell's Eaton Square town house in no time. It was chilly outside, though it was early September. Nellie was in Devon at a large gathering, ever the extra, clever guest, one who had no dowry or title and wealthy prospects so that ladies with such did not find her threatening amid their suitors or followers. Lucy wished she could pay her sister to model and promote her tea and evening gowns. Poor Nellie.

Poor herself. Lucy hated living in the hinterland of being neither wed nor single. Despite everyone's warnings against becoming a divorced woman, she was becoming desperate enough to file a case against James.

Lucy looked both ways on the gaslit street when they arrived at Morell's town house. He had written a farewell letter to her in a shaky hand, stating that he believed he was being watched by hostile elements and she was to keep safe and keep away . . . that he treasured the hours they had spent together . . . their conversations, her playing the piano for him, her friendship, admiration, and devotion that had helped to sustain him through difficult decisions and times . . . their mutual, precious love. He had never married. If things had been different, would it have been possible that—

"You are to wait for us here," she told their driver. "However long."

"I understand, that I do. Used to waiting, missus."

Followed by Bradford, Lucy climbed down, went to the door, and lifted the knocker, banging it down, once, twice. What if his butler would not let her in? What if Morell was too weak to see her or—or had died already? No, then there would be a black wreath on the door and black drapings in the few lighted windows.

The door opened. Rodgers, his butler, stood there. Morell had done away with much of his staff, but for a cook and a valet and this faithful man.

"Mrs. Wallace!" he cried. "Dear me, I did not know you were coming."

"Please let us in, Rodgers. I have to see him. Will he see me?"

"I—well, please come into the library, and I'll inquire. He's not himself now, you know."

"I do know," she said. He nodded and escorted them into the library and helped them with their wraps.

As Rodgers disappeared silently upstairs, Lucy told Bradford, "If he comes here, I'll ask you to wait on the bench in the hall. If I go up to see him, I will come for you here when I'm ready to leave. I do not—not know how ill my friend is."

"Miss Esme told Simpson she remembers the doctor fondly too, just like your mother," the girl said in her clipped Cockney accent. "She may be only six, but Miss Esme's got a fine memory, that she does."

Lucy didn't even care if the servants had been talking about this, or Esme, either. All that mattered was seeing him, saying some things, and—

"The doctor will entertain your presence upstairs, Mrs. Wallace," Rodgers said as he came back in. "So sad to see one who has healed others ill himself."

"I dare say," Lucy agreed as she followed him out. And, she thought, what did she dare say to the man waiting upstairs who had been kinder to her than her own husband ever had?

* * *

Morell's bed was mussed, and he'd obviously just had Rodgers help him from it into a high-backed leather chair as he was still settling a blanket over his legs. Lucy had been here twice before, in happy—passionate—times. He wore a nightshirt under a blue silk robe. He had not shaved for several days, and silvery stubble shone on his sunken cheeks; his eyes were shadowed, but they lit to see her. A fire burned low in the grate, and a single gas lantern glowed next to his bed.

She bent to kiss his cheek, then sat on the large ottoman next to his chair and reached for his hands. They were cold and trembling. Imagine, the skilled surgeon of many examinations and operations, trembling.

"My dearest Lucile, you should not have come, but I shall be eternally glad you did. I have missed you terribly."

"And I have worried over you."

"But you are still drawing your beautiful clothing, aren't you?"

"Thank you for that. For saying they are beautiful and knowing how important that is to me."

"You will someday lift the spirits of ladies more than I have done their health."

"No one has bothered you—tried to hurt you? Lurking Germans or others?"

"Not since the ransacking of my country place. As if then I would go on a speaking tour or some such with this shortness of breath, my chest pain and weakness."

As if to accent that, he straightened and breathed deeply and slowly, almost wheezing. His hand fluttered to his chest as if to hide the pain there. She started to speak, but he went on, "Lucile, I've seen highs and lows, and I hope you will always have the highs. Is Nellie still scandalized over us?"

"I believe she knows a good and great man when she sees one. It seems she's been a better judge of men's character than I was, except for you. I have decided to risk everything and file for a divorce, though I've agonized over it so long. I told Mother and Lucy that months ago, but I've finally 'screwed my courage to the sticking point,' as Nellie read me from a Shakespeare tragedy lately, and I've had enough of tragedy in my life."

"I admire your courage. You've told me before you have thought this out, and I pray that you have."

"Yes, well, I can only pray it won't ruin my hopes to attract some buyers who will model my fashions far and wide. But what can I do to help you? Please let me see you again, call on you to lift your spirits."

"You already have. But there is one thing. Because of my iron back brace I've hidden from most people except you—of lovely necessity—I always wanted you to sit on my lap and never told you that. I won't let this scruffy beard scratch your fair skin, I promise."

She drew her skirts closer so she could get them into his armed chair. His embrace encircled her. She lay her head on his shoulder then rubbed her cheek across his stubble, no matter what he'd said. He pulled her tighter and kissed her gently, then desperately. She felt so large in his arms, all skirts and strong body while his felt bony and thin.

Too soon, with tears in his eyes, he helped her up and made her leave. They did not say good-bye, but she knew it was exactly, painfully, that.

# CHAPTER *Eight*

Lucy drooped about the house the next day. She didn't even go out with Mother, Esme, and Simpson to the park to fly a kite, citing her upset stomach. Thank heavens, not one of them fussed or insisted she come with them, but maybe they knew she'd pull their spirits down. She sat sullen, staring at her sketches of tea gowns, which everyone called teagies. The garments had a rather naughty reputation—they were loose fitting and worn without a corset beneath so, it was rumored, that they could come up or off easily if one's lover dropped by under the excuse of coming for tea.

*Tea and me,* Lucy thought and heaved a sob. She had lost the only man she had truly cared for—after her girlhood infatuation with Cecil—and was about to divorce the one she'd married and had not cared a straw for. She tried to stem the tears, but they flowed anyway.

She heard the maid go to the front door, though she had not heard the bell. Oh, Nellie's voice. Now she'd have to hear all about the estate in Devon, the people, what fun, and she couldn't bear it, at least right now. She would beat a retreat upstairs, say she had a headache, just hide in bed and picture poor Morell in his and recall the several times they had shared a bed and—

Before Lucy could disappear, Nellie exploded into the room with, "You won't believe this!" She hadn't even removed her hat, gloves, or cloak. "I've found someone to wear your clothes among the uppers, and she loves your designs. She's a real up-and-comer, pretty, too. She'll make a better walking, talking mannequin than I ever did!"

"Oh! Oh, tell me all!" Lucy cried and broke into full-fledged tears. "I needed some good news, and you have brought it."

"Then just you remember our agreement," Nellie told her, coming over to seize Lucy's shoulders and give her a little shake. "If I fetch you an important customer, you will personally purchase one hundred copies of my first novel, ha!" she said with a wink. "That is, as soon as it's written and a publisher goes all moony over it. I just hope I have as much luck with the book as I'm having right now with admirers. I had four of them arguing over me, and they tussled in a fountain and everyone heard about it—and I might have met the man of my dreams, I mean I think I have. Prince Charming, right out of the blue."

"Nothing is right out of the blue," Lucy said as she swiped at her tears, then grasped Nellie's wrists. "You have been making your way and I, too, despite setbacks we've suffered. Only good things are yet to come, as soon as I rid myself of my husband and you find one, and—and we will go on. Perhaps Lillie Langtry was right about our glorious futures. You've made my day, and I owe you a great deal! Now tell me all."

* * *

As they bent over the cut fabric pieces on the dining room table, Lucy told Mother, "You know, I told Mrs. Brand that I would design yet another tea gown to fit her personality. She was most pleased, not only with that but with the compliments that came her way when she wore the first one. I am thrilled with new orders. And I came up with the most marvelous idea. I think I shall name each of my gowns specifically. They'll be either gowns of personality or gowns of emotion, depending on the wearer. I shall tell Mrs. Brand this one is named *Winter Wonder,* since we're in the depths of November."

"Mm," Mother said, then took away the pins she was holding in her mouth. "That will go over with flying colors, I'm sure, but you'd best concentrate that mind of yours on sewing, not promoting. If word gets round about your divorce, new orders may dry up."

Lucy shook out the accordion panels of the daffodil-hued skirt she'd worked hard on, and the material danced, just the way she'd hoped it would. "Mother, Nellie and I have both vowed to enlarge our passions—onward and upward is our motto. Young women in this modern age must have something to hope for and strive for. She is working to somehow make Clayton propose to her when he's obviously so smitten but hesitant."

"As, I dare say, any bachelor in his midthirties might be. I surely don't blame our Nellie."

"And I am working to promote myself as a designer as Lucile Ltd., not Mrs. James Wallace. I thank you and Nellie for pitching in here when you can, but I have big dreams and that does not include my sewing staff being my mother and sister."

"Oh, I hear her voice. Here she is now," Mother said, popping up. "After a ride with Clayton on Rotten Row, I hope she has some news he's asked for her hand."

"And the rest of her."

"Lucy! He's evidently wealthy enough that he may be the answer to all our dreams." She called out, "Nellie, dear, we're in here!"

Nellie rushed in, pink cheeked and out of breath. "I might not like horses, but I did fine with Clayton and in your smashing wool riding habit, Lucy. At least I didn't have to dodge other mounts, as there was hardly anyone else on the path today, so we and his man, Stephens, had it all to ourselves."

"Bully for you!" Lucy said. "You've hated horses ever since that carriage horse ran away with you."

"Yes, but now Clayton's run away with my heart. Oh, he still didn't propose exactly, but I found out so much more about him."

"I liked him from the first," Mother said, sitting back down while Nellie sank into a chair across the cluttered table and Lucy kept sewing. "Especially when I heard there are three houses on his Essex estate," she said with a sigh. "I'd love to see the large Georgian house there—what's its name again?"

"Durrington House," Nellie said. "Then there is Sheering Hall, a three-hundred-year-old farmhouse, quite redone, he says, and then a small house called Lamberts. He's a country squire at heart, stocking his fields with pheasants for shoots and—you won't believe the irony of this—breeding a herd of Jersey cows. He mixes well with aristocrats, and he's so perfect for me, and would Grandmama be so proud! Oh, by the by, he's let out Durrington House, because he's been traveling so much, but I'm sure it's where we would live if he'd just take the step to propose."

"Well," Lucy said, "before he sets out again, I hope he takes that very step."

"He's mentioned a future trip, even one to Brighton, which I am praying could be for our honeymoon. He said he would love to see me swimming with my long hair all loose. Mother, he is a man of substance, and I believe he cares for me. He's spoken of wanting children, an heir and a spare—so doesn't that sound almost royal?"

Lucy stood and stretched her back. "Almost is not good enough, Miss Elinor Sutherland," she told her. "If you want to force his hand, I will pay for you and Mother to go away for a while to see if your world traveler will follow. Will absence make the heart grow fonder or will it be out of sight, out of mind? My second client of note, Mrs. Panmure Gordon, was raving about Monte Carlo, so how about a visit there?"

Nellie jumped up and bounced like a child despite the fact she was a twenty-seven-year-old old maid. "Oh, Lucy, that might be just the ticket. To show him we can travel too, that we have some money."

"Which," Mother added, "we almost don't. Oh, I pray he'd make a good marriage settlement on you."

Lucy put in with a smile, "I can assure you I know a designer who could save us a fortune on the bridal gown and bridesmaids, child bridesmaids, too, including Esme."

"I'll chance leaving him for a while!" Nellie declared. "I'll be as bold as you have been launching this fashion business. I shall tell him Mother and I are off to Monte Carlo and say I hope he doesn't miss me—and then pray he does."

* * *

"Oh dear," Nellie said looking up from reading Lucy's letter to them. The bright Mediterranean winter sun streaming in their window illumined the black handwriting set boldly against the stark white page with LUCILE LTD. embossed at the top. "Dr. Mackenzie died of heart failure on February third. That's all she says. What a year 1892 has been so far! I know she's grieving, but I'll bet she can't even put her feelings into words. I may be the writer in the family, but I've never seen Lucy at a loss for that. Even I am grieved for his loss to his patients and profession—to Lucy too."

Mother took her handkerchief from her sleeve and dabbed at her eyes.

"He was a brilliant man," she said. "Brilliant to care deeply for Lucy, also just when she felt deserted and—and so alone."

"Best call her Lucile now, Mother. The rest of this," she said as she skimmed the letter, "is about orders pouring in, which is keeping her up all night. She's even paying Bradford to put in hems. And oh—oh, here at the bottom in a sort of postscript! She says Clayton called on her at the house to be certain of our address here, and he's coming to Monte Carlo! Now, why didn't she put that at the top with stars all around it? Oh, heavens, that means—I'm counting from the date she wrote this—he could be here today! I need to change my gown—you too. Wouldn't it be just like an impetuous suitor to drop right in? We can hardly go stroll on the promenade now, but we don't want to seem to be sitting here, waiting for him!"

Mother reached over to take her hands and pulled her back into her seat. "My dearest, you do love him, don't you? You are sure he is the one? I admit he sounds perfect too. But, after Mr. Kennedy and James Wallace, I have seen there can be a steep price we women pay for marriage. I'm not leery but—but careful. Even Clayton seems to be holding something back sometimes, to look down his nose at things . . ."

"But don't you see? That's because he is of a superior type. It's as if he stepped from the pages of *Le Morte de Arthur* or *The Romance of the Rose*!"

"Your and Lucy's happiness, little Esme's, too, that's what I live for. I have had a dear love of my own to cherish always in my heart."

"Father was God's gift to you and Clayton will be to me—just wait and see. He has that certain thing Lucy and I like to think of as 'It.'"

"It? It what?"

"A special inward charm that is like a bubble all around one's presence. A magnetic field of sorts. Charisma. A woman can have 'It' too, just like Lillie Langtry did. I'll write a story about it someday, just wait and see."

* * *

"Your mother seems overly interested in the seagulls," Clayton told Nellie with a glance behind them as they strolled the seaside promenade late the next morning. Nellie had been in such a state she hadn't slept last night and was on edge now.

"She's just giving us some privacy," she told him and squeezed his arm linked in hers against her ribs. "She knows I'm happy to see you and to have you all to myself."

"My dream with you, exactly. I long to have you off alone, no Mother, no Lucy, no chaperones. I yearn to see you swimming with your white skin just below the surface and your long, sunset hair streaming free. Nellie—Elinor—if you will have me, I would like to—love and long to—marry you. If you agree, I want to go back inside to the hotel lobby, just the two of us, because I've brought you a special gift if you will just agree—why are you crying?"

"I'm just so happy."

"Then smile. Tell me what you think—and feel."

Her feelings! This man cared about her emotions as well as her thoughts.

"That I love you. Yes, yes!" she blurted and cried the more.

"Of course I'd make a good marriage settlement for your mother," he said in a rush. "One way or the other, maybe help Lucile get her ladies' shop out of the Davies Street house. I know someone who would be a good financial adviser for that as juggling money and avoiding debt is not my bailiwick. Well?"

"Well, I always wanted to wed a man who had a herd of Jersey cows," she blurted out, though she knew she was getting giddy. "Let me tell Mother we're going back inside—and why."

"Then tell her," he said, wiping at Nellie's eyes with a handkerchief he'd pulled from his frock coat, "I bought you a large diamond ring from Cartier, and I'm sure you Sutherland women will like it—and those fine French relatives you told me about will approve too."

Despite the propriety on the promenade and Mother watching from behind, Nellie hugged Clayton. "Let's both tell her," she said. "I can wait for the ring if I have you."

Together, they turned back toward Mother. Nellie absolutely knew Clayton had solved all her problems and that from now on, everything would be perfectly wonderful.

* * *

At age twenty-seven on April 27, 1892, Miss Nellie Sutherland became Mrs. Elinor Glyn at St. George's Church, Hanover Square, in London. Lucy said she looked like a medieval princess, and she did, down to the elaborate headdress. A stunning diamond tiara—a gift from Clayton—held in place a veil of Brussels lace. She felt like Shakespeare's Fairy Queen and set a new trend since she was the first bride to wear a tiara instead of a wreath of orange blossoms.

Their French relatives attended, awed by the fact that a man of money and some position would marry a girl without a dowry. Nevertheless, their cousin Auguste gave the bride away. Esme and the two other child bridesmaids had touches of yellow in their dresses, also a break in tradition for English weddings, especially since yellow in a wedding used to mean "Ashamed of her fellow," which Elinor was not. Besides, Lucy was not about to let silly superstitions keep her from using lovely colors.

"Well, Clayton's indirectly given me a lovely gift too—customers," Lucy said to Mother and Nellie at the reception, after several guests had asked for that very yellow hue in gowns. "And he gave me the name of someone who might be willing to advise me on finances so I can hire a small staff and eventually move my endeavor out of the house, someone named, ah—here is his calling card, Sir Cosmo Duff-Gordon, fifth Baronet, no less!"

Mother looked impressed, but Nellie—that is, Mrs. Elinor Glyn—wasn't listening, and why should she? Her dreams had come true, her ship had come in. Lucy—no, she was Lucile now—had to smile at that.

After all, her own ship had come in with a new batch of orders just now. She was going to design beautiful personality dresses and gowns of emotion, frocks and teagies—even underthings, so a British bride wouldn't have to go to Paris for a trousseau of intimate items. She would make her name and her fortune, too. Yes, after being abandoned by one man and losing another to death, she would be married only to her passion for design from now on.

* * *

"Clayton, what will everyone think that you rented and closed two entire swimming pools for two entire days here at Brighton?" Elinor asked as she sat on the side of the pool and loosed her long hair for him.

"They will think I am the most fortunate man in the universe," he told her.

Clayton had insisted they both wear robes with nothing under them and then discard even those for a swim together. Their wedding night had been entirely in the dark before they left for this seaside town, but with Clayton's plans they could hardly go swimming in the sea. It was his fantasy—his romance, as she thought of it—that she should be his mermaid and seduce him and become his love. Yes, that was the tale she would spin from this, only it was real.

The last long pin that held up her tresses clacked to the tile floor, and the bounty of her hair tumbled loose clear to her knees.

Clayton leaned closer on the wooden bench and ran his hands through her heavy hair she hadn't had cut for years. "In certain Islamic cultures, you know," his voice whispered in her ear, "a women's hair is completely hidden except from her mate in their intimate times."

His other hand skimmed her spine. That touch through the

silken robe set her to trembling. Last night things had happened rather fast as if to seal the deal, but this—this was wooing, real romance, of course. It was what she had longed for, yet the pursuit was what enticed her, not the capture. Was she demented? She should have talked more to Lucy about this part of marriage.

"May I remove your robe, darling, and we'll get in the water?"

"Of course. I'm not as strong a swimmer as—as you might think, raised in the wilds of Canada."

She'd almost said, *as my sister is*. She had to stop thinking about Lucy and the ruin of her marriage to James. This was going to be grand. She loved Clayton—desired him too, surely. He was everything she'd wanted.

He lifted the robe from her shoulders, and she quickly untied it so he could pull it away. Her hair fell like a curtain round her as she rose from the bench and went down the steps into the water. It was quite warm. It seemed to caress and shelter her.

Clayton removed his robe and followed her in. His vision—his fantasy, he had said—was to see her swim with her red hair streaming out behind her, so she put her hands out in front and stepped off. The ripples caressed her. In a splash he was at her side, smiling, his hands reaching for her waist.

"Two days to touch, to know each other, to be one," he whispered as he treaded water, holding her up.

As he moved a slick knee between her legs, she put her hands on his shoulders.

Oh my, he was ready right now. What a shock to realize that she was too, and not only from the water in the pool.

He moved them into the corner where he could steady them. He pressed her against the ceramic tiles, kissing her, devouring her.

So this was really the marriage act, but not in the privacy of a bed. This was in living, moving water, a bit rushed, a bit strong, but there was power in it. She totally surrendered, her mind, too, as she had not last night when a part of her had stood aside, still thinking, thinking. But not this time. This was seduction and surrender, swirling around, sinking and soaring. So this was love.

# CHAPTER *Nine*

God forgive her, but the moment Elinor absolutely knew she had made the right choice to marry Clayton was when their carriage approached the gate of his Essex estate and the tenants were there, lining the road under some sort of wooded arch they had made to welcome them, especially the estate's new mistress. And they were cheering for them as if they were royalty.

Feeling quite grand, once the brougham stopped, she nodded, smiled, and waved to the group of all ages, at least fifty of them. Two men spoke to Clayton and then unhitched his horses, Pair and Impair, and pulled the carriage the rest of the way themselves, still shouting huzzahs in unison.

But to Elinor's dismay, they pulled them right past the big Georgian home, Durrington House, down the road to the smaller, older house, Sheering Hall.

"Clayton, why isn't the formal reception at Durrington? You said we would live there soon," she said over the noise.

"Ah, in all the excitement, I guess I forgot to tell you. A line in the leasing contract reminded me I still must honor the period for which I let Durrington. We'll be cozy at Sheering until we have a family, my dearest—much more intimate. We'll still have the run of the estate lands, pastures for the herd, forests, pheasants, and all. We'll have a fine shoot here soon and you ladies—invite your mother and sister, of course—can ride out and have luncheon with the guns. You'll love Lady Brooke, the grand dame of this area, and she can't wait to meet you. She and Lord Brooke are related to the Warwicks, lots of parties and events, dearest."

Elinor was miffed, but she tried to buck herself up. She was just tired after all that watery lovemaking, and then Clayton had even hinted at romance out on a blanket in the forest or fields here. But hadn't he led her to believe that they would live in Durrington? And she fretted that Clayton kept nipping at liquor in a flask she'd never laid eyes on before they wed.

Ah, but at last someone was cheering her on and not just adoring her sister. She forced a smile and waved stiff-wristed to their tenants, just the way she'd seen Queen Victoria do once when her carriage rolled past in London.

* * *

This was chaos, utter chaos, but Lucy, now known as Lucile, had never been happier.

Her passion for her new business consumed her. Thank heavens, Esme had Mother and Bradford to care for her. Though the dining room and parlor were stuffed to the gills with bolts of fabric and other stock, she had managed to hire four seamstresses to help out. Blessedly, two of them took things home with them to make room for the other two underfoot. Yet Lucile not only sketched each design after a consultation with the buyer either here or at her own home but fitted the garments and delivered them personally in a paper-lined box.

"Lucile, this chiffon doesn't drape like it did in your sketch of this teagie," her seamstress Margaret told her, holding up the soft drift of a golden silk skirt.

"It has to," Lucile told her. "That's one of the gowns for the charity play my sister's in, the one directed by my brother-in-law's friend, Lord Rosslyn. The charity was a grand success here, and His Lordship is taking it to Edinburgh, though I'm a bit nervous the tighter-fitting gowns, after all those stagy, bulky ones over the years, will be a shock to the Scots. They're much more conservative than we British, you know. Rebaste and drape and show it to me again."

She glanced up at the dining room wall, which sported not only sketches of her designs but also her major triumphs so far. She was most proud of the framed photograph she'd had taken of her very first nonfamily design, Mrs. Brand's gown. Next to that she had mounted the program for the charity play *Diplomacy*, in which Elinor had the role of Dora here in London. Though Lucile detested still having to use her old name publicly, she read again on the wall the encouraging words *Dresses designed by Mrs. James Wallace*.

Wrong name or not, her dreams were coming true, however cramped it was in here. She was desperate to expand her space, staff, and clientele, for many wedding gown orders were flowing in, and she had plans to begin to design underclothes. She could not bear to have her lovely garments worn over what they called "nun's veiling" or plain linen with a bit of embroidery. Her side-line of corsets would be important too. She hoped to soften them, enhance them since everyone thought they were still de rigueur. Actually, she'd love to get women out of corsets for good and not just from under robes or teagies.

But how to let a place, somewhere good but not too expensive? She had to admit she gave short shrift to juggling receipts and salaries and the price of purchases, so how to figure in fees to lease a shop? She needed to spend her time on creating, overseeing, and promoting. Now, where had she lost that calling card in this mess that gave the name of a Cosmo Duff-Gordon, someone whom Clayton had said could advise her on all that tricky numerical nonsense? He was Scottish, anyway, she'd heard, probably dour and disproving of her trendsetting fashions.

But most exciting of all, she had received an inquiry for a fitting from a name from the past, from long ago before so much had happened. Lillie Langtry! Lucile had heard Lillie had triumphed then crashed after a two-year affair with the Prince of Wales. Despite still being married, she had taken other lovers and borne a daughter and gone on the stage and been to the States—and now, she was coming here to be fitted for a gown. Oh, what scandal, but Lillie was a survivor, just as Lucile vowed to be. Wait until she told Elinor. Her younger sister was awash in social invitations in her new life, but Lucile Ltd. had their old idol coming to call!

* * *

"Is my new frock ready?" Elinor asked the moment she arrived. Mother was upstairs with Esme, and she didn't ask about either of them.

"We are to dine in just two days with Daisy, the new Countess of Warwick, not far from our home," she rushed on. "You know," she added, lowering her voice as if one of Lucile's seamstresses would overhear, "she's the one who took Lillie's place as the prince's mistress, and she's lasted a good time longer than our Lillie's two years. I still don't approve of it all."

"No, you wouldn't. And, yes, your frock is ready."

"I hope it has those lovely little touches of silk flowers and frills."

"Yes, Milady Glyn."

"That was a compliment, so don't be prickly."

"I'm not the one who's prickly lately. By the way, the woman you are disparaging is coming here for a fitting."

"Not Daisy, Lady Brooke, now Countess of Warwick! I mean, I've told them all at her parties that my sister designs my frocks, but—"

"Lillie. Lillie Langtry, who has made something of herself despite the men in her life. Our original 'It' Girl. We agreed on that."

"Daisy Brooke Warwick is that now for me. Oh, Lucy—I mean Lucile—you should see her, meet her. So beautiful and vivacious but friendly, generous. And she entertains so lavishly. Why, she's taken me and Clayton right in, as grand as she is. Anyway, as I said, I can't approve of all the liaisons, and I must admit Daisy is not good at keeping hers quiet. Some call her 'The Babbling Brooke,' you know. But she and her husband are a firm part of the Prince of Wales's so-called Marlborough House set. But we are now invited not to Easton near us but to Warwick Castle!"

"Talk about a babbling brook. You've changed, Nellie."

"Elinor, now, and you should talk with your grand plans for Lucile Ltd. I don't think your ambitions are limited at all. And of course I've changed. I'm married to a successful man with wonderful friends and—and I think I'm in a family way but I intend to lace tightly and not let my new friends know for a while, though, of course I told Clayton."

"Oh," Lucile said and bit back what she was going to say next. She went to hug Elinor. "When is the baby due?"

"About on our first anniversary, I guess. Clayton is elated, and understands it should not stop our mad whirl for a while. I will like the extra time to think and write, but the events in Essex are so—so wonderful."

Lucile stepped back and loosed her. "Do take care of yourself. It's a sea change to have a child, both physically and mentally."

"Yes, well, I thank you for that and for running some errands for me before I return next time—or having one of your staff do it for me. I have to rush back, so—the gown?"

"Here, in tissue in this box," she said and lifted the top off and laid the tissue back.

"Oh, Lucy—Lucile, it is exquisite, that striking peacock blue silk! You are using such dramatic colors, and this one will set off my eyes and hair. Daisy just loves the color of my hair, says she wishes she had it too, but she's so flaxen and fair."

Lucile almost blurted out that Elinor should have wed Daisy instead of Clayton, but then she could grasp holding on to an idol, a sort of star to light one's way, so for once, she held her tongue.

She still was tempted, though, to tear up the list of lackey chores her sister handed her to do, as if she were her servant in all ways now. She did toss it onto the mess on her designing table, oh—right next to that calling card of Sir Cosmo Duff-Gordon. She'd been meaning to write him but didn't care to be lectured about her expenditures the way Mr. Kennedy used to scold all of them or James had berated her. Clayton had said this man was good at finances, and she just didn't have time for that—or him.

* * *

Even after seeing Daisy Warwick's other splendid home, called Easton Lodge, Elinor was in awe of Warwick Castle. Of massive honey-hued stone, the huge historical building sat in the embrace of the river Avon. Ah, Shakespeare country, yet the castle had originally been located there by William the Conqueror. As passionate as she was about the medieval past and romantic ladies and knights, the castle conquered Elinor.

The most amazing thing she'd glimpsed so far was a white bear hearth rug with the animal's head intact under an array of mounted trophy heads above them in the huge entry hall.

"You're trembling, my dear," Clayton said, pulling her arm closer to his ribs as they stood in the reception line of guests being greeted by Daisy.

Their luggage had been whisked up to their room straightaway from their carriage by tall, white-wigged footmen. The prince himself was in Paris, but several of his important friends, advisers, and statesmen were here, Tory politicians all, Elinor assumed.

Most of the women wore sable-trimmed velvet or brocade with low-V necklines topped by necklaces heavy with gems or dripping with pearls. Although her gown was silk, Elinor had taken a tip from something she'd heard about Lillie Langtry years ago—simplicity to stand out amid the others. Although her Lucile gown was silk, it was a simply cut, stunning peacock blue accented by a single cameo and small pearl earrings.

Until she could describe all this to Lucile and, more important, record it in her diary, Elinor was all ears and eyes. Somehow, she must absolutely work all this into her novel she'd been writing, a story about a woman who visited fascinating people and places, though she'd hardly name her heroine Elinor. No, after all, the grand Tudor Queen Elizabeth herself had visited here, so she reckoned she'd just borrow that name and entitle her novel—for which she kept its progress secret even from her family for now—*The Visits of Elizabeth*.

Finally, they worked their way to the bewigged Groom of the Chambers, who announced their names in a ringing, deep voice to the Count and Countess of Warwick.

"Dear friend, how lovely you look!" Daisy cried when she saw her and even stooped to give her a kiss on the cheek. She smelled of lavender powder—and power. But charm, too. Daisy might spend a fortune to entertain, but she had a heart for the little people of her world too. Not that Elinor and Clayton were one of the tenant farmers or downstairs folk. She, thanks to Clayton, was climbing the social ladder and loved every moment of it.

"What a wonderful home you have made this historic house," Elinor told her, one of the opening remarks she'd rehearsed. It was true, though the vast gold-and-white grand saloon, hung heavy with painted portraits and tapestries, hardly seemed homey.

"Truth is," she whispered in Elinor's ear, "tradition rules here, not me. But it's all part of the bargain." Then she asked, "So—Clayton and dear friend, have you two met Lord Curzon?" She motioned to the person in line behind them. "My favorite, brilliant man, who will help guide our empire in the future through its foreign endeavors. George, Lord Curzon, may I present neighbors of ours in Essex, Clayton and Elinor Glyn?"

Elinor turned and met the magnetic, assessing stare of a man standing so upright and stiff he was surely a former military man. They exchanged greetings and pleasantries and chatted. His eyes glanced at Elinor, her hair, her gown, even as he spoke politely with Clayton. Then he moved on.

"Oh, he's going places all right," Clayton muttered. "You think I'm a great traveler, that man's been everywhere and to the most odd, exotic places."

"Really? I still long to see Egypt."

"You will. But about that avid-eyed hawk, you've heard that bit of schoolboy doggerel about him, haven't you? Best put it in your diary and remember it if he looks you over like a side of beef again."

"Clayton! But no, what doggerel?" she asked, as she put her hand on his arm. "Something dreadfully mean, I suppose."

Clayton rolled his eyes and recited in a quiet voice as they moved farther into the vast room,

*"My name is George Nathaniel Curzon,*
*I am a most superior person.*
*My cheek is pink, my hair is sleek,*
*I dine at Blenheim once a week."*

"Oh my. Blenheim, the ultimate in social invitations and," she whispered back, "I heard it would make Warwick look like a doll's house. That satire was a bit cruel, but it shows Curzon's superior breeding and importance."

"We'd best steer clear of him, if we can. By the way, he's wed to one of those rich American heiresses, though I don't know where he's stashed her for this. Mary something, not a home-grown English heiress like Daisy. Lord Salisbury's named him undersecretary for India, though, and I hear he likes it there."

Clayton indeed steered her sharply away from Lord Curzon, who was chatting with a cluster of people. *But undersecretary for India,* Elinor thought. That at least sounded so romantic about that rather stiff, cold man. She'd just forget that strange combination of icy and burning look he gave her and enjoy this castle. My, how blessed she was to have wed Clayton Glyn.

* * *

"I adore your brilliant color combinations," Lillie Langtry said, fingering through the samples Lucile displayed for her. "Who would think of scarlet, viridian, tyrian purple, jade, and gold, as you call them? What hue do you think I could best carry off?"

"I think you could carry off anything in any hue you choose," Lucile told her. "I know you won't recall this," she went on in a rush, "but once on Jersey, when you returned to Government House for a reception, you and the governor's wife came into the ladies' cloakroom, and there were two girls hiding under the mirrored table."

"Yes. Yes, I recall that. It seems ages ago. And someone told you of it and—Or is it that you are one of those girls?" She broke into a beautiful smile, and a faraway look misted her eyes. "Not a bit afraid were you? I toasted you with my champagne . . ."

"Yes! Yes, my younger sister and me, and you said we would make something of ourselves, and we believed you!"

"And here you are!" Lillie said and held Lucile off at arm's length with her hands firm on her shoulders as if to look her over once again.

"Yes, doing what I love and working for better."

"Don't we all, my dear—work and hope for better? Forgive me, but I believe someone said you are divorced."

"I—well, I will be soon. He deserted me and my daughter. But I've waited a while to sue because of the steep fees."

"So here we are, sisters under the skin; I too am not divorced yet," Lillie said, loosing Lucile's shoulders and stepping back, one fist perched on her tiny waist. "But everyone high and low knows I've been left in the lurch when I had my daughter. Perhaps we both shall win someday. Meanwhile, I have new friends, I have the stage and own racehorses, too. You haven't—haven't been on the stage?"

Lucile had to smile at that. "I've designed for it and hope to do more."

"If I had champagne here—the finest of it is a bit harder to come by lately—I would toast you again, Lucile. But now, please make me the most wonderful creation so when I reinvent myself again, I shall do so with beauty and aplomb!"

"I have the perfect design and color combination in mind," she told Lillie. "Let me draw a quick sketch to show you my plan."

It was as if, Lucile thought, this woman commanded the stage of life. Despite her tarnished reputation and hardships, Lillie Langtry was an inspiration.

# CHAPTER *Ten*

"I hate to ask this, Mrs. Wallace, but—"

"Please call me Lucile, Edith," she interrupted her latest hired helper. She was both a seamstress and good at fittings. She had seemed quick to learn new work, though she was a bit of a stickler, which could be good or bad. A sturdy blond girl, Edith was a hard worker. "I know you are new here, but you are to call me Lucile, never the other," she reminded the young woman.

"Yes, Lucile. I just wanted to say that the box full of receipts and notes of payment might be better separated into groupings of what we sell."

In frustration, Lucile almost sent her back into the third room downstairs of the small Davies Street house she'd nearly taken over for Lucile Ltd., but the girl probably had a point.

"I have a lovely, leather-bound order book to keeps things straight," she told Edith, looking up from her sketches of satin and lace underclothes that were selling so well among London ladies. "Frankly, I see myself as an artist, not a tradesperson."

"But the book lists what is ordered, not what is sold. We could divide the paid receipts into dressing gowns, morning gowns, walking suits, tea gowns, and dinner parties, maybe even divide those into opera frocks or theater. Then there are the bridesmaids and bridal, riding habits, debutante gowns," she went on, ticking the various design lines off on her fingers. "And now those of so lovely, naughty underthings, besides the corsets."

Lucile frowned and narrowed her eyes, but she was only thinking all that over. Despite the clever girl's Germanic-sounding last name, she had a slight French accent and that was an asset around here.

"I'm sure you're quite right, Edith. Would you have the time to—"

"Oh yes, I can do that much, but just don't ask me to add and subtract, Madame Lucile."

Margaret, one of Lucile's best seamstresses, rushed in. One thing after another, Lucile thought, and it was beginning to annoy her.

"Lucile, an irate husband is returning his wife's underclothes and saying they are indecent! That the Queen would close us down if she knew what we are selling to virtuous wives of the realm. He's waiting and insists he see you."

Lucile sighed and rolled her eyes. "In the library?" she asked as she rose.

"In the hall. He would not enter farther."

Lucile had handled this problem before, but, on the other hand, she had heard how much certain husbands adored the silk and lace garments their women wore in place of scratchy, wrinkled linen shifts and woolen winter drawers. She prayed again that her reputation would not be sullied by whispers that a woman suing for divorce was selling racy unmentionables out of her home. Indeed, they were things of comfort and beauty, and women adored them.

"Yes, I am Lucile," she told the storm cloud of a man who was pacing in the tiny hallway. He had at least removed his hat.

"And you designed and sold these to a fine, Christian, upstanding mother of four children, my wife?" he demanded, spilling the contents of his sack onto the banister of the stairs. The door opened behind her with a sweep of cool autumn wind, and a few crisp leaves skittered across the floor. Hoping it wasn't Mother and Esme back from the park to witness this dressing-down, Lucile nonetheless did not turn round to look.

She adeptly caught each beautiful silky item as it skidded off the banister before it could fall to the floor. "I designed and sold them and Lady Derby bought them," she said calmly, recognizing the articles. "She wanted to look lovely for you and for herself."

"For herself! I have told her she will shop elsewhere now, where morals, our Queen, and the empire are respected! Good day to you!" He slapped his hat on his head and started out, but encountered another man on the doorstep. "Excuse me, sir! If you have a wife," Lord Derby muttered to the tall mustached man who seemed to fill the doorway, "I would keep her far from this place of dangerous trade!"

Lord Derby ducked out, and there stood the next stranger. "Have you come to fetch your wife, sir, or to lodge a complaint?" Lucile asked, her voice so sharp it surprised her. Somehow she'd managed to remain calm during that telling off, but she couldn't take another right now.

When the new caller doffed his hat and smiled with a flash of white teeth under his mustache, she felt the earth move. No, that was just the wind on this brisk day, she told herself. As properly as he was acting, he reminded her of a pirate with that black mustache and thick raven hair—and the black leather patch over his left eye. He was taller than most men she knew and good-looking in a rakish way, which no doubt the pirate look enhanced.

"May I close the door?" he asked. "I was about to knock and it blew open, so I surmise your previous caller didn't close it well."

But it was as if, she thought, fate had opened it for them and pushed him right inside. Though she was no silly romantic like Elinor, she felt actually blown away. She got hold of herself as the man extended his calling card toward her. Suddenly, she had an inkling who he was, for he had the slightest burr of a Scottish accent.

"Oh, Sir Cosmo Duff-Gordon," she said, glancing at the card. "My brother-in-law, Clayton Glyn, mentioned you, but that was a while ago."

"It was indeed. He thought I might be of service to your new endeavor, to your schemes for expansion. He said you might need a steady financial hand, some advice. I saw you from afar at the theater the other night and remembered that I'd told Clayton I'd call months ago—and then didn't. I'm always looking for investments, offering advice to others on various trade endeavors."

She felt like a fool when he reached over to close the door soundly behind him. Why had she stood there in the brisk wind with things blowing in?

"I—I did mean to write you but things here have changed so fast, my business, I mean. Actually, I don't intend to take on investors, but to keep it in my own hands. Please, would you step into the library, and I'll ring for some tea? My workrooms are a bit noisy and busy right now."

"That would be fine. I am regretful I waited so long to make your acquaintance," he said, bowing slightly and taking her hand.

Oh no. Lightning seemed to crackle up her arm. His gaze jolted her more than had any man's perusal for years—since that silly infatuation with that boy Cecil in Jersey that had caused her so much trouble. But this was a man, one with a deep voice that sent shivers through her. *Danger!* her rational inner voice shouted at her. She must hear him out, then move him out.

"I'm afraid I cannot afford financial services, still building my fashion trade as I am," she said and indicated the horsehair sofa for him. Oh, she should not have closed the door behind them. She should have taken his coat. What was wrong with her? It was just that she hated dealing with money matters at all. And why had she said that she would ring for tea when there was no bell cord here and Mother had let Cook take the afternoon off? This man was scrambling her brain, and she didn't need that, though if she could wheedle just a bit of advice from him, before she politely turned him down . . .

Yet she found herself saying, "I could, however, pay you by making garments for your wife."

He smiled that flash of teeth again. Though it was autumn, he seemed to have good sun color on his face. No doubt, an outdoorsman, but then weren't most of his class sporting men?

"I have no wife," he told her with a steady look. "But if I did, I'd buy her those bonnie, wee fripperies you are still holding in your left hand."

She felt a huge blush begin from her throat upward. She dropped the silk and satin scraps into the velvet high-backed chair and sat on them. "A sideline. We do mostly frocks."

"I do not disapprove, lass."

That last word seemed so intimate. So—caressing. She was in over her head and she'd just met him. Probably over her head with too many orders, too few staff, too many bills yet to be paid—who knew? But she did know this man, however helpful, could be dangerous. She wanted nothing but nothing to do with the complications of a man ever again.

"I do hope to move out of these crowded quarters and let a shop and work area soon," she admitted. "My staff is growing of necessity."

"And that means more salaries. Is it true you still deliver garments yourself?"

"I—yes."

"I overheard that at the theater. That indicates to me that you cannot afford a page boy to do so."

"It's just a matter of pride—delivering gowns of personality and emotion to my customers."

"Ah, I see."

"However much you've been inquiring, I doubt if you do, Sir Duff-Gordon. This endeavor is my future, my daughter's future, and I cannot keep living off my mother."

"Mothers," he said with a slight shake of his head. "Can't live without them or with them sometimes. I have one of those at home, quite formidable yet."

Lucile nodded, and he seemed to mirror that motion as he nodded too. Instead of continuing to sit ramrod straight, he shifted sideways and leaned forward, quite intimately. "Your backbone as well as your talent, Mrs. Wallace—"

"Lucile."

"Lucile. That is a sign of sure success, your fierce passion for this endeavor. I've seen your wares and heard talk of them. But your brother-in-law is under the impression that your finances are handled willy-nilly, though he should talk. At least he knows not to counsel you about staying out of debt."

Lucile's head jerked up. Clayton had debts? Elinor had never whispered one word about that, and he had that fine estate.

"Let me tell you true," he said, "because I always do. It might serve you well to hire a bookkeeper, even part-time, to keep records and hold you to a budget, so that—"

"I don't need a budget or a naysayer, sir. I need to grow. I need a larger place than this. And I have a young woman who will be overseeing the books."

"Then be sure to oversee her. There will no doubt be a later time for expanding to new premises. If you would like me to assess your standing and then advise on how long it will take you to be able to have your own establishment, and how much you could afford to spend, then—"

"Not at this time," she interrupted. Her dander was up now. As attractive, as solid and sure as this man seemed, just crashing in like this—with a disparaging remark about Clayton, too—she had to send him away.

Almost panicked by her own feelings, she stood. He rose too. "I thank you for coming, Sir Duff-Gordon. But I am too busy now to restructure things here."

"I see," he said and gave her another little bow. "Then I shall only watch from afar and perhaps at another time you can use my services, Lucile. Please call me Cosmo as my friends do. Although I am often here in the city, my home is in braw, bonnie Scotland, and I see you are as brave as you are bonnie—that is, beautiful. But be wise, too. I'll show myself out then and call at another time."

She felt terrible that she had handled this so badly. She almost reached out to seize his arm. He opened the door to the hall and turned back to look at her again with that one intense eye. Yet he seemed to her more whole and strong than any man who had two. She felt the impact of his gaze as if he'd touched her.

Then he was gone, and she felt so very alone.

# CHAPTER *Eleven*

"Girls certainly seem to run in our family," Lucile told Elinor as the Glyns' new nanny took two-month-old Margot back to her nursery at Sheering Hall. "And she's a darling, growing fast."

"If only I felt better to enjoy her," Elinor admitted and reached back to punch at the pillows plumped up behind her on the divan in her sitting room. "This fever has laid me low too long. But," she said, reaching for Lucile's hand, "it was so kind of you to bring me that lovely traveling suit. Clayton's promised me a trip to Egypt when I'm able, but then he's also promised me the moon. Thank heavens, Clarissa was willing to come see me and amuse him with a walk on the grounds to tend to his precious game birds today."

"She bought one of my riding outfits a week or so ago. She's stuck rather close to you, hasn't she? I hardly see any of my bridesmaids anymore, except you, of course. I noticed Clayton has started to smoke cigars. I haven't seen it but his clothes reek of it, so keep smoke away from that new outfit and your other gowns."

"As if I could. Cigars and brandy, brandy and cigars."

She heaved a huge sigh, and Lucile tugged her hand free. Elinor was surprised she still held it. They'd had some spotty times lately—different lifestyles and financial positions hadn't helped.

"I'm still writing, you know," she confided. "If I can't travel right now, I shall travel through my heroine's adventures, some of that my memories of people and places, of course."

"I'm glad writing helps," Lucile said. "I suppose it's a kind of escape. And speaking of traveling, remember the doctor said that you are to get your strength back by walking. Come on then, we'll stroll this room you've decorated so beautifully. Let me help you up."

Lucile half-propped her, half-pulled her to her feet. Elinor's Lucile Ltd. printed silk robe that had been a wedding gift swirled around her feet and she nearly tripped, but Lucile held her steady. Slowly, they walked the length of the room Elinor had worked so hard to decorate to suggest the days of the old French kings with its brocades and gilt and Louis-style furniture—and the chinoiserie statue of a stalking tiger that was her pride and joy. Early in their marriage, Clayton had told her to spend whatever she wanted on the decor, to buy whatever clothes she wanted from Lucile, but lately he'd been touchy about spending money. It all sounded entirely too familiar—and foreboding—to Elinor, because Lucile had suffered through such in her own marriage. Clayton had also still insisted they live here at Sheering instead of at the Durrington House she had her eye on.

They walked back across the flowered carpet toward the divan, but Lucile wheeled her around for another turn.

"So are you going to accept help from that Scotsman, Clayton's acquaintance he recommended last year?" Elinor asked.

It helped to talk to shift her thoughts from how tired she was. Little Margot's birth, then the energy-draining typhoid fever that had followed, had nearly done her in. Clayton's delight was to tramp all over the estate, let alone shoot and travel. Even when she was healthy, it was hardly, as they say, her cup of tea, and she struggled to find time to write. But his promise they would see Egypt, see the Sphinx, that half lion, half woman . . . see exotic lands . . . none of that had materialized and she feared it never would.

Lucile was saying she was trying to watch her finances better, that she hadn't seen Lord Duff-Gordon again, but Elinor wasn't really listening. Her thoughts drifted. She was recalling that tiger she'd seen at the Gardens in Paris years ago and how her romantic beau had tried to talk her into running away with him and had whispered to her, *Belle Tigress!* How far she had come from that romantic dream, but she would live it through her book.

With a glance out the window on the next turn around the room, Lucile gasped and Elinor muttered, "Damnation!" Because there was Clayton, heading back through the flower garden from visiting his precious pheasants with Elinor's friend Clarissa. And he was kissing her. Hard. On the mouth!

Elinor's knees buckled, but Lucile held her up, got her to a chair.

"He—how dare he! But—but it's the world we live in," Elinor declared, bending over her knees as if she'd be ill. "Oh, you should see how lovers pair up at the country houses, but I thought—I thought . . ."

"Will you say something to him?" Lucile asked, kneeling by her chair.

"I don't know. I surely haven't been a wife to him—well,

physically—since several months before Margot was born. But it's the way they all act, my new friends. My dear Daisy Warwick has a long liaison with Prince Edward, her Bertie, others, too. I shall write about it, but I'll not succumb to it."

Lucile was startled at first, but it was the way of the world, at least among the so-called uppers, especially the noble and royal set. She gave Elinor's shoulders a one-armed hug and whispered more to herself than her sister, "I'll not succumb to it either, for I am never getting entangled again that way."

"Famous last words," Elinor told her and swiped at tears on her cheeks. "But then, I prefer that other old adage, I shall have the last laugh, though I don't feel like laughing."

Lucile kept ahold of Elinor while she wept.

* * *

Cosmo Duff-Gordon had not called on Lucile again, and, she fretted, he probably thought her a rude shrew with an empty head who could not control her own finances. The truth was, even with Edith's help, she really couldn't. It took a year for her to take his advice and hire a small, trustworthy lad to deliver most of her new creations to their owners. Mostly, she kept designing and fitting women, providing endless work for her staff and herself.

Fittings were taking longer now that her reputation had spread. Mamas with money, both English and American, were coming to her for debutante gowns, then later, wedding dresses and honeymoon garments. They expected Lucile herself, not Edith, to do the fittings and, to her amazement, she'd become not only a couturiere but a counselor, too.

"I can't bear to wed him, since I'm in love with someone else," a well-bred eighteen-year-old had told her just yesterday during a bridal fitting. "Mama and Papa are thrilled with the match, but he's widowed and thirty years older. I don't care if he has a stately home and a title! I'm to be a marchioness someday, but I'd rather live in a mere cottage with my true love."

Lucile had become a comforter as best she could through such stories, but the most grievous was the tragedy of her client Mrs. Atherton, a beautiful woman who had suffered through a terrible divorce case. Of course Lucile sympathized with her. But the woman's life had turned even more tragic. One day, when she was standing on Lucile's fitting platform with chiffon draped all around her, came the word that her little son had been killed instantly when a carriage overturned.

Lucile had broken the tragic news to the woman as gently as she could. She had gone deathly pale and said nothing while Lucile divested her of the half-made garment. She bid Lucile a kind farewell, as she and others stood helpless to be able to comfort her. Then, just after the boy was buried, she took a gun and killed herself by her own hand, arrayed in the black mourning gown Lucile had sent her for the funeral.

After that, Lucile cherished Esme much more. It made her realize that life must not be all work and no play—or, as the nursery rhyme said, Jack would be a dull boy.

Was she dull? she agonized far into the dark, lonely nights. Dull to life? "I love what I'm doing, but the whirl of daily duties threatens to swamp me," she whispered in her silent bed.

And then, the very next day, she received a note delivered by a messenger that said, *I hear you have hired a page boy. Is it time for a new establishment not far from Davies Street and yet so far? Is it time for us to talk again? I will call for you at four o'clock on the morrow to show you an empty shop that is ready to be let for a reasonable fee. Yours truly, Cosmo Duff-Gordon.*

She stared at the bold handwriting but only for a moment. "Wait," she told the boy. "I will send you back with a reply."

Then she wrote, *You are most kind. Yes, I believe and hope it is time. Yours, Lucile.*

* * *

Like some sort of country dolt, Lucile fussed over what to wear the next day. She also warned her staff to keep away from peeking down the staircase or out windows—they also used her bedroom and the attic now—at her gentleman caller. He was only a business associate, she told them, which, of course, was true.

She had tea served to him this time, high tea, then they set out, for he wanted her to see the building before he told her more about it. "First impressions matter," he told her with a steady look.

They strolled on a lovely spring forenoon down Grosvenor Street to New Bond Street, then turned down Clifford to Old Burlington Street near Savile Row.

"An area up-and-coming for fashionable shops," he told her. "Now, as I've said before, I want to make an investment in your product and your talent, so no denials or folderol when you hear the price of this. I believe you can well afford this address, because you now have a financial adviser and backer, and don't argue this time. Also recently, so I hear, you have attracted an international clientele."

"I'd like to storm the Bastille of French fashion someday, right in Paris, but you mean the word got out about my Russian orders?"

"I heard it from a member of Parliament, no less."

"As if it were government or men's business. Well, I didn't mean that against you, and I accept your advice—your backing, as you say—with gratitude. But as for the foreign orders, I made an array of costumes for Mrs. Willie James to take to Russia with her—ten evening gowns, house gowns, and several coats, all sable trimmed." She knew she was talking too fast and too much but she was so excited.

"I lost more than a week's sleep to get everything ready," she rushed on, "but it was worth it as it brought in orders from Russian women who admired it all, despite the fact I could not do exact fittings for them. Besides all that, I'm doing up a gown for my sister to be presented at court, though I hear Queen Victoria is too weak and Princess Alexandra may do the honors. It's one of Elinor's most romantic dreams come true."

"And your romantic dreams?" he asked as they stopped before a narrow shop with a worn façade and the faded number 23 over its door.

"I—frankly, I'm focused on only business right now."

He nodded, but she was certain he had whispered, "Pity!"

They stared together at the building. The windows were dusty and the place looked—well, droopy, but she saw the potential in it all. She envisioned gowns in the window and gilded writing on the door with her name.

"It's quite deep, though it looks narrow," he told her. "Four rooms and storage at the back."

"It looks wonderful to me," she said, clasping her hands together. "I can just see a scripted sign over the door, *The Maison Lucile*."

"And I happen to have the key," he said, producing it. He looked very happy—and so intense.

She couldn't help herself. She bounced like Esme would if she were offered a sweet.

Cosmo smiled down at her. "The key to a new beginning," he told her with a wink when she reached for it and they held it together for a moment. Even through their gloves, his big hand was strong and warm. "Let's see if you like what's inside."

As he unlocked and opened the door for them, she gripped her hands tightly as if in prayer. She was trembling, and not only because of the shop. Cosmo understood her. He'd come back to help her, after their awkward, dismal start. Despite the fact she hadn't seen him for months, it was as if they had been together a long time, standing on the cusp of intimacy, or a relationship to cherish. Before this man, that feeling would have frightened her but now it—it was exhilarating and wonderful.

"Oh yes," she said as he held the door and she stepped inside ahead of him. "Good gracious, I can certainly make do with this. I can imagine it all freshly painted and carpeted with flowers in vases next to upholstered chairs—the waiting room here, the fitting room farther back, and it isn't far from Mother and Esme!"

"Too far from Scotland," he told her, "but we can work on that."

# CHAPTER *Twelve*

"Venice! We're really in Venice! Isn't it wonderful, Clayton?" Elinor cried and swept open their French doors, which overlooked the Grand Canal. Their Mediterranean itinerary had filled her with hope—hope for the renewal of their marriage, the promise of more travel. "Of course, I'm especially looking forward to Egypt," she added. Yet it tempered her excitement when he just nodded and said nothing.

As twilight fell, she glanced back at him. He was on the sofa, reading a week-old copy of a British newspaper he'd just borrowed from a friend they'd met in the lobby. She was trying desperately to bind the rift in their relationship, but he wasn't cooperating. She had never admitted she saw him kissing her friend, but she was saving that for ammunition if she needed it. After all, the doldrums of their marriage was not all his fault. She had been ill a good long time and was unable to tramp about the estate or go on his precious shoots with him. Or share his bed.

As she gazed out at passing gondolas, most with attentive, happy couples in them, she dedicated herself again to try to be at least accommodating. There were many benefits from her marriage. Clayton always traveled first class, and she loved that, whether they were at Cowes for that yachting week or visiting country houses of the well-do-to like Daisy Warwick. Best yet, he'd spoken of taking a flat in Sloane Street in London and not only for the season in May and June. And now, a great escape to Italy, and finally to Egypt, her dream destination.

Romance was exactly what she was hoping and planning for on their gondola ride shortly, just the two of them cuddled on the seat with their boat steered by a singing helmsman through the moonlit, rustling water.

"It says here," Clayton called out as she stepped onto their narrow balcony and leaned, stiff-armed on the carved stone balustrade, "that Lord Curzon has been named undersecretary of state for foreign affairs. Now, *that's* a title. 'Foreign affairs'—I'll bet. I don't care if he's married and how stiff he seemed. Still water runs deep."

*It takes one to know one,* she thought, but she said, "Which is exactly what it looks like on the canal—still but deep waters. Do step out and see the view, Clayton."

"Seen it before. I'll wait for our ride in"—she glanced back at him as he consulted his pocket watch—"just a few minutes. Best get some sort of wrap. I say, your sister's getting cheeky with her latest summer designs. I can see right through that material to your bare shoulders."

"I'm glad you noticed."

"I pay enough for the bills," he muttered and went back to reading.

She sighed as she went into her bedroom where her lady's

maid, Williams, was laying out her evening garb for later, but she intended to wear this dress now. It irked her that Clayton had become so caustic about bills lately. If they had money for this trip, didn't they have money for clothes? He'd even fussed over toys she'd bought for Margot, though, heaven knows, he usually paid little attention to his daughter. More than once, now that she had her strength back, he'd hinted he'd like a son. But how could that happen when he hardly shared her bed?

"Oh, Williams, you're dressed too. Are you going out?" she asked as the petite woman held out Elinor's best black silk shawl to place around her shoulders.

"Why . . . why yes, madame," she said, sounding flustered, which the practical woman seldom was. "Didn't Mr. Glyn mention it? He asked me to go along on the boat ride, a treat for me, he said."

"Oh—yes, of course. It slipped my mind."

Feeling stabbed to her core, Elinor also accepted the flat, black silk handbag Williams held out. She hadn't been in charity dramas for nothing and managed to hide her hurt and anger. Clayton had done it again: either from spite or ignorance, he'd shown her that her precious world of romance was nothing to him—for perhaps she was nothing to him anymore either.

✻ ✻ ✻

Once everything was the way Lucile wanted it for now at her lovely new shop, she set out to find three perfect mannequins to show her clothing to potential customers who sometimes dropped in with little idea of what they wanted. No stuffed linen dummies others offered in their shops, which reminded her of the dreadful death masks in the crypt of Westminster Abbey. She wanted living, breathing beauties—that's what the Maison Lucile would offer.

She was looking for a particular, ideal type of feminine body, for, she'd seen, that even if a baroness or countess was short and plump, she seldom saw herself that way. Lucile thought of it as helping her patrons find their better selves. And that didn't mean she would design something unsuitable for them, just that they needed to view an ideal and then be counseled about how that could be personalized for them alone.

Although she'd seen women suitable for mannequins on the street, she could hardly just accost them. So instead she decided to go to the source: Harrods, where attractive, young, respectable women worked. Now, just having made a purchase of new satin bedsheets, she took a good look at the shopgirl who'd sold them to her and knew she'd found what—or rather who—she'd been looking for.

"One question," she said to the tall blonde. "Are you quite happy with your situation here, or have you thought of another career? For example, have you ever considered wearing exquisite garments for fine ladies to purchase?"

"Me, madame? Here?" She sounded surprised but kept her calm demeanor and controlled voice.

Yes, this girl would be perfect. Her face registered emotions but could become very still. Her long, graceful limbs were amazingly elegant.

Lucile lowered her voice even more. "Not here. You see, I own a ladies' fashion design store here in London, and I would like to hire you to display clothes, become a living mannequin, so to speak, something quite new. My name is Lucile and the shop is the Maison Lucile, if you could stop by after work," she said and extended a Lucile Ltd. card to her with the address. "I would pay you a bit more than what you are earning here, of course, and there might be some travel."

The girl stared at the card so long with her Cupid's-bow mouth pursed and her blue eyes wide that Lucile wondered if she could read. "Wear fancy clothes, Madame Lucile?" she said looking up at last. Her brows were perfectly arched and darker than her thick, honey-hued hair. She wouldn't need a speck of cosmetics and that was exactly what Lucile wanted.

Well, at least she'd picked up on her name, she thought, so she wasn't a ninnyhammer. Her street accent was atrocious, but Lucile, Edith, and the others could smooth that out. This girl fit the bill. She'd help her, advise her, soften her . . . even educate her if it came to that.

"Yes, my dear. Fancy clothes. I am on the up-and-up. Once you see my shop, you will understand. So will you come by after Harrods closes today?"

To her amazement, tears gilded the girl's eyes as she nodded. She certainly had the sensitivity to model the dresses of emotion and personality Lucile was promoting now. She'd been right to choose this girl and to recognize her sweet nature. Why, she could wrap this young woman in one of her newly purchased sheets right now, drape the material just right, and she'd look like a goddess.

And that's what she'd call her living mannequins—her goddesses.

* * *

After feeling Clayton had tried again to ruin her love for romance, real and fictional, one thing kept Elinor going: Last week they had received word she was to be presented at court in May of 1896. Even Clayton was pleased and had treated her more kindly, for it was a feather in his cap too. At any rate, it had helped her get along with him better lately. She had already written Lucile to order a gown, for there were definite rules for a presentation dress.

He'd even protested he'd not meant to hurt her feelings over ruining their gondola ride and had just thought taking Williams was "a treat for the girl."

"Yes, well, never mind a treat for your wife and the mother of your child," Elinor had said.

"A daughter," he'd countered. "I'd like a son. Wait until you see Egypt and meet Prince Hussein. Sons are elevated there. You and your sister," he muttered, shaking his head. "She wrote she's on the hunt to hire girls she calls goddesses, and you are always mooning over seeing the Sphinx, perhaps because it's a goddess of some sort too. This is still a man's world, Elinor, and likely to remain so, so let's just keep your ideas about knights in shining armor rescuing damsels in distress for your private diary or scribblings."

"For my writing, not scribblings, Clayton, and I will see my novel published someday, you just wait."

"I'll bet I do," he'd clipped out and so it went.

But today, in a fit of pique while shopping near St. Mark's Square with Williams, Elinor had staged what she considered to be the ultimate act of rebellion. She had fallen in love with a tiger skin displayed in a sales window and purchased it despite the steep cost.

Oh, how she'd felt when she stroked its vibrant, striped fur. Memories of her happy, youthful days in Paris, of her first adoring beau. He had wanted her to run away with him, which, of course, would have meant ruination, but it had sounded so romantic—still did. She could hear his whisper to her of "Belle Tigress," and that's still the way she felt, like a wild animal wanting to live free.

But to possess this beautiful creature someone had dared to kill, this splendid animal from a far-off land, compelled her. And she had dared to possess it.

The moment she heard steps and a rustling in the hall, she hurried to open the door before Clayton's valet or Williams could. She'd been promised the heavy skin would be delivered here, and that must be it.

"Expecting someone?" Clayton called and followed her to the door, drat him.

"Mrs. Clayton Glyn?" the man said and, when she nodded, he knelt at her feet and opened the wrapping paper. Out unrolled the big, beautiful orange-and-black-striped tiger skin with the proud head of the big-fanged animal settling last on the carpet.

She gasped. So proud. So beautiful and wild. And hers.

"There must be some mistake," Clayton's voice cut through her thoughts.

"No, I bought it earlier today. I wanted you to see it in all its glory before I tried to explain it. For once, words wouldn't do."

"Are you quite mad?"

But she could see him literally bite his lip as he handed over some coins as a tip for the delivery. The young man was only too glad to beat a hasty retreat.

"Isn't it marvelous?" Elinor said before Clayton could speak again. Anyway, he was sputtering with rage.

"Dare I—dare I ask how much that cost?"

"Not as much as entertaining your friends for a shoot or as feed for your precious pheasants at home, which don't look one bit this magnificent, even when absolute droves of them are shot. Clayton, I've always wanted a tiger skin and I couldn't resist it so—so romantic. Can't you picture us lying there together and—"

"Speaking of lying, you've as good as lied to me by not telling me of this, asking my permission. That tiger head on a wall at Warwick would be one thing, and of course I'd love to go trophy shooting. But with all this trip costs—never mind. Romance, romance, romance! Welcome to the real world of duties and business, Elinor. I want to know what shop you patronized, because it's going back tomorrow."

"It is not. If you're keeping track of every pound we spend now, every pence, take it out of my next birthday or Yuletide gifts. Tell everyone you bought it for me—for me, your wife, not for a friend I invited to keep you company and then I saw you pawing and kissing outside my window when I was so ill after Margot's birth."

Clayton had gone red in the face. Surely he wouldn't strike her, but she held her ground, then bent to pull the heavy tiger skin farther back from the door. Then she sat on it.

"I swear, Clayton, I shall wear this tiger skin for my court presentation and naught else, and then people will say Mrs. Glyn has lost her mind, and I'll tell them why. I repeat, you don't have a romantic bone in your body and you made me think you did with all that formal, gentlemanly talk when we met and later on our honeymoon, two days in rented water."

"Calm down. Lower your voice. We don't need the servants or the gondola boys hearing all this, now do we?"

Was he softening his stance? Had her mention of seeing him kissing her friend or her silly threat about wearing a tiger skin made him back down? Or was he somehow moved by her emotions for once?

"Let's drag this damned thing into your bedroom," he said. "I suppose Margot will like to pet it, but it will cost us an arm and a leg to ship it with us to Egypt and then home. Get up, Elinor," he insisted and took her arm to help her stand. "I suppose it's special to you like the game birds and my cows are to me."

She only nodded and did as he said. Her passion for this and what it stood for in her life was a far hue and cry from his birds and cows. But she'd won a victory here, and she felt fierce about that. She fully intended to lock everyone out tonight, including him, and lie naked on this tiger skin and claim her name as *Belle Tigress*!

# CHAPTER *Thirteen*

"I'm heeere-er!" Elinor called as she bustled into the crowded backroom that served as an office at the Maison Lucile. "I've been shopping and have to sit down," she told Lucile. "I'm carrying a big baby this time, and it absolutely *must* be a boy!"

"Sit here in my chair. Did you bring the gown?"

"Williams is having your girls unpack it in that chaos out there. And I think I'm bursting at the seams," Elinor said as Lucile helped her take off her coat and hat. She plopped in Lucile's chair and put her hands on her big belly.

"Do you mean it must be a boy because it's larger than Margot was or because Clayton has his hopes up?" Lucile asked.

"He needs a son to secure the estate, though I pay no attention to his business machinations unless he tells me to cut back—which he hasn't lately since we've been getting on."

"I see you have."

"Well, believe it or not, a tiger skin can work wonders. It's what one of your new creations does for you."

"I'll send for tea. It's cold for early December. Just wait until you hear my plans to promote Lucile Ltd. even more. I'm not sure how many guests I can pack in here, but I'm determined to stage a live mannequin parade and send embossed invitations to all my former clients, asking them to bring a guest. Both Lillie and Ellen Terry said they would help with the publicity and hostessing. Actually, I need a larger establishment again, if I could only get Cosmo to agree."

"So this event will have your goddesses walking around instead of just posing in gowns for a particular buyer? I vow, you always have something up your sleeve—if I can say that to a dress designer. Isn't it enough that you are in trade and making silky unmentionables as well as your lovely gowns? You're walking a fine line with clients—and their menfolk—who might think that sort of publicity is vulgar. Lucile, it really isn't proper to pull stunts to advertise."

Lucile propped her hands on her hips. "As proper, I warrant, as a society woman writing flippant pieces for *Scottish Life Magazine* disguised as letters from some fictional Suzon to Grizelda!"

"I'm proud of those letters and I like to think of them as articles. Has Cosmo mentioned them?"

"He has."

"And said what?"

"That they are clever essays and the pen-and-ink drawings you've done with them are charming. Actually, I agree."

"Oh, thank God. And I must tell you that Lord Rosslyn, who is my liaison to the magazine, has told me a great deal about Cosmo."

"I already know a great deal about Cosmo. He's most attentive as a business partner and a suitor. He frightens me."

"You, frightened? How? He's not putting pressure on you because he's advised you and loaned you money?"

"Not a bit of it. He frightens me because he—he moves me, and I don't want any complications with men. I've seen too much of the bad from them, and they can get in the way of one's dreams."

"Don't I know."

"A little adoration to get a girl's spirits up is fine, but Cosmo is so serious and intent."

"Frankly, serious and intent sounds like you. Meanwhile, I think Clayton laughs at my ardor for writing, yet is amused by it—sees it as a way for me to earn spending money. He's even finally keeping quiet about my book, and I'm bound to finish it as soon as this baby sees the light of day, and that in less than a month."

Edith and Hebe—whose real name was Clara, the girl hired from Harrods—knocked and came in with the gown Elinor had brought. Edith had fluffed out and stuffed tissue in the short sleeves and full skirt of white satin *peau de soir* edged with silver gauze ribbon and lace. Hebe held up the white brocade train trimmed with lace and fastened by bows of silver ribbon with diamond buttons. It was the ornate Lucile gown Elinor had worn for her court presentation before Princess Alexandra since Queen Victoria was too weak for that royal duty now. Lucile had hoped Alexandra would remember the gown and order one for herself, but no such luck.

"I think Hebe will model it in our fashion parade when I can stage it," Lucile told them, "so cover and hang it carefully. And, Edith, please send some tea in for us."

In a rustle of tissue paper and satin, they went back out. "Too many rules for that gown," Lucile said. "For a court presentation gown, the train must be not less than three yards from the shoulders and fifty-four inches wide at the end. Low bodice, short sleeves, and white, white, white when I adore colors."

"Too many rules in this world, in general, especially for women. It was difficult enough to drape that train over my left arm, hand off my name card, not to mention all those previous hours of practicing my curtsy and backing away from the royals without taking a tumble. But worse," Elinor said, lowering her voice as if someone else would hear, "was waiting all that time on the Mall in an absolute glut of carriages and then not being able to use the facilities when I needed a chamber pot so badly!"

"Not to change the subject from that lovely little fact, but what has Lord Rosslyn said about Cosmo?"

"Aha, back to that. You do care for him. I thought your putting him off was a case of 'The lady doth protest too much.'"

"Don't tease or cite your literary knowledge to me," Lucile said and pulled up a stool just as Edith came back in with a tray of teapot and cups. "Thank you, Edith. I'll pour, and please be sure Mrs. Glyn's lady's maid has a spot of tea too."

"Yes, Lucile. We'll take good care of her like you do us. Hebe's still practicing her French phrases so we'll try them out on her."

When they were alone and had managed a few sips of tea, Lucile said, "All right, let's have the straight facts about Cosmo, according to the eminent Elinor Glyn."

"Lord Rosslyn says Cosmo Duff-Gordon is above all an admirable man, a man of honor. He might as well have stepped out of some of my favorite books."

"I said, never mind all that about your books. So far, so good. Go on."

"Well, all the impressive things, of course. Educated at Eton and trained in Italy in music, no less. You have said he has a beautiful voice."

"He does indeed."

"Frankly, the thing that impressed me most is that I heard he was distantly related to the romantic poet, Lord Bryon. But if he's inherited any of his morals, beware. Byron was called 'mad, bad, and dangerous to know' by one of his paramours, of which there were many, and he had huge debts and died young."

"Sister dearest, did you ever ask yourself if someone will say of you someday that 'a little learning is a dangerous thing'? So far, Cosmo has been nothing but wise, good, and wonderful to know."

"But has he asked you to travel to Kincardineshire to see his estate? Good heavens, it's on the northeast coast of Scotland. And I thought Clayton's lands were too far out of London. I should have made him take me before we were married, so let that, at least, be a warning to you."

"I do know Maryculter is a longtime family estate near Aberdeen. It sounds beautiful there, but I haven't gone yet. Too much going on here and—it would be a commitment somehow. He said he didn't intend to ask other people to go along if I agreed to visit but planned to invite a few in to meet me once we were there."

"But let me fly another red warning flag for you. Like most gentlemen today, he is a sporting man, bird shoots and all that. He'd have you off by yourself farther than Clayton has me, even though we have a London flat now, even if Cosmo does seem to be in London a good bit. And Lord Rosslyn said that's how Cosmo lost an eye—in a hunting accident."

"Yes, I did know that. But I'll tell you that one eye sees more than most with two. And it can challenge and flirt as well."

"And seduce one's heart if not one's body? Hmm, perhaps I can use that description too, if not in this book, then another."

"Another? Anyway, Cosmo's reputation is not primarily as a gamer or hunter but as an athlete. Did Lord Rosslyn tell you he's a noted fencer? One of Cosmo's goals is to represent Great Britain in the Intercalated Games. He's also a self-defense enthusiast."

"Perhaps you're the one who'd best study that art. Well, he is a man's man, and that's always attractive to a woman. I trust you to know his family is very wealthy from way back. In the 1700s they founded the Duff-Gordon sherry business in Spain, which still produces strong wines. And one other thing that may come into play here. Lord Rosslyn says Cosmo's beloved father made him promise on his deathbed that he would honor his mother's wishes, take care of her. She's strictly old Scottish school—or church, I should say."

Elinor put her teacup down and went on, "Lucile, Lord Rosslyn said that Cosmo's mother would never permit him to wed a divorced woman. I just wanted you to know that lest he makes promises or—well . . ."

"Tries to seduce me into an affair instead of marriage?"

"Well, yes. I wanted to get round to that, but I felt I had to screw my courage to the sticking point, so to speak. I admit he does have a certain allure about him. Besides, it seems to be the way of the world among the uppers. It might be all right for my friends, like Daisy Warwick, but I detest that in general."

"But you said at the first that Cosmo is an honorable man. Frankly, he's more than intimated his feelings for me. They shimmer from him, however serious he can be," she whispered.

"Hmm," Elinor said, going back to her tea. "*They shimmer from him*. I shall use that."

"Why don't you set your story in Egypt since you adored your time there so much? Or in India?" Lucile reached for the copy of the *Standard* newspaper on her drawing table. "That famous man you met who seemed so grand—ah, Lord Curzon—has just been named viceroy of India, and there's to be almost a royal reception for him there where he will rule as a king."

She pointed to the article, and Elinor reached over her big belly to snatch it up. "Oh, his American wife and two young daughters are going to India with him," she read aloud. "It means certain riches and titles to serve the Queen there, it says.

"They have two young daughters," she went on. "I can only hope and pray that was not to be my fate soon. Clayton's drowning in brandy lately and toasting with expensive champagne a son he's sure is on the way. But, my, doesn't the mere name and title of Nathaniel George, Lord Curzon, Viceroy of India, sound romantic and grand?"

* * *

Only a fortnight later, Cosmo took Lucile home in his carriage when Elinor's warnings were still fresh in her teeming brain.

"I'd best not ask you in since Mother and Esme are visiting Clayton and Elinor in the country, waiting for the birth," she told him as she was ready to ring the bell.

"No better time then."

*Oh crumbs.* Even his voice got to her, deep and resonant with that slightest Scottish burr. She gave a nervous, little laugh that sounded so ingénue. The man did make her nervous, a shivery kind of delicious tingle. "Well, for a few moments if you don't mind your driver waiting in this bitter cold. Perhaps he can drive round to the back and Cook will take him in."

"Thank you for being so thoughtful. I would have sent him somewhere warm and told him to come back later, but that would be fine. And we are not going to argue further about your needing a larger place for this live-women parade you are set on. We'll search for a bigger venue and then you can stage your event."

Lucile let herself in while Cosmo talked to his driver. She held the door open for him and held her tongue. She knew he was right, and she was in too much of a hurry to move again, but she'd never fit all the guests she planned to invite into that small space.

As for Cosmo coming inside, she could handle this. The man had been ever the gentleman, although they still had tiffs over her plans for more spending. Well, he was from Scotland, and they were notoriously frugal, but somehow she knew he'd rattle her poise even if he was from the moon.

She called for a light supper to be prepared, and they sat in the library where Cosmo himself stoked up the fire.

"I have a confession to make," he said, bending over the grate with the poker after jokingly making several fencing feints with it to make her laugh. "Although I am happy to advise you and invest in you, I might not have done that for anyone with such a stubborn streak and high-flying plans. But I am willing to consider the expansion plans for your—our—business you have in that pretty head of yours."

Her stomach flip-flopped as he sat down close beside her on the sofa and turned slightly toward her. It suddenly seemed so hot in here when he barely stirred the embers.

"I thank you again for your help and concern, Cosmo. I hope you don't intend to call in my debt to you, because you know I'm not ready to pay you back. And yes, I would love to expand."

"I am totally intrigued by that. Financially, you are not ready. But emotionally? You and your gowns of emotion your clients adore with those exciting names like *Sweet Surrender* and *Promises to Keep* heat my blood. Lucile, sweetheart, I'm not rushing you but—lass, I adore you, and not just as a business partner."

Despite how close he was and the scent of fresh, outdoor air that always seemed to emanate from him, she told herself to set him back, to hold him off, this beautifully built athlete, this intense man. But the moment he moved toward her, she found herself leaning into his embrace.

She'd been kissed by a few other admirers since James had left, of course, and had felt deeply for Morell. But the strength, the power of this man and his carefully guarded emotions nearly drowned her, and she kissed him back with wild abandon.

His lips slid lower, down her throat, as she mindlessly arched back for him. His mustache tickled. She had needed his strength, encouragement, and help, but she had not fathomed she had needed him.

He kissed her again, devouring her sanity. Suddenly Scotland didn't seem so bad, so far away. But this was what she could not do, respond like a wanton, surrender her strength and power she'd fought so hard for.

"My beautiful sweetheart," he whispered, tipping his head back a bit to look at her.

Was the room spinning? She felt like a schoolgirl back in exile on Jersey, wondering if she'd ever find someone to love. But she'd learned it was safer to love her own dreams and desires and not to trust a man again.

"Cosmo," she told him, out of breath, "wait."

"I don't want to. Not for you."

"They'll be in with supper soon," she whispered, feeling quite the silly coward.

"I'll buy you a thousand dinners, anywhere you want."

"Dinners in a bigger shop?"

"Business," he muttered. "Too damned much business, always business. Just now, that was not business between us, lass, but something else, and don't forget it."

He cleared his throat and set her back as Cook knocked on the door and rolled in a cart with several covered dishes and a bottle of Duff-Gordon wine he'd sent them. But her maid, Bradford, bustled right in behind, waving a white envelope.

"A message just came from your sister, not by post but a messenger," she said and bobbed a curtsy to Cosmo. "Since the baby is due soon . . ."

"Yes, of course," Lucile said and took it from her and broke the red seal. But it was from Clayton. He'd written in a hasty scrawl,

*Come to help your mother if you can. Elinor has been delivered of another daughter. Large baby, hard birth. She's ill and the doctor says no more children. Clayton*

# CHAPTER *Fourteen*

Elinor was afraid she was going to drown. She was swimming with her red hair wrapped around her in thick, black water. But why was her mother on her honeymoon with them? She kept hearing her voice, and was she crying? She would have to include that scene in her book. Oh, and Lucy must be here too. How old were they? This was awfully hot for Canada, and what would her strict, French grandmama say to her hair being down?

"She'd delirious again. The fever seems to hang on. More ice and we'll try to bring it down," a man's voice said, not Clayton's.

Icy looks. Icy looks from some of those women she'd tried so hard to entertain with her drawings and stories. But they were kinder when they learned she had no dowry, and why would anyone want an ugly, red-haired girl? Lucy was prettier, made pretty costumes for their dolls, too, and perhaps one of those dolls had been presented at the palace . . .

"Elinor, dearest, it's Mother. You have a lovely daughter. I know you said that it was a boy. But if a girl, you wanted her to be named Juliet."

"Her story is a tragedy," someone whispered. "They both die."

Suddenly, Mother's face was gone, and Lucy's was there, her grown-up face.

"Lucy!" someone said. "I'm going to drown! Hold me up!"

"Listen to me, Elinor—Nellie," she said. "I will hold you up. No one is going to die. You rest now and get your strength back. Do not let go of all we've had, all that we can be. Your daughters need you. Your book needs you, and you must finish it. Be strong, and I'll be right here with you."

She felt better after that. Lucy held her hands and surely wouldn't let her go off this cliff above the sea. They were looking out the window of Elizabeth Castle in just Jersey, and she could see from here her heroine Elizabeth from her book. She would not let her die. She would finish her story and share it with people, with Mother, with Lucy and even Clayton.

Elinor was sure she pulled a frightened child named Nellie next to her and held her tight so she would not fall into the water and drown.

* * *

Elinor was impatient with how slowly she came back from Juliet's difficult birth and the rheumatic fever that plagued her after, and her temporary need for crutches plagued her, too. But the truth was she did not mind the doctor telling her she could not risk more children. Clayton was upset, though he was kind enough to lease a small cottage, Lamberts, on the estate for her mother so she could help care for her in her convalescence. But while he'd promised to try to show someone he knew at a newspaper her book when he returned, he was already off to Monte Carlo on his own for a month.

That hurt. Partly because he had proposed to her there. In

her own heart, Elinor knew they were at the very least emotionally estranged now. No putting the broken pieces together this time. Let him caress his bottles of brandy. She accepted that their marriage—except for their little girls—was a failure, but she refused to believe she herself was.

* * *

"Admit it, Cosmo," Lucile told him, stooping to give him a peck on the cheek. "This new shop is perfect for all my plans. I adore the pale gray painted walls with the mirrors and the thick carpet to set everything off. I tell you, this mannequin dress parade today will be a feather in my cap."

He was quick to turn his head so that she caught his lips with her mouth instead of his cheek. "I told you, lass, all this on the condition that you one day model an outfit you have made especially for me, like one of those silky Oriental-type robes with some of the garments under it like you had in your hands and then sat on to hide the first day we met."

"Cosmo! You're to help with all this today, not distract me."

He sighed and rose from one of the little gilt wooden chairs they had set in a circle around a raised stage bedecked with white gardenias, stephanotis, and orchids he thought had cost too much, an arm and a leg he'd said with a narrow look at her arms and legs. The man was absolutely driving her to distraction and on a day like this.

How did she know Lucile Ltd. was doing well? Because important designers were spreading rumors about her, calling some of her designs indecorous. Yes, she was doing away with some layers of petticoats and big bustles and putting slits in some of the tighter skirts. The corsets she sold now were form enhancing, not form shaping. She had introduced the French *brassiere* and worse—in the eyes of the fashion establishment—insisted on doing away with calling women's arms and legs "limbs" as if they sprouted from trees. And her expansion to this new address at 14 St. George Street just off Hanover Square was a threat to other couturieres, who believed any sort of publicity, like the embossed and gilt invitations she'd sent out for this newfangled event, was "cheap."

Edith bustled past. "Hebe looks wonderful in Mrs. Glyn's presentation gown. All six of the living mannequins are nearly ready, Lucile."

Lucile patted Cosmo's shoulder and hurried out after her. "The musicians should be here soon," she told Edith, amid the nervous, chattering girls. "And I intend to decide which of my sister's jewels go with which gown of emotion. Have Mrs. Langtry and Mrs. Terry arrived yet? Oh, I pray nothing goes wrong today. How I wish I'd dared invite some of the royal family, but we're not there quite yet. Down with those horrid old wax-faced mannequins. We are going to give them our beautiful goddesses—reality, though fanciful and fantastic!"

"Yes, Lucile," Edith said in a loud voice. That was evidently a cue, for all her living mannequins and seamstresses began to applaud. There was Lillie Langtry, who had slipped in too, not only smiling but lifting an early glass of champagne in a toast to Lucile's creations.

* * *

Once Elinor heard what a roaring success Lucile's dress parade had been, she was even more driven to finish *The Visits of Elizabeth*. Although she and Clayton were married in name only now, he had kindly taken the manuscript to a man named Mr. Jeyes, who was a subeditor on the *Standard* newspaper. Clayton had also read parts of it at his men's club and said it had elicited some "good laughs."

"Which I take means good in general, not derisive," she said. "So then . . ."

"So then Jeyes, good old chap, has an offer for us that it be run in segments in a publication called *The World*."

Elinor rose to her feet without leaning on her crutches when she heard that. "Well, after all," she said, "Charles Dickens was successfully serialized."

"But he suggests a pen name, and I do too. After all, women of our class don't write, not for publication."

"And if it fetches in money? Or is praised?"

"Still keep your real name secret, I'd say."

"Even for other novels I intend to write?"

"Elinor, what in the deuce do you want? A little pin money would be nice, of course. Don't let your sister's fame go to your head. As much as you two care for each other, I fear you try to top each other too."

"Quite untrue," she told him. But, she thought, just wait until Lucile and all her fancy clients finally figure out who had written a book, one men, too, had deemed delightful.

* * *

"You did what?" Lucile demanded as they celebrated the periodical publication of *The Visits of Elizabeth* two months later in the library—now Elinor's writing room—at the Glyn flat in Sloane Square. "You are supposed to be keeping the identity of *Elizabeth* a secret and you told Daisy Brooke Warwick? Don't you recall even the newspapers used to call her 'The Babbling Brooke'? She won't keep your secret, at least with the uppers she cavorts with, including the Prince of Wales, so you . . ."

Lucile's voice trailed off, and her hands shot to her hips. "Why, Elinor Sutherland Glyn, you told her on purpose!"

Elinor only winked and smiled. "I certainly hope it doesn't leak out, but Clayton can hardly scold Lady Warwick, can he? You know everyone's talking about it, saying *The Visits of Elizabeth* is clever and funny. I can just see you putting an anonymous name on your designs and replacing those tall letters touting the Maison Lucile on your new building."

Lucile sighed and sank into the chair across Elinor's writing desk. "You are right as rain, of course."

"I appreciate your saying so. Dear Lucy, my girlhood friend and ever my sister, I've decided that Elinor Glyn sounds a bit like a nom de plume, anyway. I intend to write more novels, and I've started another to be called *The Reflections of Ambrosine*, with the main character modeled on Daisy Brooke Warwick and the hero based on this handsome young man Daisy introduced me to, Major Seymour Wynne Finch, one of the Prince of Wales's Marlborough House set. And oh, he has such style and panache—like your gowns, only quite in a different way."

Lucile picked up more than the inspiration for a fictional character in the way Elinor's eyes lit and her pale skin blushed nearly as red as her hair.

"If you'd been able to come to the dress parade, dear Nellie," Lucile said, picking up on her tender use of her own girlhood name, "you could have taken part in the toast Lillie Langtry proposed for me. You don't by chance have any champagne round here, do you?"

"No, but something else that will surely do." She went to the sideboard, opened a cabinet drawer, and dug under a stack of papers. "Ta-da!" she sang out, producing and holding out stiff-armed a bottle of Bodega sherry from the Duff-Gordon collection. "Clayton is drinking more and more of his expensive brandy, but this should do the trick for two girls from just Jersey. Now where are those glasses he hides? Ah, yes, no fluted goblets but old cut-glass crystal tumblers."

She poured two liberal glasses of the sherry. They clinked them together.

"To my sister, Lucy alias Lucile, fashion trendsetter and artist par excellence," Elinor said.

"To my sister, Nellie alias Elinor Glyn, published author and artist par excellence," Lucile said. "Onward and upward!" And they drank to that.

# CHAPTER *Fifteen*

"Oh, Madame Lucile, can we not peek at them when they are here?" Annie, one of Lucy's best seamstresses, asked.

"You may look up and curtsy, but no one but Edith and I will be in the Rose Room while we do this fitting. This is a special day, and I want no missteps. We will fit the gown to her, so even Hebe won't be needed this time," she told her assembled staff and shooed them all back to work.

Lucile had hired four other "living mannequins," every one of them nearly six feet tall with perfect curves. They all had fair hair and classic features. She had them sitting so they would not tower over their royal guests, but she wanted her "goddesses" to be able to see them so close—and here!

When the new century dawned in 1900, word was that old Queen Victoria was ailing. But the Maison Lucile was not. Lucile had seldom felt more professionally energized—or personally desperate.

Energized because her new client Mary, Duchess of York, was actually stopping by for a fitting of a stunning blue satin, heavily embroidered gown Lucile had created for her after a visit to

St. James Palace to show her the sketch of it. Previously, designs for the duchess had been carefully packed and sent off in a carriage, but this gown was special to Her Grace, and so to Lucile. The entire staff was thrilled because her husband, Duke George, was going to accompany her. At Victoria's passing, he would become Prince of Wales when his father, "Bertie," was crowned King Edward VII. And then someday, hopefully far distant, George would become King and their Queen would be in Lucile's frocks. Let the other fashion salons like Norman Hartnell's over in Bruton Street, which had been so snide, chew on that!

The only cloud that hovered over her excitement was that she hadn't seen Cosmo in over a fortnight, since he was in Scotland. His mother was also ill, that pillar of Victorianism whom he had vowed to protect and honor at his father's deathbed. Lucile pictured her as looking like Queen Victoria, still mourning her long-departed husband and the grand old days. Cosmo had sent Lucile a letter now and then, but she was shocked how much she missed him, and, worse, she feared that his ardor for her was cooling. And hers, more and more, was not, and that terrified her too.

"And do not be peeking out the window at them," she threw back over her shoulder as it was obvious the royal carriage, one pulled by four horses instead of a pair, clattered up just outside the door. Yes, they were precisely on time. Lucile had been told that the duke was always prompt if not early. Obviously, he was a stickler for propriety, so everything had to go quickly and properly.

With Edith behind her and the others standing back, Lucile greeted them at the door with a curtsy and pleasantries. The duke was bearded and smoking a cigarette, no less, but no good to fuss about the smoke near all the fabrics as she had with other men. Women smoked now too, but she had no compunction about scolding them.

The royal couple often lived in their country home called Sandringham in Norfolk and, despite her excitement, Lucile found herself wondering if it was anything like Cosmo's Maryculter in the Scottish countryside.

"This way, please, Your Graces," she said and indicated the carpeted hall toward the private fitting room at the rear she had dubbed the Rose Room.

"A beehive of activity," the duke said with a quick glance around. "Just the way I like to see our children at worthwhile tasks. Lead the way, then," he added, she assumed to give her permission to walk ahead of them.

Oh, just wait until she wrote Cosmo all this. It had worried her so that Elinor had said his mother would never accept a divorced woman as a daughter-in-law, but if royalty approved of her, wouldn't that count for something?

Things went well, though she could tell the duke did not like being penned in this small, frilly, pink room. He sat only briefly in the armed chair she'd brought from home, then stood or paced. Everyone knew he was an outdoorsman, a sportsman, but weren't they all, from the squires to the noble males of England, including Cosmo—even Clayton, who had turned out to be a wretched husband for intellectual, emotional Elinor.

The dark-haired duchess was not as stunning as her mother-in-law, Princess Alexandra, but she was pretty. She held herself stiffly erect, head up, shoulders back as she was fitted. It was rumored she did not get on with her mother-in-law and—oh dear . . .

Lucile's elbow knocked into the box of straight pins Edith held for her and they spewed all over the flowered carpet, even to the duke's feet.

"Oh, sorry," Lucile cried. "Edith and I will get them."

"Not to worry," the duke said. "Keep working there, as we are going to see the Queen. Here, let me help." To Lucile's surprise and embarrassment, he knelt next to the small dais on which his wife stood and helped Edith pick up pins.

Lucile didn't know whether to laugh or cry. The future Prince of Wales and King of England was kneeling at her feet. Wait until she wrote that to Cosmo!

* * *

"But I can tell you care for me, my darling Elinor," Seymour pleaded. He shocked her by kneeling next to her chair at their private luncheon table and taking both her trembling hands in his. "Can you not be mine in body as well as in soul, as you have said?"

They had met several other times for luncheon at this Amphitryon restaurant in London, which had private dining rooms intended for discreet liaisons. She loved this man madly—Clayton liked him too—but she had not been able to take the final step, the plunge to surrender her body to him as she had her heart. For some insane reason, she was still faithful to a husband who now detested her, who said he was sick of her histrionics and temper tantrums.

Seymour Wynne Finch was all she had idealized and desired, as if he had stepped full blown as a hero from her heart and head. He was what she considered to be "the best type of Englishman," well born and well educated, widely traveled. He had served his nation and was still a major in the Royal Horse Guards. He was a member of the Prince of Wales's so-called Marlborough House set. And, nearly fifteen years ago, he had enjoyed an *affaire de coeur* with her onetime inspiration Lillie Langtry. Yet, he had been eating strawberries from her hand and kissing and licking her fingers with each bite today. She was nearly insane with desire, however much it must be the man's first move. And yet she meant to—she must—put him off again.

"I told you, dearest," she said, her voice trembling, "I know it's de rigueur among our friends, but I am just not ready to become your lover, however much I love you. It's not you—it's—it's me."

He laid his head on her knees as if he were a little boy. She could feel the heat of him, fancied she could hear his heart beating. She shifted her hips slightly as he embraced her thigh and derriere with one arm.

Elinor knew full well that if she was discreet about the affair, Clayton would not give a damn. He'd gotten on well with Seymour when he'd visited them at Sheering Hall or their flat here in London. But however tempted she was to give in to her passions and his, it just was not her way. Yet in this moment she nearly swooned. This was truly romantic love, even without the blending of bodies.

He raised his handsome head and looked up at her. "I'm not worthy of your ideals, am I?" he asked. "It's your moral code only to love those who fit your elevated sensibilities."

"No, it isn't that. You are my ideal man, and that makes this even more difficult."

"I am so tempted to ravish you, my darling. But you know I would never presume that far."

"And I am so tempted that there is only one thing to do, and that is not to give in. We—I must stop meeting you like this. I fear I'm fragile and will break—break my promises and rules."

He suddenly looked so angry that she feared him for a moment. "Since you've decided, then so have I," he said, clipping out his words with almost military precision. "I shall leave you now because it is so difficult to be near you and behave. And you would detest me forever if I acted the cad on my deepest desires not only to please but to possess you."

She sucked in a sob as he stood and stiffly stepped back two paces.

"I won't forget you or what we could have had," he told her in a measured tone. "I wish you well in your marriage and your future."

As he turned away, she almost screamed his name and ran after him. Her vivid imagination pictured her on the settee, even the floor, clinging to him, crying out his name as he pulled her skirts up. Her passion was so vivid when he quietly closed the door that she nearly imagined he had taken her.

She hated herself yet admired herself at the same time. She sat alone for a good hour, listening to the silence of the room and smashing strawberries she had been feeding him by hand.

* * *

"You've seemed so unhappy lately," Lucile told Elinor as they left the theater together and waited in line for a hansom cabriolet.

"You should talk. You hardly smiled, let alone laughed at Ellen Terry's jokes. You're missing Cosmo, aren't you?"

"Terribly. Once he'd been through the funeral for his mother, I thought he'd be back, but I only received a short note. Now that she's gone, maybe the divorced woman is not such a diversion. Maybe I was his rebellion—but I thought he cared."

They climbed up into the hansom and gave the driver Elinor's address.

"And you?" Lucile asked. "Things with Clayton are . . ."

"Dreadful. At first I thought he would be proud of my writing, at least the money I earned. But he's out of sorts that I'm the so-called first society woman to write under my own name, as if it were a shameful thing. Well, it's his last name, so can't he be proud of that? But listen then. Why don't you do what I did to push Clayton to propose, as risky as that was? I recall it was partly your and Mother's idea."

Lucile gave a little laugh. "Run off to Monte Carlo, you mean, and hope he'll follow?"

Elinor turned to her on the seat. "Is it not worth a try? After you're gone, I could let on to him in a note that you are looking forward to events there, the dinners, the balls and theatricals—new people. Take Mother with you. Heaven knows, she's sad enough seeing what's become of me."

"Nonsense. She's proud of you."

"She had such a happy first marriage and she wanted that for us. I'm beyond the pale for that, but you and Cosmo—who knows?"

"I'd hate to leave the shop right now, but I do have several workers I can trust to be in charge. He might worry about that, too, that I'm off having a good time instead of minding his investment. I'll do it, if you'll play your part too."

"Playacting—that's my forte lately, on the page and off."

They shook gloved hands on that.

# CHAPTER *Sixteen*

There was a terrible banging on their hotel room door the fourth night Lucile and her mother were in Monte Carlo.

"Good gracious!" Mother said. "I pray someone has the wrong room."

"Who's there?" Lucile called out, standing near but not at the door.

"If he's in there, I want a word with him here and now!" a deep male voice bellowed. A voice with a distinctive and disturbing Scottish burr.

*Cosmo! Cosmo was here!*

Holding up a hand for her mother to stay where she was, Lucile fumbled with the latch and lock and swept open the door to find him looking quite magnificent with a sword drawn from a scabbard. He was in full Scottish regalia to knee stockings, belted kilt, and loose-sleeved, laced shirt with a black wool jacket and tam. For once, he smelled of whiskey instead of Highland air.

"Cosmo, whatever is it? What are you doing? And put that sword away."

"Is he here?"

"There's nobody but Mother, and you're frightening her out of her wits."

"Lord C was all Elinor would admit to me. I saw her before I sailed, having to chase you halfway across Europe. Is it true he's been courting you and turning your head? Pray God you haven't given him a promise or he's laid a hand on you."

*Elinor, indeed,* she thought. The great romantic and fiction writer had embellished the story they'd planned. She remembered how Elinor had been talking about that regal, powerful Lord Curzon, viceroy of exotic India, as she'd put it. Is that where Elinor had dreamed up Lord C? Even if it was, she had no intention of telling Cosmo.

"Cosmo, sheathe that sword, and we will talk."

"Is he British? Who is he? I intend to challenge him to a duel over your honor."

"Now that you're here, I can hardly recall his name. Put that down, I said, and sit."

"Good evening to you, Mrs. Kennedy," he said, finally noticing her. He lowered his voice and seemed to steady himself as he slid his sword back into its scabbard. He looked a bit sheepish as he came in.

"Good evening to you, Lord Duff-Gordon. How kind of you to drop by. Now if you will excuse me, I shall let you two hash this out and be in my room, Lucy dear, if you need me." And she made an exit worthy of Ellen Terry.

Lucile closed the door behind her. She was in one of her Oriental silk robes with little underneath, and it was—she glanced at the clock—nearly ten thirty.

"You can bet you won't so much as recall his name now that

I'm here," Cosmo insisted as he dropped the scabbard and sword onto the carpet and reached for her. "He better not have laid a hand on you, but I intend to." He gave her a resounding, earth-shaking kiss until he nearly lost his balance, then sank to the sofa where she'd been sketching designs. She sat beside him, pulling her split robe closed over her bare knees.

"If you're going to marry anyone, you're going to marry me," he went on. "Did he pressure you? Did he propose?"

"I suppose he proposed some things—which, of course, I did not accept."

"Thank God. But why did you leave London with nary a word?" he demanded, turning toward her. His breath was as sharp as his expression. Yes, he had been drinking and not his usual Duff-Gordon sherry. For a moment that bothered her. Clayton was forever in his cups, and maybe, now that Cosmo's strictly religious mother had died, he'd taken to it too, but no. She'd studied this strong, honorable, and loyal man. And because he was strong, she'd decided what she must do if he ever proposed—and was he proposing now?

"You see," she said, reaching gently for his big hand clenched on his knee and unflexing his fingers, "I thought you had grown weary of me, oh, maybe not as a business partner, but you hardly said you so much as loved me lately."

"I haven't grown weary of you. I've loved you, damn it, for over seven years, almost from the first time you stood with little silky underthings in your hands and then put them under your pretty bum before you rather quickly tossed me back out on the street."

"But I tried to retrieve you later."

"Ha! That makes me sound like a hunting dog. And you did

not. You let me make the first—the second move—and then played hard to get." With his free hand, he reached out to finger the fine, silky material of her gown at the neck, as if he would pull it awry to bare her to him. In a quiet, coaxing voice he went on, "Sweetheart, don't you remember I told you that you must wear such bonnie things for me someday? Do you think a dour Scotsman and sporting man would ordinarily invest time and money in a ladies' fashion house if there wasn't something there he wanted? And you don't do men's clothes."

"Not yet—but," she told him, reaching for her design sketchbook on the table and flipping to a back page, "if I ever do, this will be the first. It's what I have dubbed a 'Cosmo sporting suit.' See? I've labeled it thus."

"Damn good looking," he said, leaning closer, almost on her shoulder. "Tweed and then leather there on the lapels, I hope."

"Cosmo Duff-Gordon," she said, tossing the sketchbook on the table, "I haven't given a flying flip for any other man since I met you. But because you are a strong man, one who usually gets your own way—"

"I intend to with you."

"—we need to come to an understanding before some sort of arrangement."

"Arrangement? I'm marrying you, lass."

"But, as you know, I have another love besides you, and I don't mean another man. The arrangement I'm speaking of," she went on, pulling her dressing gown together again under his steady stare, "is that I simply cannot abandon my business, my shop, and my career. And a Scottish estate on the river Dee, however lovely, I am sure, is far from the Maison Lucile in London."

"Don't I know. You haven't set one foot in Scotland yet, and it's the place I love most. So I would want the woman I love to be there—though back and forth to London, too."

He put his hand on her knee, caressing and gripping it through the slick material. But she must not be distracted or deterred.

"But as my bulwark of strength and adviser for the shop," she went on, "you understand that it takes a great deal of my time. You've always counseled well, that I not jump ahead of my resources, but I have dreams and plans to open a shop in Paris and—"

"The fancy frogs won't patronize a British woman's shop."

"They will if they love the clothing. And America, not that I have an exact plan for that, but I want to visit there, see the opportunities, so—"

"So give me one of those sheets of paper, maybe the one with the Cosmo suit. I'll cut my finger, my wrist, anything and sign in blood to all that if you'll wed me, lass. My lass," he said and reached for her.

He lifted her so easily onto his lap, then held her there a moment, staring intently into her face. "If your mother wasn't in the next room, probably listening at the door, I'd seal our bargain another way. Lucile-Lucy Sutherland Wallace, will you marry me? After all, maybe being able to have the name *Lady* Duff-Gordon will help with sales when you take over the world. I'll be there beside and behind you. I know you have a hard time trusting men, but we can work on that."

Her head spun at his words and at his touch. "Agreed," she told him. "With that plan, I agree. I don't know what I would have done without you over these last years, but I believe I do know what to do with you now."

"Quit talking about your plans and kiss me. I have no intention of being put off or losing you again—ever."

* * *

They were wed two weeks later, May 24, 1900, in Venice at the house of a friend of Cosmo's who was in foreign service there. He'd even found a bagpipe to blast—it was really called skirling, she learned—Scottish tunes at the intimate reception.

Mother attended, but not Elinor or Esme, who was staying with her aunt. Lucile's only other regret was that, considering all the sumptuous wedding gowns she'd made for others, she wore her favorite ball gown, an old one. But what mattered was that she was marrying the man she loved.

Cosmo was so proud and happy, and, yes, she was happy too. So indeed, she was now Lucile, *Lady* Duff-Gordon.

He took her to a beautiful site called Abazzia in western Croatia for their honeymoon, a spot where they knew no one. They swam in the warm bay of the Adriatic Sea each day and sat in the shade eating seafood and sipping wine. This setting seemed so open and so real, not closed off or made by man. The second day in a row, when she beat her muscular athlete in a swimming race, she realized she loved the feeling of winning. She'd won her dream career and the man of her dreams.

That night with their hotel suite's double door open to the July night breeze and the stars, they sat naked in their bed and watched the moon rise over the sea with the music of its crashing waves on the shore.

"I'm used to winning races and matches," he whispered, "but you beat me twice fair and square, so you get a prize."

"I already have a prize," she said, flashing her heirloom engagement ring and gold wedding band at him in the glow of moonlight that illumined their bodies and their bed.

"A new prize," he said. "Something I wager you've never had or done, my sweet, wild lass of a wife." He turned to her and put one hand on her shoulder, one on her waist. His mere touch made her shiver with desire. "I'm proud of you for not drawing one sketch of a costume while we've been here, and you beat me fair and square at swimming, so name your prize."

"Besides your helping me find and open a shop in Paris?"

"Yes, damn it!"

She laughed deep in her throat. "All right then," she whispered, moving her thigh to press against his. "No more teasing or cat and mouse. I want to show you I can win at more than a swimming race. And at building a business. I know you are the man in the family, but I can lead too."

She amazed herself at her boldness, but, good gracious, times were changing. Just wait until Bertie took the throne. Elinor thought so too, and had talked about an idea for a novel where the woman seduced the man—novel and naughty indeed in Queen Victoria's world.

She pushed Cosmo back on their pile of pillows and mounted him, settling in at once. Despite his bravado, he gasped, but cooperated fully, gripping her to him. He barely managed to whisper, "And I used to think fencing was my favorite athletic endeavor."

She gasped too. It was strange to be the one on top, the one in charge. But she reveled in it and found that it led to a strange surrender too. And, for one mad, shattering moment, there was no one or no thing in the world besides this man she loved.

## CHAPTER *Seventeen*

Cosmo and Lucile greeted guests for the reception they had arranged for Elinor's latest book, called *Three Weeks*, when Mrs. Severton, their cook, hovered in the hall, frowning, motioning to Lucile. The woman hardly ever came upstairs, so something must be very wrong.

Their London home in Lennox Gardens would soon be filled with more than family, including their childhood inspiration, Lillie Langtry. Elinor's publisher was here; even Clayton, who had promised to be on good behavior, was here. He liked Cosmo tremendously so Lucile hoped he was telling the truth. But he'd arrived in his cups early, and without Elinor. Lucile just hoped he wouldn't make a scene.

"I'll be back in a moment," Lucile whispered to Cosmo. "I hope Mrs. Severton's soufflés have not fallen—just jesting." She gave his arm an intimate squeeze.

After nearly seven years, their marriage was still a delight to them. Granted, she didn't get to Scotland as much as she knew he would like, but she had redecorated grand old Maryculter House and had even gone out tramping the estate with him each visit.

"What's amiss, Mrs. Severton?" she whispered as the plump woman kept motioning her farther back into the hall. At least Lucile smelled nothing burning.

They stopped before the closed door of Cosmo's study, which Lucile had decorated with tartan curtains, leather chairs, and prints of Scottish scenes. He'd been ecstatic. Even now, as intrigued and perturbed as she was, she pictured how they had made love on the maroon, brass-tacked leather couch in celebration of his "Scotland in London room."

"It's your sister, milady. She come to the back downstairs door, she did. Insisted I fetch you to this room before she—I think she said before she made her entrance out front."

"Good heavens, is she ill?"

"Looked a bit peaked and shaky, she did, but—"

"Thank you, Mrs. Severton. I'll let you return to your duties now. We are looking forward to your excellent meal."

Lucile turned the knob and pushed the door inward. Elinor's plumed and ribboned hat was tossed on the ottoman. She wore the most recent gown Lucile had designed for her and for which she had not yet paid. But that, amazingly, was the way of the world right now. Even fine families seemed to be deep in debt, trying to keep up with King Edward's grandiose expectations of hospitality to him and others of his set.

"Elinor, what—"

"Just sit down, and I'll tell you. *Three Weeks,* my dear book, my dream novel has all gone wrong!" She burst into tears and sank onto the couch with her face in her hands.

Lucile perched beside her and put a hand on her shoulder. "It isn't doing well? It's only been on sale for a few days. I've barely had time to start reading my copy. But you said it was the best thing you've ever done, better even than *Beyond the Rocks,* which was so well received. Did the publisher mention your weak spelling and grammar again, so—"

"It's been called immoral in a review" came muffled from behind her hands. "Immoral! I'm going to be attacked on all sides. No one grasps the nobility of the book. They all harp on the breaking of morality in the story. After all, everyone sins. Wait till you get your newspaper tomorrow. And let me recite a piece of doggerel being bandied about that Daisy Warwick warned me of. You see, in the novel, main characters make love on a tiger-skin rug," she said and took her hands from her face. Her expression was one of hurt and contempt as she recited,

> "*Would you like to sin*
> *With Elinor Glyn*
> *On a tiger skin?*
> *Or would you prefer*
> *To err*
> *With her*
> *On some other fur?*"

"Oh my! That will spread like wildfire. But it is promotion."

"Promotion! That's my Lucile! Thank God, Clayton's leaving for the Mediterranean on his own, because I can't stand his drunken lectures on money, let alone this. I've had hate mail from several early readers, actually nonreaders. I can tell that the worst of the critics, so far at least, have not even read it. They make mistakes in their comments."

"Slow down. Tell me the story in the novel."

"All right," she said, blotting at her tear-streaked face with a wadded handkerchief. "I know I said it's the book of my heart and it is. I know I told you I didn't want to talk about *Three Weeks* even to you before it came out. The story is of a foreign queen traveling incognito in Switzerland who seduces a younger Englishman she, obviously, is not wed to."

"Oh, I see," Lucile told her, recalling vividly the night on their honeymoon—and some since—where she had taken the lead with Cosmo.

"You don't see," Elinor insisted. "She doesn't only want his body—and even that for a noble purpose to have an heir to save her kingdom. He's culturally an ignoramus in art, music, history, and she wanted to change that. His character was inspired by an admirer of mine Clayton sent away—not Seymour Finch but Lord Alistair Innes Ker."

"What? The young man who went to Paris with you and Clayton? I—I didn't know he and you . . ."

"Well, obviously nothing came of it. I'm still faithful to my husband at least that way. Alistair was only the inspiration for this book, what I was yearning for, not what happened. But never mind all that. It's over, but the aftermath from this story is not. The point is that the critics and early readers of *Three Weeks* are scandalized, absolutely in a frenzy, so how can I face the others out there today, let alone later in public?" she demanded with a new flow of tears and a nod at the door through which they could hear the growing buzz of voices.

"Well, welcome to the Sutherland sisters' society," Lucile told her, "and I don't mean having young admirers."

"You have all those young men you call acolytes about the shop, who adore you."

"Who want to learn from me. About designing clothes, dear sister, not about love."

"And what sisters' society? You don't write more than letters and names of those emotional, personality titles you give your frocks. Whatever is Mother going to think? I don't give a flying leap about Clayton's opinions, but she's still of Victoria's times, through and through."

"Don't underestimate her. As for Clayton, he came drunk to the door a bit ago, and Cosmo stashed him upstairs to sleep it off for now. But don't you see? Some have accused me of indecency for years, for creating clothes that were immoral, that showed a flash of leg and offered small, silky lingerie instead of bustles and break-back corsets. Some blue-blooded snobs snub me for 'keeping a shop,' especially since I'm now Lady Duff-Gordon. And yet the orders for more and the happy and assured women who wear them, including Princess Alexandra and the Duchess of York, keep coming. The right people will surely admire the uplifting and noble parts of your novel."

Elinor blew her nose and shook her head. "As I get older, I can't continue to write just fun and frippery. But you mean the book might be popular anyway, despite the so-called scandalous parts?"

"Your publisher, Mr. Duckworth, evidently believed in the book and its author, and he should be here any minute. I say, dry your tears, square your shoulders, and bluff it through. Defy them all. If it's the book of your heart, I am certain I will love it and recommend it to my clients and friends."

"Oh, as much as we don't get on sometimes, old girl, as much as you pooh-pooh my literary allusions, I am so grateful for you.

But then—that's right. Now that you write fashion advice for the *Royal Magazine*, perhaps you understand my literary aspirations more."

"Women must have aspirations beyond their families—passionate goals. I've agreed to design for the theater here in London, and I intend to take on French fashion in the heart of Paris, to open a shop there someday. Even your frivolous friend Daisy Warwick has turned to socialism in her struggles to help the poor."

"What would I do without you?"

"Hide out more than you do writing in rural Essex and mope about, I suppose. Wait here, I said, and I'll order some wash water from the kitchen for your face. Cosmo said just the other day—and I agree—that you are at the height of your beauty. And aren't we at the height then of our creative goals and dreams, but with better yet to come?"

"Just a moment then," Elinor said and grasped her wrist. "One other thing before I face family and friends. You recall Lord Curzon, whom I've mentioned?"

"Yes, of course. Former viceroy of India, now the Right Honorable Lord Curzon serving as a civil servant with parliamentary ambitions. So sad his wife died last year and left him with those three little girls to rear alone. I suppose like all ambitious men, he wanted a son."

"The thing is, I met him at a—a function again. So kind and dashing. Terribly witty. Well, through another friend, Alfred, Lord Milner, I sent Lord Curzon an early copy of the book. He read it and wrote that he understood the true purpose and passion of it."

"Understood the *passion* of it?" Lucile said with a knowing laugh.

"Don't look at me that way. He meant that there was a beauty in the love of my characters Paul and the mysterious lady and the child that came from their union. And that my ending was moral because she paid the price for her adultery with her life, but that their son would go on to rule, to be a noble man. Lord Curzon saw good parts in it, of her teaching a young Englishman to appreciate not just love but the arts and travel. And since I have the lady in the novel seduce the young man Paul while she is lying on a tiger skin, he sent me one he brought back from a hunt in India. I—I have two of them now, and I cherish both."

"Oh."

"Do say more than 'oh.'"

"I've heard you speak of Lord Curzon, but you've spoken of other admirers too. So he has become special. I'd best read the book, but if you wrote it and it came from your heart, Cosmo and I will support you with all we have. Now let me get that wash water, and it looks as if you've been tearing at your hair. Then we'll face first the lambs here tonight and you can face down the lions of literature another day."

* * *

Elinor managed to get herself together, put back on her cloak and hat, and walked round to the front door. At her entry, everyone applauded, but then, she thought, they hadn't seen tomorrow's newspapers or heard the scuttlebutt.

Her publisher, Gerald Duckworth, seemed to think early sales were good and whispered, "Buck up, Elinor. Scandal can be a boon to sales."

"Before it goes on sale in the States, I will write an explanatory introduction to my American readers. Perhaps they will grasp what our countrymen seem not to, that the one motive that makes a union moral in ethics is love."

"I'll second that," Lillie Langtry said and gave Elinor a hug. She recognized at once Lillie's frock, a Lucile gown of emotion—that was her specialty. This one, if she recalled correctly, was *Do You Love Me?* Lillie had been a scandal to many and loved by many—too many—yet she held her head high and radiated the sort of passion for life that Lucile had just preached to her. The three of them, Elinor realized, were somehow all sisters under the skin.

"Auntie," Lucile's daughter, Esme, said, and gave her a kiss on the cheek, "I think it's so terribly exciting that you have American readers, and Anthony agrees and Grandmama, too!"

Elinor gave her niece a hug. At age twenty-two—though much too young, Lucile thought—Esme was engaged to Anthony Giffard, Viscount Tiverton, a good catch. They were so in love, holding hands even now. Her fiancé was from a fine family, for his father was an earl who was Lord Chancellor and had written a book on English law. The young couple's insistence on their short betrothal and coming marriage next month reminded her and Lucile of their own mother's loyal love for her first husband, so passion obviously ran in the Sutherland family. Yes, whatever slings and arrows assailed her, Elinor decided right then she would hold her head high.

Even Clayton came downstairs to join them for the toast to the release of *Three Weeks*. Of course he wouldn't miss a chance to raise a glass, even to his own wife he'd emotionally abandoned long ago, even if it was champagne and not his favorite steady slugs of expensive, imported brandy.

"To Elinor Glyn's continued literary success," Cosmo said and everyone agreed with a chant of, "Here! Here!"

"To a long and fruitful writing career," Gerald Duckworth added.

"Good luck, Mummy!" her daughters, Margot, age fourteen, and Juliet, age nine, cried in unison and lifted their glasses of pink punch.

"To my very talented sister!" Lucile said and clinked her glass to Elinor's.

Their mother said, "I am so proud of both my girls, but I don't know if I'll read this book at my age, dear. But a good love story, well, perhaps."

Lillie Langtry said, "I love America, and I think you would too. I hear *Three Weeks* goes on sale there soon, just the time for you to pop over for a visit. Mr. Duckworth, can you not send her there on a sort of tour? I say, 'Go west, young woman!' and that means to new places, new people. You'll adore it there—you would too, Lucile. New horizons for all of us 'just Jersey girls'!"

Elinor's gaze connected with Lucile's. New worlds to conquer. Why, dear Lord Curzon had done that, and she admired him so. Now that he was back and had looked kindly on her—in his own aloof way, of course—she wasn't set on a foreign jaunt, but she could do without Clayton's grim face and penny-pinching ways for a while.

Go west, young woman? Maybe so.

# PART III

# New York City

1907–1912

# CHAPTER *Eighteen*

"The grand finale! So your maiden voyage to America was done in style," Consuelo, Duchess of Manchester, said to Elinor as they stood side by side along the portside railing of the *Lusitania*. New York Harbor was awash with tugboats and pleasure craft as their big vessel came slowly in. "There, you see," Consuelo said, pointing at a huge statue on a small island, "the lady with the lamp holds it high to greet you."

"She's magnificent. And if it's been smooth sailing for me on my first Atlantic crossing, it is partly thanks to your kindness and hospitality on board, Your Grace."

"My dear Elinor, have you not heard that hospitality is my middle name?" she asked with a smile.

Consuelo was one of the first of what was called "a dollar princess," a bride from a rich American family who wed an Englishman for a title, reputation, and grandeur in exchange for her father's wealth saving a family estate and name from bankruptcy. Consuelo had wed a viscount, who became a duke when his father died. Perhaps she'd use that in a future book,

Elinor thought, that is, if she survived the impact of her current novel.

This grand lady, who insisted her friends call her by her first name—though Elinor slid in a "Your Grace" now and then—had an American mother but a Cuban father who had made a fortune as a merchant in the American South. Not only had she blazed a trail through the English upper classes, but she had been one of the numerous mistresses of the Prince of Wales, now King Edward. Currently in her midfifties, Elinor guessed, this outgoing woman's Cuban heritage was revealed in her dark eyes and glossy black hair, now going a bit silver. Evidently, money was still a problem for the Manchesters, and it was said that the flamboyant Consuelo had accepted gifts for introducing later dollar brides to their titled mates.

Patting Elinor's gloved hand, Consuelo went on, "It has been a joy to know you better than when we were 'ships passing in the night' in London or at country house parties. When one's entertaining King Bertie, batten down the hatches."

Elinor laughed at Consuelo's clever banter. Not only had the woman been kind to her during the days of the Atlantic crossing, but she had invited her to come along to her friend's home on the Hudson River for a few days rather than going directly to the Plaza Hotel in the city. The place was called Hyde Park—it sounded so English—and the hostess was Mrs. Frederick Vanderbilt. Consuelo was godmother of the beautiful and popular Duchess of Marlborough, Consuelo Vanderbilt, her namesake, whom Elinor had met twice at London social events.

Everyone knew King Edward loved American hostesses, especially the clever Consuelos, for they found new ways to amuse him. "Oh yes," Consuelo had answered a question at the dinner table one evening on board. "His Majesty loves us upstart American climbers and comers. He loves good cooks, too, and I always have those—entirely worth the money to raid one from a fashionable French restaurant. And more than once, I hired a singer for a private concert when we entertained him. Our king is a connoisseur of everything and hates to be bored, but don't we all?"

Thanks to Consuelo, Elinor had not been bored on the voyage, although she had come alone with just her lady's maid, Williams. Clayton was off for a visit to Japan with their daughters and his mother-in-law, filling in for Elinor, who had at first intended to go with them. They were all to meet up in the American West and traverse the huge country together, back to New York and then home. She would have loved to see exotic Japan, but, to her, the United States of America was exotic too.

As they watched the flotilla of tugboats surround their big vessel to edge them toward the pier, Consuelo spoke again over the noise.

"Now, don't you fret about those nasty British reviews for your novel. Banned at Eton—how overly prudish! I thought it was a perfectly splendid story, and other discerning readers will too. Besides, I believe you will find that we born-and-bred Americans are not as—well, as hidebound in hypocritical ways as our dear English. After all, everyone's reading *Three Weeks*."

"Not for the wrong reasons, I hope."

"Some, of course. A friend told me her daughter, age sixteen, was reading it in secret. Her governess was appalled and told her mother but then was caught reading it herself."

Elinor smiled. "I have heard similar tales, Your Grace. But the critics and churches have been brutal in condemning it—and me. I'm afraid that my publisher, Gerald Duckworth, sent word ahead to some American papers that I was coming for a visit on this ship. It's been that sort of newspaper and magazine journalist who has caused me so much harm, so I wish he would not have done that."

"Nonsense. Word of mouth is what sold the book like nothing doing in England. Nothing ventured, nothing gained, my dear, that's my motto. And in my homeland here," she added with a sweep of her arm at the crowded array of buildings beyond the piers, "that's a good one to remember."

But upon their disembarkation, the motto Elinor wished for was "Help!" Curse Gerald Duckworth, for at the bottom of the ramp onto the busy pier like a swarm of bees stood men who were shouting her name. Some held up signs with her name or a photograph of her face or the cover of *Three Weeks*. She almost turned round to march directly back to her cabin to head home where she knew where to hide. But she would face them down, no matter that she was off to a rocky start here where she had hoped for so much.

Consuelo, surrounded by her two maids and men carrying a great array of luggage—both the duchess's and Elinor's—was motioning for her to follow. Elinor saw Consuelo was greeted by a man who gestured toward the exit. Elinor had only one-third as many trunks, though she had brought an array of Lucile fashions and sixty pairs of shoes, for who knew what she would face in this wild country? But as she moved toward the bottom of the ramp alone but for faithful Williams cowering behind her in the hubbub, the swarm of newsmen hemmed her in.

"Mrs. Glyn, can you give the *New York Herald* a statement on your new novel? What do you think of the moral values of the rich in England?"

"Over here, Mrs. Glyn!" another man shouted, waving a copy of a newspaper. "Our readers want to hear from the woman who wrote the runaway seller *Three Weeks*! Is it based on anyone you know? Is it true that the lady in the novel is based on a real person?"

"Authoress Glyn! Just a short statement about your newfound fame, if you please!"

Elinor moved aside off the bottom of the busy ramp. "As you can imagine," she said in a clarion voice that almost didn't quaver, "I am looking forward to my first visit to your country and need to rest now. But if you will give my companion your cards, I will let you know quite soon when interviews are possible."

*There,* she thought. *Lucile would be proud.* And, oh, thank God above, that Americans might be rude and crude—or so she had heard—but she liked them so much already she could have hugged each one.

* * *

In her office, Lucile stopped midway through the letter she'd received from Elinor in America just this morning. She'd only read bits of it en route here, for Lucile Ltd. was presenting a huge mannequin parade by invitation only today, and people were already arriving.

It seemed the newspapers in the United States were not attacking Elinor but extolling her as "a famous authoress extraordinaire." She had been feted by a Vanderbilt relation at their lavish mansion and befriended by the Duchess of Manchester.

"No time for all that right now," Lucile muttered to herself as if speaking to Elinor through this letter. "This will be lavish and elegant today, too, with my goddesses wearing my new collection."

Elinor had gone on and on—she'd get to all that later—about the thrill of now living in the elegant Plaza Hotel. About how she was considering what Lucile had called self-advertisement, which Elinor had always pooh-poohed before. About a visit from some popular American author who had read *Three Weeks* and said he understood it, a humorist named Mark Twins or something like that, whom she called a "terribly witty creature."

Actually, Lucile hated to admit it rankled a bit that Elinor's book, so degraded here, had now become a cause célèbre in the United States. As Elinor had put it, *The Americans here in what is called "God's own country" are indeed different from us. More color in their faces, more kindhearted. Even commoners on the streets seem full of vitality, intensity, and determination.* She had gone on and on, not that Lucile had read the entire rambling letter yet.

For heaven's sake, Lucile groused silently, how dare Elinor turn on her own countrymen—perhaps including her own family. Did Elinor not know her older sister was full of vitality, intensity, and determination? She was doing smashing work here, and today would prove that. The audience included the queens of Spain and Rumania and noble ladies, including several HRHs. Also, the influential theater crowd would be here, such as Lillie Langtry, Ellen Terry, and Lily Else, the famous singer for whom Lucile had created costumes in her *The Merry Widow* triumph, including the new rage called the merry widow hat. Quite a few ladies had worn a version of that big-brimmed, bird-of-paradise-plumed fashion today, so it had been wise to build a slightly raised stage here so everyone could see.

Most of all, Elinor's letter did not sit well with Lucile because she herself intended to influence American women with her clothing, perhaps even designs for the common woman, for that seemed the American way. And she did not want to be known in America only as Elinor Glyn's sister.

After all, Lucile Ltd. was doing well, but until she conquered New York and Paris, it would not be enough. If her little sister could be a raving success in America, she could too. She intended to let Elinor know that the designer Lucile now commanded twenty guineas for a consultation, a mere consultation! When women had five to six changes of costume per day, and needed hats, shoes, and gloves to harmonize, the sky was the limit—not just in England and America, though, you might know, Elinor had gone on about expecting foreign translations of *Three Weeks* to sweep all Europe, too.

Lucile tossed the letter onto her desk and went down the hall into the dressing room, abuzz with women's voices. She clapped her hands for silence and made a little speech: "My dear goddesses, every seat is taken by ladies thrilled to see you presenting the Seven Ages of Woman. Quick costume changes will be necessary and done with whispers. Listen carefully for your cues, and I thank you all for what I know will be a smashing success."

As she swept back out in a new, rainbow-hued chiffon gown, she felt a bit of guilt. Actually, before she sailed, Elinor had come up with the concept for this presentation, something about Shakespeare and "the Seven Ages of Man" she had rattled off.

Some of the goddesses were wearing jewelry borrowed from Elinor as well as from herself. But when she'd asked her sister to stay until after the parade, she'd said she couldn't.

From backstage, she peeked out through the curtain. Her four young male assistants, whom Cosmo jokingly referred to as her acolytes, had everyone seated. Her acolytes were all so eager to learn design, to have their names on fashions of their own someday, but today they were serving as ushers to escort the guests to their proper places. All attired alike, they enhanced this large room as much as did the newly done decor.

Before Lucile stepped out onto the stage in front of the blue silk curtain to introduce the different ages of fashion in a woman's life, she glanced down at her notes: *the Schoolgirl, the Debutante, the Fiancée, the Bride, the Wife, the Hostess, and the Dowager.* Her seven goddesses, each nearly six feet tall, were well prepared to show her new designs off so alluringly. Despite being upset by Elinor's letter, she was ready too.

Applause swept at her like a wave as she stepped out before the curtain. The scent of roses and lilies in huge bouquets on both sides of the stage nearly made her swoon as she smiled and began.

"Welcome to Maison Lucile for our mannequin parade to share with you, entitled *The Seven Ages of Woman.*" Her voice quavered a bit, perhaps because she was trying to project it. My, she was nervous and hadn't planned on that, but she went on, "The early sections of the Seven Ages we will present today have just a few frocks, the later sections, many, but is that not the way our lives blossom? Just like each one of you, each gown you will see today has its own name and personality, evoking emotions. See if you can tell which are 'When Passion's Thrall

Is New,' 'Give Me Your Heart,' 'The Sighing Sound of Lips Unsatisfied,' and 'A Frenzied Song of Amorous Things,' to name but a few. The gown I am wearing today is 'Dreaming of the Rainbow.'" She slowly pirouetted to let them view the high-waisted, daring shimmer of pink, lilac, pale green, and orange chiffon with the intricately embroidered, beadwork, and Belgium lace at the hemline and the garland of silken and pearl roses round the neckline.

Several oohs and aahs and another round of applause washed over her. Lillie Langtry in the second row was nodding and clapping louder than the rest. Lucile smiled and bowed, wishing Elinor were here to see and hear all this. They had once teased each other that Lillie was going far, that she had that difficult-to-define quality they called "It," part charm, part charisma, which sometimes boiled down to just plan animal magnetism.

Elinor had cheekily claimed she felt she had "It" when she was lying nearly naked on her most recent tiger skin. Today, Lucile felt she had "It," too.

# CHAPTER *Nineteen*

"There you are, at last!" Lucile cried and popped up from the sofa when Elinor came in the door of her small suite in the Plaza Hotel. "So busy you could not meet your big sister at the pier? I simply had to come visit you in New York when I received your long, excited letters."

Elinor dropped her fox stole on a chair, and they kissed on both cheeks. "I'm glad you arrived safely and hope it was a good crossing. Sorry I'm late, but I was at a luncheon in my honor arranged by Emily Post. She's quite the social arbiter here. She writes about etiquette, something I agreed with her is important. I didn't say so, but especially in this country, the so-called gentlemen could use a bit of polish. All rush, rush and money, money."

"Yes, thank you for asking about the voyage," Lucile said, frowning at the gush of words, but Elinor didn't notice her sarcasm. "From what you've written, you are always busy."

"I just couldn't change these plans today. Reporters were at the event from *New York Journal* and *New York World*. Those papers are known for some sensational stories, so I supposed

*Three Weeks* is cannon fodder, but with this novel, I'm starting to learn that any promotion is still promotion."

"I've always told you that, and I've proved it too. Women are coming to me in droves for fashions," Lucile said, annoyed that Elinor had not asked her how things were at home. "But your letters with such detail make it sound as if you have another novel in the making." She sat back on the sofa, and Elinor perched beside her and pulled out her long hat pins.

"Always. Lucile, it's made me famous here! Mrs. Elinor Glyn, authoress!"

"I hope some of that admiration spills over to our own countrymen," Lucile said as Elinor spun her big-brimmed merry widow–style hat onto the floor, no less. Lucile tried to ignore that despite the fact she'd seen her popular creation on the ship and in the streets of New York. "You realize I received, just in time, your last post about not having room for my staff to stay here in your suite. I've put my secretary, Miss Francatelli, and poor Simpson in a room just down the street, but how to do without my lady's maid on-site? If she's late some morning, I may have to borrow your Williams. Someone who's been dubbed 'the best dressed woman in the world' can't go about looking slapdash."

"Ha! As if you ever would. But speaking of that, I have found the most wonderful treatments to preserve youth and beauty. A facial elixir called 'The Secrets of El-Zair' is simply all the rage here among some of the social elite. It's part of a belief in what is called 'New Thought.' We must always think of and send out 'golden lights' in our thoughts, and the thought force will help you to obtain anything you desire."

Lucile gave her a narrow-eyed stare. "I'm afraid that all sounds a bit hobgoblin to me, like those old fairy tales full of magic you used to be obsessed with."

"I'll say no more. I didn't really expect you to understand. And how is Cosmo doing, as they say here, holding down the fort?"

"I miss him terribly already. He's overseeing things in Scotland and London, but, of course, my staff is highly capable of forging ahead without me for a short while."

"You'll be here a short while?"

"Don't sound too hopeful. I intend to find a place for a Lucile's New York while I'm here, and my old friend Elsie de Wolfe is going to help me."

"I've seen her here and there. You're right to choose and use her, as it seems she knows everyone from way back, but then she is a native New Yorker. I recall she bought oodles of clothes from you when she was on her dollar-princess husband quest, but she just didn't find a suitable title—or man, did she? I swear, Lucile, no man would have her if he really knew her," Elinor said, leaning closer and lowering her voice as if someone would hear. "You do know that about her—don't you?"

"Yes, I know she prefers women. She's made no secret of it since she has so many sapphic friends."

"She wasn't pretty enough to find a man either, though I heard someone say just last week she had such willpower that she could persuade you that she was beautiful. Well, her stint on the stage here made her known not for her so-so acting but for her fabulous clothing, some of it probably of your making. I'd ask her for advice in a minute. Actually, remember when Lillie said to me, 'Go west'? Well, Elsie and my publisher here have said the same, and I'll be heading out west, clear to Nevada and California this spring."

"What an adventure! I intend to conquer this continent too, only with my designs."

"I've been meaning to ask if you smell faint smoke in here?" Elinor asked, squinting at the room and fanning her face.

"I don't even smell it anymore," Lucile said, leaning away to the end table to produce an ivory taboret she opened. She plucked out and held up a long cigarette.

"You—you smoke? But you always had a conniption if someone lit up near your materials or gowns."

"Straw tipped so the smoke isn't as strong," she said, holding it out. "Quite calms my nervous demeanor sometimes. Well, Cosmo smokes an occasional cigar or pipe, so he doesn't mind, and it's the rage among the uppers. In London, I also carry what's called a Bo-Peep walking stick with a crook on the end. I tell my assistants and my sewers, fitters, and the rest of the staff that I carry it so I can pull them back from disaster like a little flock of sheep if they stray. And I've taken to wearing ropes of pearls over my gowns, not to mention I always take my little Pekes and pugs to work. I adore having them about my feet, though I suppose, the others have to watch where they step. You do know Queen Victoria always had pet dogs hiding under her skirts? All that is my persona, Elinor, and you have yours with your many spoken and written golden thoughts."

"And you think I'm long-winded? Well, at least you didn't bring your little dogs."

"But just like Elsie and you, I brought bags of ambition. I say, do you have anything to drink round here or can we order something up? Here we are in New York with new worlds to conquer, and a toast has become our tradition."

"Yes, as long as it isn't imported brandy. Clayton nearly bathes in it, and it might as well be rotgut. It's ruining him, that is, ruining him more."

"I'm sorry. Really, I am," Lucile said, reaching out to touch Elinor's arm.

"I too, but I'm happy to be away from him, even if he's off again on one of his first-class travel adventures. Mother will keep an eye on him, and I pray he won't make a fool of himself in front of our daughters. So, shall I order up some good Scotch whisky in honor of your Scottish husband, and we'll drink to your better marriage than mine?"

Despite the fact they'd been subtly at each other since Elinor walked in, Lucile tugged her closer and hugged her. "Sorry, Nellie," she said, "but you carry on with style and aplomb through it all."

"Well, we aren't our own 'It Girls' for nothing!"

* * *

Elsie de Wolfe exuded confidence and cleverness. The one time Cosmo had met her in London, he'd said she reminded him of a "house on fire." Today she was taking Lucile in a hired hackney to see a building on fashionable West Thirty-Sixth Street that Elsie was sure would do for a New York Lucile's.

"But the key to self-advertisement here will be not the name Maison Lucile or New York Lucile's, but Lady Duff-Gordon," Elsie insisted. "Please trust me on this. Americans are simply mad for English titles. It will pull them right in. It would be worth the money to hire a local publicist, too, instead of thinking everything up yourself. You are in a different world here, you know."

"So Elinor says. But if you send your friends, the shop will prosper under any name," Lucile told her with a smile.

*My, the traffic is busy here,* she thought. They might as well have been near Hyde Park, but things got calmer when they turned off Park Avenue onto a more residential street. Now was as good a time as any to ask her friend the big question. "Would you like to invest in my New York shop, Elsie?"

"Believe it or not, I'm living a bit on the edge. Despite family money, I'm hardly being frugal to have my daily open-door tea times and to help keep up the Washington Square home. I was paid a pretty penny to decorate the Colony Club here—it's the first women's club in the city. I'll take you there another day. But I just cannot tie up too much capital right now. However, Lady Duff-Gordon," she said with a little laugh that showed her large, uneven teeth, "I can find you several investors, I promise."

"Of course, Cosmo and I will put money in, but I would be ever so grateful if you could. I'll make it up to you with some new frocks."

"Speaking of that, will you be able to design enough frocks to open a shop here soon? If you take a lease out on this place—there," she said, pointing at what she'd described earlier as a gothic brownstone town house. "You'll need to get it decorated, staffed, and inventoried soon to make it more than pay for itself in this fashionable district, of course."

"Oh, it's lovely. Reminds me of my second shop in London. Today, New York, and soon—Paris! I can't wait to see the inside."

But suddenly, she recalled that long-ago day that dear Cosmo had taken her into her first shop she could let. She supposed that neither Elinor, with her disappointment in Clayton, nor Elise, with her disdain for men, cared to hear one word about her love for Cosmo, but, indeed absence was making her heart grow fonder. How she wished he were here to assess the possibilities—and the finances. As they disembarked with the driver's help, the horse stamped and nodded as if he knew this was the right place too.

"Once I look inside, I'll have to consult my husband," she told Elsie. "But it looks perfect. And if it is, give me two months back in London to design at least one hundred American styles and fetch my mannequins and we'll take the town!"

"I think we Americans call it painting the town red."

"There won't be many shades of red in a new spring American collection, I think," Lucile said with a little laugh. "As for the interior of this handsome house, I'm planning on dove-gray walls and a rose room for lingerie and lots of gardenias for the first parade here. I swear, I'm phasing out that pouter pigeon-breasted silhouette that people liked so much and tapering the lines and—well, let's go inside, and then I'll take you to that restaurant you mentioned to celebrate. What was its name again?"

"Delmonico's. And I bet my bottom dollar we'll find at least two or three of the investors I have in mind eating luncheon there."

* * *

*Cosmo, my dear love,*

*I will be coming home soon now that I have financing for the new Lady Duff-Gordon Shop. I will be in a whirl to design enough for a new American collection and then hurry back with the goddesses to show my work. But I must tell you that Elinor and I have had an opportunity to meet the American President, Theodore Roosevelt, at the White House in Washington, no less!*

*However, I believe you would have done better with him*

*than I, for he is a sportsman too. And, would you believe that he went on and on about my book 'Memories' his wife had read? I tried to tell him that book was written by your late, departed aunt Lucie, but he seemed not to either hear that or accept it. Elinor thought it was great fun, of course, that he believed I was an author too. At any rate, I would rather be with you than with any man on earth, however well known and powerful.*

*Clayton has decided to bring Mother and their girls home via the Trans-Siberian railway and not via the Pacific and America. First class, as ever, of course, but I worry that it is another sign their marriage is on shaky ground. When he arrives, do see if you can warn him about mitigating his drinking.*

*And you may be right that there are sad signs he may have overspent, especially since he's moved his family into Mother's house in London when they are there. At least he's given her that little house Lamberts in Essex. Worse, I have heard Elinor tell more than one person that Clayton is independently wealthy and she writes merely to amuse herself, when I know she quickly sends her royalty checks home to help support Margot and Juliet.*

*I will see you soon and hope you will return with me next time to America if you are able with all you oversee at home. Meanwhile, kiss Esme for me. What a blessing that she, like us, has a happy marriage.*

*Shall I claim some sort of prize from you when I return?*

*Your loving wife,*
*Lucile*

# CHAPTER *Twenty*

A man with a megaphone on board the ship kept announcing, "All ashore that's going ashore! All ashore that's going ashore!"

"I wish you could go back with me, darling," Lucile told Cosmo as they stood on the deck of her ship. "I so want you to see the new shop, and we could 'do' New York, as they say." She was heading back nine weeks after her first trip there, armed with one hundred fifty new frocks for the American market and planning to make more. She had already shooed her female entourage down the deck so she and Cosmo could have some semblance of a private farewell. As others who would not be sailing vacated the vessel, she clung to his arm. "You would love the so-called newfangled cocktails they serve at parties."

"I would love being with you *after* the parties, so we could have our own private one. You've been so busy designing since you've been back, but the time we've had . . . Well, I will miss my 'best-dressed woman in Europe,' though I must say I prefer you in undress."

She hugged him hard. Here she was in her midforties, feeling like a young girl leaving her first beau. Yet her time home had been worth it. Just last week, a parade she had staged had drawn over five hundred people. She felt sad, in a way, that her sister would not be in New York, but Elinor had gone out west and that perhaps was for the best. As strange as it seemed, the more success each of them achieved, the more they argued and didn't get on at all.

"Next time, I promise I'll go with you," Cosmo vowed as they clung to each other. "I have a friend who knows J. P. Morgan, the owner of the White Star Line ships, and they're going to build a massive ocean liner, an unsinkable one. It's supposed to take over three thousand men to complete it in Liverpool, but it will sail out of Southampton to New York City and back. Its maiden voyage will be a great, memorable event, and he's suggested we be there for the parties and the memories."

"Mm. Sounds like our kind of ship—unsinkable, like us."

They kissed each other again.

"Best of luck, darling, and hurry back," he said.

"After Lady Duff-Gordon's designs have conquered another country," she told him with a smile but tears in her eyes.

"If it wasn't for the promises I made you before you said you'd marry me, I'd cart you off this ship right now, slung over my shoulder, like a pirate seizing a maiden, but I'm not and you're not."

She watched him turn quickly away and hurry toward the canvas-covered disembarkation ramp. For once, she wished she was a character in one of Elinor's romantic novels to be carried away.

But she went to join her staff and wave from the railing when the ship set out.

* * *

Elinor had seldom been so excited. The Wild West of America was a whole new world, a land she was coming to think of as the realm of rawhide romance—that is, romance in the truest sense of the word, a story with heroism, adventure, and even mystery. She was already planning a novel called *Elizabeth Visits America*, which would present her experiences here. Years ago, she'd devoured Western-themed books by writers like Bret Harte and Owen Winter, and what she saw now brought all that to life. The dashing heroes of those stories were her hosts today, for she was visiting a primitive mining camp called Rawhide, about an hour away from another picturesque place called Goldfields, Nevada. Indeed, this was a distant land, so different from anyplace she'd ever seen.

What impressed her most was not the sagebrush bumping past her skirts in the wind when she was helped down from a stagecoach they had sent for her, nor the tents and board shanties, nor the signs of DANCE HALL AND SALOON where they went inside. It was the men themselves, who, through her host, had invited her here. They were polite and had a strict moral code. She had heard there was no lawlessness here, or else they meted out justice themselves. She'd seen a hand-printed sign that read, DON'T CROSS THE LINE!

But what moved her most was that these miners had read her book and wanted to thank her for writing it! She'd take that praise any day over snide English hypocrites who attacked her and her writing without reading it, or, if they did, without grasping that what made an out-of-wedlock love right was real romance. Besides, the uppers of England were deep into illicit, serial affairs themselves, including the King!

"We got us two things we want to present to you today, Mrs. Glyn," a weather-faced man named Wally something or other told her after their meal in the cleared-out dance hall. "From me and the men, here's a medal saying much obliged for your visitin' us in Rawhide and for your fine writin'."

Applause and a yippee or two followed. She was so deeply touched. On the oil-cloth-covered lunch table she'd shared with them still stood a small, ragged bunch of yellow daisies that someone had ridden nearly ninety miles to bring back, since it was such barren land here. That meant more than a bower of roses at the Vanderbilt house or the clouds of fragrant gardenias at one of Lucile's mannequin parades.

Looking down at the medal with her name and *Special Guest of Rawhide* engraved on it, she told them in a loud voice, "I thank you so much for your hospitality and kindness to me. I will always treasure this and the lovely time here."

"That's not all, though," another lanky man told her, standing up. He wore a six-shooter at his side, and his spurs clanked, though most of the men had forgone spurs today. She believed he was the one they called simply "Irish." His freckled skin looked like leather, and his hair was bleached blond in the sun. Bowlegged and dusty as he was, she thought of him as a real hero, one who would appear in her new novel.

He cleared his throat and went on in a raspy voice, "We thought a lady like you better have some hidden protection when she travels. Not for here, 'cause we'd fight for you to the death if some polecat came near, but out in so-called civilized land."

Murmurs and nods. Someone at the back of the group evidently hacked into one of the spittoons. How she wished she could explain to these men what an English "dance hall" was like at a grand

London town house or country home—and that this place was just as good—but that was impossible. Besides, somehow, right now, this was better.

Irish gave her a small, mother-of-pearl-handled pistol. "We give you this here gun, Mrs. Glyn, 'cause we admire your damn—I mean, darned—pluck to write your book and then stand by it. You got courage, just like us."

Tears blurred her view of the pistol. "Again, I cannot thank you enough," she told them. "This means so much to me because it is a true gift, one from the heart and one that symbolizes—that is, stands for—the fine, upstanding men you are. No matter if I visit New York City or San Francisco or Los Angeles, where I am headed next, I will never forget the men of Rawhide."

The applause and whoops rang in her ears. Even when she rode away in the coach, the whole thing seemed like a fantasy. She looked down at the medal and the pocket pistol on her lap and realized how far away she was from what she knew and what she loved. But it was true that she'd always remember Rawhide and the chivalrous men, like knights in shining armor, like the lords of their own exotic realm. She'd always picture them in what they'd called their best duds with their fine, saddled steeds and high moral code. She decided then that the only man she'd ever admired more than the lot of them was Lord George Nathaniel Curzon, and he was as far from her in possibilities as the miners in Rawhide, Nevada.

* * *

Even Elinor's visit to the two, vibrant young cities in California—young by British standards, at least—could not top her day in Rawhide and Goldfields. Especially because the San Franciscans criticized *Three Weeks* nearly as much as some English had. The city was recovering from a devastating earthquake, and the condemnation of *Three Weeks* shook her to her core after her acceptance in the East.

What fascinated her the most about Los Angeles, which meant "The Angels," was not the city itself but the small, nearby growing but grubby set of cinema buildings in a small town called Hollywood where Americans produced the new fad they called moving pictures.

Later, as she made her way back home, she stopped in New York and saw one for the first time. She was fascinated by the medium, but dismissive of the title cards—words written to convey dialogue or emotion that appeared on the bottom of the black-and-white screen. "It will never replace the written word as experienced in book stories," she told anyone who would listen. However, she was fascinated by the idea that maybe, someday, some way, her work, especially *Three Weeks*, might be made into a moving picture.

She herself moved in a dream after her adventures in America, planning her next book, lost in thoughts that she was at least famous some place for the right reasons. It seemed a dream, that is, until she returned home and saw Clayton.

When he greeted her, she tried not to show her dismay. He looked dreadful. Stouter. Bloated. Distracted. His cheeks had a violet tinge to them. Heart problems? Her mother's letters had said nothing of this.

"Were you ill on the trip?" she asked him, trying not to show her surprise. "I know Mother was, but I—"

"It's not only that. I need to explain—some things."

"Yes, of course. I'm sure a lot has happened since I've been gone, and I want to hear all about your trip."

"Elinor, let's sit down. Here, over by the window at the table."

"Are you quite well? The girls looked fine, so it isn't that and—"

"I am not quite well, but it isn't what you think. Haven't you seen the signs, my clever observer of people and things? What the deuce!" he swore. "It's not my physical health, but my—our—financial health."

"Oh. Bills coming in from the long trip you all took, or mine. Clayton, the royalties from *Three Weeks* and those yet to come after my tour should cover all that, and I'm hoping to eventually stage the story here in the theaters, if I can just make the right contacts, maybe with Lucile's help, so—"

"Can you just listen for a moment without words, words, words!" He smacked his fist on the table and the inkwell shuddered. She saw he'd been writing out a long list of numbers. "Your ship may have come in but mine's sinking. My debts have finally caught up with me and everything's caved in. Creditors, threats, gambling IOUs."

"Gambling! Not again! I—you should have told me earlier. I guess I should have known."

"You're seldom here! And when you are, your head is spinning with flights of fancy. I just wanted to live well, live fully. I have no illusions that I will live long, never thought I'd outlive what I inherited or could get in rents from Durrington House. I did not worry about you, because you have your original marriage settlement from me as well as so many admirers and could surely marry one of them."

"Clayton, I have been faithful to you, and—"

"Physically, perhaps. But I was never the knight in shining armor you once fancied me to be. We haven't been truly wed in a heartfelt way for years now, have we? And you have that restless, what you call romantic, spirit. Elinor, no more fantasies for either of us! We are going to have to move out of here and in with your mother in little Lamberts. Sheering Hall will be sold. We must cut back expenditures severely. Your books or not, good foreign reviews or not, we are worse off than deep in debt, we are bankrupt!"

* * *

"Celia, I believe we have found the proverbial pot of gold at the end of the rainbow here in New York," Lucile told her store manager she'd brought with her from London. "I cannot keep up with orders and even charging five hundred dollars for a personal consultation has not kept American mamas from scheduling with me for their daughter's coming-out seasons or their own events."

"And you've buffaloed the newspapers, Madam Lucile. *Buffaloed*—that's something I heard here the other day. Despite that one sniping paper which called you Lady Muff Boredom because your self-advertisements are all over, everyone is singing your praise."

Celia, so prim and plain looking amid the chaos of fancy fashions, goddesses, and rich clients, picked up another clipping scattered on the designing table. These last two months, Lucile could not have done without this young woman's intelligence and energy. More than once Lucile had shooed someone away from trying to "pretty up" or change Celia, for Lucile admired how she dressed her personality in straight dark skirts and plain blouses or shirtwaist dresses. No-nonsense Celia was one of the few in the Lucile organization who knew the business was bringing in over forty thousand pounds a year, but, of course, not all of that was profit, and it did not count the swelling profits here in New York.

Celia said, "*Harper's Bazaar* says you are the marvel of two hemispheres. And this one says you offer 'the Society's 400' New York ladies a 'fairyland of frocks.'"

"A fairyland of frocks. It sounds like something the famous authoress Elinor Glyn would say. My favorite quote is the one—ah, here it is," she said, reaching for another newspaper article. "'One of Lady Duff-Gordon's allures is her talent with "the fascination of suggestion." Just a slight revelation of an ankle here, or the shadow of a thigh, sets one's thoughts to spinning for both sexes.' My, that sounds like something my sister would write too. Perhaps Elinor and I are more attuned than we like to admit."

She plunged into fretting again the moment that was out of her mouth. Clayton had declared bankruptcy, and the family had moved out of Sheering Hall, when it had galled Elinor from the first that they did not live in the larger Durrington House on the estate. Lucile hoped her sister would accept a loan or even a financial gift when she returned to England, and Cosmo had offered some assistance already. Elinor had vowed to write books as quickly as she could to be able to pay off some of their debts, holed up as she was in a separate room in the small house called Lamberts, which Clayton had originally given to Mother. But of course she'd decorated her cubbyhole outrageously fancy, modeled after Marie Antoinette's pied-à-terre Trianon at Versailles.

"Here's my favorite, though," Celia broke into her agonizing. Again, she thought, what would she do without this woman? Her good business sense and organizational skills kept her from going crazy here, kept her, a little bit, from missing Cosmo's financial aplomb.

"Oh, the quote from *Vogue Magazine*," Lucile said, peering over her shoulder. "'Lady Duff-Gordon is the high priestess at the shrine of clothes.' Still there's a snide undercurrent in that comment. I am not asking my clients to worship clothes, just to enjoy them, though, I suppose, certain American women spend much more on their Lady Duff-Gordon wardrobes than they do at church, where they should be worshipping. But I strive to create an identity for individual women, not just a frock. I want them to feel confident, beautiful, interested, and interesting. That's always been the goal of my gowns of personality and emotion."

"We all admire that, Lucile, your staff here and at home."

"I'm honored and grateful," she admitted and reached out to squeeze Celia's hand. "But the truth is, all that is not quite enough—and I don't mean the money or the respect. I want to share my vision for how women should look and feel with more than the English, Americans, and a scattering of foreigners. Paris is in my sights, Celia," she said with a little laugh. She loosed her hand and pointed her finger, as if it were one of Cosmo's hunting guns, at the fabulous bridal gown just completed for a New York 400 daughter. "Sooner, rather than later, Paris, here we come!"

# CHAPTER *Twenty-One*

Elinor drove herself hard, writing her book set in America. She felt as if she didn't come up for air. She needed the money, needed to care for Clayton, needed to spend time with her girls before they went away to their boarding schools again—if they could afford that.

But she forced herself to take a break and eat lunch with them. Mother presided now at the table. Perhaps because she had suffered through a dreadful second marriage with a tightfisted, irascible husband, she thought Clayton, with his apparent easygoing nature and generous spending habits, was an ideal son-in-law. Besides, he'd given her this house and taken her on trips.

"Grandmama, remember how pretty the pagodas on our trip were?" sixteen-year-old Margot asked, dawdling with her spoon in her strawberry pudding. "I've drawn some pictures I want you to see."

Elinor crumpled her napkin in her lap. Why, she fumed, did Margot not want to show her own mother the drawings? The girls knew she used to sketch people and places. And why didn't Margot explain what a pagoda was, especially since she hadn't been along on their trip to Japan? She hated to feel stupid and left out. It seemed no one included her in their conversations, and when she tried to start a topic, it quickly petered out.

Ten-year-old Juliet piped up, "And, Grandmama, I hope you'll have time to help me hang the hem that ripped out. We can pretend we are Auntie Lucile—ha!" Juliet added with a little laugh. "That is, if you and Father aren't going to play piquet all afternoon again."

"Oh, you know how your father loves card games," Mother told her with a wink.

"Excuse me, please," Elinor said and rose from the table, tossing her linen napkin—a torn and mended one, no less—in her chair. She was afraid she would burst into tears. "Someone has to go to work here."

Juliet's simple request galled worse than Margot's. And her mother used to hate cards after all the hands she'd had to play with her own husband.

"Ta, ta, Mother," Margot said, then turned immediately back to those at the table. "And I hope you have time to look over my letter to the headmistress."

Elinor turned back, thinking finally she was to be included, but the girl was still talking to her grandmother. Drat! She was only half-finished with her novel, and the middle of the book was always what she considered the muddle of the book: too many plot lines and characters to juggle, like real life here lately. It made her as crazy as this skewed family did.

And that last comment was the nail in the coffin. Who was the famous authoress here, who knew about writing, and who would be paying for a finishing school abroad for their eldest child and a boarding school for the other? Yet her own mother had supplanted her in her children's interest and affections. Some of it was her own fault, of course, for being busy or away, but now, more than ever, she had to write to put so much as pudding in their mouths!

Elinor bit her lip hard and blinked back tears as she hurried from the room, feeling as if she were running from her daughters instead of just Clayton this time. All of this was his doing, and there he sat, stuffing his face with food they could hardly afford and with his third lunchtime imported, expensive glass of brandy as if he ruled his world, when—as far as she was concerned—he had ruined it.

* * *

Although Elinor had spent more time with her daughters before they went off to school again, she had tried to avoid Clayton. She couldn't help it. She was working herself to the bone and needed to get out of little Lamberts before she went quite mad. She needed outside stimulation, ideas. How could she write deep, emotional, fulfilling stories when her own heart was starved for affection and love?

This autumn evening in London, where she was staying at Lucile's for the night so she could see her publisher tomorrow—to ask him to help her find some fast money somehow, somewhere—she had accepted an invitation to a ball given by her friend Consuelo, Duchess of Manchester. She hadn't seen her since their voyage to and time together in America. Fortunately, the duchess was also back in London, and the timing was perfect.

This was also a reception for Russian royalty Elinor had met once before in London, the Grand Duchess Kiril, a client of Lucile's. But while she thought this evening would be so relaxing, two men in attendance were making her more anxious. One was a Marlborough relation, a young man named Winston Churchill, who kept chattering and hanging on. And the other, the object of her secret affections for several years, Lord Nathaniel George Curzon, was just across the crowded room.

This clever Winston had an American mother too, but Elinor wasn't sure if she was a dollar princess or not and she wasn't about to ask him. He could go off on tangents on absolutely any subject. Though she'd heard he was a climber, she thought the comment was intended to mean in career ambitions, for anyone related to the Duke of Marlborough must be well set in society.

She finally managed to move past young Winston and head for Lord Curzon's group when the grand duchess herself, with a small entourage, blocked her path.

"Dearest Mrs. Glyn," she said. "My mother-in-law and I so did like your novel. I meant to write, but I will ask. This winter, we would be honored to host you in St. Petersburg. Perhaps a new setting for a novel? We have a small society there, to compare to this," she added with a gloved sweep of the room, "but we would count it an honor."

Elinor was stunned. "I—the honor would be all mine."

"New people, new stories," the dear woman said with a smile and tapped her arm with a fan she expertly flipped open, then closed again.

"I will write a formal invitation," the grand duchess assured her. "My people will write about arrangements. Think now of the possibilities," she concluded as she swept off with her coterie of friends again.

"Think now of the possibilities," Elinor whispered to herself as she saw Lord Curzon smoothly detach himself from the cluster of people where he seemed to be the center of attention.

She studied him again, a luxury after her memories and all her daydreams of him. Actually, she'd heard that he had taken an interest in and corresponded with other writers, even a woman, but had he sent a letter to anyone else, saying he understood her book? And had he sent anyone else a tiger skin when that was obviously a symbol of passion and love—and seduction—in the story?

The man most people addressed as Lord Curzon or simply George, if they were of his intimate circle, looked a bit exotic, however staunch his English roots. She knew he was about five years older than she. His skin was slightly olive hued, and his dark hair, frosted with silver, accented his high forehead. He had a narrow nose and an expressive, sensuous mouth. His bearing was strictly military, ramrod straight, but she'd heard that might be from the metal brace he'd worn for years due to a back injury in his youth. Strange, she thought, but Lucile had mentioned that Dr. Morell Mackenzie she'd been so attached to had worn a brace. Perhaps such instruments put out a magnetic pull to any Sutherland sisters in the area.

And best of all, George Curzon seemed somehow above the common man, a lord of destiny, somewhat cynical, a wry observer, yet—

Dear heavens, he was looking her way and had caught her stare. Their gazes held. She was so startled that she was slow to smile. Hopefully a friendly smile, not come-hither, though that's how she felt.

She stood rooted to the spot, feeling almost as if she were waltzing with him, spun round and round. As he nodded in recognition and began to walk toward her, she almost felt the floor give way.

Never, *never,* not even with Seymour Finch had she felt like this. Admiration, passion—destiny?

"Dearest Elinor," he said, his voice steady, somehow both sharp and sweet. "I've been wondering how your trip to America was, for I intend to go myself when duties and single fatherhood let up a bit. We must meet for lunch so that I can hear all about it."

"The tiger skin you kindly sent me—as I wrote to you—amazing."

"I appreciated your letter—and the sensual scene in the book with the tiger skin."

He still held her hand. Tingles shot up her arm to her breasts, the tops of which peeked over the top of a low Lucile neckline. She tried to control her breathing and her voice. She almost blurted out that she used to think of herself as *Belle Tigress.*

"Yes, amazing, that tiger," he said as he studied her face. "Beautiful. One-of-a-kind stripes and vibrant colors in the tiger fur. I stalked and hunted it myself in India."

"I—you said that. It made me cherish it the more."

Surely she wasn't going to be tongue-tied, she thought. But she could not have created better dialogue in her novel that said so much below the surface.

"Luncheon, how kind," she managed.

"Tomorrow then? There's a hotel on Jermyn Street with excellent food, if you are here for a few days in London."

She had to see her publisher tomorrow. Then she had to head back to work on her book in the country. She'd told them she'd be back.

"That would be lovely," she said.

"Tell me where you're staying, and I will send my carriage for you."

"Oh yes." Heavens, she sounded like an idiot who couldn't put more than a few words together.

"I must admit," he told her, loosing her hand at last, "I heard there were some—some family financial arrears."

What if he was making an assignation, expecting to pay somehow. But everything aside, her schedule, her sullied reputation for *Three Weeks,* or the Glyn bankruptcy, this was her chance. She had long admired this man from afar. Surely she could control this.

"Yes, but everyone has ups and downs," she told him with a smile. "It would be lovely to have some time to hear more of India, and I shall tell you of the wild, wild American West."

He nodded and smiled, showing his teeth. "Then we shall plan exactly that, and who knows where our talk may take us?"

She might be forty-four years old, but, in the middle of a crowded ballroom, she nearly fell at his feet.

* * *

"I love the mingled hues of the heather and the gorse, especially on a windswept, sunny day like this one," Lucile told Cosmo as they sat on a woolen blanket with their picnic lunch not far from Maryculter mansion. "I shall use those colors in a collection soon."

Now and then their nearby horses nickered, but they were content eating grass. And despite all that filled her head, Lucile was content today too.

Cosmo wore a kilt and, despite the brisk wind and his knee-high woolen socks, didn't seem a bit cold. Beneath their view stretched bonnie braes he owned above the river Dee. Hawks sailed above in circles, and three kinds of clouds fought to rule the Scottish sky.

"I love it all too, especially when we are here together," he said, leaning back on his elbows. "You are so busy and famous now, my bonnie lass, but I know those looks when your head is spinning with ideas again. Ambitious, far-off ones. When will enough be enough?"

"Conquering Paris will be enough. I know most of the French look down their Gallic noses at the English—our food, our sense of style. But I'll show them."

He pulled her down beside him on the blanket with one arm under her head and one hand on her waist. As they stared up into the restless heavens, he told her, "With Lady Duff-Gordon, is even the sky the limit?"

She turned on her side to face him. "You will go with me this time, won't you? France is just across the channel, and the Scots have always had closer relations to the French than the English have. Cosmo, I need you in Paris to navigate things, at least to get started. We could lease a little house and enjoy the City of Lights even if I have to work hard for a while."

"You always work hard. But today and this week, I cherish. Yes, I'll go too. You'll take a staff, and I'll take our menagerie of dogs. But despite your stakes in London, New York, and Paris, here is the home of my heart and I pray—for sometimes, at least—of yours. I'll go with you to New York sooner or later too, at least when that new big liner is completed. I hear they've decided to name it the *Titanic*, for its massive size."

"Wherever we go, you are the home of my heart, my dearest," she vowed and ran her finger along his lower lip under his mustache. It needed trimming. It made him look so rakish, like the pirate he had mentioned when she'd sailed to New York without him.

In his rich voice, low and musical with that touch of Scottish burr, he said, "I hope the warmth you feel for me will keep the braw, chill wind from your legs and mine, because I want to seal that promise here and now. We have always sealed our vows well, have we not? People sometimes ask why we Scots wear the kilt. My love, you are about to find out one reason."

His gaze was so intense it heated her all over. How brazen that he lifted her cloak and skirts out here and fumbled with her lingerie. "Is that all there is to this?" he asked, looking annoyed, as his fingers snagged in her silk panties. "I don't mean to ruin it."

"Let me do that."

"That's the story of my life, my love, letting you do whatever. But I will always be along for the ride."

She reveled in the ride. When he possessed her body, her beloved Cosmo was like this land, strong and wild and brave.

# CHAPTER *Twenty-Two*

Lucile slid the sketch of the ball gown across her desk to Elinor. "I can't believe you're going to be a guest in imperial Russia. Thank heavens I've designed for Russian nobles before."

"As if," Elinor said, squinting at the drawing, "I'm noble too. Ha!"

"It's going to be cold there, so I've tried to strike a balance between bare throat for your necklace but a higher décolletage and cap sleeves. Some velvet inlay because that will keep you warmer than satin and lace everywhere. And it flows."

Elinor heaved a huge sigh. "It flows like money. I can't thank you and Cosmo enough for the loan, and I will pay it back."

"You will, not Clayton?"

"You can see he's to be trusted for nothing but eating, drinking, and being merry, even as our ship goes down. I've had several people dear to me offer a loan, but—"

"Several people," Lucile echoed, putting down her sketch pen and leaning closer. She put her elbows on the table and her chin on her clenched hands. "Including Lord Curzon?"

"He is a dear friend, an adviser. We have many interests in

common, the classics, for example, and travel. And I adore hearing about his days in India."

"Excellent change of topic, madam authoress. But you are seeing him in private?"

"For long lunches, so don't you read more in. I am yet faithful—physically faithful—to Clayton."

"I must tell you people are talking."

"Let them. I'm used to that after becoming the notorious author Elinor Glyn of *Three Weeks*. I know it didn't help that I tried to produce it as a play with my own money, until the wretched, priggish Lord Chamberlain banned it—when I had totally toned down the scandal in it everyone was expecting to see! So yes, then that was money down the drain in tough times, but it was my money, and I'd planned to make a windfall from it."

"I know. But a woman who bought some frocks last week here—a good many of them—said I should actually warn you to steer clear of Lord Curzon."

"What?" Elinor said sitting up straighter. "Warn me? And are you? Who was she, one of his so-called Souls, I suppose."

"Let me not answer that, since I promised I would not use her name. But the Souls? What sort of group is that?"

"A clique of Lord Curzon's longtime friends, mostly women, who dare to advise him on his personal life. They didn't even like his wife, said she was a social-climbing American, when I know from what he's said she loved him dearly and waited years until he proposed. But these so-called Souls are meddlers in his life and now mine!"

"You said you two are just friends, so guard yourself and guard your heart."

"Too late for that, big sister," Elinor admitted and fumbled in her purse for a handkerchief. "I'm deeply in love with him, whatever happens. I feared his 'blessed Souls' would speak against me. I'm not worthy of him, that's what they must believe, though he speaks well of them and hasn't said they are talking me down."

"Would you divorce Clayton for him?"

"And then think he'd marry a divorced woman, the immoral author? He's an honorable, idealistic, grand man with an important, public reputation who aims high, to be in the cabinet, perhaps to be conservative prime minister someday." She wiped her eyes and blew her nose. "Lately, we have had a tiff. He advises against my going to Russia, however much I'm to be feted there, shown simply everything, and get a new book out of it. He believes Russia is a dark place, a powder keg, he said, just waiting for something dreadful to happen, especially after that so-called Bloody Sunday massacre when the czar ordered peaceful protesters fired upon."

"He's right that was terrible. And to think he's cousin to our Prince of Wales."

"Well, I must go," Elinor said, popping up. "I'll stop by here myself for the gown and the frocks you've done for Margot for finishing school. I'll be taking her there myself and stopping at Heidelberg on the way back."

"Heidelberg? Whatever for? On your own? You said you weren't taking Williams with you just to drop Margot off. Elinor, you are blushing."

"It's warm in here," she said, fanning her face. "I must run and I do thank you for putting my gowns on a tab lately. What would I ever do without you?"

"Probably be able to keep a safer secret that you must be meeting someone in scenic Heidelberg on the way home, perhaps for a liaison, perhaps someone whose name I could guess."

Elinor turned back at the door. "If you must know, despite the ruin of my marriage and my finances, George Curzon is the light of my life right now." She pulled the door open and ran right into Cosmo.

"Elinor, leaving?" he asked. "Are you all right? Both of you?" he added with a glance in at Lucile, who had followed Elinor toward the door.

"Onward and upward, dear Cosmo," Elinor told him. She looked back at Lucile and added, "Here's to Heidelberg!"

* * *

"My love, I can't believe we've managed this," George told her and swept her into his arms. "Privacy—real privacy at last where no one knows us."

He had been waiting at the Heidelberg hotel for her, sitting at a back table in the little first-floor restaurant where they had agreed to meet. "Your luggage?" he asked as he pulled out the other chair for her.

She didn't mind that she was looking only at the oak-paneled wall behind him, because she was, at last, really alone and looking at only him.

"It's at the front desk to be taken up to the room. I registered as you said, Mrs. Nathaniel, and they said you were already here and in the Rotrosen Room."

"So my middle name Nathaniel is worth something for once. Sit, sit, then we'll go up for a while before dinner. So lovely to be open about this and not behind closed doors, though I relish the idea of that. Does anyone know you're here and not staying longer in Dresden?"

"Lucile. But she doesn't know where. I vow, she reads minds—mine, at least. She guessed. I didn't exactly tell her."

He gestured to the waiter for a glass of wine for her. "And she said?"

"She said one of your Souls bought a gown and warned her to warn me to stay away from you."

His high forehead, so aristocratic, furrowed right to the high bridge of his aquiline nose. "They have no right, and I'll tell them so," he promised. "They are another reason we are here instead of at some rural inn in the Cotswolds."

"You are too well known for even there."

"Mostly my name. And you too—your name. So we shall consider ourselves Mr. and Mrs. Nathaniel here," he asked, looking intently at her, as her wine arrived.

"It's a lovely fantasy—the best fiction I could imagine," she said, blinking back tears.

"We shall make time both fly and stand still." He raised his glass to clink it against hers. "Not three weeks, but nearly three days. Just two people in love."

"Yes!" she said. "Oh yes."

* * *

Here she was on a train, having left cold Russia behind and she was still heated by the memory of her and George's passionate days and nights together in Heidelberg two months ago. The countryside near Warsaw, Poland, blurred by. She had cut short her visit to Russia because everything had gone wrong.

The worst was that Clayton had written that creditors were actually knocking at their door in rural Essex. She had to go home to see her publisher to get some sort of advance, promise something serialized, a new novel quickly—anything for some money. She'd managed to get them out of dire debt once, but this was even worse. Next their creditors would be hounding her and the girls.

Besides that, her time in Russia, armed as she was with new gowns and accessories, had been ruined by the death of Czar Nicholas's uncle, which had plunged the entire court into mourning black of which she had none. Events were canceled, her plans disrupted, though she did manage a tour of the Winter Palace. Her maid, Williams, had become ill, so she'd sent her home and replaced her temporarily with a Russian maid—a sullen girl with whom she could barely communicate.

However, she had been helped by a Russian official to get this string of tickets home, at least as far as Warsaw. She was to stay in the Hotel de l'Europe tonight, then take a train to Berlin tomorrow morning. She would be met there, according to the man who had kindly made her arrangements, by a carriage to take her to the hotel.

She was so physically and emotionally drained she couldn't wait to get to a bed. Her head was nodding and kept jerking her neck, though her mind wandered again. How sweet and thrilling it had been to curl up in bed against George after their lovemaking, to put her head on his bare shoulder. Before he undressed her, he had rid himself of that terrible iron contraption he'd worn since he was a boy. He had been freed to be himself with her, a daring, darling man. Even in their lovemaking he was controlled, but wonderfully so. He had teased her to tell him what was her coded, private name for him in her diary, but she had not told him. She had two of them, one *Milor,* short for my lord, and *Superior Person*, or S.P. Both pet names would show him she adored him and that wasn't good for—

"Warsaw! Warsaw!" the conductor cried. Then he said in several languages, "For this train, end of the line, end of the line."

A muted screeching sound and jolt further woke her from her daydream—or night dream. Despite the lights in the train station, it seemed dark. Few people were on the platform and few other trains moving. Oh, so unusual to be on her own, to be carrying just a dressing case all the way home while her luggage was sent. Just outside the entrance, as she'd been told, there was to be a waiting carriage. And, once she disembarked and walked out, there was one.

Two dark-suited men were on the high box seat. She was so used to seeing the newfangled motorcars at home or at least small cabriolets in the city that she hesitated.

"Madame Glyn?" the man beside the driver asked and climbed down. "Let me help you in and pass your luggage in. Then we'll be off."

"Just this bag," she told him. His face was in shadow under his brimmed hat. His accent seemed Russian, not that she could pick out a Polish one. "To the Hotel l'Europe, you understand," she said.

"*Da*, madame."

Was *da* how to say *yes* in Polish as well as Russian? Well, all she wanted was a good night's sleep, and she was grateful to her Russian contact for this carriage.

But she was disturbed, then appalled, at how fast the vehicle went. They plunged into a dim neighborhood through nearly deserted streets. Surely they could not be heading toward the center of Warsaw to a hotel.

Despite the blast of icy air, she opened the window and shouted to the driver, "The Hotel l'Europe! Here in Warsaw!"

Her stomach cramped when he said nothing and the carriage plunged on. Her creative mind snagged on one plot possibility: She was being abducted. But by whom and to where?

* * *

"Don't cry, lass," Cosmo said and pulled her into his arms when they read the post that their bid for the Paris shop had been rejected. "And don't take it out on me. I said I would support you on a Paris opening of Lady Duff-Gordon when the time is right and ripe, but this indicates it isn't. We must concentrate on the London and New York stores and save Paris for another day."

"Another year, you mean." Standing in their London parlor, she leaned into his strength, yet she couldn't help but think he was secretly pleased. Her husband might be a cosmopolitan Cosmo, as she had often teased him—when it came to London, at least—but he was at heart a Scottish Highlander. And Scots, as generous and well-off as Cosmo was, were known to watch their money and stay home in the Highlands. He'd looked at the prices to lease or buy other shops in Paris, even in a suburban arrondissement instead of the city itself, and said the other places except for this one were too risky a financial venture for now.

"But both my shops are making money like hay at haying time," she protested now, trying not to whine or scold. Their big St. Bernard, Porthos, pressed against her, nearly toppling them while their Peke, Mr. Futze, cavorted, yapping as if scolding her for protesting.

"But you've been spending money hand over fist on the new craze of fashion photography and buying promotions in the papers. So," Cosmo said, "when there is enough to secure both the London and New York stores in case times change—"

"Times change? You mean the king being so ill? Surely no war is on the horizon, certainly not in France."

"Germany is unstable. But that aside, again, I promise we shall lease or buy a Paris shop and house when it is time. Lass, I know you are used to having things your way—"

"I am not. Don't you recall how long you made me wait for my first shop?"

"And how long I made you wait to entice me into marriage?"

"I did not!" she insisted, but then realized he was trying to cajole her. "Indeed, though," she added, swiping at her tears, "good things are worth waiting for."

"My beautiful lass—with a good brain," he said, lifting her chin and quickly kissing her. "Just to make it up to you, I'll go with you to your dear New York City, and you can show me the shop and the sites. You talked about wanting a motorcar and a small place on Big Island, so—"

"It's Long Island. And yes, I long for both."

"Righto. Your sister will be back soon from her daft jaunt to Russia, and the *Titanic*'s maiden voyage is to be quite some time after her return, so I will be sure we get first-class tickets. You can go back on your own once before that, but I promise you a braw, bonnie time with a devoted husband after that."

"Then your very-much-in-love wife promises you that the two of us together will have an exciting time on the *Titanic*."

# CHAPTER *Twenty-Three*

Elinor was completely panic-stricken. These men must indeed be abducting her. But why? Had she made enemies in Russia, done something wrong? Should she risk throwing herself from this careening, fast carriage on this dark, rural road?

Again, she put her head out the window, shrieking and screaming for help. Nothing from the men. No lights in sight, no buildings, only blackest, cold night with stars stabbing the sky.

Eyes wide open, she gripped her gloved hands together and began to pray. She should have prayed more, clung to the God of her youth, not gone off on new thought tangents. In her jumbled thoughts, images of Margot and Juliet flashed through her mind. She'd been a terrible mother. She was an adulteress, however many times Clayton had betrayed her. She and Lucile had argued so much lately.

Again, she grappled with the reason for this outrage. If she could fathom that, perhaps she would know how to argue. Had someone followed her to a foreign place to make her pay for writing an immoral story no one understood? Were Clayton's creditors going to hold her for ransom or make her pay with her life? Anyone who knew them must realize he did not have sixpence to pay a ransom.

*Oh, dear Lord, help. Help me!*

Her worst childhood fear of a horse running away with her wagon screamed at her. She was a terrified little girl again, frozen in fear, hurtling toward destruction and death.

Yet, as if her plea had been instantly answered, the carriage came to a hard halt. She slammed into the opposite seats and hit her head on the interior wall. Grabbing her purse, she intended to jump out, hold up her skirts, and run, but—but she heard other voices and peered out to see two men on horseback alongside the front of this carriage. Oh, the men on horseback were in uniform and held some sort of guns, blessedly pointed at the men on the box and not at her.

"Stay inside, madame," came a voice in heavily accented English. Polish? French? Definitely not British.

"The Hotel l'Europe in Warsaw!" she called out, her voice breaking.

"Shortly, madame. These men have made a dreadful mistake."

It would do her no good to run. Had she been saved and from what and by whom? George had been right to warn her not to come to Russia nearly unescorted, and then she'd sent poor Williams home with a bad stomach ailment. Could someone have slipped her maid something to make her ill?

Thank God, the carriage turned round, and, with the two men on horseback riding alongside, she was taken at a more normal pace back to Warsaw to the hotel. It was late, but how late? In the glow of gaslights outside the entrance, she unbuttoned her coat and tried to read the timepiece pinned to her gown. The train she had hoped to catch to Berlin was leaving in four hours, hardly time to get a good night's sleep. Not that she could rest, especially after both her abductors and rescuers had disappeared the moment she alit from the carriage before she could so much as speak to them.

Planning to just wash up and nap, then be certain she made the Berlin train, she went up to the reception desk to explain that she was here late for her reservation her Russian contact had made for her. She realized she knew only his first name. She wasn't certain she could trace him to tell him what had happened, to see if he could discern who might have caused this nightmare. Or was he the villain behind all this, working for whoever was her enemy?

"I am sorry, Madame Glyn," the man at the desk said, squinting at her, "but there is no reservation for you here last evening, or this one. Regretfully, we have no rooms, and . . ."

Exhausted, frightened but grateful she was here among people and not lying dead in some ditch, she nodded and walked away, even more shaken. Someone had carefully planned that she not arrive here, so why make a reservation? Would she be pursued farther? For once, she longed to be home. Dearest George had been right that the Russian empire could be a dark place, however kind some of the nobles here had been to her.

At least, if she could not get a thrilling mystery plot for a novel out of this trip, she was not worth her salt.

* * *

In May of 1910, King Edward VII died, and Britain, like Russia, was plunged into mourning. Lucile's shop produced black gowns, and Elinor wrote books, short stories, and articles as fast as she could to pay off debts. *Hack writing,* some accused, and, she had to admit, they weren't her best efforts. But then when had the critics liked her?

Sheering Hall, sadly, was sold, and she and Clayton lived with her mother in her little house on the grounds. Clayton still drank and traveled as if he were king of the world, though Elinor felt it was worth the cost to have him gone, until she heard via the grapevine that he was stupid and selfish enough to be gambling in Monte Carlo.

That was nearly the last straw, like a straw smoked down just the way Lucile did on those cigarettes of hers—until Elinor learned there was something worse when George let slip that Clayton had asked him for money, and he had given it to him!

"What?" Elinor cried and sat up in bed. They were in Carlsbad, a spa town in Czechoslovakia in the off-season, just for a few stolen days. "When? He told me nothing of that, but you should have! It makes it sound as if you are paying him for the use of my—my favors!"

They were naked in satin sheets she had brought along, but, for the first time, she nearly assaulted him. She swung the pillow at him, wishing he were Clayton to hit. George seized the pillow, then seized her and sat up beside her, grimacing at the ever-present pain in his back. For once, she did not care.

"I knew, of course, that your family was in dire financial straits," he explained, holding her wrists in his hands, while her hair streamed loose between them. "It was a loan, not a gift, so calm down. I thought nothing of the sort about buying your favors, though I do have plans for a famous artist to paint a portrait of you for me. I'm going to commission a full-length painting of you by Philip de László, a society portrait painter. You can wear some fabulous gown your sister designed and the sapphire earrings I gave you. Your red hair, white skin, and green eyes will dazzle—"

"Don't try to smooth-talk, change the subject, or bribe your way out of this, sir politician!" she demanded. "I will pay you back for the loan as soon as we return home! I won't have it! Besides, that means he knows about us."

"That surprises you? And he is going to do what to you, the breadwinner of the family he has deserted? And he might do what to me? I was happy to help."

She could not hold back but burst into tears. She'd felt helpless and ashamed since the night she was nearly abducted and still did not know why. George had said he'd told her that she should have heeded his warning about not going to Russia. He would not have set that up, surely not to teach her a lesson, she'd told herself. But here he was with a financial hold over her, through her wretched husband.

"If I loose you, will you attack me, tigress?" he asked.

She shook her head. He scooted back to put himself against the headboard to prop up his back and pulled her to him, holding her tight. She tried to stem her sobs, tried to be stoic, controlled, the image she had strived to project to this man she adored. At first, she held herself stiff in his embrace, then just clung to him.

"You see," he said when she quieted, "I believe in you. Even if I had not loaned him a small sum—"

"I'll bet it wasn't small."

"A small sum to me. Even then I did it to help you, Elinor, yes, I suppose to bind you to me, to make you grateful. For, whatever comes our way, I don't want to lose you."

She put her arms around his neck and pressed her mouth to the side of his throat where his pulse beat hard.

"I'll pay it back," she said, her voice muffled against his skin. "With money, I mean."

"Of course you will. But you work too hard, when someone should be taking care of you."

"As much as I love knighthood and chivalry, it's new times, my dear lord, the Right Honorable George Nathaniel Curzon. Lucile has her designs and I have my writing, and that's the way of it. Now let me dry my tears, then tell me all about how it happened and how much you loaned him so that he could gamble it away in Monte Carlo—or was that part of your plan?"

"In a perfect world, I would have you all to myself, just like this—and, of course, still enjoy our intellectual talks and arguments, too," he said and slid them down to lie flat on the sheets again.

And when he pulled her to him, despite anything he might have done amiss, she knew any sacrifice was worth any price she paid to love this man.

# CHAPTER *Twenty-Four*

"Who needs the Ritz or the Waldorf Astoria when we have the *Titanic*?" Lucile asked Cosmo as they swayed together on the dance floor. The ship was swaying too, so they didn't move much, unlike those who insisted on a swirling waltz. Although the eight-member string orchestra was playing Strauss and others were sweeping past them, they stayed off to the side in their own world.

"An amazing little city unto itself," Cosmo said. His mustache tickled her earlobe as he spoke over the music. "My time in the gymnasium and the Turkish bath today really woke me up. Shipboard living agrees with me."

"I haven't waked up yet from this dream. Such a glorious setting. Why, I'd love to have my goddesses float down that grand main staircase. I wouldn't mind having Maestro Hartley and his violin play for my next parade, too," she added with a nod at the exuberant leader of the musicians.

"Always business in mind with my sweetheart," he teased. "So how did you assess the ladies' shops you were in today?"

"Mm, spent more time in the beauty salon, but I would have redone several of the layouts in the shops."

"With Lucile, Lady Duff-Gordon, creations on display out front, of course."

"Now who's talking business?" She moved closer to press her breasts to his chest and her hips to his. He held her tighter. She lifted her head to gaze into his face. For a moment they forgot to sway, let alone waltz, though the orchestra swept into the opening chords of "The Blue Danube."

Cosmo cleared his throat and said in a husky voice, "I'd like to skip dinner but not from the captain's table. It was good of Captain Smith to include us tonight."

"I heard he's a stickler for being on time, though it's said he's pushing for the ship to be ahead of time in New York. Best we go join them then."

They made their way into the elegant first-class dining room and joined the people gathering at the captain's table set for eight with crystal goblets, sparkling china, and an array of silver. They were introduced to an American named Margaret Brown, who declared, "But call me Molly."

Lucile was excited to see, according to the lettered place-name cards, that she'd be seated next to the co-owner of Macy's Department store, the bearded Isidor Straus, while Cosmo was next to Mrs. Straus. They chatted with the couple briefly and with Captain Smith. Lucile wasn't sure whether Straus himself or his wife would be best for this, but she intended to pitch her clothing to one or the other of them.

Even the hand-lettered menus they were given looked grand, just as did this entire floating universe of the *Titanic*. Caviar and a choice of wines began the meal; she ordered quail and Cosmo chose lobster—although they could have had both. Amazingly, in this chilly mid-April at sea on the Atlantic, fresh peaches were part of the table decorations, intermixed with pink roses and large white daisies.

Even as the bearded captain stood to propose a toast, the violinist-maestro Lucile had admired stopped by their table to play a Puccini aria she couldn't name, but no doubt, Elinor could have. Puccini loved his heroines and gave them soaring songs, so Lucile never could understand why so many of them had to die tragic deaths.

She smiled at Cosmo over the top of her champagne glass. Heading for New York in luxury with the man she loved . . . conquering New York as she had London . . . hoping yet for great success in Paris . . .

Life had never been so lovely.

* * *

"I'm not sure I've ever been happier," Lucile told Cosmo the next night as she sat back down by him at their lounge table on the A deck of the *Titanic*. "You were so right to counsel me to wait for the right price for the Paris shop on the rue de Penthièvre, and now we have it not only staffed and stocked, but ready to go. I'm excited that, after this quick trip to New York to see to things there, we're off to Paris to attract and build our clientele! And in New York, I just know you'll love my little suite at the Ritz and the motorcar. Not as fancy as ours in London and Scotland, but, after all, American made. Oh, just a minute. I see someone I must greet."

He reached across their little table and snagged her wrist to pull her gently back down. "Lucile, do you need to keep popping up to have people sign that *Confessions* book of yours?" he groused as she flipped it open again. He seemed tired and snappish to her today, but then they'd been up to all hours making love last night after dancing and dining.

"Getting a signature is one thing," he went on, "but personal questions under headings such as 'likes, abominations, and madnesses'? I think it's all a bit mad."

"Now don't fuss. You know it's all the rage."

"Sleep is all the rage for me tonight, lass."

"I use my *Confessions* book not for rubbing shoulders with the elite and famous but for connecting with people, getting to know them better, just as I need personal contact with my clients. You are too much of a stay-at-home, my dearest. See here?" she asked, leaning across their table to slide the little leather book toward him. "John Jacob Astor and his bride filled in their likes and pet peeves and favorite things. Ben Guggenheim wrote in it too. This little book will bring us important New York contacts and business."

"Always the self-advertiser. It's in your blood. And you are in mine. But speaking of that, I have a bloody headache and need to turn in."

"Sorry, love. Too much champagne for your head, do you think? I'm afraid that though it's after midnight, I'm wide awake. Maybe it's that chill wind outside I can hear keeping me up. If you feel bad and want to sleep, I can spend tonight in my own cabin for once and have Miss Francatelli come keep me company." She reached up to push a stray lock of his hair back from his forehead.

"I imagine I've had too many late nights staying awake making love to you," he whispered. "And, yes, I'd best stick to my Scottish whisky instead of all this fancy Paris bubbly stuff."

"All right," she said and downed the rest of her goblet. "But I've been on such a whirl, I don't know if I can sleep."

They headed toward their cabins, feeling the slight roll of the massive ship. Others had remarked on the rough seas, but after all, it was mid-April in the northern Atlantic. Not only the engineer but the designer of the vessel were aboard and so proud of this break-speed liner on its maiden voyage. And why not, with such elegance and beauty everywhere they looked on board? Lucile saw it as a luxurious, floating palace with decor like something she would design, and she'd seen three Lucile gowns besides the one she was wearing this evening.

"That's not the champagne making me sway this time," Cosmo commented, zigzagging slightly again.

"Nor the remnants of our dancing three nights straight when I know you'd rather they do a Scottish reel."

"Not tonight with a pounding head."

"Poor Franks won't know what to make of my actually using my cabin," she told him as they strolled their corridor.

He kissed her quickly on the lips and rapped on her cabin door for her. "I'm going to turn in. Call me for a late breakfast. Good night, Franks," he said when Lucile's secretary opened the door.

"G'night, my lord," she said, obviously surprised Lucile was stepping in past her.

Lucile sank onto her bed with a sigh. The cabin was very pretty with pink curtains and several bouquets of flowers. She'd needed the closets and drawer space here as well as in Cosmo's cabin, but most of her jewelry was in the ship's safe.

"Wait until my sister hears about this ship," she said as she sat on her previously unused bed and took her shoes off. "She's holed herself up writing like mad, but when I tell her about the *Titanic*, she'll want to use it for a lovely, romantic setting."

* * *

Elinor was struggling to find the words to write. She knew things were stacked against her. She had to write fast, at least thirty pages a day to make her deadline. Since she was desperate for money to pay off Clayton's debts, Gerald Duckworth had promised her a thousand pounds for a novel to be serialized if she could do it quickly. She wasn't sure she was composing up to her usual standards, and that scared her. It didn't seem to flow. And it wasn't only her layabout husband's flight to distant Constantinople to escape his debts that was worrying her, but George Curzon's activities right here in England—or the lack thereof.

Quite simply, they didn't include her lately, not even snatched, private, hidden moments like lunch in their old hotel. Sometimes he didn't write or telephone for days—eleven days and counting right now. Of course he knew she was busy. No doubt he was busy, too, with his daughters and government service, but she felt panicky when thinking he had wearied of her.

Thanks to her publisher, she'd paid George back for his loan to Clayton, every bit of it, despite how he'd never mentioned it again and others were hounding her. Could he have taken offense at that? Or had his Souls' friends sabotaged his passion for her when she'd been certain he meant to tell them to steer clear of that? Or was he simply bored with her when she needed his strength and attention desperately?

"Curse it all!" she cried. She wadded up the new, half-written page, despite getting ink on her hands, and threw it across the room against the wall. What if this novel was utter rubbish? Should it all be in the dustbin? Why weren't her golden thoughts working to attract her beloved Milor, as she called him in her diary. Even her last novels had been letdowns. *The Reason Why* had not been well received, and *Halcyone*, which she'd hoped would be her intellectual book, her masterpiece, had been misunderstood and even mocked for its pretensions. And now she had ideas to write a book she would call *The Man and the Moment*, and had that somehow passed her by with Milor? Had she given him too much too fast?

Drat, she actually wished Lucile was here to talk to, even though lately they went weeks in their own worlds without a word, or subtly sniped at each other when they were together. But whatever would she do without her, even if it was to argue and scold, trying to one-up each other? Sometimes, though she'd never tell Lucile, she envied her for Cosmo and for her new shops and designs—and her luxurious, glamorous maiden-voyage trip on that new wonder of a steamship.

She glanced at the clock. Mother used to say that nothing good ever happened after midnight, so maybe she should try to sleep or at least send both her daughters some golden thoughts and Lucile and Cosmo, too.

Elinor pulled out another sheet of paper and stared hard at its vast, white blankness. It seemed so big, so cold, almost dangerous. Though it was quite warm in here, she shivered.

* * *

Trying to go to sleep, Lucile said a quick prayer and fretted briefly about how Elinor had gone overboard for Lord Curzon. She hoped Cosmo would be in a better mood and rested in the morning. He was a dear to come on this voyage with her, and she was worried he wouldn't like New York with all its bustle and rush—and how busy she was there, so busy . . .

She stepped off into sleep but something woke her. A jolt

nearly flung her out of bed. She bumped her head on the wall above her pillow. One of the vases of flowers in the room crashed to the floor.

"Franks, are you all right?"

"I'm up. I felt something earlier. I just looked out in the hall. The lights are out. And what's that funny rumbling noise?"

"Sounds like the engines straining. I wish they wouldn't try to set some sort of speed record on this first voyage."

She had been chilled, even with their electric stove, so she had not completely undressed. Now, especially with the glass on the floor, she jammed her feet back in her shoes, seized her fur coat from the foot of the bed, pulled it on, and got up.

"I can't believe there would be anything wrong with the engines on this ship," she said. Her voice shook. "It sounds like someone rolling large balls on a wooden bowling alley. I'm going to check on Cosmo."

She wrapped her coat she'd been using for an extra blanket tightly around her. Fumbling for her purse in which she had both cabin keys, she went across the hall. Amid many voices and some people rushing past, a man's voice down the way carried to her, though he was speaking to someone else: "I hear there's ice on the deck. Can we have hit something? Someone said an iceberg."

The corridor lights were flickering now—perhaps it was only some sort of electrical problem. She unlocked her husband's door and went in. Unbelievably, he must be sound asleep because he was snoring.

"Cosmo, dear, the ship is having some sort of problem. People are most disturbed and many are up. I heard someone say we might have hit an iceberg."

She touched his shoulder. He startled. "Lucile, it's damn cold out there and so is the draft from the hall. Go back to bed. This ship is built with watertight compartments. It may slow down their race for the crossing record, but go back to bed and don't worry."

Upset he was so gruff, she went back out. But, with Franks standing in the door of their cabin, she told her, "I'm going out on deck to see what I can learn. I'll be right back."

The night was blank black. The ice cold wind cut right through her coat and froze her face. "Nothing but temporary trouble," she heard someone down the deck say. "Word from a steward is not to worry."

She exhaled a sigh of relief that turned to a puffy cloud the wind ripped away. But as she went back to her cabin to assure Franks all was well, a deadly silence fell. The constant hum and slight vibration of the ship's engines had stopped. The sudden silence was terrifying, especially when it had been filled with the distant sound of raised, panicked voices.

She ran back to Cosmo's cabin. He was up and getting dressed. "Strange sounds," he told her. "I'm going to check things out. Get dressed—doubly dressed—and not in those flimsy dance shoes, just in case."

*In case of what?* she wondered. Thank God this was an unsinkable ship.

* * *

However exhausted she was, Elinor could not sleep. She wrapped herself in an old lilac-and-pink Lucile cape and jammed her feet in shoes. Taking an electric torch, she went out the back door of the small house, hoping not to wake her mother, and stepped out under the fading stars that the rising sun was devouring. She clicked off her light, wishing she'd managed more sleep.

The wind was a bit chill for April fourteenth—no, it was the fifteenth now, the Ides, as Julius Caesar would have called it. *Beware the Ides of March,* she recalled the line from Shakespeare that was to warn Caesar just before he was assassinated.

She went out and sat in the swing her daughters had once enjoyed when visiting their grandmama. It creaked, and the wind rustled the new leaves of the apple tree. What time would it be aboard the *Titanic* now? she wondered. If the ship were close enough to New York, it would be about seven hours from daylight for them. Well, she'd hear it all from Lucile, whether she wanted to or not.

Elinor scratched her ear and was surprised to realize she still had Milor's gift of emerald earrings on. He had said those would remind her that he wanted to remain her close friend, no matter what, through thick and thin. Now she feared, they were a farewell gift. Her trust in golden thoughts and angel guardians was useless. So hard to say good-bye. But if this separation of theirs was to be permanent, she somehow knew how it felt to die.

* * *

Cosmo, thank God, returned to the cabin quickly. "I'm glad to see you both warmly dressed, though I've been assured it's nothing dire. Still, they are taking the covers off the lifeboats, and it is captain's orders we are to wear our lifebelts. Just keep calm. Think of it as a drill, and I'm certain we will be all right."

Cosmo's deep voice had always calmed her, but Lucile sensed his alarm. They helped each other don and strap on the awkward, clumsy belts. The three of them went onto the port side of the ship and there saw a scene of horror.

"Who the hell is in charge?" Cosmo asked, as if speaking to himself.

They huddled back against the ship wall—was it tilting slightly?—as screaming people charged the lifeboats. They rushed for places on them, shoving others aside, even screaming women and crying children. From somewhere in the chaos, officers on megaphones roared, "Women and children first! Stand back! Order! Order here!"

Cosmo's arm came tight around her. She leaned into him, and Franks pressed close to her. "I'll get you two on a boat," he shouted over the noise. "It might be more serious than they've said. I think the deck is listing."

Just then a lifeboat in front of them tilted from its uneven weight and cast shrieking people into the cold blackness of the sea. Everyone on deck gasped, but the shouts for help far below soon quieted.

"No!" she told Cosmo, gripping his arm. "I won't leave you, no matter what! Maybe we can put Franks—"

"I will stay with you!" Franks cried over the renewed noise on deck. "Please let me stay with you, milady!"

A sharp noise split the night, and the flare of red rockets overhead screamed into the sky. "SOS flares," Cosmo muttered. "From the other side of the ship. Let's try that instead of this hell here."

He seized Lucile's elbow and propelled her inside with Franks following. He nearly bounced off the door on the shuddering deck but managed to open it. People fled at them, pushing at the door. They staggered across the width of the ship as it jolted, lurched, and went even more atilt. That pressed them into the wall of the corridor, but they fought their way on.

# CHAPTER *Twenty-Five*

Amazingly, on the starboard side of the ship, relative quiet reigned. They saw only some of the crew preparing to launch a small boat, calling to one another. And the boat had empty seats.

"Hey, there!" Cosmo shouted. "Any room in that boat for three?"

"'Tis the captain's boat, sir, and we be firemen, and I a petty officer, a seaman. An officer said to take it 'cause the captain, he's still on board till the ship be righted. Sure, then, there's some room."

Lucile was shaking uncontrollably. If the captain was going to right the ship, wouldn't it be better for them to stay on board? It was so cold, so dark and dangerous out there in the utter void. But then there was the horror on the other side and—

Cosmo gave her no choice and held her upper arms hard as he handed her, then Franks, to the man, who indicated seats in the prow. For one moment she feared Cosmo would not come. Since he was always a man of honor, she would not have put it past him to go fetch some women and children from the other side of the ship. She saw him hesitate for a moment, staring at her.

"Please, Cosmo!" she cried and held out a hand toward him.

"Got to shove off now, sir," the petty officer said.

He climbed in, followed by two other male passengers who appeared from somewhere and said they were Americans as they clambered in without an invitation.

"Cast off!" the officer shouted to the oarsmen. "Once we hit the water, pull away as fast and far as possible, mates!"

Sitting next to Cosmo with Franks in the closest seat next to one of the other male passengers, they held on as the boat was lowered into the water. It hit hard and began to rock, even knocking against the side of the listing ship at first. Waves and wind threw icy spray. Struggling, the men rowed away from the vessel, with its rows of lighted portholes on each deck above growing smaller and smaller.

If the electricity was back on, Lucile thought, surely it would stay afloat. On their voyage from Canada to England when she and Elinor were young, they'd tossed and turned but a much smaller ship had ridden it out and—

Her stomach roiled and churned. She bent over the bow just in time to spew her supper and cocktails into the inky, white-capped sea. Worse, she saw floating in it, blank, jagged pieces of ice as if someone had ripped up huge pieces of paper.

Franks handed her a handkerchief to wipe her mouth, bless her, and Cosmo gripped her to him. Dear heavens, she was going to be sick again, right now, but not as sick as picturing all those poor souls who might still be fighting for a boat on that great, grand vessel. But—but maybe things were under control, because she could swear, even now, she heard the orchestra they'd danced to last night still playing.

The men rowed on. Someone said something about not wanting to be sucked down when it went. When what went?

She opened her teary eyes to look back at the *Titanic*, only to see its stern suddenly tilt sharply upward. Had it cracked apart where the iceberg had hit? Franks screamed, and they watched in horror as row after row of round portholes lights slipped beneath the sea until the unsinkable ship was gone.

✻ ✻ ✻

Two hours later, Lucile lay curled up in her wet fur coat on the floor of the lifeboat with her head on Cosmo's booted feet. She wasn't certain whether her retching over the bow was physical or spiritual at the shock of it all. The others sometimes whispered and sometimes tried to buck themselves up, but they sounded delirious, as if this were some sort of feverish nightmare—and it was.

"You shall have to lend me another Lucile gown for New York," Franks said, her voice quaking. Someone had a canteen of water aboard, and she washed Lucile's face with a wet handkerchief, not salt water for once. They were all trembling from the temperature and wind as well as from shock. She could tell even Cosmo was shaking.

"What about us poor lads?" one of the firemen asked. "We've not only lost our pay but our kits, too, when she went down."

Cosmo told them, "I'm sure you'll get another ship and have tall tales to tell."

"If we're not cursed from being on the one that went down," the petty officer said. Lucile recalled he'd said his name was Hendrickson.

"Tell you what," Cosmo said, his lips so numb with cold that he didn't sound like himself. "I'll give you each a five spot toward a new kit when we are taken up somewhere. I hope those distress rockets in the sky bring a rescue vessel if the wireless didn't put out an SOS."

"Heard the closest ship didn't respond but another one, thank the Lord, must have. The second one had a name something like the *Corinthian*," said a young, shaky voice.

"*Carpathia*," an older voice corrected. "A steamer. Stoked its boiler fires on one round-trip. And thanks for your kindly offer, your lordship. Got a wife and three little ones at home, and grievin' I am for those kind went down with the ship, even for those in all those other boats out on the sea like us here. Was wishin' some o' them had found us 'fore we launched, but glad you all did. No good empty seats in a tragedy like this. And they said she would get to New York fast and never sink."

Just when Lucile thought she was feeling a bit better on this rocky, black sea, she pictured people fighting for lifeboats, some saying good-bye forever to their menfolk who remained on deck. She pulled herself up to be sick over the side again, though she had nothing left to lose. In the crest of the waves—no more ice floes right now—she saw her own daughters' little faces years ago and she thought of the young Irish cabin girl who had been so sweet and helpful that she'd given her a woolen robe she'd brought.

Franks handed her the damp handkerchief wet with seawater this time, and, still sitting in the bottom of the boat, Lucile leaned against the strength of Cosmo's legs as his shaking hands gripped her shoulders.

Just then, the sun peered over the edge of the eastern sea.

* * *

The next evening, as the sun set, Elinor was finally writing again. Yet she felt exhausted. Drained. So sad. She jolted when Mother called from outside her closed door, "Elinor!"

"Working, Mother!"

"I know you don't like to be disturbed, my girl, but you have a telephone call! I don't know what those calls cost since I don't use the contraption Clayton insisted on, but the way things are, you had better hurry!"

Elinor's hands trembled as she jumped up and rushed out. She was expecting Gerald Duckworth saying he needed the book soon. At least he was going to take it in segments for serialization, but that was so dangerous. Who knew that the first part written would work with the way plot and character developed later? Sometimes amazing things emerged that were even a surprise to the author.

She hurried into the parlor to their mounted wall phone, lifted the earpiece, and stood on tiptoe to speak into the mouthpiece. You might know, Clayton had it hung for his height.

"This is Elinor Glyn."

"Elinor, it's George."

Her heartbeat kicked up. Curzon. Finally. Finally. She closed her eyes as tears squeezed out onto her cheeks.

"No doubt you've been busy," she said, trying to sound breezy and light.

"I'm sure you have too. My dear, I'm here at Parliament, so I can't talk long. I have . . . news. This hasn't been announced to the public yet but will be soon. I hear the *Daily Mail* and other newspapers will be all over it. I'm not sure of all the—ah, the results of this." She heard him hesitate. She pictured that little frown that sometimes perched above his nose when he was upset or hurt.

"So," he went on, "did your sister sail on the *Titanic*'s maiden voyage as you mentioned?"

"Oh, yes she did, with her husband and a secretary. What does that have to do with anything? What hasn't yet been released to the public?"

"It's on the wireless, since it's a British ship. Word is that—dear Elinor, I'm sorry to tell you that it's reported by another vessel in the area that the *Titanic* sent up emergency flares and radioed ships in the area for help. Soon its captain wired that it was in danger of sinking. I fear it has gone down."

"That can't be. Not that ship. Gone down?"

"In the North Atlantic. Evidently, the captain wired they hit an iceberg, so I wanted you to know—and I wanted you to know I miss you. I thought it best if I not call, but now I've brought you bad news, and I wish I could comfort you."

She stood there, sucking air, not really dissolving into hysteria as she wanted. Mother would, though. She might have been through the terrible loss of her first beloved husband, but this might do her in. Yet something calmed Elinor, something strong like that iron rod poor Milor had to wear to keep him standing without pain.

"I am sure, whatever the dangers, Lucile will come through," she told him in a steady voice hardly her own. "Somehow she always does. And I am sure, since you say you miss me as I do you, you will arrange for us to see each other soon. Thank you for your call."

She amazed herself by hanging up right then. She had to show him she was strong, not beg or cry, despite the fact she collapsed against the wall, clinging to the phone box. But that big ship sinking? With all those people? Lucile. Cosmo. How dreadful the danger, and yet she knew somehow she'd see them both again—and, from this tragedy—see her beloved Lord Curzon, too.

* * *

When Lucile lifted her head to peek over the prow of their lifeboat, she saw chaos surrounded the waters near the *Carpathia*. Relief at last, but a different horror from the sinking of the *Titanic*. They were only one little craft among those hovering close to their rescue ship. So few boats—so few people survived?

Feeling dizzy and faint again, she collapsed next to Franks, who also lay freezing and exhausted in the bottom of their boat. All of them were shaking uncontrollably; Cosmo's feet beat a regular rhythm against the slanted wooden floor as the crew rowed them closer to the massive side of the ship, like a huge, high wall to climb to safety.

Cries and sobs mingled from the other lifeboats with people being taken up rope ladders thrown over the side. Some were so weak or injured that they had to be hoisted aboard with ropes tied under their armpits or round their waists.

Cosmo helped Lucile sit up again as they waited their turn. A glance behind them revealed huge icebergs, but in the pale morning light, they seemed almost like giant pearls or opals. Was she losing her mind the way so many had lost their lives? What she and Cosmo had lost—jewels, clothes, papers—were nothing next to that.

A woman in the closest lifeboat, waiting like them to be taken on board, was screaming at boat after boat, "I can't find my son. In your boat—is he there? Sixteen, red hair . . . my son Ronald! Has anyone seen my son?"

In shock and sympathy, Lucile would have sobbed herself into hysteria if she'd had the strength.

When it was their turn, neither Franks nor she could manage to climb the rope ladder they let down from the ship, and it took Cosmo and two of the *Carpathia* crew to get them aboard. Lucile fell to her knees, eternally grateful to be on a solid deck. A stewardess immediately put a warm blanket—a heated one!—round her shaking shoulders. Even before they were led away to companionways where the ship's guests and crew had given up their cabins, they were offered brandy and hot coffee.

Once off the chilly deck, Lucile smelled baking bread, and in her near delirium imagined she was a little girl again in Canada with Grandmama helping Elinor and her in for supper. She overheard someone say the ship's bakers had been baking bread to feed three thousand—but, surely there were not that many aboard here who had been saved.

"Count's up to about seven hundred on board," she heard a man say as if to worsen her fears. "But that's all offa that huge ship what went down? Heard tell their manifest was over two thousand. And we got us some near death here, too, some died already on board. No more survivors in sight, though, Cap'n says."

She wondered if Captain Smith, their host last night—was that just last night?—had gone down with his ship. And her sweet Irish cabin girl? Their table companions? Those who had signed her silly "madness" book? Though offered bread with butter and jam, she could eat nothing. Guilt rode her hard for the caviar and champagne they had too easily, carelessly downed on board that now dead ship.

"Ma'am, hot baths for you now, and we'll help you walk to your guest cabin," the stewardess was saying. "This way, ma'am, your husband, too. Here, let me help you."

Cosmo actually ate breakfast while Lucile soaked in a tub of hot water. She felt too ill to eat but was given a sedative and put to bed in the cabin, which two kindly passengers had given over to Cosmo and her while Franks was just down the hall with some other women.

Lucile slid into darkness and slept, on and on, wandering long hallways, swimming through rough water. At first when she woke, she was confused. This wasn't their cabin. But when she saw Cosmo bending over her in clothes that weren't his own, with a frown on his face, it all rushed back at her. She must have slept around the clock, because sun dared to stream in the porthole behind him, gilding his silhouette, promising a new day.

"Are we headed for New York?" she asked him, her voice not her own as he took her hands in his. Finally, warm and steady hands.

"Yes, lass. But life—maybe New York, too—will never seem the same after our salvation when so many died. I sought out the men who saved us and wrote checks for them—just on paper since so much was lost. It was the very least I could do. They were so grateful and wanted to do something for us, so they've signed our lifebelts as a thanks. We'll have those as a reminder of the lads who saved us."

"A lot of new frocks gone too, but none of that matters," she whispered, looking up at Cosmo as he sat carefully on the side of her narrow bed. He nodded and sniffed back tears. "People matter," she went on. "Oh, my love, life is so dear! Hold me, please. Don't ever let me go!"

* * *

Four days later, her legs still shaking, Lucile and the other survivors of the tragedy disembarked the *Carpathia* in New York Harbor. Though she always had prided herself in her erect posture, she leaned on the railing for stability and strength.

"A horde of people, including journalists and thrillmongers," Cosmo muttered, glaring at the waiting crowd below. "Of course they can't just leave us alone. I heard they've already written up stories on both the living and the dead, rumors and the like, cabled here and there, including ones sent to this ship."

Cosmo had been right, she thought, recalling the silly signatures written in her *Confessions* book. She'd been shocked to realize that everyone who had autographed it the night the ship went down had drowned, millionaires and moguls, along with much of the crew, the captain, and most of the steerage passengers.

"Look, Cosmo," she said, pointing. "Right at the bottom of the ramp, I see my friend Elsie de Wolfe. Why, I'll bet she's here to meet us with a motorcar and spirit us away from that noisy crowd. I have no desire to do interviews about this horror."

"Not even for self-advertisement for once?"

That shook her a bit. Did he think she was too forward, too rapacious with all that? Or had this near-death experience just made her realize what really mattered in life?

Without the worry of their luggage, they headed down the ramp with Franks close behind. Strange, but Lucile recalled Elinor carrying on about how the newsmen pursued her about her illicit novel when she first disembarked in New York. It must have been a scene like this, noisy, raucous, jostling.

"There they are!" a man's voice shouted. Lucile saw he tried to shove Elsie away. "There's the English lord that paid a near empty lifeboat to row him and his rich wife away when people were dying!"

The words didn't even register with Lucile at first, but she heard Franks gasp and felt Cosmo tighten his grip on her arm. How could they know of that incident already—and have perverted it so?

"Keep going," Cosmo said out of the side of his mouth. "If they mean us, they are dead wrong, and I'll not grace that with one word."

Somehow Elsie fought her way to them. "Follow me!" she shouted and elbowed a man with a camera back, though he popped a light in their faces. Other blasts of light and clicks of cameras followed. Lucile lifted her pocketbook to shield her face.

Ordinary men were no match for Elsie or Cosmo as they made a path for Lucile and Franks and half-pulled, half-shoved them along through the press of people.

"Not far now!" Elsie cried. "I'll get you to your apartment at the Ritz!" They walked faster, still pursued by men shouting questions. Ordinarily, Lucile would have laughed as the intrepid Elsie led them into a warehouse and managed, with Cosmo's help, to pull a sliding door closed on their pursuers.

"Walk through here," Elsie ordered. "It's as close as I could get through the traffic and crowd. Despite the rumors and the yellow press, I never fathomed it would be that bad."

They piled into the two backseats of her big motorcar, and her chauffeur drove them away from the docks.

"Elsie, again, I can't thank you enough," Lucile told her.

Elsie extended her gloved hand to Cosmo and shook his hand. "Your lordship," she said. "Lovely to see again the man lovely Lucile loves." She gave poor Franks, who sat beside her facing them, a one-armed, big hug. "Sorry to tell you, but there is much ado about the lower classes being drowned when the uppers bought their way out of that catastrophe, despite the fact many famous people drowned. I know you had big New York plans, Lucile dear, but there's to be an inquiry back in Britain soon, and, I'm afraid, the names Lord and Lady Duff-Gordon have been fastened on like a dog with a bone. I've booked return passage for you both on a liner—if you're courageous enough to get back on one—because you're going to be hounded here. They are saying the most dreadful things, especially about his lordship."

"They accuse him of bribing our way into a boat?" Lucile asked.

"And rowing away while others drowned."

"It's so untrue. That is not what happened!"

"I believe you," Elsie said with a roll of her eyes. "But will they? Times are changing. No one knows their proper place anymore, and class jealousy, at least in this country—well, enough said for now."

Tears sprang to Lucile's eyes. Cosmo had done nothing but protect them and try to help the men who had been kind enough to row them to safety, men who were following the captain's orders to launch that boat just then when they happened upon it. How desperately she had wanted Cosmo to love New York, to commit to staying here with her from time to time—and now that might be ruined.

Lucile choked out, “Even if we flee now, we shall return.”

“Or you, at least,” Cosmo said, frowning out the window. He was biting his lower lip. Her beloved man of honor was shamed, and she could only pray he wasn’t shattered, though he looked it right now. He’d always sat and carried himself so straight, her handsome athlete. But his head was down and his shoulders slumped. How would this charge of cowardice and cruelty be received in England, Scotland, too, his beloved home?

She reached out to hold his hand as tightly as she could. He was trembling, perhaps with fury as well as shock. Her stomach went into free fall, as if this motorcar were a small boat again plunging them into the rough, black sea.

# PART IV

# Paris and Beyond

1912–1919

# CHAPTER *Twenty-Six*

As Elinor took a side seat in the Scottish Drill Hall at Buckingham Gate in London a month after the *Titanic* disaster, she was glad no one looked her way. She wore a large hat with a veil so that she didn't have people staring at her. It had been bad enough this last month with Lucile and Cosmo at the center of attention of journalistic ridicule or even nasty comments to their faces, however much their friends stood by them. Even today, a crowd of newspapermen had gathered outside waiting to get in for this Board of Trade Inquiry on the loss of the *Titanic*.

Despite her own trials with the so-called press, Elinor wanted to be here to support Lucile and Cosmo. How ridiculous and scurrilous a lie that they were cowards willing to use their wealth to escape drowning and leave others behind. A good deal of class jealousy stirred the pot too when, after all, she and Lucile had fought their way up from next to nothing. Granted, Lucile had married well, and she had not. Clayton was hiding out of the country. At least she didn't have to deal with him here, but only pay his distant hotel, gambling, and drinking debts.

A stir swept through those seated, but it was not yet the entry of the president of the court, Lord Mersey, nor even the Duff-Gordons' defense lawyer, Mr. Tweedie. Just more of the swells, as she and Lucile used to think of the elite of the land. And—oh no, it couldn't be—but there came Gordon Selfridge, a wealthy department store owner and one of Elinor's latest admirers whom she had not turned away as she had some others. He was a brash American, wealthy, gregarious, and, unlike someone else, he enjoyed being seen with her. She had nicknamed him her American Napoleon, and he sometime called her his Josephine.

She had actually tried to make her beloved, secretive Milor jealous, and Gordon's attentions had done the trick. She'd dared to take a small house in Paris partly because Milor had vowed he would come to visit her there.

Lucile looked stunning when she entered, and poor Cosmo looked stunned. Of course, he was hurt and angry, which he controlled with his iron resolve. Elinor listened intently to the opening remarks and sat forward as Lucile was called to testify.

"Lady Duff-Gordon," the accusing lawyer began the questioning after she was sworn in, "is it not true that your husband promised the men rowing the rescue boat five pounds each to get you away from the sinking ship?"

"No, sir. He offered them five pounds each because they had lost their entire kit, as they called it. That was long after they rowed away. We never would have been in that small boat if we had not simply happened upon it when they were launching anyway, and at Captain Smith's orders."

"I see," he said, leaning toward her with a shake of his head that bounced his periwig. "An interesting slant on things."

"I don't think you do see, and isn't that a slanted comment?

Terrible rumors have been spread and distorted by those who were not in this great tragedy. For example, Captain Smith was not drunk, and we have heard that bandied about, even in the newspapers. Colonel Astor hardly shot off a gun to force women from their places in the boats, because he died aboard."

"As most honorable men did, Lady Duff-Gordon."

"Is it not true, Your Honor," she said, turning to look up at the presiding Lord Mercer, "that a greater percentage of third-class passengers were saved than those of first class? Not, of course, that that would excuse so many precious lives lost above- or belowdecks. But why so many vile and untrue rumors about what happened on board among those like us who did our best to survive along with my secretary, Miss Francatelli? Neither she nor I took up a place in the large, public lifeboats so that more could survive. My husband's writing a check for five pounds each for those men the next day was an act of charity and gratitude, not some bribe or payoff."

Lord Mercer banged his gavel down, and the lawyer sputtered, "You will not address Lord Mercer directly, my lady. You will answer the questions put to you and not ask them nor lecture the court! And your husband after you!"

But that was Lucile, Elinor thought as her sister didn't flinch but stood erect at the bar until the hubbub died down and the questioning went on. Some in the audience applauded her when she stepped away after another half hour of being grilled. She had given not an inch, and neither did Cosmo thereafter during his two-hour, brutal cross-examination, though he was obviously suffering from being accused and dragged into this shameful show. Anyone who knew Lord Duff-Gordon knew he was honest and honorable to the core.

Titanic *cowards, balderdash!* Elinor thought. They were sacrificial lambs but lambs that roared.

* * *

"You did splendidly, my love," Lucile assured Cosmo as they left the courtroom, arm in arm, as if to prop themselves up. She knew they both felt utterly drained. What a skewed proceeding! Cosmo had called it a roasting.

But they hadn't been prepared for the raucous crowd they faced on the street. Newspapermen, of course—they'd grown used to them and to snide remarks—but this was a group of obviously working-class people, and so large a one that their motorcar had been forced to park on the other side of it, so they'd have to run the gauntlet.

"Maybe we should go back in and around—" was all Cosmo got out before they were spotted and something was thrown at them. It knocked off his hand and splattered his face. Rotten strawberries? No, it smelled worse than that.

Spoiled, raw eggs smacked at both of them and shouts to echo that: "Rotter! Cad! Paid a fee to go to town, letting all the poor folk drown!" a chant began over and over.

Suddenly, someone pulled Lucile back toward the hall. Cosmo, still holding her arm, turned away too. Elinor!

The three of them retreated quickly, though mud, slime, and horse dung followed, some clinging to them. Others trying to leave the building behind them screamed and scattered. An official-sounding voice from the doorway shouted, "Order! Order, you rabble out there, or the magistrates will have you all in here!"

But the crowd's insults and the pelting of ordure grew.

"I—I can't believe it," Cosmo huffed out as they backtracked into the courtroom where several people blatantly turned their backs on them, but at least didn't pelt them with garbage.

"Keep moving," Elinor insisted. "There must be a back door into a square or an alley. If we must, we will walk to a cabriolet stand. How dare the rabble act like that, led on by lies in the newspapers! Oh, I've suffered from that before, so welcome to the club!"

Lucile wiped Cosmo's face and dabbed at the rotten egg on the bosom of her frock. So it had come to this! Fleeing New York was one thing, but to have to flee London, too?

"Elinor, I'm sure I've said this before and may say it yet again, but what would I do without you?"

"Sisters are meant to stick together—unless they are arguing," Elinor answered as they still bucked the flow of courtroom traffic to finally get out the back door into a quiet, shady square lined by buildings.

"If I didn't smell like a stable, I'd kiss you, Elinor," Cosmo said, dabbing at the mess on his face and his frock coat. His voice caught and shook, but as lately, he was putting up a good front.

But Lucile could see he was wiping away tears, too.

✻ ✻ ✻

"Isn't this French pied-à-terre perfect, darling?" Lucile asked Cosmo as he carried her across the threshold of their newly purchased, small house near Versailles. She kissed him soundly on the cheek before he put her down.

"Are you speaking English or French, lass?" he asked. "Peed a what?"

She laughed and hugged him again, trying to buck him up

as she had ever since they had testified at the Board of Inquiry and been attacked and hounded in the London streets. They had been completely exonerated, though that had not stopped slurs that still deeply wounded Cosmo. So deeply that, though he'd said he'd probably not go to the United States again, he had agreed to come here for the autumn with her to get away from snide remarks and sideways glances, even in Scotland. It was, she thought, as if he bore a scar of melancholy she could hardly heal.

"Let's look round, while the chauffeur unloads our things and the dogs," she said, grasping his hand and tugging him along. Neither of them had seen the house, though she had talked to its seller and received photographs of the interior and layout.

Cosmo sailed his hat onto a silk settee and let her lead him through the narrow stone house and out toward the walled-in backyard. The slant of the afternoon sun had shaded most of the grass. Already they could hear their big St. Bernard, Porthos, and their yipping Pekingese, Mr. Furze, scrambling behind them with their nails skidding on the polished stone entry. She unlocked the back door and pulled it open to the autumn air.

"At least, at last," he said, "privacy not far from Paris, to keep us both happy. We shall enjoy sitting out here."

"And entertaining. You said we could."

"Of course. And since Elinor has somehow found the money to take a place on Avenue Victor Hugo just a short motorcar ride away, no doubt, we'll have guests you both invite here, not to mention Elsie de Wolfe's Villa Trianon nearby. That woman knows everyone everywhere we go."

"About Elinor—you aren't implying Lord Curzon's given her a loan again? She said she has money from the sale of little Lamberts since she has moved into Mother's London Green Street house while Clayton's still hiding out in Constantinople."

"Let's face facts, even if she can't. Lord Curzon is ambitious to serve in the government and he not only won't marry a divorced woman but one who is a notorious authoress. I'm afraid she's going to be hurt, because she obviously adores him, and he's out for himself, and that's it. But let's just concentrate on us right now."

In a splash of sun and crisp breeze with the dogs bounding around the yard, Cosmo pulled her to him in a hug. "I want to make you happy, lass, and I'm proud of how you stuck by my side in the *Titanic* mess."

"They weren't just after you. Besides, we are a team."

"France for a while it is, but turnabout is fair play that you'll go to Scotland with me. And no more of America with those brash people and rabid reporters. We Brits may be tenacious, but the Americans—of course our own countrymen have proved to be nasty, even brutal, too . . ." His voice trailed off, and he shook his head.

"Perhaps you'll feel different later. You know I must go back, and I hope to have you with me. It's more of a rough-and-tumble place even in New York but—"

"Elinor claims the Western wilds are more civilized than the cities. But let's just enjoy this now," he insisted again and, tucking her arm through his, walked her out farther into the yard as if he were escorting her to a formal event.

She kept quiet for once, though later she must find a way to get him back to New York—get herself back there at least. She had purchased a larger shop than the one on Thirty-Sixth Street, at the corner of Fifty-Seventh Street and Fifth Avenue. Wealthy

American women loved her designs, and some had even taken to wearing her mannequins' colored wigs, though that fad was short-lived. Lucile never forgot that although the *Titanic* had helped her put life—and her passion to design—in perspective, she was still thrilled to make women happy, to make them feel they were special.

Of course it hadn't been so smooth going here in couturiere-crazy France, where she'd been snubbed at first as an audacious Englishwoman, but her designs had begun to entrance and conquer. Once again, her dreadful experience on the *Titanic* and afterward with Cosmo had even strengthened her backbone more. Besides, she wasn't just designing for "pretty" as Esme called it years ago, but to make women feel better about themselves, more free.

One of her biggest triumphs lately was doing away with the terrible, high-boned collar that was always poking at women's necks. Her lower collar she'd named after Peter Pan—Elinor's suggestion, since it sounded a bit fairytale-ish and looked like a boy's collar—was most popular in the States. But meanwhile, tango-crazy Paris was also Lucile-fashion crazy; still, she wanted more and more for her customers here, in America, and at home.

Forcing her thoughts back to the present, she strolled the fringe of their new property with Cosmo. The lilac bush would be lovely in the spring, she thought. Two wicker lounge chairs awaited with a table between, perfect for morning tea or late lunches. One wall had a trellis with ivy, and birdsong welcomed them from the only large tree in the yard. But she wouldn't be sitting here as long as he thought, oh no, she would not.

Cosmo sighed so hard she felt his chest rise and fall. "I like it here, at least for a while," he admitted.

"You can just feel the romantic history here," she said.

"You're sounding like Elinor."

"Maybe just a little. We do agree on some things and support each other when push comes to shove, you know."

"I do know. She was a gem to come to court, and she rescued us from that mob."

She loosed his arm and whirled in a circle as if she were one of her own mannequins, showing off a new gown. She wanted to get him off brooding about that terrible day so he didn't get depressed again. His honor had taken such a terrible hit that it had changed him greatly.

"Speaking of Elinor's love of romance—and mine too, Cosmo—just think that this house was once given to Napoleon by Mademoiselle Mars and has the lovely title Pavilion of Mars! Names matter, you know. I've proved that."

"But Mars was the god of war, and that may be coming here in Europe."

"Don't even say that if you mean Germany's saber rattling. Paris is very gay now, and everyone wants to have fun and buy new things. So I want to learn to tango and you must too!" she said, clapping her hands above her head and bumping her hip into his.

But instead of laughing or taking that bait, he frowned. "Not me, lass. I draw the line at that. Some say it's indecent with all that thigh thrusting amid sultry looks and hip grinding. Let's just save that for our bed. As for this place being given to Napoleon once, I do relate to that. The poor bastard thought he had the world at his feet and ended up in exile too."

✻ ✻ ✻

"You came!" Elinor cried as she opened the door to her beloved Lord Curzon the moment he rang the bell. She'd even sent Williams away for the day and told her to come in quietly at night and go directly up to her dormer room.

He stepped in, set down a portmanteau, apparently his only luggage. The hired hack he'd engaged drove away. He closed the door behind him before she could and glanced around, perhaps to see if they were alone, and, still in his coat and hat, picked her off her feet in a crushing hug so unlike him. She embraced him, too, arms tight around his back, surprised not to feel the iron brace he always wore under his clothing.

He didn't kiss her as she had hoped and expected but buried his face against her throat and held tight. "Of course," he murmured, his words muffled against her skin, "I only came so you could give me a tour of your beloved Versailles. No one knows I'm here, do they?"

"Only my lady's maid, and she's out for the day and utterly loyal. I have eighteen days to finish my next novel, entitled *Guinevere's Lover,* but I'd toss it all away for our two days here together. The story is about two star-crossed lovers, and the hero has a rather cynical attitude toward things at times, but love wins, Milor."

He lifted his head; his gaze devoured her. "Are you calling me my lord after all our times together?" he asked, his usual stentorian voice low and raspy.

"No, it's *Milor,* m-i-l-o-r, and I've just given away my private diary name for you that you have asked to know, but I said no."

"I shall hope that my darling will tell me all then." He smiled, though his lips still looked taut. Would he ever realize that the stoic hero of the novel was greatly based on him? But he would probably be too above it all to care for such trivia.

He went on, "Shall we talk of the classics, authoress Glyn, or more about your writing, or about how I hope to attain the vaunted position of Lord Privy Seal in the coalition government in Parliament?"

"No, Milor."

"Then let the only privy seal between us be our love and our lovemaking."

He swept her off her feet—though, indeed he'd already done that nearly four years ago.

# CHAPTER *Twenty-Seven*

Nineteen fourteen had started out so well for Lucile; her business had grown and demand for her fashions increased. But then the unthinkable had happened in August: war. Germany had attacked France after marching through Belgium, leaving King George with no choice but to send England into war against his cousin Kaiser Wilhelm.

Some hoped the Yanks—the Americans Lucile loved so much—would get in, but there was no sign of that yet. Although Paris still seemed safe, Lucile had left the city she loved so much and, after a short trip to London and Scotland, persuaded Cosmo to come with her to the United States. She tried desperately to keep him happy here but knew he was yearning to go home.

"Cosmo, another good review for *The Perils of Pauline*!" she told him, looking up from the *Chicago Tribune* she was reading on the sofa next to him while he studied an issue of the London *Times* that was at least two weeks old. "They adored my costumes in it. William Randolph Hearst is going to run the series in his papers, and he's put money into the moving picture serial. He's been quite pleased with my fashion column in his magazine *Harper's Bazaar,* you know. And to be asked to teach at the New York School of Fine and Applied Art—well, what an honor. See—this country is good luck for us."

"For you, lass, not a homesick Scotsman."

"But we're a team, remember? What would I have done without your advice all these years?"

"Spent too much money too soon."

"But the money keeps rolling in, so how can you say that? Flo Ziegfeld wants me to design costumes for his shows, and Sears and Roebuck in Chicago is interested in my adapting my designs for their stores. That's my new mission here, lifting the spirits of the average American woman through an affordable but stylish clothing line."

"Your mission, eh?" he teased, peering over the edge of his paper. "You're sounding like a saver of souls in some far-off jungle. You work too hard, and it's beginning to show. And how's your stomachache doing? Too much rich food at your soirees, too many desserts fetched by your acolytes."

"My stomach pain is still there, and it pains me to hear that innuendo. You know I need my apprentices, not only to help at the shop but to learn to emulate my styles, so they can lighten my load in the future."

"Too damn many of them underfoot at your events," he muttered, crunching his paper into his lap. "Especially that Italian Bobbie what's-his-name. If he's a rising opera star, why hang about a dress designer?"

"But he's such a beautiful singer. He'll become famous soon enough and then we'll lose him, but his lovely voice has set the mood for the mannequin parades and receptions. My customers adore him."

"So you don't need to. He's too doting, almost fawning. Other than for a good aria or two, not to be trusted."

"That's not true! He's not bad at designing ideas either."

"My point is he has designs on you, if you ask me—and you didn't—so enough said. Lucile, my love, here in this city house, however prettily done up it is, I'm missing Scotland, the fresh wind, the scent of heather, my horses, and our home there." He reached over and covered her knee with his big hand. "Come here on my lap, lass, and give me a kiss to make me forget it all."

She sailed her newspaper on the floor at her feet, twisted toward him with her arms outstretched, and—and felt sliced in two by the most horrid pain she'd ever felt.

She cried out, pressing both hands to her belly. Falling, falling, but he caught her and laid her on the sofa where she gasped for air, and the world went screaming red and then all black.

* * *

"Over there, farther to the right," Elinor ordered the two men holding the portrait of herself that Milor had commissioned and she had sat for in Paris. She pointed to the right, then back again. "Now up—the bottom of the frame about your waist height. You'll have to heft it up the ladder once you get the hooks in the wall."

The portrait was in the style of Reynolds or Gainsborough, just the sort of dreamy painting she used to moon over back in adolescence on the Isle of Jersey. She looked every bit the grand dame in a three-quarter portrait with a hazy background. She was wearing the sapphire earrings Milor had brought to their love nest in Paris.

She'd told both the artist, Philip de László, and Milor that she'd wanted to have a tiger skin in it, but that had been nixed by both. Yet this was a seriously stunning portrait, a far cry from the little drawings she used to do to entertain people when she had no name or fame.

Her dear Lord Curzon surely was taking their love seriously. He had leased this romantic, old Jacobean mansion named Montacute in Somerset and had asked her to come to live here while she redecorated it for him. It seemed to her a dream come true, to be important to him, to live in a grand house with him, worthy of his love. Surely, with her long estrangement from Clayton and him now so ill, this was a sign she had a future as Lady Curzon someday.

"Yes, yes. Exactly there," she told the workmen as they struggled to hold up the framed portrait. Like everything here, it had to be placed just right. But now she must choose material for the draperies. Green, she thought, perhaps a jade green to highlight the color of her eyes, staring out so straight from that painting.

As she hurried from the high-ceiling, walnut-paneled dining room, she sighed. Wait until she showed this estate and palatial home to Lucile and Cosmo when they returned from America. So many rooms to decorate, but how blessed she felt to have a large budget. With Milor, perhaps her days of scraping and saving were over. She felt invigorated and thrilled, even though her dear lord and master was not due back until the weekend.

Yet she still did worry about poor, ill Clayton—who didn't want to see her any more than she did him. So she struggled to write to pay his bills, and she telephoned frequently to their daughters, who helped tend him. He was living with Margot and her husband in Richmond, being spoiled, even to still having his rich foods and brandy.

And yet, Elinor worried, as she fingered through the drapery samples of sleek satin and brocades, this was a remote mansion, so she had not mingled with any of Milor's friends. She supposed his so-called Soul group still spoke against her, however much she tried to waylay that with golden thoughts sent their way. So, as far as she knew, no one outside their families knew of her time and task here. Surely Milor did not plan to stash her away as his mistress while he spent most of his public time in London. After all, his daughters were in and out here; she'd met them and thought they liked her, another good sign.

Whatever happened, nothing—but nothing—would ever change her love for George Nathaniel Curzon.

* * *

"Keep sponging her off to bring down that fever," a man's voice said, dragging Lucile from deep sleep. "It's making her delirious. Tell her husband he can come in to sit with her again in a few minutes. This raving might upset him."

Her eyelids fluttered open. Who was raving? But her lips felt cracked, and she wet the chapped skin with her tongue. She saw a man in white in a room she didn't know. Not her bed. Not her robe or nightgown, but a plain white drape over her. Had the *Titanic* gone down and she was in that stranger's stateroom on the *Carpathia*? But where was Cosmo?

Her midriff was bandaged and hurt like the very devil. She dared not move her hands to touch it. The same woman—oh, a nurse—who had sponged her neck and arms was now holding her wrist and looking at her watch. Exhausted, floating, Lucile drifted off to sleep again.

But thoughts and pictures kept dancing through her brain. She felt dizzy. Had she been dancing and fell? What had she been wearing? Had that crazy client of hers, Isadora Duncan, refused to wear the gown she'd planned for her?

"I want to wear classic clothes!" the young woman shouted in her Paris shop.

"We make classic clothes here, Isadora," Lucile had said, trying to calm her raving.

"I mean, classics—a flowing robe, a toga, a chiton like they once wore for their sacred dances in Athens, even on Mount Olympus!"

Now why didn't this notorious, famous dancer agree to wear regular Lucile styles? At first, Lucile had scolded her: "Look, I've dressed the likes of Mata Hari, Sarah Bernhardt, and Lillie Langtry, but we can adapt all that."

So she had designed for her just what she wanted, and Isadora had hugged her and promised to come to dance for her guests. But she was late arriving after Lucile had promised people a dance on the back lawn.

It grew dark and the party was over. Lucile was embarrassed and angry, and so very sad, felt so very heavy, like she would never dance again. But someone pounded on the door, and a woman's voice floated to her, "I'm here, let me in! I feel better now. I've been drinking, but they had to operate on me."

And she began to dance, whirling around. Her white mantle spun away and she was naked, dancing, yes, the famous dancer naked—or was she a designer? She was lying under the lights while they put a mask on her face and said they would help the pain, but she knew they meant to cut her open. They would see her fears then, her pride, her determination. But Isadora danced and danced in the moonlight with her eyes closed and then she opened them and—

Lucile struggled to open her eyes. Oh, a hospital room, a doctor and a nurse.

"Can you tell me your name?" he asked.

She was tempted to fling off the white cover and dance. But her lower belly hurt when she even moved her hand.

"Lucile, Lady Duff-Gordon," she told him.

"Summon his lordship," the doctor told the nurse, who scurried from the room. "You had an abscess on your womb, milady, so we had to take it out—part of the womb. You will have pain for a while but should make a good recovery."

Oh, thank heavens, Cosmo was here, leaning down, taking her hand in his big one. "You gave me a scare, lass," he said. "Doctor, I will get her out of the city for a while, rest and recuperation."

"And not back to work right away," the doctor said, with a nod that was almost a bow as he backed from the room.

"Did you let Esme and Elinor know?" she asked. "Is all well at the shop?"

"Yes, of course. I've taken care of everything. You are not to worry, my love. I've let a house called the Anchorage for us on the shore of Long Island at a place called Mamaroneck, that area you liked. I need to get you out of this frantic city for a while. People have been worried. I won't even complain if Bobbie comes and sings you a song or two. We need time for you to regain your strength and for me to regain you. As I said—I was worried."

She squeezed his hand back as best she could and pursed her lips when he bent to kiss her. She trusted this man with her life and always would.

* * *

Elinor's obsessive attention to the inside of old Montacute had spilled over to the outside. She had just ordered hundreds of blooming plants for the stone urns along the back stone balustrades and the beds surrounding the gravel drive. With each improvement she made, she stamped herself on this place—and, she hoped, on Milor's heart.

When the telephone in the sitting room rang, she jumped and snatched up the earpiece. Expecting Milor's voice, she realized it was Margot's.

"Mother, he's not going to last long. Daddy—he's going fast, hardly breathing."

"I have a motorcar and driver here. I'll leave straightaway. Has he—has he been asking for me?"

"Once. But he thought you were swimming in some pool somewhere and kept saying you had your hair down."

Elinor sucked in a sharp breath. Their honeymoon, when she'd had so much hope. He was dying, and after all the troubles between them he still thought of their honeymoon long ago. Lucile had nearly died in the States and now this. She knew Clayton was deathly ill, and yet the reality of it was such a sad shock.

"I'll be there as fast as I can, Margot. Tell him."

She hung the earpiece back on the hook and turned away to run upstairs for some things. "Thatcher, a dear friend is near death, and I need to go to him," she told the butler Milor had just hired. "Please call the driver to bring the motorcar round and inform his lordship that I will be in Richmond at my daughter Margot's for a few days."

"Of course, Mrs. Glyn."

*Of course,* his words echoed in her head. Of course she was still Mrs. Glyn, and with her author's fame would always be. But, God forgive her, how desperately she wanted to be Lady Curzon someday.

# CHAPTER *Twenty-Eight*

In November 1915, the late autumn sun poured in Lucile's window on Long Island Sound, and Bobbie's voice came pouring through it too when she opened it. He was serenading her with one of her favorite Neapolitan songs, "O Sole Mio." She knew the lyrics were about a lover's song to his lady on a sunny day. For some reason, Cosmo had left the room in a huff, and then, she realized perhaps why, though he and the young man had been getting on well enough lately.

Cosmo had enjoyed his voice training in Italy years ago. He used to sing to her, and she loved his voice, but could he be jealous of Bobbie, his youth and adoration of her—and his romantic song? No need. Absolutely, no need. Why had she always understood women better than she had men?

Bobbie's real name was Genia d'Agarioff and he was actually a Russian émigré, a very talented, handsome one too, with fierce ambitions to become an opera singer, though he was so creative she'd given him a job overseeing the cutting room in the New York shop. One of her acolytes had brought him to the shop, not really to learn the design business, but to entertain her staff and clientele during parade shows. Of course, her mannequins adored him, and he seemed to get on with everyone. He had little money, so she'd invited him to stay here at the beach house. Cosmo had disagreed, yet allowed it since she was still healing months after her operation, but now . . . now she wondered if her husband was trying to think of a way to make Bobbie leave.

She rose from her chair and waved to Bobbie below. Then she took her cane, not an affectation lately but a necessity, and went after Cosmo. She found him in his bedroom, staring—actually glaring—out a window at the restless, white-capped water in the sound. He turned to stare at her.

"Your voice is precious too," she told him, taking his stiff arm. "You never sing anymore."

"Bird in a cage or fish out of water here," he said, turning away again. "Lucile, I need to go home to Scotland for the winter, and I want you to come with me. You're strong enough to travel now."

"But we'd be snowbound there, and I've been away from the shops here and in Europe for weeks. What about my outside commitments, my dreams to—"

"To design for all of womankind before you're content?" he demanded, and his voice broke. "To be waited on hand and foot—and voice—by an army of your acolytes?"

"You have waited on me hand and foot through this, my love. Please try to underst—"

"I understand, but it doesn't help. Yes, I know I agreed before we wed that you must have your career, too. I only wish I could be half as dear to you as sewing and cutting and your voracious self-promotion. I feel cut to pieces here, and I may not be put back together again like that . . . that damned Humpty Dumpty if I don't go home. I see you're not going with me. I can read that plain enough. You're back on your feet, and I've got to find mine again. I'm booking passage as soon as possible, solo, I believe. O, poor me, solo mio," he muttered as he pulled away and stalked out.

Lucile's knees went weak; she collapsed into a nearby chair. She should say she'd go too but she couldn't. Not now at least. Soon. The London store needed her too, and the Paris store with the threat of the Huns . . . Why had it come to this? Cosmo was her bulwark, her adviser, her strength. But despite his denials, he had broken his vow to support her design empire, so she might just have to continue building it alone.

She put her face in her hands and sobbed.

* * *

The moment she stepped out of her motorcar in Richmond, Elinor could tell she was too late. Clayton must have died. Margot ran out to meet her, her face ravaged by tears. She looked both grieved and angry.

"I was hoping you'd be here in time," she choked out. "His sisters and a cousin made it in time but—"

Elinor pulled her into her arms, then propelled her up the walk toward the house. "I'm sorry, my dearest. Sorry for him—even after all these years."

"But you could have patched things up. You should not have been doing up a house for you know who."

"Please, Margot, not now. Let's try to pull together on this."

Margot, even with her lighter hair, looked so like her sometimes, especially around the eyes when they weren't swollen and reddish from tears. Both girls had their mother's backbone, thank heavens, and not their father's dissipated ways, though they'd loved him dearly for his generosity—which he could not afford—and his fun and first-class outlook on life. The foolish man could hardly expense the way he'd lived, but he had taken the girls along for the ride.

Margot pulled away and blew her nose. Juliet burst from the house, arms wide. "Oh, Mother, he was living high right till the end!" she cried, hugging her hard. "But—but I think his soul kind of left us about five years ago when—when—"

Elinor finished for her, "When nothing could stop his headlong rush toward escape from his problems, including me, I suppose—and toward wearing himself completely out."

Margot, sounding stuffed up, said, "He's in a coffin now, but they will come to take him tomorrow. We're going to have him cremated, then have a memorial service. Everyone's agreed."

That comment about "everyone" hurt more than the others. She was not included in that decision, as in "everyone who had mattered." For the first time she began to cry, dreading going in to see his sisters and cousins and whoever else was behind the buzz of voices drifting through the door Juliet held open.

Her damp handkerchief wadded in her hand, Elinor went inside to find a sea of black-clad women sitting in the parlor with Clayton laid out in a handsome wooden coffin on a table. She steeled herself for the comments, the hard looks as she went up to gaze at his white, round face, so still now.

His eldest sister stepped up to hug her. "We can never thank you enough for keeping him financially afloat," she whispered. "We are grateful you allowed him to live the way he wanted until the end."

His cousin, the sternest and most staid of the lot of them, came up and took her hand. "We are so appreciative of all you did to support him . . . in—in more ways than one, especially when he overstepped to lose the properties that were his heritage. He just did not have your grit and go, and you've been a godsend to us all."

Amazingly, so it went. They were grateful to her, perhaps since they didn't have to pay his debts and take him in. They showed her great respect that day and during the memorial service. Margot and Juliet saw it too and softened toward her. Professionally, Elinor was used to being surrounded by admiring people, but this was better. Despite the tragedy of her and Clayton's life together, this was family, one perhaps she had ignored too long.

* * *

The longer Lucile stayed in New York, the more it seemed there was to do. She ignored the advice and pleas in letters from her mother that she come home and a short cable from Cosmo that he expected her soon. You might know, somehow Esme was on her stepfather's side. And how dare Elinor take her to task for not living with her husband when she'd spent years apart from poor, departed Clayton. Elinor had gushed that Curzon had inherited his family estate of Kedleston and the title 5th Baron Scarsdale. She'd said she hoped to help redecorate that great neoclassic expanse of a mansion someday too.

Now why, Lucile groused to herself, would she want to go home to hear more of that? Good heavens, did that bright sister of hers believe, now that Clayton was deceased, that the ambitious Curzon would marry her? And Esme hardly needed a mother at the age of thirty-one with her own family. Besides, she and Anthony were living in the country and seldom came to town.

Yet, feeling guilty at her family's scolding and missing Cosmo,

Lucile wrote him frequently. He answered in brief one-page notes that smelled of his pipe and—did she imagine it?—fresh, brisk Scottish air. She feared he did not believe her when she wrote how much she missed him and she could only pray he did miss her because the tone of his letters was businesslike, as if he were her adviser again but not her beloved. Well, she'd see to all that once she got back to England, though in one note he'd threatened that they should let out or sell the Lennox Gardens pied-à-terre since they were never there anymore.

And worst of all, he dared to lecture her long distance about spending so much money. He was keeping an eye on the London store but said it needed her there. You might know, he didn't say he needed her. Surely her flagship London store was on solid ground even in wartime. It was her new ventures here in the thriving United States that needed her time and attention.

When she was in her New York apartment or at the Long Island house, to stave off depression, she filled it with her staff, her friends, her acolytes—and Bobbie. He cheered her up. He sang to her. But when there were stirrings that America would enter the war, he seemed convinced he should enlist.

"My homeland, Mother Russia, she fights on the side of England," he told her, his face impassioned. "If my adopted country goes to help them, I will too."

"But you are important to the New York shop. You can lift hearts here with your singing career—keep people's spirits up as you do mine," she'd protested.

But what really kept her spirits up was the shop she'd opened in the most fashionable area of Chicago. Cosmo had tersely advised her not to pay the high rental, but he didn't exactly say no, so she clung to that as his approval. She could chuck her entire career for all he cared if she just came home to cold, snowy Scotland. But she could not and would not, not yet, at least. The passion within her to succeed, to share her vision of beauty, to lift women's spirits, prevailed.

"Franks, this shop is in an ideal location," she'd told her secretary when they'd first entered the new building at 1400 Lakeshore Drive, set like a jewel among millionaires' homes who had made their fortune in the meatpacking business and had daughters galore they hoped to marry well—even to English titles. Ah, she'd heard it all before, but what customers they would be, and they all wanted to meet and consult with Lady Duff-Gordon.

It made her feel wanted, but it also made her feel old. Well, she had turned fifty-three this last June. Where had the years gone? But she felt ready to take on new tasks and challenges just like in the good old days—didn't she?

Yet how desperately she wished that Cosmo were here. She wanted him to sing to her, not Bobbie. But she laid her cane aside at last and stood squarely on her own two feet in the main room of the Chicago property, the design of which she was still working on.

"I want something wildly dramatic here," she told faithful Franks, thinking how Elinor was nearly finished decorating Curzon's Montacute mansion. Would he even want that leased estate, now that he had inherited his family legacy of Kedleston? And where would he get all the money for his private empire-building?

"Purple rugs, I think," she went on, as Franks took notes, "bordered with emerald and definitely pale lilac draperies. And then my first design line will be splendid and set new trends—

but be cuts and looks I can adapt to a much more middle-class woman who wants to look and be her affordable best."

"You are the best at all this, milady."

"Sometimes, in what really counts, I wonder."

* * *

Elinor wondered when Milor would come again, this time to view the finished product of redecorated Montacute, but he had been so busy in London now that he was formally in the wartime government cabinet. When he came again, they would dine alone over an intimate dinner in the dining room, and she would seat him to face her portrait. She would escort him from room to room, pointing out particular objects, color schemes, views, and next spring, they would walk through the new gardens she had planned.

But the place felt so big and empty without him as the early December wind howled outside. The huge fire that Thatcher, the butler, had started in the fireplace crackled and trembled. The logs shifted and sparks flew.

To take her mind off her apprehensions and loneliness, perhaps she should write to Lucile again. Did that woman intend to take over each big city in America with her designs? And she'd tried to tell her that, after a certain point, absence did not make the heart grow fonder, but rather, it could lead to out of sight, out of mind.

At least Cosmo didn't drink himself to death or gamble and run off to anywhere but Scotland. Since Lucile's first husband had run off with a silly pantomime girl, was her older sister just building walls between herself and Cosmo so he wouldn't hurt her if he did the same? But not loyal Cosmo, and Lucile should realize what a gift she had in him. Granted, he had been different—more melancholy, even wounded—since the debacle of his honor being attacked after the *Titanic* disaster, his own disaster, in a way, though he was innocent of all charges.

Elinor went into the paneled library and dropped into the large armchair she'd had upholstered especially for Milor in burgundy leather. Thatcher had brought in the December 11, 1916, London *Times*, yesterday's issue here in exile as they were, with every crease ironed out of it as Milor requested when he was here.

As ever, she skimmed articles for his name. She completely understood his being ambitious. That streak ran in her blood too, and just look at Lucile.

"Oh, not this again!" she said aloud in the empty, chilly room, as if she were arguing with the vaunted paper. "He's always been so loyal and does things for good reasons, so must they keep carping on this?"

The paper was rehashing last year's huge headlines declaring that the Right Honorable Curzon of Kedleston had "betrayed" former Prime Minister Asquith and joined Lloyd George's coalition government just to obtain a place in the cabinet. "The government needs good minds in these perilous times we are at war," she continued her diatribe. "So of course he had to switch sides."

Rather than getting upset over all this again—Milor had explained it to her—she flipped way back to the pages that covered society. And there, almost immediately in the various birth, marriage, and death announcements, her gaze snagged on Curzon's name again.

She skimmed it and gasped. Wide-eyed, she read it again and screamed. This was a nightmare! This could not be!

George Nathaniel Curzon, the right Honorable Curzon of Kedleston of the PM's cabinet is betrothed to a Grace Duggan, and they are to be married on 22 December of this year, with a ceremony in the United States and a smaller, later ceremony in January 1917 at the Ritz Hotel in London.

The paper slid to the floor, and she stamped on it as she clutched her throat with one hand. She knew who this woman was, a very wealthy American widow with two sons. No doubt young enough to give him sons—and her fortune.

Elinor tried to get up but her legs gave out and she slid to her knees with her elbows on the chair seat as if she were praying at a prie-dieu. Sobbing silently at first, she felt stabbed in the heart and soul. To lead her on, keep her here, betray her. Her adored and beloved Milor, faithless and vile.

Gripping her hands together, she burst into tears and flooded his chair until Thatcher found her slumped there hours—or maybe eons—later.

# CHAPTER *Twenty-Nine*

It was cold and snowing hard, but Elinor didn't care. She felt as if she were being tormented in the depths of hell.

How dare George Nathaniel Curzon and his new wife hold their second wedding for all his friends—oh yes, the Souls would be there in fine fettle—in the Ritz Hotel, a place that had often been her personal home away from home. He'd secreted her away in tiny hotels, but he was proud to show off his new bride in the grandest.

So Elinor was in the backyard behind her mother's small London house, and she was going to erase that man from her mind. What the deuce, but she had been out of her mind to trust him, to love him! The heart had its needs and reasons, but he had ruined her lifelong belief in true romance.

The wind and snow—tiny pellets now—peppered her face and bare hands, but she didn't care. This had to be done now. Perhaps it would help the burning pain inside to burn the past.

She scraped a wide circle of snow away with her foot and dumped the big box of his letters to her on the damp, crushed grass. Stirring the pile with her foot, she took yet another letter from her coat pocket and tried to light it with the box of lucifers she'd brought out. It flared fast and burned her fingers. She hardly felt the pain. It was nothing next to real agony.

She tried again, shielding the lighted envelope. Oh, she had admirers still, one in particular who had been attentive for years. But never would she play with the fire of passion and romance again, except in her novels. There would be only happy endings. Lucile would understand. She was desperately unhappy without Cosmo but she wouldn't give in to abandon her goals and come back to live in Scotland—not even just have the London and Paris stores as he wanted and let the American ones go.

"The 'It' girls are burning their bridges," she said aloud as she bent to touch the flame to the waiting pile of paper.

"Elinor!" came a sharp voice behind her. "Whatever are you doing out here in this snowstorm? I thought you were lying down."

Her mother. Her long-suffering, blessed mother. She could not have done without her, tending her and Lucile and then her granddaughters over the years. Mother had cared for Clayton more than she had, but that was because he was generous, so unlike Mother's second husband, the horrid Mr. Kennedy. Besides, she had never let go of the deep love for her first husband, their father, yet so handsome when he died, never to weaken, ever young.

"I'm burning some letters, Mother. Go back inside."

"Do not order me about. You will catch your death of cold out here. Can you not cut them up and throw them away?"

"I want them destroyed. I want them burned."

"Oh, I see," she said as she came closer and looked down. "His love letters."

"Ha! Love letters! Lying love letters. Perhaps I should use that for a book title."

Despite the wet ground and snow, the pile of them finally caught fire. She wished her mother would go back inside. She always saw right through her.

"I thought I would die when I lost your father," Mother said. "And look how I've gone on all these years without him, thanks to you and Lucile being so—well, strong and active."

"And quite mad, both of us."

Mother put her arm around Elinor's waist. She'd come out so quickly her coat was not buttoned nor did she wear gloves or a hat. Elinor dug her gloves out of her pocket and put them on her mother as if she were a child.

"Dearest, Elinor, you will go on without him, the wretched cad and betrayer that he is."

"It's not only that. I'm burning another letter too. It came yesterday and kept me up all night. My request to the government for copyright to protect *Three Weeks* has not only been denied, but in the most cruel way. I wanted to protect my story from others who still make fun of it after all these years. Someone planned to make a bawdy sham of it in some dreadful, cheap London review."

"May I see the letter before you burn it?"

"It was the firebrand I used to set the others aflame. But I will tell you—only you—what the judge's decree said. It is going to make it so hard to write the book I'm starting now. The right *honorable*—that word means nothing to me anymore—judge decreed that I am not to have copyright protection for the novel because—and I quote—"It is vulgar, grossly immoral, and deserves no protection as a literary work.""

"Oh, my dearest, how unfair," Mother said, tugging Elinor back from the spreading flames the wind now fed. "So, what do you plan to do?"

"Well, not throw myself on this blaze as if it were a funeral pyre where the Hindu widow immolates herself with her lost man. I shall follow your pattern. Lift my head and pick myself up somehow. I must tell you my next novel has a terrible, cynical, cold hero I've based on Curzon, but I shall have to give it a happy ending to not let my readers down. Also, I think I shall help in the war effort, here or in France. I shall do it for England, for our countrymen and for dear France. We Sutherland women forge ahead, don't we, mistakes and tragedies and losses, no matter what? We go on."

Arm in arm, they stood together in the snowy cold until the flames burned out.

* * *

Lucile looked up from her drawing board in her New York shop. For once, Bobbie's singing was annoying her, and the bustle of the others in and out was distracting her. She stabbed her pencil point into the flowing gown she had just drawn and didn't really like. It did not have "It."

"I need some quiet!" she announced.

All the buzz stopped. Even her new designer, Peter, who was bringing her a cup of tea, froze in half step. Bobbie, who was feeling his oats a bit too much lately to order the others around, rolled his eyes and frowned, fidgeting. Could he not sit still lately?

"I can't think, that's all," she said, amazed anew at how everyone seemed to orbit around her whims and schedule. It had to be that way, didn't it? She was the sun, and they were the stars in this heaven of fashion and design. But, for once, she felt she'd overstepped.

"I am frustrated by the new trends in style," she told them. "I know America will soon be declaring war, and some will be 'going over there' to help stop the Huns, but we must not let women lose sight of beauty and their very special, individual personalities. Some of the new trends I've seen elsewhere than in this shop make women look like boys. They might as well be wearing men's clothes with those straight skirts and jackets and those plain hats. Where is the feminine elegance, the grace and flow?"

Several of her acolytes looked at one another but no one answered. For once, her dear Franks wasn't even taking notes. And Bobbie dared to storm from the room.

Lucile took two sips of the tea Peter set down silently for her, then got up and went out to see what was ailing Bobbie. It had annoyed her that he'd insisted on singing patriotic songs lately—in both English and Russian—instead of romantic ballads. Sometimes she thought of him as a friend, sometimes almost a son. She adored how he adored her, especially since Cosmo was being so stubborn and difficult, even an ocean away.

She found the handsome young man pouting in the dim, deserted showroom with his arms crossed over his chest. He leaned against the elevated walkway she'd recently had installed so that the mannequins could strut off the small stage through the seated audience, turn round, and walk back.

"What is ailing you, Bobbie?"

"I might ask you the same, dear Diva."

"I told you not to call me that nickname. This is not some grand opera, and don't be cheeky."

"It might be a tragedy but one only in the third act, I think. It's wrong of you to try to keep me from enlisting. Don't you think," he asked, obviously forcing a stiff smile as he came toward her, "I would look smashing in a doughboy uniform?"

Instantly exhausted by another go-round with him on this topic, she collapsed in one of the chairs. He perched sideways in the one next to her and leaned his elbows on the arm of the chair and clenched his hands together as if in prayer.

"Shall I beg, oh, great one?" he demanded. "I can't just sit here singing to you and your women clients and friends day and night, besides helping with froufrou frocks, when men are dying for a cause."

"Doughboy—what a wretched name," she said, hoping she could drag him off his usual subject. "Those uniforms make a soldier look like a lump of dough in the middle."

"Of course you could have designed much more handsome ones to get shot up in the trenches, ones colored red perhaps to hide the blood."

"I resent your tone and topic. Bobbie, what is really wrong?"

He jumped to his feet. "If you could see—see and really know—how others feel, you'd know what is wrong with me! There is a world out there beyond your talents and ambition and shops. You've been so kind, Lucile, Lady Duff-Gordon, so good to me, but I'm not some piece of cloth you can cut and stitch to your own design and then keep in a drawer or closet! This country has been good to me, and it's going to fight the kaiser over there, and, no matter if you are always used to having your own way, I'm going to enlist!"

He actually saluted and turned about in a most mocking and military manner and marched out, ignoring her when she shouted, "Bobbie. Bobbie! You come back here so we can discuss this again."

She had a good notion to get up and chase him, try to save him from his frightening, perhaps fatal mission. But she felt frozen in her chair while his words echoed in her mind. *There is a world out there beyond you* . . . She knew that, of course, but what terrified her was that Cosmo had more than once written or said nearly the same thing.

"My lady," came a quiet female voice behind her.

With Bobbie's words pounding in her head, she turned slowly round. Franks. Faithful Franks standing there for who knew how long.

"I'm all right. Whatever is it?"

"Flo Ziegfeld sent a messenger with a letter for you. Mr. Ziegfeld wants to attend your next mannequin tableau and parade, because he wants you to design for his *Follies* here in town. For what he calls his 'showgirls.'"

"Read it to me, will you?" she asked, still not wanting to get back on her feet since that dreadful display Bobbie had just dared. Why, she'd sacked people before for such an outburst, and he knew it.

Franks squinted at the page in the dim light. "I recognize some of these names from the show we saw. He requests that 'The Empress of Fashion' design for him—oh, siren gowns, Egyptian, Chinese for this list of ladies. Irene Castle. She's that dancer, remember? Also Marion Davies—"

"William Randolph Hearst's latest squeeze."

"And Billie Burke. Why, that's Flo Ziegfeld's wife!"

Lucile stood at last, holding herself erect, however deflated she'd felt after Bobbie's accusations, which had made her think of Cosmo again. Except for businesslike notes back and forth between them, she'd tried to shut out thoughts of her husband, because it made her long for him and hate herself.

"Yes, Billie Burke is indeed Mrs. Florenz Ziegfeld! Oh, Franks, to design again, to design elegant clothes and for the stage, the best advertisement ever!" She clasped her hands between her breasts, then reached for the letter to read it herself. "I may have signed with Sears and Roebuck, but how I've longed to return to my first love of designing really ethereal clothes."

But she thought of Cosmo again. He'd no doubt be glad to hear that Bobbie was leaving his luxurious life for a hard cot and wretched food and being yelled at to march in step, and not by her anymore.

She skimmed the letter herself. Yes, Flo Ziegfeld promised all that, but wanted to see her next mannequin tableaus to get ideas. Oh, she had a million new ideas. Here Cosmo was always fretting that she was spending too much money, and this would be another new contract to appease him. Yet how she wished she had him here to care for the boring business end of things so she could just design, design, design.

Cosmo had recently written that she was too much of a "designing woman." He meant her never letting up—never letting down to relax. But that's the way she'd been born and bred, Elinor too, who had written she was volunteering in the English war effort, delivering candy and flowers to wounded soldiers, no less, and she was planning to head to Paris to do even more.

Well, she'd show them all that she could lift spirits too. If only Flo Z's productions weren't called the *Follies,* because that's something else Cosmo had accused her of—as if in an afterthought—in the postscript of a note just last week. She wondered if he'd taken the quote from Elinor, who adored the classics, since it was a line from Homer.

Lucile had only read it once because it annoyed her so—and hurt her too. It went something like this: *People blamed the gods for evils, but in fact it was their own follies causing their woes.*

Well, she didn't like the tenor of that, but she did like her brilliant plans to design for Ziegfeld. It opened up a whole new world, an escape from all this dreadful war talk, from Bobbie's desertion, from Cosmo's, too. Ah, but wouldn't it be wonderful to just create and not worry for the business end of things? Now what was the name of that man Hearst had mentioned who might like to buy a big part of her business and manage the boring parts, maybe buy Cosmo's share out here?

"Come with me, Franks, and we shall make the exciting announcement that this next fashion parade and tableau must be perfect, all two hours of it, down to every stitch and frill and step. Ah, we're back to silks and satins, bows and lace and ruffles and flounces. Do you realize this will mean Flo Ziegfeld will do our promotion for us? Oh, and see if we can get that string quartet back, and if they can bring a romantic tenor since, sadly, very sadly, we have lost the one we had."

# CHAPTER *Thirty*

Lucile paced back and forth in her private office in the New York shop, reading more of Elinor's letter and becoming more angry with every line.

> *Lucile, you simply owe it to your country to come home and help in the war effort, at least in London, but Paris could use you too, and not just to oversee your shop here.*

"How dare you tell me what to do!" Lucile sassed the letter. She should have taken time to read it at home—left it at home—but she'd put off reading it yesterday when it came. More of the same, Elinor's grandstanding, now that she was finally looking at the contents.

> *I really cannot believe you are sitting the war out there in lush, plush conditions.*

"Lush and plush, indeed. I am working very hard!" she cried, planning to write back those very words in her own letter when she had time.

*I can't tell you how hard I worked on my new novel. The book has been well received so far, although I've had several letters saying it has a terribly cynical heroine, especially because of the theme, which, more or less, says that it is wiser to marry the life you like, because, after a little while, the man doesn't matter. I suppose since you and Cosmo seem quite estranged, you would agree with that.*

"If you mean I'd be imprisoned in Scotland for good—or for bad—I agree with you for once, sister. Speak for yourself about what was your dreadful marriage. You would have been better off to have left that years ago!"

*I must tell you that William Randolph Hearst has made me a healthy offer to bring out my latest novel in America, but he wanted me to soften her character somewhat and not make her so brazen as to decide she wants to lose her virginity. I told him, no, she is a modern woman, and he has said he still may take the novel!*

"Terrible!" Lucile said even louder. "That's what I shall write you back. Cannot you hold to the better ways of the past? Must you, too, always be pushing forward? Next you'll be wearing those tight, plain hats that smother one's hair and straight-skirted, skinny girl clothes." She almost didn't read on, but her eye caught Cosmo's name again.

*Your countrymen need you, not to mention Cosmo. Oh, yes, he cloaks missing you well, but I saw him before I left*

*London for Paris, and I can see you have hurt him to the core and—*

"As he has done me. And you too. I shall do what I need to do, and if you are not careful, prancing near enemy lines, you will prove yourself as foolhardy as you always have, but gambling with your life this time—not just writing some romance about a real-life cad who betrayed you."

*So many women of all classes have stepped up at home, and I am so proud of my girls. They both volunteered for the Voluntary Aid Detachment, wretched but worthwhile jobs, and both have worked their way up to acting as secretaries for important men. Margot is working for the deputy chief of air staff and Juliet for Admiral Richmond while Mother pitches in to care for the grandchildren. Although I began working at the canteen in Grosvenor Gardens in London, then moved on to deliver cigarettes and candy to our wounded boys here in Paris, as I mentioned before—but did not hear your response—I am honored to now be named vice president of the Secours Franco-Americain Society to bring relief to devastated battle areas. I will soon be touring regions which need help, and, I'm sure you'll agree 'if I screw my courage to the sticking place,' it is worth the risk, and so—*

Lucile sank into her desk chair and sucked in a huge sob. Yet again, her sister's literary reference to Shakespeare. The *sticking place*, indeed!

She wadded up the long letter and threw it in the rubbish basket, then yanked it out again and smoothed it open on the desk. Her tears wet the paper and blurred the ink.

Elinor had no right to lecture or scold her, or blow her own horn. The war effort! Bobbie was insane to have volunteered and was now stationed in Chicago. She supposed next time she was there, she might try to look him up, despite how he'd abandoned her.

Meanwhile, Cosmo's letters had become more scarce, though he still warned against overspending in such times. But she did have funds, on paper, coming in soon, at least. What a burden it was to worry about future money, so she needed a business manager she could trust, actually a full-fledged American partner to tend to taxes, insurance, pricing, and things like that that Cosmo had been so skilled at.

"Well," she said aloud, "it takes money to make money."

She blew her nose and wiped under her eyes. She had a staff meeting soon and would look like a harridan. So what, she thought, if she'd purchased new furniture for the beach house and still kept her New York apartment and had redecorated the front rooms of the Chicago and New York Lady Duff-Gordon establishments? She'd thrown a lovely, garden-themed party for her staff here, who had worked so hard to dress Flo Ziegfeld's glorious, glamorous showgirls for his *Follies*.

And just yesterday, she'd hired several additional skilled seamstresses, but she'd needed them. Oh, and a chauffeur for her new motorcar because she couldn't abide driving in New York traffic.

After all, she was contributing to society too. She was certain she must have lifted the spirits of many New Yorkers with her fantastical costumes, not to mention the Midwest farmer's wives who bought their clothes from the Sears and Roebuck catalog, which featured her 1917 collection, designed especially for them. How strange there had been negative comments about her note in the catalog touting the personality and fantasy of every dress, not to mention that some frocks were judged "too fancy." Perhaps they all just worked too close to the soil to grasp the meaning of romantic clothing.

She skimmed the postscript of Elinor's letter, another long paragraph. Her sister was going in some sort of vehicle behind former enemy lines and could find danger there. Elinor was risking her life, not her pocketbook. A great wave of guilt and self-loathing washed over Lucile, and she put her head in her hands, covering her eyes.

Then there was Cosmo, she thought, and began to cry again as she felt the stab of guilt, regret, and longing. So, let alone Elinor with all her bragging, was her own husband behind his own enemy lines against her now?

* * *

"This isn't my first venture into a devastated area, you know," Elinor said in French to the officer, *General d'armee* Jacques Presque, who accompanied her in the big motorcar. With other press representatives, she had been assigned to the Third French Army. Actually, she was relieved to get out of Paris for a while, since life there went on madly as if no danger lurked and no men died, and Elinor thought that quite immoral. German aeroplane air raids had hit Paris, so why did that not sober up the populace? They fiddled while Rome burned, just as she felt Lucile was doing in America.

"*Oui, madame,*" Officer Presque told her, obviously pleased with her good French, "the Huns were here for a while. You will soon see the name we have for them—the Vandals—is well founded."

Though they had an excellent chauffer driving, the roads were full of holes, and their journey was so jerky and bumpy that she did not take notes but studied the ruined countryside and listened to him. Officer Presque had suggested she take the front passenger seat so she could see better, but she had said the backseat would be fine so they could converse more easily.

They were entering an area just this side of the front. The fact that she wrote articles for American newspapers, and the French needed the Americans in the fight, was her pass to such adventures. She reported on what she'd seen, and it bolstered the foreign support effort in what was being called the Great War. In short, she was proud of risking her neck and hoped she'd inspired Lucile to join the effort in some way, though she could hardly picture her here in one of her fancifully named tea gowns, smoking a straw-tipped cigarette and leaning on her Bo-Peep walking stick.

Nothing "great" about the so-called Great War, Elinor thought, but of course *great* meant widespread. She understood that even more as they passed through little towns that were now behind the French lines, places the Germans had devastated. The once beautiful pastures, small villages, crops, gardens, and cottages now lay ravaged by battle. She'd heard terrible tales of livestock slaughtered, people brutalized, and women raped.

How painful it was to see that the retreating Huns had hacked off the tops of new cherry and apple trees, obviously just from pure spite and hatred. She saw few civilians, and those looked hungry and dazed.

They passed massive rolls of barbed wire and poles among

signs in French and English directing convoys toward the front. Huge, gray lorries lumbered past on the road with a honk of the horn. More than once their vehicle stopped at railway tracks as boxcars full of what the men said were ammunition and guns chugged past. Occasionally, they saw rows of ditches that had held retreating or advancing men, the sites of the terrible trench warfare stories.

"These trenches have been evacuated for two months," Officer Presque told her. "The fierce battle raged here for days. I am sorry for the stench, Madame Glyn. Death still hangs here, *oui*?"

Before she could answer him, they heard the growing buzz of an approaching aeroplane. They craned their necks to the windows, looking up. It was coming right at them, swooping low.

"It's a German Taube—a bomber! Go! Go!" Officer Presque shouted in French to their driver.

They sped up, when Elinor thought they should be fleeing in the opposite direction, but they obviously wanted to get past the plane before it could drop a bomb. The holes in the road made her bounce into the ceiling and the window. The officer shoved her down behind the front seats as if that would help and shouted at the driver, who began to weave on the road as the plane roared over them.

"It's circling!" the driver shouted. Officer Presque hunkered down to look up through the side window again. "It's coming back!"

A huge blast boomed behind them. The car lurched. Debris flew, breaking the back window and spewing glass shards at them. The driver accelerated even more. Another boom at closer range shook the car before the scream of the plane lessened as it veered away.

Lifting her head at last, Elinor saw why. Ahead of them, through the smoke, blasts came from huge, hidden guns shooting madly at the plane.

"A hidden antiaircraft battery!" the driver screamed. "It's ours, but I don't know if they hit the Taube!"

Chaos, noise, smoke ahead. As shells burst skyward again, the plane was gone—hit, she hoped—as the battery went silent and was hidden by its camouflage of trees once again.

Keeping an eye on the sky, both men got out to look at the motorcar. Besides the broken window, they told her the boot had been hit by flying stones or shrapnel, and three of the four tires were punctured and ragged.

"I'll radio for help," Officer Presque said. "But we'll take shelter over there in that village until someone arrives. I think the sign said we're in Peronne. Let's leave the vehicle right there and hike, find a cellar. Perhaps the men in that battery will come for us or send help, but that bomber could return."

He hauled his wireless apparatus out of the maimed boot of the motorcar and, keeping low as if they were being attacked again, they scuttled like crabs in a ragged line toward the ruined village.

# CHAPTER *Thirty-One*

My dear, old friend, so lovely to see you!"

"Now, don't you dare call me old," Lillie Langtry said with a smile as she swept into Lucile's private office, "but I know what you meant."

Lucile was greatly cheered when her longtime idol Lillie Langtry stopped by the shop in New York for several new frocks. Though Lillie was sixty-four now, Lucile thought she still looked fabulous, and she told her so.

But how, even without reminiscing, Lillie's mere presence brought back powerful memories: Lucile pictured herself and Elinor as girls, hiding under a dressing table to catch a glimpse of their shining star from Jersey. And when they had heard she was the mistress of the Prince of Wales—well . . .

"Keep looking forward, not back, that's my motto," Lillie said as she stood on the fitting platform while Lucile draped satins on her to see which colors she preferred. She had instantly known what her friend would want for an evening gown, or so she thought, though Lillie had said to forget some of the silk roses and what she'd called "froufrou." Lucile frowned at herself in one of the many mirrors in the room. However she had complimented Lillie, it was amazing how time passed, how people aged. She herself had silver hairs threaded through her hair. And Cosmo—she hadn't seen him for several years. Would he have silver in that handsome mustache?

"Hard to believe America's finally thrown her might and her men in with dear, old England," Lillie said, drawing back Lucile's attention.

"If we could only have that horrid war end before Americans lose their lives too," Lucile muttered through her mouth of pins. She almost never did fittings or suggested samples anymore, leaving that to her ample staff, but with Lillie, it was different. "A dreadful business! But on this skirt, a bit less swag and sway, I think. I must keep up with the tighter, straighter skirts now, though at least we're out of that terrible hobble skirt style. Women need more freedom today, not to totter along as if we must have someone to lean on."

"I never could abide those, as they made the silhouette so choppy and broken—no grace and flow. But we designers are trendsetters, not followers," Lucile insisted, after taking her pins from her lips and sticking them in the pin cushion on her wrist.

"Another goal is to never look my age!" her friend said. "Never have and never will. That's been one lovely thing about your styles over the years, they just floated along, but now there's more hustle and bustle to life, more—well, plain reality than some of your frocks show."

Lucile almost felt as if Lillie had slapped her. "I—I guess my heart belongs to the past and nothing plain. We need romance and escape and beauty, especially, in these trying times."

"Of course we do, but the trappings are different in different times. Those sleeve ruffles you sketched—can we smooth them out too? Oh, I hope my skin stays tight for all the sleeveless frocks that are so in style now. I swear, I work on lifting books each day to firm up, and I adore those shiny jet beads in place of those heavy ropes of pearls. No way I shall advertise I belonged heart and soul to an older generation and age, so . . ."

Lucile froze inside as she chattered on. For one strange, shattering moment, she felt so depressed she'd just as soon be dead.

* * *

"Is she dead?" Elinor whispered to Officer Presque in the dim cellar.

They had run into an underground haven of a bombed-out house that still had parts of four walls, half a ceiling, and rickety cellar stairs. The remnants of the remaining structure reminded her of a skeleton, and they had not expected to find anyone inside.

But a young woman lay on a hemp sack with another one pulled over her for a meager blanket. They could not make her out well as dusk fell above them until their driver produced an electric torch and turned it on.

"Not dead," the officer whispered. "Sleeping. With something stuffed in her ears, maybe to mute the bombs."

The girl heard them or sensed the light. She woke and sat up, cowering against the damp wall, hands to her throat, shrieking. The officer tried to quiet her and assured her they were French. Elinor knelt, pushing him away with her shoulder and tugging pieces of rags out of the girl's ears. As she had hoped, the sight of another woman halted her hysteria. Elinor spoke to her in French, telling her they had come out from Paris, that a battery of guns was nearby to protect them and shoot down any more planes.

The girl wore a dress that reminded her of more ripped-up rags. Had she no coat or hat? When she calmed, Elinor asked, "What is your name?"

In a small, shaky voice, she said, "Fleurette, madame."

"Are you alone here?"

"I came back from Paris. My family's house—gone. The village gone. I thought I could help. I cannot. No one can."

"Perhaps we can. We will take you back to Paris with us when we go."

Fleurette was slender and shaking. Even in the dim, reflected light, which their driver no longer shone in the girl's face, Elinor could see she was beautiful, with shoulder-length auburn hair and a classic face with high cheekbones, perfectly arched eyebrows, and Cupid-bow lips. When she tried to cover her torn, filthy clothes with the hemp sack blanket, Elinor shrugged out of her coat to wrap it around her, and Officer Presque gave Elinor his big, warm coat.

"Madame, I used to be a mannequin and wear the most lovely fashions for women—before the war," Fleurette said, starting to cry again, though she must know she was quite safe with them now.

Elinor drew in a sharp breath. "Not—not for Lucile, Lady Duff-Gordon's shop?"

"For Monsieur Worth," she told her, swiping tears from her sooty cheeks that made gray streaks, yet still looking heartbreakingly lovely. "But I had to come home, to see my people, my family. How could I stay in the famous fashion world when all this was going on? But then, they were not here," she repeated as she collapsed into sobs.

This girl was a gift from God. While Fleurette cried on her shoulder, Elinor held her tight and thought of another way to prod Lucile to champion the war effort and not just hide behind her own mannequins.

* * *

Lucile had not mocked or ignored Elinor's next letter. *With all your brilliant talent in fashion, cannot you do something for this girl we've brought back to Paris? Or beyond that, something to raise money for displaced, broken people like her?*

Elinor's lengthy description of Fleurette and her past had haunted and inspired Lucile. Grateful and glad to have a cause—one that could combine promoting fashions with the war effort—she had leaped into action with all sorts of schemes. Charity shows were de rigueur in the city, so why not design one around the story of Fleurette?

Calling her creation *Fleurette's Dream at Peronne,* Lucile presented a short drama she wrote herself with a prologue and eight scenes. Elinor, she told herself, could not have done better. She hired a small orchestra for background music to set the various moods. In the show, while the pitiful girl slept in her cellar, she dreamed of her dear Paris and the clothes she used to wear for her designer—not Worth, of course, who had criticized Lady Duff-Gordon designs as passé from time to time, but her own Lucile fashions.

"I adored the dream scenes," a reporter—a female, fashion-only reporter—had told Lucile at a party. "Especially the one where she dreamed she took a walk with a friend and the one where she went to a dance with a beau. Did you create those scenes from your own past or memories?"

"I chose universal events, ones we all can recall," Lucile told her. But the truth was, as she had created the scenes and designed garments for them, they did come from her own memories. Times with Elinor when they were young, but especially thoughts of Cosmo. He'd written he was proud of her for raising money for the war effort, but that she could surely do that in England and Scotland, too, that she should come home to present *Fleurette's Dream* there.

She was besieged by other women who had seen the presentation and wanted to order the fashions. She reminded them that a part of their orders would go to the war effort as did the ticket prices for the show she intended to take on the road at least on the East Coast and Midwest, first to Chicago.

But her thoughts still clung to Cosmo. He had not said he still loved her, but at least he had only warned her once in his latest note about too much spending. True, she had paid for all this herself, so that every penny could go to the war effort. But, for the first time, she seriously thought about his request that she come home. Whether he lived in a castle or a cellar, yes, wherever Cosmo was—really, wasn't that home?

* * *

If she'd been completely truthful with herself, Lucile thought as she strode through the lobby of her Washington, D.C., hotel a month later, she would have admitted she hoped to see how Bobbie was doing while she was here, where he was now stationed. Everyone else with the show was excited that President Wilson would be in the *Fleurette* audience this evening, but she had hoped Bobbie would attend.

She and Franks were heading out to take Lucile's dogs to a park for a walk. Lucile had her big chow, Mahmud, and two Pekingese, which she always traveled with, but she kept thinking of Bobbie.

Raising money for the war effort, even though it profited her business, too, had made her forgive him for enlisting. She would track him down, tell him so, give him a ticket for tonight. After the war, she would gladly give him a position again. You might know, the army had realized his talents too and, though he'd been commissioned in the 5th Engineers regiment, he'd been given the job of directing the choir. Good, she'd thought. That would keep him safe.

Despite the demands and triumph of taking *Fleurette* on the road, she planned to at least visit England soon. She missed Esme and her family—of course Cosmo, too, though he still tried to control her from afar. She needed his advice for business and financial affairs, but since he was sitting tight there, she had decided to find an American partner to shoulder some of that responsibility. If that freed her up to go home, how could Cosmo, Esme, or her attorney son-in-law, who all had a large financial interest in the company, argue with that?

But she had already scheduled six months on the road in eighteen different towns with *Fleurette*, including here in the nation's capital city. Surely that would shut Elinor up about her doing nothing to aid the cause.

"Lady Duff-Gordon," a busboy called as he caught up with them and gestured back toward the lobby desk. "A notice just arrived for you over the telephone from your office in New York."

Dear Franks went over to get that for her while Lucile held the three leashes. She opened the note while Franks took the two Pekes back.

"Oh!" Lucile cried. "Oh my."

"Bad news from New York, milady?" Franks asked, coming closer.

"From here, really. I mean, about here—Bobbie's in a hospital, quite ill with pneumonia. So maybe this is a gift from God that I am here now. Billy Sunday says things like this are not fate, but from God, you know."

Billy Sunday and his wife were two of Lucile's most unusual friends, for he was a hellfire-and-brimstone Christian evangelist, but she cared deeply for him. So many different Americans, and here—despite Bobbie's plight—she was longing for a Scotsman.

Pulling the big dog, she went straight to the desk. "I need to telephone this number at once," she said. "I need to visit an ill soldier."

The man dialed the number for her and handed her the receiver. It felt so heavy in her hand. Dear Bobbie, so full of life and song. His voice—she imagined she could hear Bobbie's beautiful voice, but she could hear Cosmo's deep, lovely one too.

She learned on the telephone from the commanding officer's aide what hospital Bobbie was in, weak and very ill with pneumonia, which was the result of serious influenza that had swept the troops.

She left the dogs with Franks. She wouldn't take the time to call for her own motorcar, but rushed out to find a taxi.

* * *

What terrified Lucile the moment they drove up to the side of the hospital, where she got out because of traffic in front, was a simple glimpse into a loading bay. Within were stacked rows of coffins! Surely not with bodies in them, soldiers' bodies from disease if not war.

She rushed inside to the main desk, claiming to be next of kin for Genia D'Agarioff. She had almost asked for Bobbie, but she was the one who had nicknamed him that. Did they think she was his mother, sister—even his older lover? She didn't know or care.

Others milled around in the corridors, some whispering, some crying. They sent her up one flight of stairs to a ward with lots of beds filled with young men. How she wished she could have known; she would have arranged a private room, but perhaps in these dreadful times, this was normal. The nurse led her to his bed. She perched carefully on the edge of it.

"Bobbie. Bobbie," she said louder, "it's Lucile. I'll get you out of here, special care."

He moaned and slitted both eyes open. A good sign, she thought, though he looked so pale, so—almost invisible. She took his hand. His face was flushed so she expected his skin to be hot, but it was cold. His hand was cold and thin.

"Mama," he whispered so quietly that she had to read his lips. "Mama."

"It's Lucile, dear. You must rest and get better, so you can sing again. Bobbie, listen to me. The war surely will be over soon, and now you won't be sent over there. You must save your strength and get better."

"Sing. I will sing." He closed his eyes.

"Sleep, dearest. Sleep and get strong and you will sing again where everyone adored you and applauded and—"

His hand relaxed in hers, and he seemed to slump deeper into the white sheets of the narrow bed. He breathed out in a long, deep sigh. Though she could swear she still heard his voice, she knew he would never sing again. Well, maybe with an angel choir in heaven.

# CHAPTER *Thirty-Two*

"Quite strange to see a woman here," the London *Times* reporter Nigel Paige told Elinor as they entered the Hall of Mirrors at Versailles with the rest of the press members for the signing of the peace treaty. The room was abuzz with muted, male voices.

"How strange for you to say such when half the population of the world is women," Elinor replied. "I believe many of them have brains and are able to read. Of course, though, women did not fight on the front battle lines—which I have seen quite close—they too fought the Huns in their own way and suffered. This is peace for women today also."

"Oh, well, didn't mean to imply differently," he told her and went as red as a ripe pippin.

Reporters from the *Times* always thought they could lord it over everyone else, she thought. While they had waited in line, he had made several snide comments to imply that articles on the peace treaty being signed today would be better covered from "a male point of view." She simply could not let the remarks pass, though she knew the press permit in her gloved hand could be revoked at any minute. God bless Lord Riddell for getting it for her and for paying well for her observations of the war for his paper, the *News of the World*.

She turned her back on and moved away from the old curmudgeon Paige. Despite his disdain, she almost had to pinch herself that she was here. Not only in her beloved Versailles but here to report on the formal end of the war.

She stood on tiptoe to survey the room near the signing table. The German representatives looked as if they'd like to sink through their seats. She could see British prime minister Lloyd George and the American president, Woodrow Wilson, both seated far to the front, as she took her seat in the back row.

If she had an opportunity to say a word to Wilson, she'd tell him that she was the one who had rescued the real Fleurette, the inspiration for the presentation he'd seen in Washington. She'd make clear that she was the one who had insisted that her sister produce the charity show. Lucile's letter about the president's attendance had been the only happy note in the sad news she had sent about the demise of her employee Bobbie, whom Cosmo had distrusted. Elinor would tell the president that Fleurette had located her mother and sister and that they were all being supported by profits from the show, as were other French refugees. Lucile had even promised the girl a job when business picked up at the Paris shop again.

Elinor heaved a sigh as she perched on a small, gilt chair. If only Lucile would return to Europe, perhaps they could make peace with each other, especially since Elinor had picked up hints in her letters that—for once—Lucile's American endeavors were suffering from a shortage of funds, something Elinor had lived with for years. Cosmo said Lucile didn't listen and that she had overreached her previous extravagance, but when did her older sister really listen to anyone? Full steam ahead, that was Lucile, though Elinor had to admit she had a bit of that in her, too.

She took off her right-hand glove and began to take notes, but when she glanced up, it was the glorious, massive room that still stunned her anew, however packed it was with black-suited men and one other woman she saw come in. The ceiling soared high overhead, seeming to float as if it were held up by the over three hundred floor-to-ceiling mirrors on one side and tall glass doors that overlooked the gardens on the other. The parade of mirrors doubled the people. She turned to glance at herself in the one behind her.

Dear heavens, at least she didn't look fifty-four, despite her hard work and her own money worries. Yet she planned to take another trip to Egypt and Spain—had to travel while she still could. Money was well spent if it kept her young and provided fodder for her fiction. She had no desire to be a grandmother who stayed home and only tended her grandchildren, however much she adored them.

*28 June 1919*, she wrote at the top of the page. *Use mirrors as a symbol to make readers think about their own observations of the war and the need we all have for peace. Between countries, family members, husband and wife, loved ones . . . In a way, haven't we all been at war over something, with someone, from time to time?*

For one moment she let herself remember when she'd brought George Curzon, her Milor, here to Versailles, that monster who had betrayed and hurt her so badly. She had not forgiven him yet and perhaps never would. She looked up from her notepad again, frowned into the mirror, and turned around just as the room quieted and the German representatives stood to sign the treaty first.

* * *

"Sign right here, then down here," John Shuloff's lawyer told Lucile, pointing to the blank spaces on the long document. She nodded and began to sign *Lucile, Lady Duff-Gordon* and affix the date. So much tightly spaced, small print here. She adjusted her glasses. Her own lawyer, a friend of Elsie de Wolfe's, had already gone over the agreement thoroughly. She was seated on a hard wooden chair, so why didn't this man have some leather padded seats in his office? Worse, the lawyer seemed to hover over her.

Yet she felt a great weight was about to be lifted from her shoulders. Now she would have an American partner to oversee finances and business affairs, to free her up just to design and find a way to enjoy life again. This agreement would buy herself, Cosmo, and Esme out of their interests in the New York, Paris, and Chicago stores and leave them the London shop. Surely everything would stay the same, except she would receive a monthly executive director's salary. Her income would no longer fluctuate, especially since she disdained the postwar, dreadful boyish styles of chemise dresses and those tight cloche hats to cover that dreadful shingled, lopped-off hair. She was not completely cutting ties here. Though she was thinking of going back to Europe, when she visited New York, she expected to keep an eye on her new design studio in the Flatiron Building.

She looked up from all her signing with a sigh. Shuloff was here, watching her, sitting at the end of the table, since he'd already signed. His scrutiny was fine with her, because it meant he had an eye for detail, that he was the sort to take charge and observe people, just as she had always been. She knew the imported lace and brocades were a thing of the past and that the prices of frocks would have to come down and cut profits, but she still meant to have a hand in holding on to some of the signature details of Lucile designs that had made her famous.

"You're free to return to Europe now," Shuloff said the moment the ink was dry.

"Oh yes, but I want to keep an eye on things here in the transition."

He ground out his cigar in one of the glass ashtrays with JS etched in their depths. Spittoons crowded each corner of the room, which added to the masculine but common feel of the place. She could have had it redecorated to be more welcoming and sophisticated in a trice.

"I don't think the hand-sewn promise will last for long, though," he told her, leaning forward with his elbows on the table. "The future is mass production to keep prices down. Your outreach to the Sears and Roebuck buyers that didn't fly might be a possibility now."

She felt so tired, so relieved, that his words hardly registered. Guilt over being away from her family and Cosmo, her tense, tenuous relationship with Elinor, her grief over Bobbie's death all weighed on her. She'd given every penny from the Fleurette tour to the war effort, but those six months on the road had taken a further toll on her work here and in Chicago. Numerous new designers she used to call her acolytes had taken over much of the day-to-day work.

Shuloff stood and offered her his hand, so masculine, so American. She rose and shook with him, wondering how she'd had the courage to part with any of this that she controlled—and wondering, if she did go home, if she would lose control there with her first Lucile's shop and with her loved ones.

* * *

Elinor was recently home from Spain when she received the telegram at her mother's house. At first, she just stared at it. It was from her agent, who had received the message from her publisher, dear Gerald Duckworth. He was forwarding an offer from a Mr. Jesse Lasky in America, and the main message read: *The Famous Players-Lasky Studio wishes you to come to Hollywood, California, and write for the moving pictures. Stop. Salary would be $10,000 per picture, plus traveling expenses and better terms if the "movies" do well. Stop.*

She read it again. The postscript said they had read her books. They liked her books! She blinked back tears and read it all for a third time. Below the momentous first five lines were details that other "admired" writers had promised to come also to elevate the storylines and characters of Hollywood moving pictures. Somerset Maugham, whom she had read but had not met, was one such writer.

She collapsed on the bench by the umbrella stand and began to cry. Approval. Admiration. Adventure. A financial windfall. Amazing, new people. Something and someplace new, though she'd glimpsed old Hollywood when she'd been out west years ago. Perhaps they would do *Three Weeks* or *Beyond the Rocks*, her favorites. She was completely ignorant of screenwriting, but she'd learn. She would learn fast.

Jumping up, she ran for the telephone.

* * *

After the formal signing of the contract, Lucile stayed away from her design studio for two weeks while she kept busy socially and wrote home to test the waters about returning to oversee her flagship London store—hers and Cosmo's. Esme had written back, *It's about time. Your grandchildren won't even know you.* Cosmo had scribbled hastily, *I'll believe it when I see it. And I want to see it—and you.*

So today, she steeled herself and took her limousine into the city from Long Island to visit her studio at the Flatiron Building. Although she would probably return to England for a time, it would do her staff and the new management good to see her, to be encouraged.

Granted, it would be hard to see someone else in charge, as she realized a few new staff would have been hired. She hoped none of her employees had been let go. She should have insisted on that in the contract, but it wasn't her contract. She felt a bit lonely, for she'd sent dear, loyal Franks home to England to her ailing, elderly parents, whom she hadn't seen in years. Except for her canine menagerie, and, of course, her social friends, she felt greatly on her own in her apartment and her lovely Long Island home.

Wanting to make a grand entrance as always, Lucile had dressed to the nines this October afternoon in a teal wool suit and fox stole, of course with a signature plumed hat. In case she had time to leave the staff with a few new designs after she'd looked everything over, she'd brought her favorite sketchbook with a few drawings to share. How she wished she'd walk in to hear Bobbie singing to the staff or to see her mannequins chatting as they prepared for one of her lovely fashion parades.

But oh—the front office looked different as she stepped inside. Spartan. No flowers in vases, and the large window was bare with no satin draperies, none at all, though that offered a spiffy view of Broadway far below. A young man she did not know looked up from his typewriter and asked, "Are you here for a fitting?"

She stared at him so hard he flinched. "I am here to see my staff. I am Lucile, Lady Duff-Gordon."

He bounced up. "Oh, of course. We were not told you were coming. Please have a seat while I inform—" He got out before she rounded the desk—where was that Aubusson carpet that lay here?—and opened the door to the hall. She walked as quickly as she could, not leaning on her signature walking stick but carrying it like a weapon.

Her eyes skimmed the first room for familiar faces. She saw two of her junior designers, but strangers, too, hunched over drawings, sitting at long tables. There were no swatches of fabric samples in sight. At least these workers looked industrious, for only a few glanced up, and only one—by his shocked expression—seemed to recognize her. Had she been gone for decades? Was this a nightmare?

"Lady Duff-Gordon," the receptionist said, scurrying behind, "please wait until I call Mr. Shuloff, or tell the manager. Mr. Shuloff isn't here, but not far away, and the manager, Leon Green, is on the telephone to suppliers, so—"

Leon Green. Whoever was that? Rather than set this man straight, she ignored him. In the next room, she saw none of her dear mannequins, women she'd so carefully chosen for size, shape, and face. Instead, on slightly raised platforms, stood dreadful, faceless, stuffed, cloth dummies with strangers pinning fabrics or constructed clothing on their lifeless forms, clothing that was plain, close cut, and so cold and dreadful. Other dummies were stacked against a wall like pale, naked corpses.

The receptionist had left her now, running toward the back office that had been her studio with its lovely views of Fifth Avenue and the park. She could not bear to see it now. Had they sold her antique furniture there, its carpets and draperies? If so, it was her own, stupid fault.

She had made a terrible mistake. She had sold out, ruined things. Her dream of design for the new world was over, shattered.

"Lady Duff-Gordon, just a moment, please. Mr. Green, the new manager, will see you now!" came the receptionist's voice behind Lucile as she turned and fled, even shaking off the hand he dared to lay on her arm. Mr. Green had not even come out to greet her. And John Shuloff was a barbarian, a proletarian who had no sense of beauty in his soul—if he had one at all. From now on, she would think of him as Attila the Hun, slayer of the gilded past, no better that the kaiser, whose soldiers had ravaged France.

As she headed for the door to the hall to make her escape, she was nearly sick to her stomach on the new linoleum floor of the reception room. She was certainly sick to her soul.

# PART V

# Hollywood and Home

1920–1926

# CHAPTER *Thirty-Three*

This entire, glossy-looking Hollywood deal was starting to make Elinor feel ill. Four other authors had left in a snit already—including Somerset Maugham—because their scripts and advice were not being heeded. But Elinor had decided to take a stand with Jesse Lasky after she'd suffered through several months of being challenged at best, ignored at worst.

"Mr. Lasky," she called out to him, rising from her canvas deck chair on the set of *The Great Moment,* the first of her books for which she'd written the screenplay. He'd actually taken over the director's tall chair this morning, saying things were moving too slowly. The cast, standing on their marks, ready to go, stopped to look her way.

"If this set is to be an English castle," she announced in a loud voice, since everyone was used to orders through those dreadful megaphones, "there should not be spittoons lined up on the floor nor those modern art, florid works on the wall. You have imported me, so to speak, to elevate the script, and it has been grievously rewritten by your so-called continuity staff of your scenario department or by their stenographers, no less."

She waved the rolled-up script at him as if it were a sword.

"Cut! Cut the action!" he called. "Elinor, dear," he told her from his elevated chair, "I don't expect you to grasp how different this is from words simply lying there on page, but—"

"Words in a novel—or a script—are never simply lying on a page! They leap at the reader or listener. They go deep into the mind and heart, if written correctly, and that is a huge 'if' around here! They express feelings, and a fictional reality, and—"

"And," he interrupted, now shouting through his megaphone, "you must learn to be the cog in the machinery, as are we all. Time is money, so we need to get back to work."

"My high and mighty lordship," she said, hands on her hips, "money, money, money is all I hear around this town! But what matters is that the heightened suspense you asked for in my second revision of this script is becoming a farce in the filming! I do not wish to turn tail as have your other excellent writers, for I believe in what you are doing to reach and entertain the common man as well as the culturally sophisticated, but—"

"Elinor, your ending just won't work," he insisted, putting the megaphone down. "As for the set, we can do away with the spittoons, but that space needed to be filled. All right, clear away the spittoons, all but one," he called, picking up the megaphone again.

The men she'd come to think of as Lasky's lackeys these last months jumped to obey. Ignoring them and Lasky, she strode over to the back wall of the set and lifted down a hastily daubed painting that looked to be of a tropical isle. That's where she wished she was. So many of her hopes had been dashed about her Hollywood career. She might as well be on a desert island for all the attention they paid her. Her goal to glorify romance on the cinematic screen was about to go down the proverbial drain.

She set her jaw firmly but blinked back tears. She'd met many big names, as they called them here, and several actors and actresses she admired who were waiting to be big—just as she'd hoped to be "big" behind the scenes. She'd spotted the handsome but shy Rudolph Valentino at once, a young unknown whom she longed to cast in *Beyond the Rocks*. Gloria Swanson seemed talented as did Gary Cooper and even the saucy Clara Bow. She'd been to two parties thrown by the so-called king and queen of the moving picture industry, Douglas Fairbanks and his lovely wife, Mary Pickford. They were as close as anyone came to royalty around here.

Yet she was tempted at this moment as she hid the painting behind the set to also hide there and just cry. No, she told herself, she had been built for stronger stuff than that, been through worse than this. Still, as different as this situation was, she kept remembering feeling terrified and out of control when that carriage had abducted her from the Warsaw train station and had driven her off into the dark, snowy night.

"Places again, everyone!" Lasky boomed through his megaphone. "We'll do this scene, then take a break while I confer with Mrs. Glyn. And someone, get another painting for that wall. Something 'terribly English,' as they say. But we need to stay under budget, something perhaps foreign authors don't understand," he added, with a narrow glance her way again. "All right, one more run-through, then we'll shoot."

When Elinor stomped back to her chair, a bald man with dark brows, some years younger than her, stood there as if waiting for her. He was smiling broadly. Was he laughing at her?

"You're right, you know," he leaned forward to tell her in a calm, assured voice. "It may all be pretend, but it must seem real.

Step over here, Mrs. Glyn, and let's talk. I'm Cecil B. DeMille, also a producer, one with—I dare say—a bit more heart than Jesse Lasky."

Elinor had never heard of the man, but there was something about him she instantly related to—trusted in. Certainly not like she'd trusted Clayton once, or Milor back home. But this was Hollywood, and money men ruled it. As the Americans liked to say, "She still intended to give it a go."

* * *

Lucile was at sea again, though this time, alone and feeling very much that way. No Franks and certainly no Cosmo on the ship. Just her three pet dogs she'd left in her cabin, where she'd taken most of her meals. Now she stood at the railing as the huge liner plunged through the night waters toward England. Music sifted in from outside, but the whine of the wind and slosh of the waves against the hull almost muted it.

Strangely, it felt good to be alone just to let memories of grand times wash over her, warm her. Mostly times with Cosmo, though her thoughts drifted far back to her first voyage that she, Elinor, and Mother had endured when they'd left Canada for England years ago and later on to Jersey. Elinor had always become ill with *mal de mer,* but she and Mother had weathered the voyage well, preferring to be on deck instead of having to listen to Mr. Kennedy's complaining. She had even played the piano on the small ship to entertain others. Why didn't she take the time or have a piano to play anymore?

She recalled that dreadful, deadly night on the *Titanic.* But Cosmo had been there, steady and strong. He'd found them that boat and been shamed for it later, stalwart, proud, upright

Cosmo. He'd saved them all, and that night she was the one who got sick on the waves.

She began to walk fast along the rail, right into the teeth of the autumn wind. She held her hat in her hand now because the wind even ripped at her hair, her—as she liked to think of it—not graying but silver-frosted hair. Did the sea spray speckle her face or was that her tears? She had done so much, reached out to so many, but she had been a terrible mother and wife. Cosmo had promised before they wed that he understood, that he would support her designing career, and he had, but then things had just—just gone overboard somehow.

She'd written them when and where she was coming home, but she wouldn't hold it against them if they didn't greet her, for Lucile, Lady Duff-Gordon, felt quite the failure now.

She'd been a wretched sister, too. Why couldn't she and Elinor get on together, even when they were apart? Lucile had to admit she should not have written Elinor "I told you so!" when things went so wrong for her in Hollywood at first, though she'd weathered that storm, not only working for a new director Cecil-something but mending bridges with that Lasky movie mogul too. Her letters seemed an endless list of famous names from the cinema, and she'd decided to stick it out and bragged that she was making money hand over fist. My, the common way she worded her letters now made Lucile realize that her sister was becoming Americanized. Sometimes she even sounded like the man Lucile thought of as "Shameful Shuloff."

She shook her head to clear it. She was terrified even now that she didn't have it in her to make up with her family for her long absence and her fierce ambition. Her sale of the New York, Chicago, and Paris stores had been a disaster. Lucile's wasn't hers anymore. It was some cheapened, quick-made assembly line, like those men who made Henry Ford's Model Ts one after the other, all the same. No more personality dresses to suit the wearer. The elegance of what they now called the Victorian or Edwardian eras was gone. The belle epoque in Europe was dead, and in her darkest moments, sometimes she wished that she was too.

* * *

Elinor had been to many a Hollywood party, but no one staged ones more glamorous than the wealthy publisher William Randolph Hearst at his grand estate of San Simeon on the central California coast. His home here was called Hearst Castle, and she could see why. Though she'd been in some of the most magnificent castles in Europe, this quite new one screamed MONEY AND POWER! and—another American phrase again—"impressed the hell out of her."

Though its decor was not French, it was like an American Versailles, and how she wished Lucile could see it—and realize that her own sister was staying here for the long weekend. It stood on a rocky promontory above Hearst ranch land with a view of the azure Pacific. Grand and sprawling, a mix of Spanish Colonial and Italianate styles, its towers stretched into the sky with terraced gardens below. Pools and statues reminiscent of her beloved Versailles reflected everything from clouds to strolling guests.

Room after room of stonework and wooden carvings, imported art inside and out, gave testimony to the genius of San Simeon's female architect, Julia Morgan, someone who, Elinor had just been telling her friends Charlie Chaplin and Clara Bow, would have made a perfect third Sutherland sister to her and Lucile. Of course, she'd had a bit too much champagne, but that wasn't much of a stretch, was it?

"I see what you mean!" Clara said in that shrill, Brooklyn-accented voice of hers. Since the young woman had looks and charisma, Elinor only hoped the movies never became talkies. Clara could emote like crazy and lure one right in—if she kept her pretty mouth shut. On the silent screen, the young woman was the epitome of what she and Lucile used to call "It," that definite but indefinable quality that acted like a magnet with men and women, too. Elinor was proud that her suggestion that Clara be publicized as "the It Girl" had really taken hold.

"I see what you mean too, oh esteemed fellow Englishwoman," Chaplin said to Elinor. He was British also and was putting on an upper-class accent right now. But he was also in his cups and had been ogling women right and left tonight, though he was married and had enough sense not to play fast and loose with Clara or Elinor, who had taken the younger woman under her wing.

Elinor told him, "I'm not a 'fellow Englishwoman,' Charles, because you are a man."

"I've noticed that much," he said with a waggle of his eyebrows. "You're always nitpicking, my dear Nellie, but I know your heart's in the right place," he added with a wide-eyed, comic ogle of her breast. "Admit it, you are as ding-dong impressed with this American Taj Mahal and the greenbacks behind it as the rest of us. Money, money, money! Hollywood does that to one, doesn't it, Clara, and don't answer that, at least out loud. Just think what you would say in that pretty head of yours."

And he was off again to the bar set up nearby the Neptune Pool. He even did that funny, little tipsy walk of his, though Elinor knew well he wasn't that intoxicated yet. Always the entertainer. But she was upset that he had implied Clara had bats in the belfry, which she did not. She was just new, naive, and overwhelmed, and Elinor spotted that well enough from the old days.

But what bothered her the most was that he insisted on calling her Nellie, which no one else did anymore. It made her miss Lucile and Mother. She also disliked his implication that she was as money hungry as the rest of them here in boomtown Hollywood, riding the waves of America's passion for the movies and its stars. Why, women sobbed and screamed when young Valentino came on the screen, so Elinor felt proud to have spotted him first.

Of course, with her past need to support Clayton and the girls for years and then herself since, Elinor admitted she was conscious of her finances. Lucile had become that way too, finally facing hard times, when she used to just roll her eyes at her younger sister and pooh-pooh Cosmo's firm foot on the budget.

A rush of emotion hit her hard, and she sank onto the wide lip of the Neptune Pool under the tall temple façade. The evening breeze from the Santa Lucia mountains blew fine fountain mist in her face as if she were at sea.

Lucile was headed back to England, maybe was there already. Elinor regretted telling her how much money each script was making for her when she knew full well Lucile's fashion shops had hit hard times. But she'd wanted to make the point that her writing had done well, done as well as Lucile's designs. Not only that, but she had lasted into the future, and she'd rubbed that in, when she knew Lucile's romantic designs were under assault for being old-fashioned and impractical. Oh, she hated herself for her smallness sometimes!

"Are you all right?" Clara's voice pierced her agonizing as she leaned closer. "I mean, you look kind of funny, not funny like

Mr. Chaplin. Elinor, I want to thank you for being so sweet to me and convincing everyone to call me the 'It Girl,' 'cause no one knows exactly what that means—like maybe sexy or not—so it makes me kind of mysterious."

Elinor just nodded. "Would you get me another drink, Clara?" she asked. "Just tonic or soda water this time."

"Oh sure. Be right back with 'It'—get it?" she asked and patted Elinor's shoulder before she hurried off.

As darkness fell, Elinor stared down into the aquamarine depths of the pool with its shifting waters, lit by torches. She saw her image in the water, lost in its wavy lines and broken swirls.

But she was thinking that, after all their differences and years apart, she and dear Lucile had been the original "It Girls."

## CHAPTER *Thirty-Four*

Not even one of Lucile's mannequin parades with London's royal and noble in the front row or opening a new shop in the most famous cities in the world had set her so on edge as when her ship came into Southampton. After these five years away, after the mistakes she'd made, would Esme or Cosmo come to meet her? Could she resurrect any of her old professional or personal life again, and if so, on what terms?

She stood shoulder to shoulder with other passengers at the rail as the ship edged closer to the waiting, waving crowd on the pier. Leaning over, she squinted to skim faces but saw no one she knew. She bit her lower lip hard and blinked back tears.

It hurt her to see some arrivals being greeted with cheers and huzzahs, perhaps just a fortunate, normal person whose family was elated to have him back. Though she used to be such a social butterfly, she'd kept to herself so much on this voyage that she hadn't heard whether any personalities were aboard. Some sort of confetti dusted the air, and people hugged each other on the gangway below.

Well, she thought, she'd made her bed and she must lie in it.

She would work to win Esme back and play with her grandchildren and design dress-up clothes for them. As for her life with Cosmo, that remained to be seen. Now here she was alone with no one she knew waiting below.

She disembarked and made arrangements at the porter counter for her pile of luggage to be handled clear to the taxi stand on a rolling cart. Now she'd have to get herself and that to the Ritz Hotel in London. Not for years had she been forced to fend for herself dockside like this. She knew she couldn't afford the Ritz for long, but she'd find a small house to let or buy outside of London. She wouldn't have a motorcar anymore, but there were always cabs or trains. The Ritz had been her sister's "hangout" once, as the Americans would put it, so she'd write her next time on Ritz stationery. She couldn't bear for Elinor, or anyone, to know the real state of her financial affairs.

It annoyed her that, with the rolling stack of luggage behind her, she would have to stand in the queue for hired motorcars. But then as she walked that way through the thinning crowd toward the line of people . . .

"Mother! Over here!" came a familiar voice, and Esme broke from the stragglers, waving like mad and tugging her little daughter, Flavia, along. Her husband, Anthony, Viscount Tiverton, was just behind her with their son, Tiverton, in his arms.

"Wait," Lucile told her porter. "Wait right here."

But she wasn't waiting. She threw her arms wide, and Esme hugged her. No Cosmo, but kisses from her dear grandchildren who had grown so much she didn't know them. But neither did they know her, and Flavia cowered when she kissed her.

Esme was still talking. "We had a tire puncture on the way, and the men had to fix it, and once we got here, they had to wash up. Sorry we weren't here when your ship came in, because I wanted the children to see that."

"The *men* fixed it?" Lucile asked. "Did someone stop to help?"

"Oh, no, it was Cosmo's motorcar, and he can fix anything."

"Almost anything," came the deep voice from behind her she had so longed to hear.

She turned. She had forgotten he was so tall. Much more silver in his hair and mustache. He looked fine—grand.

"We've come to take you home," he said, and his voice cracked. "Wherever you decide is home."

She stepped closer to him. Even in the press of people and noise here, she was sure she scented Highland heather and fresh air. He extended his arms, and she threw herself into them, her cheek against the rough tweed of his jacket. He felt so strong, so good.

She wanted to tell him that home was wherever he was, but she wasn't sure how her ruination of these last years in America would sit with him. But she was sure that she couldn't wait to see London, to recapture the grandeur and the grace of it all. For that much, at least, and mostly for these beloved people, she was home.

* * *

Elinor was ecstatic. For the movie based on her novel *Beyond the Rocks*, two of her favorite players had been cast—Rudolph Valentino and Gloria Swanson!

After all, she was the one who had first noticed Valentino's impact among bit players so she had coached and promoted him. Unlike others who called him Rudy—which did not enhance his Latin charisma at all—she always just called him Valentino. Like

Clara Bow, he had "It," only the male variety, which was much more dangerous. Elinor herself, whom he called Madame Glyn, or "My Madame," was totally susceptible to his charms, despite the somewhat large gap in their ages. She knew not to play with fire anymore, but she didn't mind being warmed by it.

"No one dances the tango as well as you," Valentino told her with one of those long, narrowed-eyed looks as they went back to their table in the nightclub to join Gloria and her companion. This was no mere lad, she reminded herself, but a twenty-seven-year-old man with much experience of all sorts. He just acted like a spoiled child sometimes, so she must be careful bringing him along for his role in the movie.

"And you are the tango king," she told him as he held her chair for her. The dancing had made them both warm. "We will make a place for your tango in as many of your movies as long as I have anything to do with it," she promised. "But this is not all pleasure this evening, my dear. We need to discuss your big love scene with Gloria."

"This evening is pleasure to me," he insisted and gave her another of his smoldering stares that so lit up the screen—and, she was sure, would help to make *Beyond the Rocks* a roaring success. But his screen chemistry, as they called it, had not bubbled over yet with Gloria, however excellent a sultry actress she could be—which is exactly what was wanted for this movie.

That last look almost made Elinor swoon, but she heard Gloria sniff sharply, so she turned to her and said, "Let's call it a night, as Mr. DeMille always says. We need to go over that one scene, so I hope your friend won't mind heading home alone."

"I told him it was not all play and no work," Gloria said and downed the rest of her martini. "Come along, and I'll walk you out," she told her companion. Gloria was between husbands, definitely her weakness for such a bright girl.

Unfortunately, when they left the table, Valentino was recognized, and two women sashayed up for autographs and breathless wonder, just staring at him. It annoyed Elinor but amused her too. There might be only one Valentino, but he surely topped any so-called acolyte Lucile had always kept in swarms about her, including that Bobbie.

But these women hanging on annoyed her even more. "Come on, then," she repeated, standing. "I see Gloria coming back, and we'll take her right out to the limousine." She picked up Gloria's little silk purse from the table and took Valentino's arm to gently tug him away. They were running a tab on Mr. Hearst's dime—actually, more than a dime—since this was his and Marion Davies's table.

In the limousine, Elinor sat them on the main seat and took the back-facing one. She called to the chauffeur, "Drive slowly, please, and close that sliding window behind me." When he complied, she went on, "Now, you two, I am going to teach you what your director evidently cannot. Specifically how to be romantic in the European way, gently, but with leashed passion."

Strange, but right in the middle of this important moment, even with Valentino staring at her, she remembered how she had loved to sprawl half-clad on her tiger skins for inspiration. She'd brought the oldest one with her to Hollywood, but seldom was so foolish anymore. *Would you like to sin with Elinor Glyn on a tiger skin?* The words of that old, naughty doggerel darted through her mind. She had bought the first skin years ago in Venice, infuriating Clayton, but Milor had given her the other—one he had slain himself, even as he had slain her dreams.

She shook her head to stop the memories and cleared her throat. "Now, our director, Sam Wood, is very nervous about the censors, you know. No kiss can run longer that ten feet of film. And they will be shooting two different, culminating kisses in the climactic scene with the more passionate one for the European market. The Americans have that—what do they call it?—Puritanical streak yet. Now, slowly, with feeling, with leashed passion. Of course, look into each other's eyes. Gloria, concentrate. Valentino, emote. Now kiss at least for half a minute."

Surely, Elinor thought, Gloria could sense the electricity. If a woman in her fifties could, she could!

Elinor knew she could do a better job of directing a movie than some of the men in Hollywood. She'd prove it right now. "Slower. Slower! First, kiss the palm of her hand, lingeringly, looking deep into her eyes. Gloria, look a bit stunned, a bit unsure, then change the expression to surprise and segue that to desire. Then come closer—pulled inevitably together. No kiss on the mouth yet, but you are breathing as one, becoming one in heart and mind—later in body. Everyone will feel it . . ."

Elinor felt she would die of the heat in here, but was it just her? Not since that rat Curzon had she nearly fainted at someone's feet. If Gloria didn't feel that and act on that . . .

When the two of them kissed tentatively, then powerfully, Elinor flopped back in her seat and fanned herself. Oh, to be young and stubborn, but hungry for life again. But as fake and phony as the movies and written romance could be, there *was* such a thing as living through others instead of for others. Did that and her continued quest for emotion and wealth, even power, make her unique? Or just more like Lucile than she ever wished to admit?

* * *

Lucile happily agreed to stay with Esme at their country home for a few days before heading back into London to the Ritz while she looked for a small house, one maybe she could afford on the outskirts of the city. She'd heard Hampstead Heath had some places like that to let or purchase.

Cosmo didn't stay long that first night, but it was obvious that he was more at home here with her family than she was. Little Tiverton sat happily on his lap and played toy soldiers with him, and Anthony and Cosmo got on well.

But Cosmo was back the next day, and Esme suggested just he and Lucile take a motorcar ride.

"Town or country?" Cosmo asked her when she was seated beside him. They were still rather stiff with each other.

"Since I am with you, the countryside. Esme tells me she seldom goes into London."

"Good girl, your Esme."

"I do mean to visit the London shop soon."

"Like Londoners, it's much changed since you left," he told her, starting the engine and pulling away. "Women worked hard during those tough war years. Fancy fripperies are not so common now."

"And styles are plainer. I know what you're hinting at. I learned that the hard way in New York. Cosmo," she went on, turning toward him on the leather seat, "I'm sorry I made a mess when I sold the U.S. and Paris stores. I just wanted desperately to get out from under them—everything but the design part, which is very different now. The styles are so—not Lucile anymore."

He frowned but kept his eyes on the road. The countryside was lovely, but she kept her eyes on him.

"You always were a disaster with finances, lass."

She teared up that he had finally called her by that simple pet name again—*lass*. "And you weren't there to advise me," she added.

"Because you let me down, and I couldn't bear that again."

"I never loved or trusted anyone the way I did you."

"Did, not still do or could again?"

Her insides cartwheeled. "You know what I mean."

"I fear I don't and haven't for a long while. Look, Lucile, let's not argue. Let's just be together and remember the good times, not the bad. And see what we can salvage for the future."

She wanted to ask him if he meant a future together but she was afraid to make another wrong move, professionally or personally. She wanted to promise Cosmo that—if he wanted—she would like to visit Scotland again, but perhaps he had his own life there now, even another woman. She glimpsed for a moment how badly she had hurt him.

"Yes," she said and reached out to briefly lay a hand on his arm, "it is a lovely day, partly because I am, at last, again with you."

# CHAPTER *Thirty-Five*

"Elinor, darling, of course you would be here," actress Pola Negri greeted her and pressed her cheek against Elinor's, one side and then the other through their stiff, netted veils as they emerged from their chauffered motorcars. Elinor hoped the veils and hats might help the stars hide from the screaming crowds along the street. It was blazing hot in the sun—blazing hot in her grief.

Not only was Valentino dead, but his fans were tearing their hair and clothing and shrieking despite their proximity to the Beverly Hills Church of the Good Shepherd where the memorial service was to be held today, August 30, 1926. Clara Bow, across the way, waved and blew her a kiss, and the crowd screamed again as if that were for them. But most of the hysteria was for Valentino.

Elinor was glad the police were holding back the crowd from rushing the arriving guests. Shameful to mourn like that, for it said, *Look at me, me, me!* But then how appropriate for Hollywood, however great the tragedy of Valentino's loss from appendicitis and peritonitis at age thirty-one. He'd died in New

York City, and his funeral there, she'd heard, had been chaos, so she should have expected it here, too. The thing was, in her heart, she could have joined that mob, crying, wailing, falling to the ground near the heaps of dying flowers and scribbled love notes.

Because, bad enough to lose Valentino, but Curzon had died last year, and she'd smothered her grief when she'd received Lucile's letter about his sad end. Curzon and his second wife, Grace, had been estranged for several years and hated living together. Grace had not given him the heir he'd so desired. He had lost his life's goal to become prime minister when Stanley Baldwin was elected instead.

Ironically, Elinor thought as she gripped the iron railing and headed up the stone stairs of the church, Curzon had been sequestered at Montacute where he'd stashed her away until she learned the devastating news of his engagement to Grace. So he hadn't been aware of the political machinations in Parliament until too late. He had died what they called "land poor," and all that would have been rich revenge, except she still missed and mourned him. And forgave him at last.

And now Valentino was gone too.

"Chin up, Elinor," Jesse Lasky whispered just inside the vestibule and put an arm around her shoulders. "I know many claim to have discovered Rudy in the mix of hopefuls, but you truly made him shine, him and our Clara Bow 'It Girl,' eh? What a loss! He could have made himself and everyone even more of a fortune."

Elinor almost agreed, but that sounded so crass—and what would she have been agreeing with? That she had more or less discovered Valentino and helped to shape him—or that he was worth only money to her and everyone else here? It wasn't true in her case, for she had cared for him deeply.

As Lasky melded into the crowd of mourners, Charlie Chaplin appeared as if he'd been watching for her and held out the crook of his arm to escort her into the sanctuary. At least he looked truly grieved.

"Hello, fellow Brit," he said and squeezed her arm against his ribs. "Funny how funerals make us think about past losses, eh?"

"You are hardly the 'little tramp' of movie fame, but a serious, astute thinker. I see you read minds."

"Remembering your husband's death today?"

"It was my father who died young," she admitted, though she hadn't realized she would share that until she blurted it out. He escorted her up the aisle as if this were a wedding. "And Mother always used to tell Lucile and me how dashing he was, how strong and handsome and clever. We never knew him," she said with a sigh. "But even when she wed again of necessity, our departed, fabulous father was somehow always hovering in her heart—in the room."

"So maybe Valentino was like a long-lost, dashing, strong and handsome, and greatly missed young father to you and not a younger boyfriend or a son."

She turned sharply to look at him, but he hadn't meant it as a dig or joke. And had he been right? Those young, handsome men over the years, some Clayton sent away, some she did—was she looking for her lost father, not a lover? And Lucile had adored those so-called acolytes she had mentored and had suffered bitterly over the loss of that singer, Bobbie. Yet as bright as they both were, neither of them had ever thought of this, and of such were lives and longing made.

Elinor could hear what the two men behind her were saying once she was seated and Chaplin settled down. He looked not mischievous, but almost wise and benign, like some modern-day Buddha as the pipe organ began to play sonorous and sweeping music. The congregation stood as the priests and altar boys entered with the casket rolled down the aisle amid the scent of smoky incense from the censers swinging on their chains.

Yet she heard from behind her, "His sex appeal would have taken him to the top of the money heap. Women around the world would have paid anything to see him—and then fantasized he was their sheik in their tent ready to ravish them."

"No kidding. Money talks. He's to be interred in the Hollywood Forever Cemetery on Santa Monica Boulevard, I heard, and they could probably sell tickets to have a glimpse of the crypt."

She turned to glare at the two men, who ignored her. She was struck again by the fact people here were thinking of Valentino in terms of money, not a young life gone. Had she, too, become greedy and crass? She'd noticed the attitude of avarice and self-importance among movie people before, but had she been part of that? She'd heard others call it the Hollywood curse or the Hollywood disease, and was she feeling so sick to her stomach because she'd really caught that—was like that?

The so-called religion of New Thought had ensnared her for a while with its "golden thoughts" and its worship of wealth, success, fame, even youth. But what good had any of that done Valentino? At least he was being buried as a Catholic, a believer in the Good Shepherd who cared for his flock whether they were rich or poor. That had mattered to her during the Great War, but she'd lost that all in Hollywood.

On the right-hand side of the church, she saw a lovely stained-glass window of the Good Shepherd, the Lord Jesus with a lamb on his shoulders. Sunlight streamed through it to cast a kaleidoscope of colors onto Valentino's flower-covered coffin on its catafalque.

She jolted when the presiding priest intoned, "The Lord be with you." But only a few in the congregation knew to reply, "and also with you."

* * *

Lucile admitted to herself she had never felt so anxious over being alone with a man, well, not since she was young and went to her first dance on just Jersey the year she came out. She and Cosmo were here in Scotland at his Maryculter estate, alone but for his staff. He'd been courting her during the time since she had returned to London—or had she been courting him? Dinners out, motorcar rides, his help with her finances in the shop just like old times.

Despite a kiss or a hug here and there, Cosmo had been protective but entirely proper. Was he waiting for her to make the first move? Perhaps he was working up to telling her this was the way it would be—only friends? She supposed she deserved that. Despite the fact he was the one who had left her, she was really the one who had deserted him.

The Lucile, Lady Duff-Gordon Shop had surely seen better times, for few women were buying fancy frocks after the war with a looming recession and international tensions. In a way, she thought, as she looked at herself in the pier glass in her bedroom adjacent to Cosmo's, she hoped her floor-length Scottish skirt and frilled lace blouse she planned to surprise him with tonight would further send a message to him that she wanted back permanently in his life—and as his wife.

The wooing of each other would make a good plot for a movie script or novel for Elinor. She'd never dared to offer ideas before, but her thoroughly modern sister was coming to England for a visit next week. How they used to fret and fume back and forth about "Nellie" always having her nose in a book while "Lucy" was more adventurous. She recalled one huge argument they had on Jersey when Elinor acted completely scandalized because she saw her reading the end of a book first to decide if she wanted to read it at all.

"You are ruining everything!" Nellie had shouted. "It's the journey that matters—the getting there, what happens along the way. How can you be so foolish—so insecure?"

"Me, insecure? You're the one hiding from real life, just you and pages and printed words! How can you waste your time on a story that may end unhappily!" Lucy had shouted back and thrown the book at her. They hadn't spoken until Mother forced them to make up. Had they ever really made up? She still longed for happy endings, however rough the journey, despite the glorious, bright times.

Lucile jolted back to reality when a knock sounded on the door that linked the two bedrooms. Cosmo had told her it was locked, as it had never been years ago, and the key was on her side. Had he meant something suggestive by that? Perhaps that it was her decision to join him? When he'd escorted her here after dinner last night on the day of their arrival, he'd left her at the hall door with a simple kiss on her cheek, and she was astounded how sad that had made her. But, if they were to be man and wife again, shouldn't he make the first move? He'd agreed she would keep her newly purchased house in Hampstead Heath so that she could afford to be near the shop most of the time, but she'd vowed to visit Scotland more than she ever had, and he'd simply nodded. At least he'd kept the way she redecorated Maryculter upstairs and down years ago.

She hurried to the door and unlocked it. The mere turning of the key seemed incredibly loud. She swept open the door.

"My Scottish lass is back," he said as he put one hand up on the door frame, just leaning there and studying her. He wore his favorite kilt and dinner jacket. "You must have designed that skirt," he added.

"I did. Ordered the material and had it made as a surprise for you. I know it's a local plaid," she said, turning round once, then backing up several steps until her bottom bumped into the high, four-poster bed.

"It's called a tartan, lass. And that one's a dress Stuart, the royals, you know. I see I need to give you some Scottish tutoring."

"I'm always willing to learn."

"Then let me serenade my lady love," he said, coming closer. He took her hands in his and sang slowly, almost sadly in his beautiful, deep baritone, "*Should Auld acquaintance be forgot and never brought to mind?* . . ."

Tears filled her eyes. She stood as if mesmerized, longing to throw herself into his arms, but he stopped in midword and said, "My beautiful, beloved lass, you are always brought to my mind. I may have been a cad, and you've been a wee bit daft, but shall we try our marriage again—for old times' sake?"

"I say yes. But how about for new times' sake?"

She threw herself into his arms. Just as in the old days—surely like times yet to come—he picked her up and carried her to the big ancestral bed in his adjoining room. He lay her down and nearly ripped off his jacket.

"The lord and lady of the manor are going to be very, very late to dinner," he told her and proceeded to show her why.

* * *

Chaplin and Marion Davies, Hearst's mistress—Chaplin had somehow been allowed to bring her without Hearst—insisted on taking Elinor back to her suite at the Ambassador Hotel after Valentino's memorial service, so she sent her car home without her. Truth be told, Hollywood was a crime-ridden area, evidently as thieves realized how many wealthy people were running around in real jewelry. Douglas Fairbanks and Mary Pickford had taken to having a guard in another motorcar follow Elinor home after dinner at their lovely mansion Pickfair. A woman alone—well, it was so kind of them. And somehow lately, she had really felt alone and was longing to take a trip home.

Lucile was in England now, though she'd heard little from her lately. They'd hardly seen each other in years. Besides, long absences from Elinor's daughters and her grandchildren sometimes made the bright lights of Hollywood seem very dim.

"Come on then, old girl, let's lift a toast to Valentino," Chaplin said to her as his motorcar pulled up to the curb at the hotel. "Marion, pull that hat down but not the veil, because that makes people look at you. Hopefully, you will not be recognized, and we'll go up with Elinor for a nightcap. Heaven knows, we need one."

Marion gave him a quick punch in the shoulder. "And you think people in the lobby won't recognize you?"

"My dears, I shall just look serious and walk straight and no one will turn a head."

"I can't stay long, though," Marion said with a sigh. "It's a miracle the old man let me out on my own for once. I do think Elinor looks like she needs friends right now, but you know who will have a rip-roaring fit if I'm late. Hearst is jealous of everyone."

"Except me, which is a mistake," Chaplin said as they went in single file, looking neither right nor left as the doorman opened the lobby entrance for them.

Elinor had once prided herself in being recognized from time to time as a famous authoress, but compared to the on-screen people, she could go anywhere without stares.

They were glad to snag an elevator with no one in it except the uniform-clad operator, but his eyes popped when he saw Marion. They piled out on Elinor's floor and made the turn toward her suite. She was grateful for her friends, but suddenly, it made her so lonely for her family again, even for Lucile. Why had they not gotten on at times when so much bound them, past and present? Their lives, full of fame and fortune—and a wretched first marriage—had the blessing of daughters. They were so much the same.

"Oh my, someone's drunk," Marion muttered when they heard, then saw two men down the corridor, fighting. One was on the floor and one—oh, the other one was lifting a fist—no, a knife—and plunging it down again and again.

"Stop, there!" Chaplin shouted.

The standing man vaulted over the prone man's body and ran the other way, toward the exit stairs down the way.

"Right outside my door," Elinor cried.

"Go back down for help!" Chaplin ordered Marion and pushed her back toward the elevator.

She cried, "I can't be seen here or Hearst will murder me. But I'll tell them at the desk, then wait in the car!"

Chaplin rushed down the hall after the running man, though the villain had a head start. Elinor hurried to bend over the injured one. She had to tell herself this was real, not some moving picture. Blood puddled on the crimson carpet outside her door. She didn't know him—couldn't think what to do until help came. He lay face up, suddenly very still.

She hated to touch him but she ripped off a glove and felt for his wrist pulse. His skin was slick with his own blood. Nothing. No pulse. She felt for his neck artery. On this day of all days—a man dead, literally at her door.

Rushing down the hall came a portly man with a boutonniere in his lapel—oh, she recognized the hotel manager—and a security policeman with two other men behind them.

"Mrs. Glyn, are you all right? Do you know him?"

"Yes, I'm all right—and no. A stranger. He's—he appears to be dead."

"Frank, get a tarp or stretcher up here fast," he ordered one man. "Have him taken down the fire stairs. Mrs. Glyn, you realize this never happened here. You saw nothing."

"No, I saw the man who knifed him, though from afar. Won't the police want to question what I saw? There was another witness, but . . ."

She glanced down the hall toward the fire escape door where Chaplin had run. Where was he? Surely he hadn't caught or accosted a man with a knife.

"I don't know where my friend went but I—"

The manager cut her off her words with a slice of his hand through the air. "We can't have this happening here. Like the novels and movies you write, Mrs. Glyn—mere fiction. Reputation—everything here. In gratitude, of course, we will reduce the rate of your suite. Say nothing about this to anyone. It never happened."

Elinor leaned against the wall for support. Shocked at their reaction as much as by the corpse, she just gaped at them. Too much today. Too much lately. But how could she be part of a cover-up of a man's murder, especially not for a bribe? Did they intend to recarpet this entire hallway so those bloodstains would not show? So she would not have to see them and step over them every time she went in and out? Had both Marion and Chaplin known it would be handled like this? Had Chaplin really chased the killer, or did he just want to save his own skin?

Elinor's hand shook as she walked around the men and, hugging the wall, unlocked the door of her suite and went in. She locked and bolted it, then barely made it to the sofa before her legs gave out. She was under contract here for almost three more years and was making good money and mingling with fascinating people. Even *Three Weeks* had finally been made into a film, somehow a justification for the attacks on it and her agony over it all these years.

But she'd been living a hollow life, a tarnished one, and—at least for a while—she was going home. Outside was a stain on the carpet and inside was a stain on her soul.

# CHAPTER *Thirty-Six*

Lucile's entire family came up to Scotland on the train for a Saturday-to-Monday holiday: Mother, Esme, Anthony, and their little brood; Elinor with Margot and Juliet with their husbands and children. It was early September, and the gorse and heather lingered on in the mild weather. The first full day, they took a huge picnic, four baskets full of food, up to the lookout over the glens and braes and the river. All three young mothers had brought their nannies to help watch the children, so the adults sat on a tartan blanket after their repast and chatted.

"So beautiful and wild here," Elinor said, inhaling the crisp, fresh air and looking out into the distance. "I shall set a novel here someday."

"That would be nice," Lucile said, taking Cosmo's hand and beating down the urge to mount a comeback. For once she didn't scold Elinor for always talking about her writing.

"Scotland is most invigorating and unique," Elinor went on, "as I hope my stories always are, on the page or on the screen."

"Scotland would be a fresher location than the books you've set in Continental Europe or even England," Lucile said before she realized, as hard as she was trying, she and Elinor might argue again—and she didn't want that. She was finally so happy, and she wanted poor Elinor to be too after her difficult days in California working away at her so-called dream career.

"Although Sir Walter Scott has set many a novel here," Elinor said, evidently refusing to drop the subject. "But I don't mean to lecture. I think I shall stretch my legs and see the view out the other way."

"I'll go with you, and leave Cosmo and you younger folk to talk," Lucile said.

Mother put in, "And I shall go help the nannies with my lovely great-grandchildren. I may be up in my eighties now, but I can still get round and intend to."

Cosmo helped her up, and Elinor and Lucile went over to steady her. Cosmo winked at Lucile as Mother headed briskly down the path toward the barking of the hunt hounds and high-pitched laughter of the children. No hunting grouse or partridge today, Lucile thought, though the men planned on that tomorrow. Today was for just family time—finally, a family.

Lucile led Elinor to the brow of the hill with the best view. They stood there unspeaking for a moment, skirts blowing, hair flying in the brisk breeze, watching an eagle riding the currents.

Elinor said, "You're back with Cosmo, really back. I can tell and I am happy for you."

"Yes. You and I have had our ups and downs with men, haven't we, and often not at the same time, so we could advise and help each other."

"Don't take this wrong, like I'm chattering too much about writing—I know I overdo that once in a while—but I've been thinking of ideas for a novel, maybe a movie script, called *Know-*

*ing Men*. Do you think I'd be a brazen idiot to write something with that title? God knows, I've made some terrible choices, loved and lost men, hardly seen the way they really were, including Clayton and Curzon."

"I, too, made an early mess of things—before Cosmo and then I nearly lost him since I was so self-centered."

"At least you escaped that now—and here I am, headed back to fantasy financial land in Hollywood soon."

"But you'll handle that and rise above. The thing is, at times I've had to protect my designs, my staff, my visions, but still . . . as to your question, I think it's right for you to do that novel and script if you are ready to. A man would. And both of us have done well in a world no longer completely run by men."

Elinor smiled, and her eyes lit. "Thank you for your trust and love, Lucile. You know something my friend Charlie Chaplin said once? He's quite the sage, you know, despite his silliness on screen. He said, the only way to predict the future is to create it. But you and I—sometimes we've been clinging to the past."

"Just like Mother, I have no intention of acting old," Lucile insisted. "We women need to forge ahead. If I cannot abide the new boyish fashions, I shall just not design them. But I meant to tell you I've had an offer to write fashion advice for a newspaper. I shall call my column *Letters to Dorothy*, a pseudonym, but everyone will still know the author is Lucile, Lady Duff-Gordon. So now two writers in the family."

"You'll do splendidly. But the thing is," she said, turning toward Lucile and seizing her hands, "my idea for *Knowing Men*—don't you think that's a lovely double entendre, if you know what that means in the Bible?—could be adapted for the stage in London, too, and you could do the costumes for it. I'd set it all in the past, and you could create the most delicious flowing frocks, all chiffon, satin, and lace again."

Lucile sighed. "I've had to try to let go of that past, but yes—yes, perhaps. It would be good to work together, wouldn't it?"

Elinor bit her lower lip and nodded. Their eyes met and held. They dropped hands and leaned against a granite boulder with their shoulders touching.

"If only we could have done that more," Elinor said with a sigh that matched Lucile's. "One of our mutual mistakes. But we're together now in purpose and outlook—in sisterhood and friendship, too. And even when I head back to slapdash Hollywood, we shall stay in touch, really in touch."

They held hands again. "We will go on, my dear Nellie," Lucile vowed. "Onward and upward, as we used to say before things pulled us apart."

Elinor laughed and elbowed her lightly. "Lovely Lucy, we'll show the world how things should be done."

"We 'It Girls' always have!"

P.S.

Insights,
Interviews
& More . . .

*

## About the author



## About the book

About the author

# Meet Karen Harper

Jeffrey A. Rycus

*New York Times* and *USA Today* bestselling author KAREN HARPER is a former Ohio State University instructor and high school English teacher. Published since 1982, she writes contemporary suspense and historical novels about real British women. Two of her recent Tudor-era books were bestsellers in the United Kingdom and in Russia. Harper won the Mary Higgins Clark Award for *Dark Angel,* and her novel *Shattered Secrets* was judged one of the best books of the year by *Suspense Magazine.*

# Behind the Book

This is the second novel I've written set in the Victorian/Edwardian eras and beyond, and I hope to write another soon. These books are inspired by and based on real women, although, of course, scenes and dialogue are fictionalized—what Alex Haley, who wrote *Roots,* dubbed "faction."

I have stayed as true to real people and events as I could—although these "It Girls" had such amazing careers and knew so many fascinating people that I had to ignore some events and occasionally collapse time a bit. I tried to be careful not to simply name drop, because their friends and acquaintances were a list of who's who of two continents and several historical eras, and, in many cases, deserved development of their own.

I discovered Lucile while reading a research book, *The Real Life Downton Abbey* by Jacky Hyams, for my previous historical novel, *The Royal Nanny.* Three short paragraphs convinced me to look into Lucile's life—and what a life! She was a survivor of the *Titanic* to top all that off! And then to discover she had a sister who was an early romance novelist who also wrote for early Hollywood was a special gift. However, having two dynamic heroines made this the most challenging book of the many I have written.

By the way, I didn't create any of the sisters' antics or adventures—for example: Elinor's abduction in Warsaw really happened and was never solved. Elinor and her friend Charlie Chaplin did discover a murder right outside her hotel door. Perhaps truth is stranger than fiction.

The sisters did go on to present the ▸

play *Knowing Men* together, though it relied on the past so much that it wasn't very popular in the new Jazz Age.

Both Sutherland sisters were famous enough to have been mentioned in *Downton Abbey*. If you were a fan, perhaps you'll recall that Tom Branson mentioned that Mrs. Glyn "writes scandalous books" in one of the episodes. And way back when Edith was first to be married but then was left at the altar, her family members planning her trousseau mentioned putting her in Lucile lingerie.

By the way, there is still a modern lingerie company that banks on Lucile's reputation; take a look at their wares at www.lucileandco.com. These are definitely not her designs, though she might have approved that they are lovely and risqué. And more trivia: Audrey Hepburn's fabulous ball dress in the movie *My Fair Lady* was based on Lucile's design for Snow Princess for the opera *The Merry Widow*. Lucile's dress designs, like her hats, swept London fashions.

In case you would like to pursue any reading or research about these original "It Girls," here is a list of some of the works I consulted. These are books focusing specifically on the sisters, though I also read others about the general culture and times.

*Lucile, Her Life by Design* by Randy Bryan Bigham, MacEvie Press Group, Los Angeles, 2012. This is a huge, expensive book with many illustrations. I want to thank Gayle Strege, curator of the Ohio State University Historic Costume & Textiles Collection, for obtaining a rare copy of it for me. Gayle and her staff have been very helpful. The amazing costume collection they oversee at Ohio State includes a 1916 Lucile ivory silk wedding dress, which can be viewed at this website gallery: http://fashion2fiber.osu.edu/items/show/3766. Additional Lucile designs can be seen on Pinterest or other sites by entering her name.

Other books I read and consulted include the autobiographies of both women:

*Discretions and Indiscretions* by Lady Duff-Gordon, Frederick A. Stokes Company, New York, 1932.

*Romantic Adventure, Being the Autobiography of Elinor Glyn* by Elinor Glyn, Ivor Nicholson and Watson Limited, London, 1936.

Because researchers need to be careful with autobiographies, since the authors may omit, bend, or enhance facts (and both women did), I also consulted these nonfiction books:

*Addicted to Romance: The Life and Adventures of Elinor Glyn* by Jcan Hardwick, Andre Deutsch, London, 1994.

*The "It" Girls: Elinor Glyn, Novelist, and Her Sister Lucile, Couturiere* by Meredith Etherington-Smith and Jeremy Pilcher, Harcourt Brace Jovanovich, New York, 1986. (Note: I had decided on the title *The It Girls* before I found this book and couldn't bear to change it. As you probably know, it is not uncommon for books to have the same title.)

I also couldn't resist reading Elinor's "scandalous" novel *Three Weeks,* published by Duckworth, London, 1907, and recently reprinted by IndyPublish.com in Boston. Of course, by modern standards, the book is quite tame, but it was the *Lady Chatterley's Lover* or the *Fifty Shades of Grey* of its time.

I was impressed and surprised by how "modern" these sisters were, in the pursuit of their careers and in that they were at times the major breadwinners of their families. I was surprised that divorce was as common as it was, especially among the upper classes. Both women believed in self-promotion, which was quite unladylike at that time. They were definitely among the leading "lean in" CEOs of their day.

If you'd like to see a clip in which Elinor describes "It!" take a look at https://www.youtube.com/watch?v=gAoFIYulf90.

Thanks as ever to my husband, Don, for proofreading and serving as my business manager—and for putting up with a writer. Also, much gratitude to my wonderful team of Annelise Robey, my agent, and Lucia Macro, my editor.

Lucile and Elinor's relationship reminded me of a quote from Nancy Mitford, which Lucia shared with me: "Sisters are a shield against life's cruel adversity." To which Nancy's own sister, Jessica, replied, "But sisters *are* life's cruel adversities." Those of you with sisters—wish I had one—are they both right?

I do love two special quotes by the It Girls themselves, which, I think, summarize not only their lives, but what women should strive for today.

Lucile Sutherland, Lady Duff-Gordon: "It's a tragedy for a woman to have too little to wish for."

Elinor Sutherland Glyn: "The journey matters, not just the ending."

I hope reading this novel mattered, not just the ending.

For more information, photos, and facts about these It Girls, please visit my website at www.KarenHarperAuthor.com, and www.facebook.com/KarenHarperAuthor.

# Excerpt from Elinor Glyn's *Three Weeks*

It is not a very easy thing to fold up a huge tiger-skin into a brown paper parcel tied with string. But it was accomplished somehow and Dmitry disappeared noiselessly with it and an answer to the note:

"I will be there, sweet lady.

Your own PAUL."

And he was.

A bright fire burnt in the grate, and some palest orchid-mauve silk curtains were drawn in the lady's room when Paul entered from the terrace. And loveliest sight of all, in front of the fire, stretched at full length, was his tiger—and on him—also at full length—reclined the lady, garbed in some strange clinging garment of heavy purple crepe, its hem embroidered with gold, one white arm resting on the beast's head, her back supported by a pile of velvet cushions, and a heap of rarely bound books at her side, while between her red lips was a rose not redder than they—an almost scarlet rose. Paul had never seen one as red before.

The whole picture was barbaric. It might have been some painter's dream of the Favourite in a harem. It was not what one would expect to find in a sedate Swiss hotel.

She did not stir as he stepped in, dropping the heavy curtains after him. She merely raised her eyes, and looked Paul through and through. Her whole expression was changed; it was wicked and dangerous and provocante. It seemed quite true, as she had said—she was evidently in the devil's mood.

Paul bounded forward, but she raised one hand to stop him.

"No! You must not come near me, Paul. I am not safe to-day. Not yet. See, you must sit there and we will talk."

And she pointed to a great chair of Venetian workmanship and wonderful old velvet which was new to his view.

"I bought that chair in the town this morning at the curiosity shop on the top of Weggisstrasse, which long ago was the home of the Venetian envoy here—and you bought me the tiger, Paul. Ah! That was good. My beautiful tiger!" And she gave a movement like a snake, of joy to feel its fur under her, while she stretched out her hands and caressed the creature where the hair turned white and black at the side, and was deep and soft.

"Beautiful one! Beautiful one!" she purred. "And I know all your feelings and your passions, and now I have got your skin—for the joy of my skin!" And she quivered again with the movements of a snake.

It is not difficult to imagine that Paul felt far from calm during this scene—indeed he was obliged to hold on to his great chair to prevent himself from seizing her in his arms.

"I'm—I'm so glad you like him," he said in a choked voice. "I thought probably you would. And your own was not worthy of you. I found this by chance. And oh! Good God! If you knew how you are making me feel—lying there wasting your caresses upon it!"

She tossed the scarlet rose over to him; it hit his mouth.

"I am not wasting them," she said, the innocence of a kitten in her strange eyes—their colour impossible to define today. "Indeed not, Paul! He was my lover in another life—perhaps—who knows?"

"But I," said Paul, who was now quite mad, "want to be your lover in this!"

Then he gasped at his own boldness.

With a lightning movement she lay on her face, raised her elbows on the tiger's head, and supported her chin in her hands. Perfectly straight out her body was, the twisted purple drapery outlining her perfect shape, and flowing in graceful lines beyond—like a serpent's tail. The velvet pillows fell scattered at one side.

"Paul—what do you know of lovers—or love?" she said. "My baby Paul!"

"I know enough to know I know nothing yet which is worth knowing," he said confusedly. "But—but—don't you understand, I want you to teach me—"

"You are so sweet, Paul! When you plead like that I am taking in every bit of you. In your way as perfect as this tiger. But we must talk—oh! Such a great, great deal—first."

A rage of passion was racing through Paul, his incoherent thoughts were that he did not want to talk—only to kiss her—to devour her—to strangle her with love if necessary.

He bit the rose.

"You see, Paul, love is a purely physical emotion," she continued. "We could speak an immense amount about souls, and sympathy, and understanding, and devotion. All beautiful things in their way, and possible to be enjoyed at a distance from one another. All the things which make passion noble—but without love—which is passion—these things dwindle and become duties presently, when the hysterical exaltation cools. Love is tangible—it means to be close—close—to be clasped—to be touching—to be One!"

# Reading Group Guide

1. The status and struggles of women were different in the late Victorian and Edwardian eras. How do Lucile and Elinor both triumph but also pay the price for pushing the envelope in their careers?

2. Take another look at the two quotes by the Sutherland sisters at the end of the "Behind the Book" essay. Would those statements be true today or are they dated? What single inspirational statement or piece of advice would you share about a woman's journey through life today?

3. The acquaintances and friends of the Sutherland sisters are a list of who's who of two continents. Of the various famous people who figure in the story, who would make a good central character for a novel of his or her own? And have you read a book or seen a movie about one of these secondary characters? I recall a 1978–1979 Masterpiece Theatre series on Lillie Langtry called *The Jersey Lily*. Amazon has the complete series on DVD, and some episodes are archived through PBS's Masterpiece Theatre to be watched online.

4. The concept of "It" as being a charismatic character trait is still around today. It is first mentioned in chapter eight of this novel, and most people associate it with Clara Bow. Do you know or have you known someone who emanates "It"? How or why did they stand out to you? And how would

you explain that personality phenomenon to someone who hears about it for the first time? Do all famous people have some sort of "It" today?

5. Both Elinor and Lord Curzon had derogatory doggerel written about them. Was this the negative social media attack of their day? What other social pressures are mentioned in the novel? And how does the press of that period compare to the media of our time?

6. The novel illustrates that sisters can be a blessing or a curse. Why didn't the Sutherland sisters get on at times? Have you experienced similar two-edged family dynamics in your own life or observed it in that of others'? Have you read fiction or nonfiction about other "sister acts"?

7. It has long been noted that women who lose their fathers early may later tend to gravitate toward older men. Lucile and Elinor lost their father early; they didn't really remember him, and he was kept alive and young through their mother's memories. Have you seen women try to replace a loved and lost parent in their lives?

8. The traditional concept of "romance" (meaning not just a love story) played a part in the lives and careers of both Lucile and Elinor. Did their clinging to their ideal of romance (based on chivalry and adventure with the idealized woman on a pedestal) help or hurt them in their respective careers as designer and novelist? ▸

**Reading Group Guide** ***(continued)***

9. Who are the noted women today who are "leaning in" and breaking barriers through unique careers or endeavors? Do they have it easier or harder than women in the past? (And do they have "It"?)
10. As a reader, what do you think of historical novels that are what Alex Haley, the author of *Roots,* dubbed "faction"—that is, a well-researched novel about real people that has fictional scenes and dialogue and some invented characters? How would a faction novel work differently from a well-written nonfiction book on the same subject?
11. Do you agree with Elinor or Lucile about whether to read the end of a novel first before investing hours into reading the whole book? Have you ever done that or have you known others who did? What were their reasons?
12. What did you think of the style and content of the *Three Weeks* excerpt?

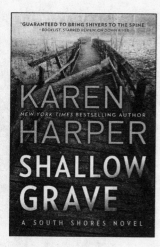